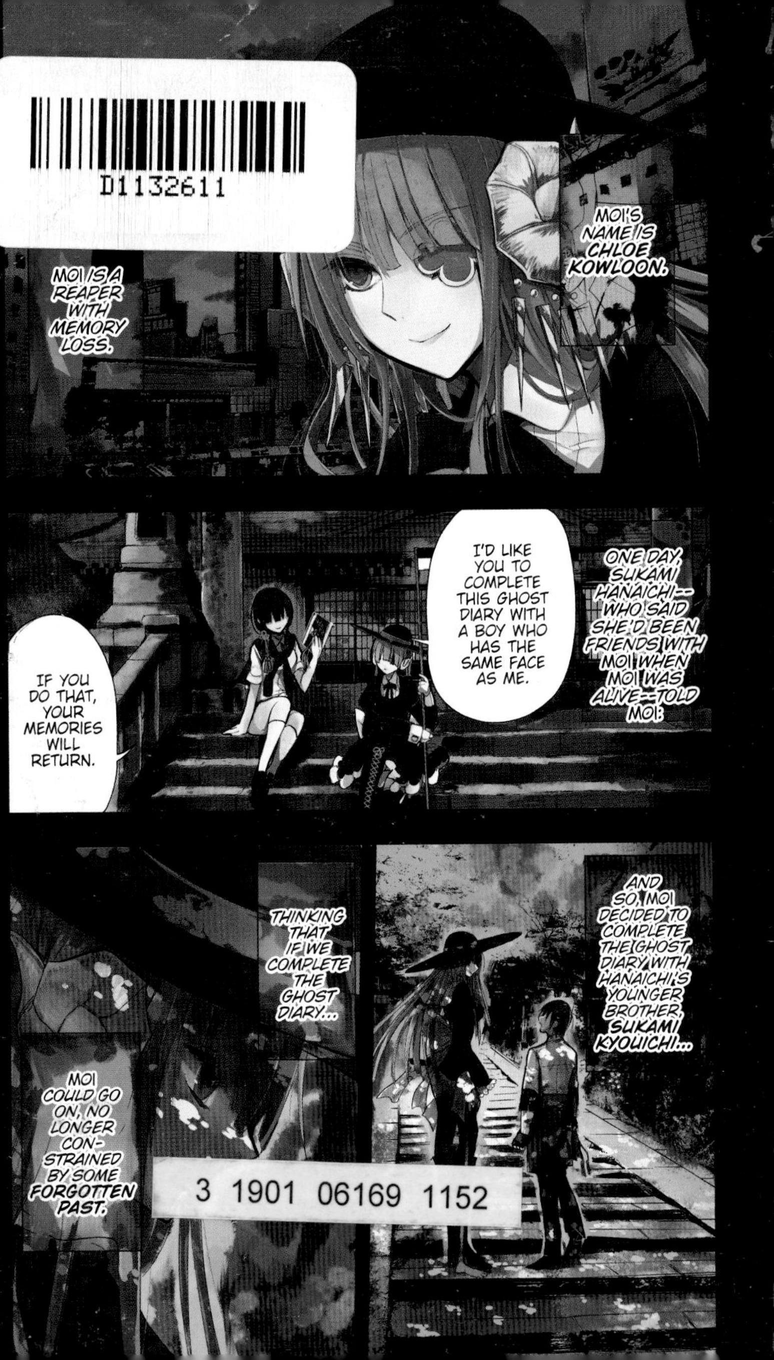
MOI'S NAME IS CHLOE KOWLOON.
MOI IS A REAPER WITH MEMORY LOSS.
ONE DAY, SUKAMI HANAICHI--WHO SAID SHE'D BEEN FRIENDS WITH MOI WHEN MOI WAS ALIVE--TOLD MOI:
I'D LIKE YOU TO COMPLETE THIS GHOST DIARY WITH A BOY WHO HAS THE SAME FACE AS ME.
IF YOU DO THAT, YOUR MEMORIES WILL RETURN.
AND SO, MOI DECIDED TO COMPLETE THE GHOST DIARY WITH HANAICHI'S YOUNGER BROTHER, SUKAMI KYOUICHI...
THINKING THAT IF WE COMPLETE THE GHOST DIARY...
MOI COULD GO ON, NO LONGER CON-STRAINED BY SOME FORGOTTEN PAST.

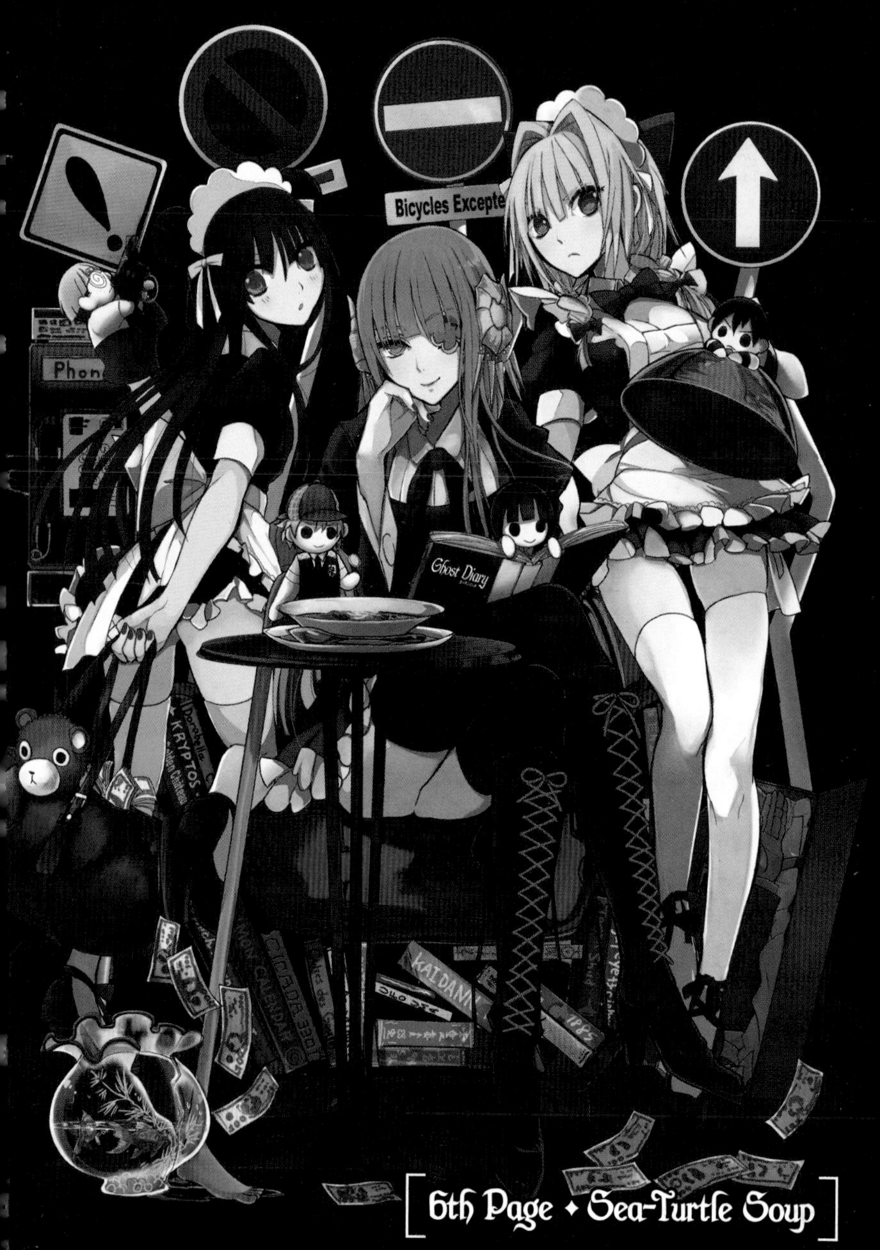
Bicycles Excepte
Phon
Ghost Diary
KRYPTOS
KAIDAN

6th Page ◆ Sea-Turtle Soup

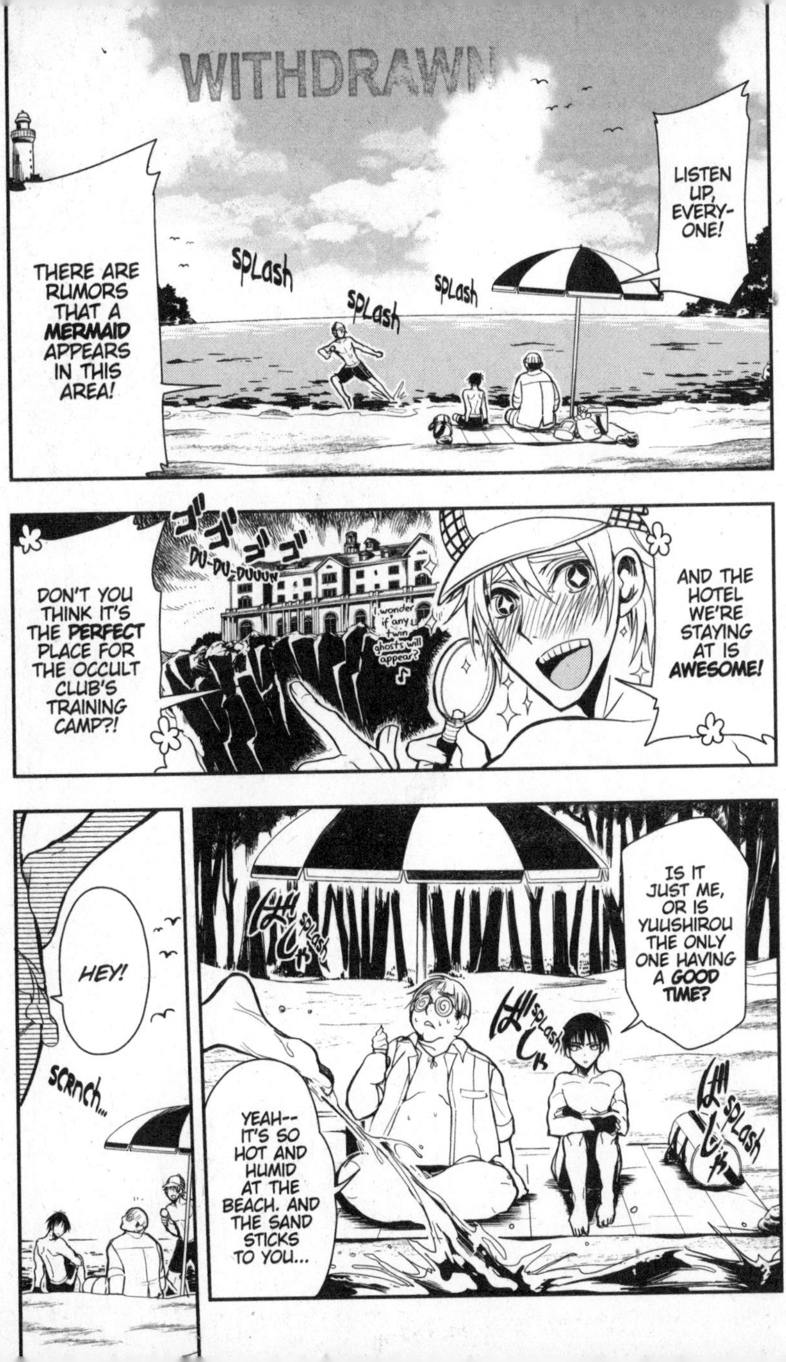
LISTEN UP, EVERY-ONE!
THERE ARE RUMORS THAT A **MERMAID** APPEARS IN THIS AREA!
sPLash
sPLash
sPLash
AND THE HOTEL WE'RE STAYING AT IS **AWESOME!**
DON'T YOU THINK IT'S THE **PERFECT** PLACE FOR THE OCCULT CLUB'S TRAINING CAMP?!
DU-DU-DUUUN
I wonder if any twin ghosts will appear? ♪
IS IT JUST ME, OR IS YUUSHIROU THE ONLY ONE HAVING A **GOOD TIME?**
YEAH-- IT'S SO HOT AND HUMID AT THE BEACH. AND THE SAND STICKS TO YOU...
sPLash
sPLash
sPLash
HEY!
scrnch...

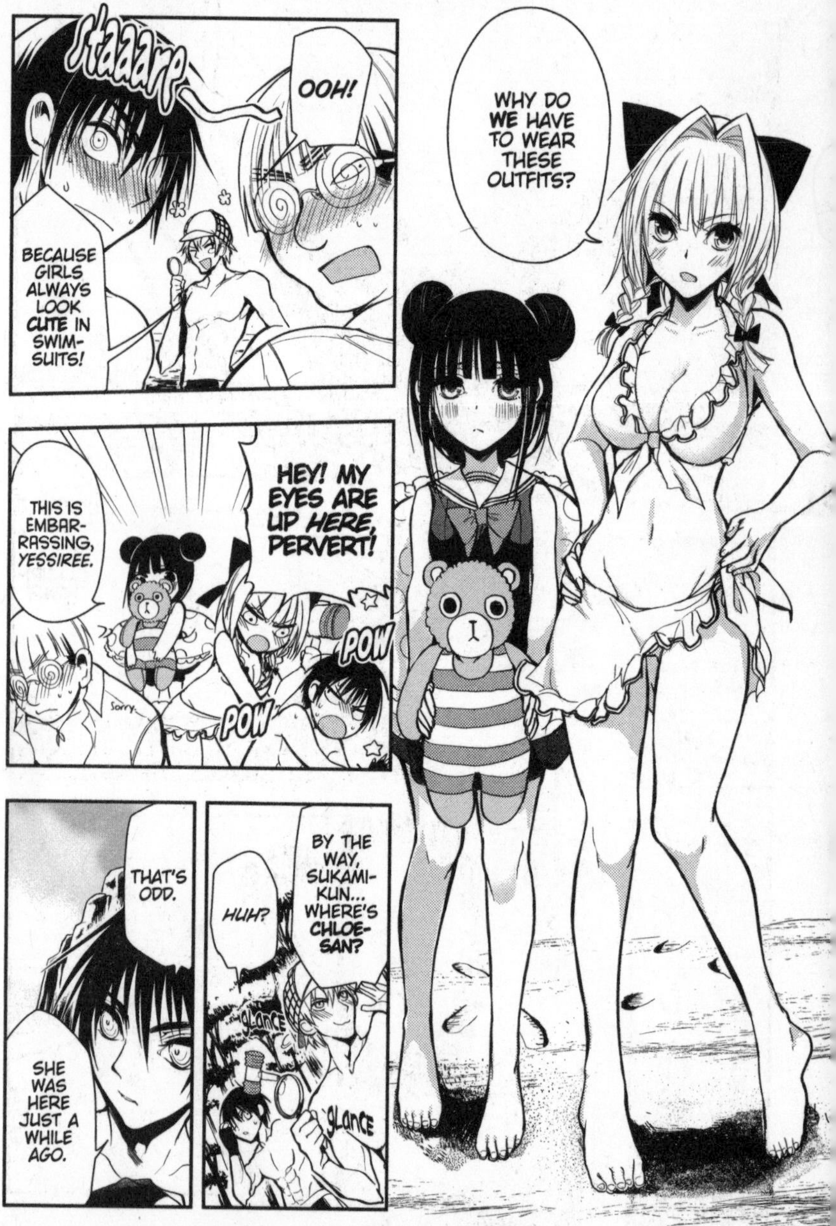
WHY DO WE HAVE TO WEAR THESE OUTFITS?
OOH!
staaare
BECAUSE GIRLS ALWAYS LOOK CUTE IN SWIM-SUITS!
HEY! MY EYES ARE UP HERE, PERVERT!
THIS IS EMBARRASSING, YESSIREE.
POW
POW
Sorry.
BY THE WAY, SUKAMI-KUN... WHERE'S CHLOE-SAN?
HUH?
glance
glance
THAT'S ODD.
SHE WAS HERE JUST A WHILE AGO.

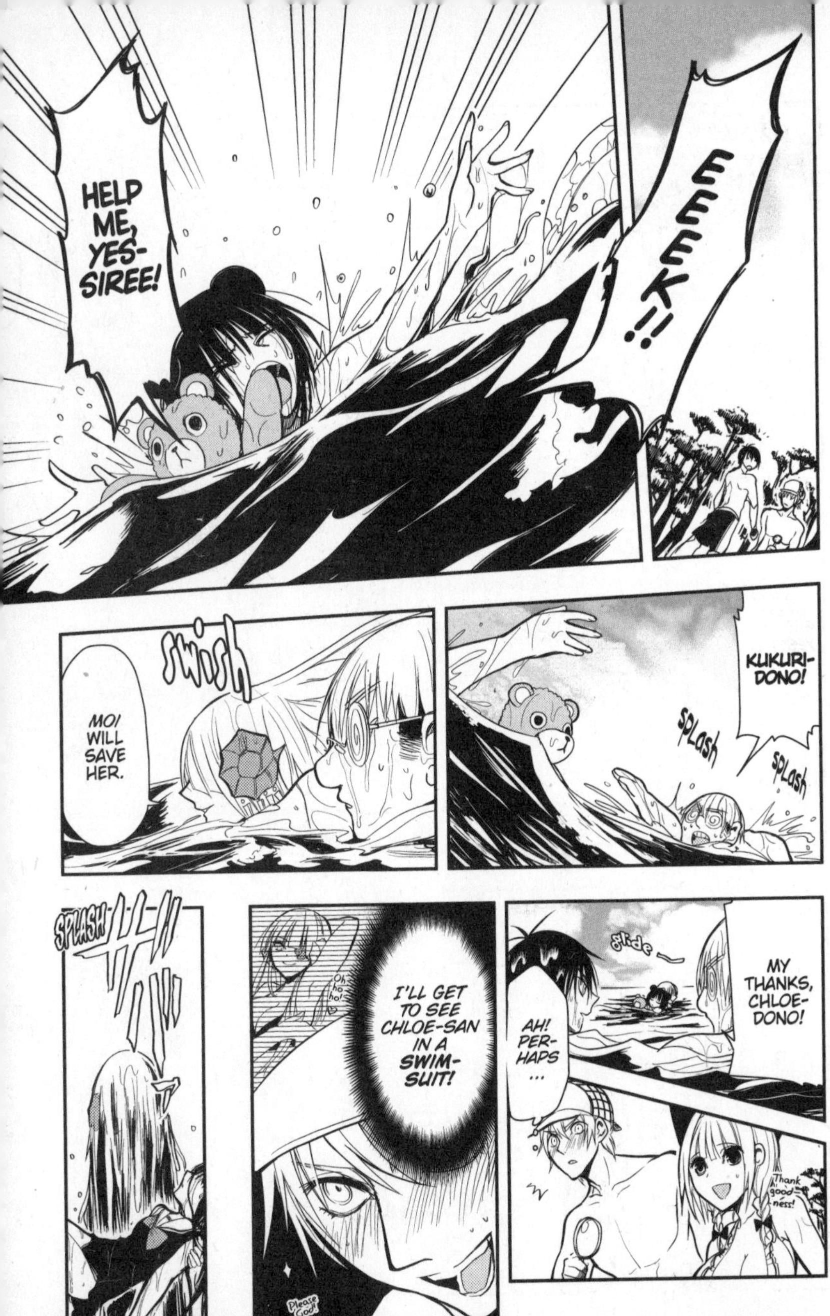
EEEEK!!
HELP ME, YES-SIREE!
KUKURI-DONO!
splash
splash
swish
MOI WILL SAVE HER.
glide ~
MY THANKS, CHLOE-DONO!
AH! PERHAPS...
Thank goodness!
Oh ho ho!
I'LL GET TO SEE CHLOE-SAN IN A SWIM-SUIT!
Please God!
SPLASH

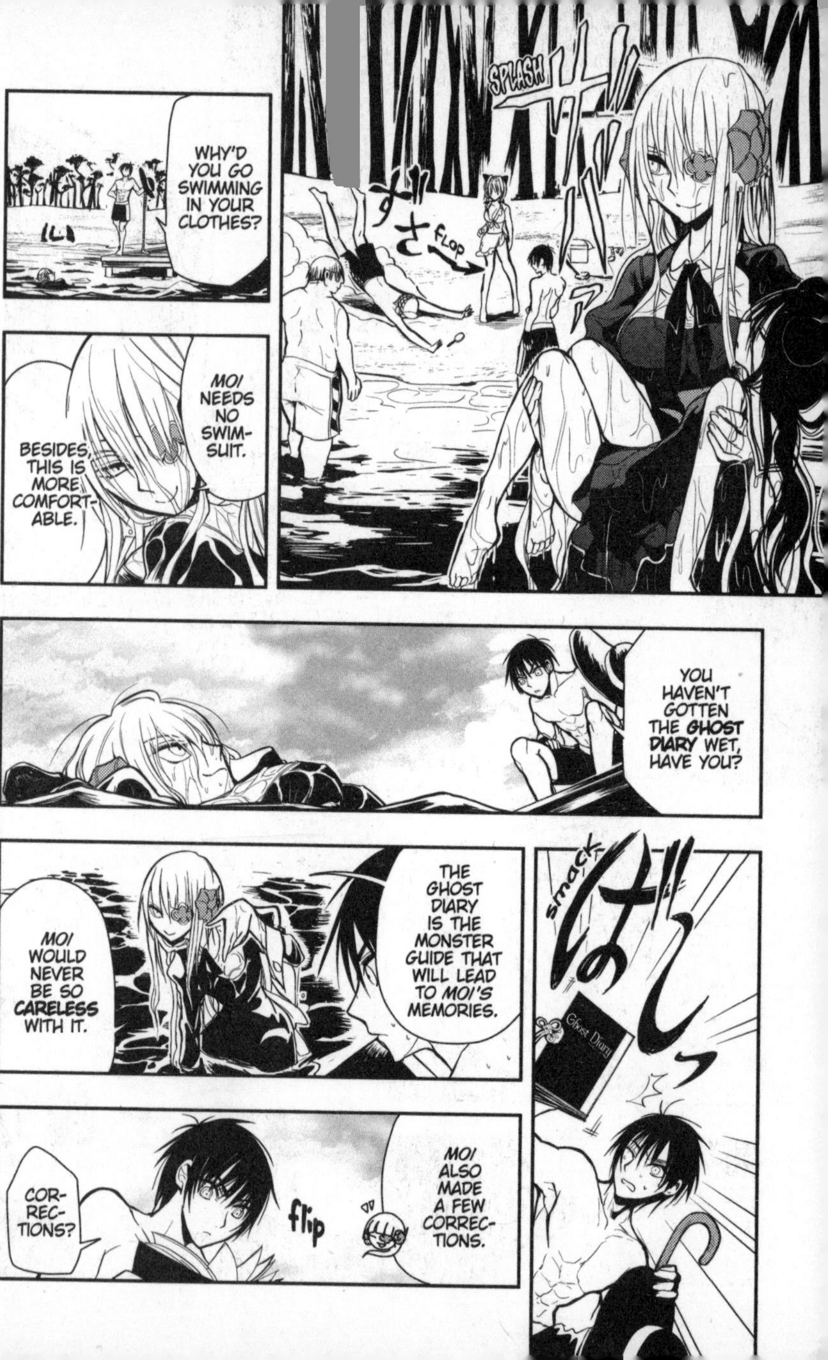
SPLASH
FLOP
WHY'D YOU GO SWIMMING IN YOUR CLOTHES?
MOI NEEDS NO SWIM-SUIT.
BESIDES, THIS IS MORE COMFORT-ABLE.
YOU HAVEN'T GOTTEN THE GHOST DIARY WET, HAVE YOU?
smack
Ghost Diary
THE GHOST DIARY IS THE MONSTER GUIDE THAT WILL LEAD TO MOI'S MEMORIES.
MOI WOULD NEVER BE SO CARELESS WITH IT.
MOI ALSO MADE A FEW CORREC-TIONS.
flip
COR-REC-TIONS?

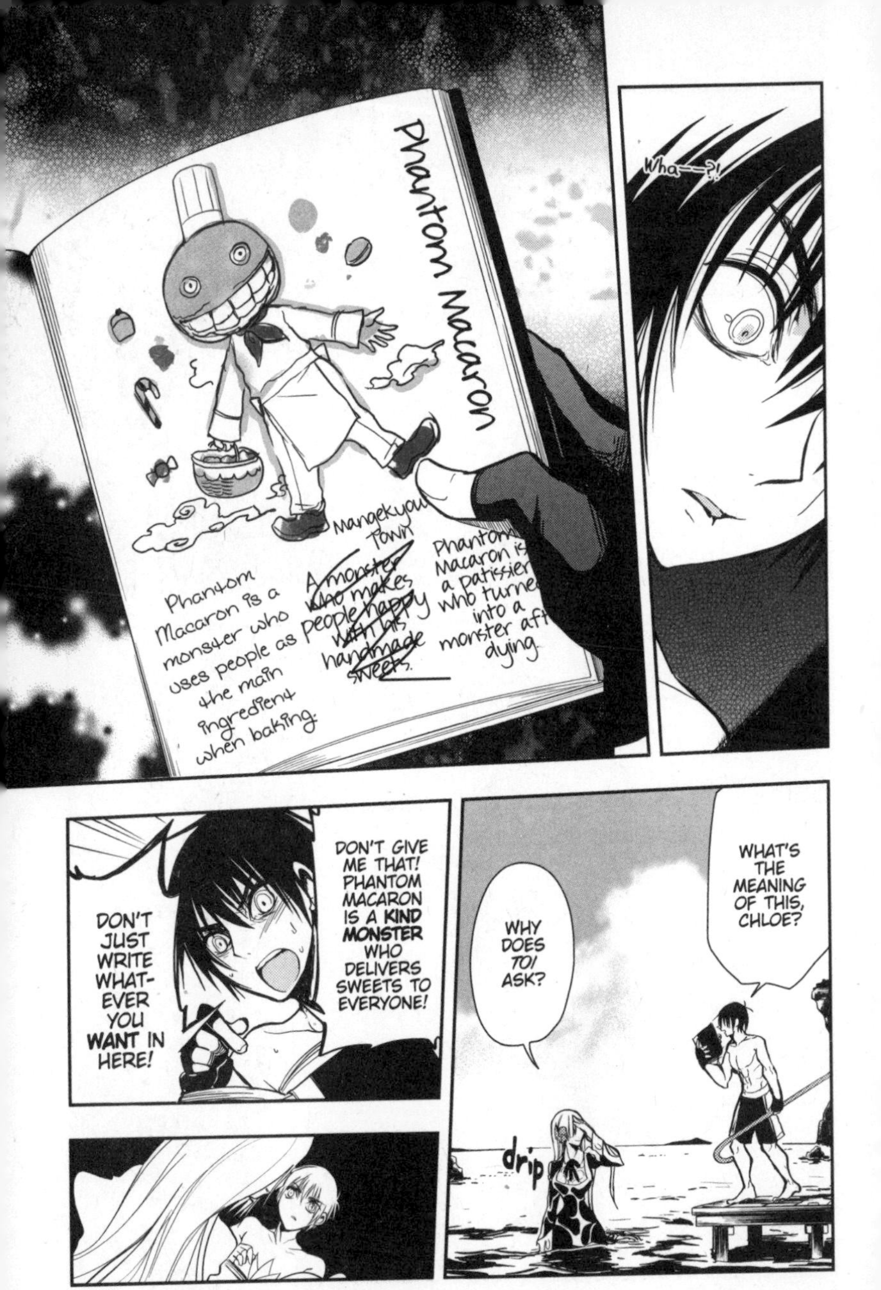
Wha---?!
Phantom Macaron
Phantom Macaron is a monster who uses people as the main ingredient when baking.
A monster who makes people happy with his handmade sweets.
Mangekyou Town
Phantom Macaron is a patissier who turne into a monster aft dying.
WHAT'S THE MEANING OF THIS, CHLOE?
WHY DOES TOI ASK?
drip
DON'T GIVE ME THAT! PHANTOM MACARON IS A KIND MONSTER WHO DELIVERS SWEETS TO EVERYONE!
DON'T JUST WRITE WHAT-EVER YOU WANT IN HERE!

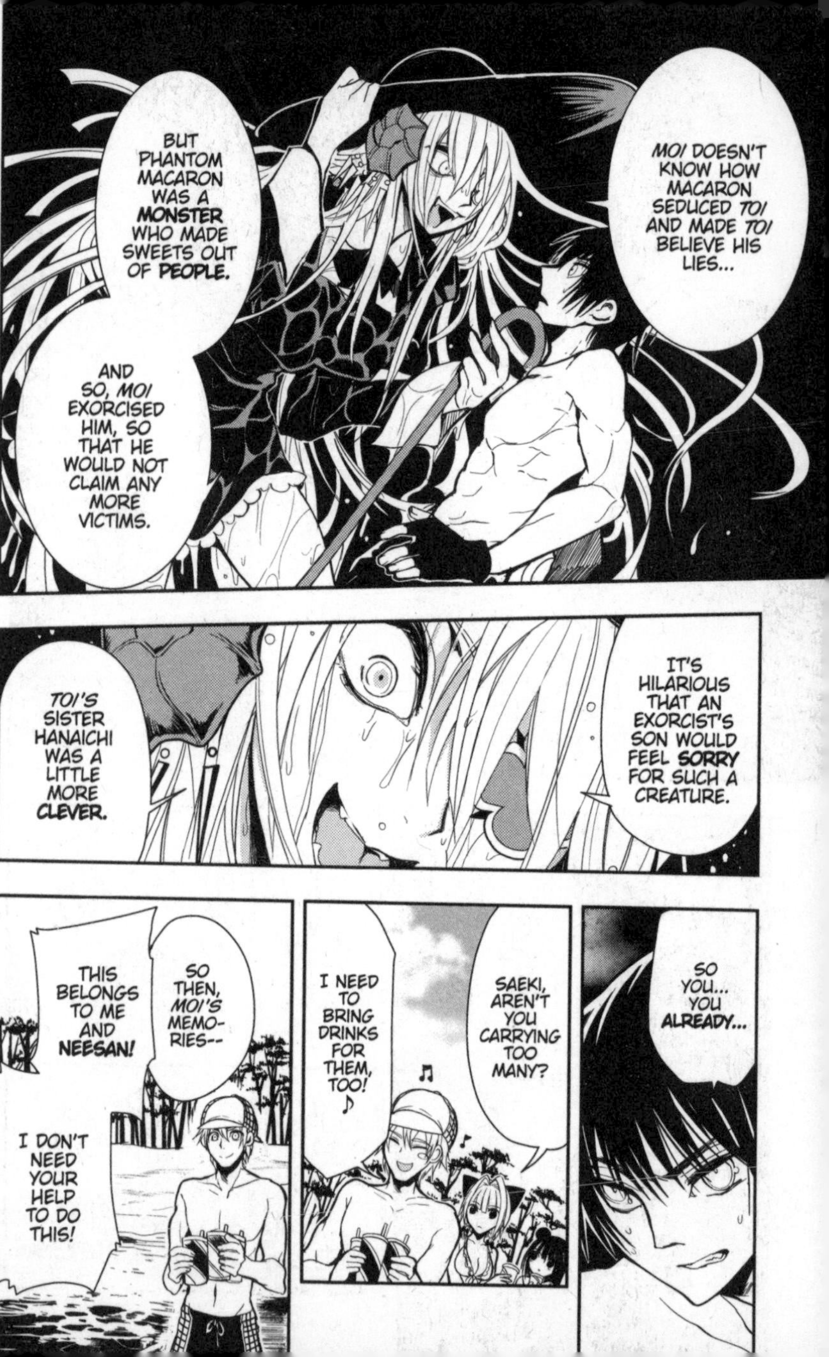
MOI DOESN'T KNOW HOW MACARON SEDUCED TOI AND MADE TOI BELIEVE HIS LIES...
BUT PHANTOM MACARON WAS A MONSTER WHO MADE SWEETS OUT OF PEOPLE.
AND SO, MOI EXORCISED HIM, SO THAT HE WOULD NOT CLAIM ANY MORE VICTIMS.
IT'S HILARIOUS THAT AN EXORCIST'S SON WOULD FEEL SORRY FOR SUCH A CREATURE.
TOI'S SISTER HANAICHI WAS A LITTLE MORE CLEVER.
SO YOU... YOU ALREADY...
SAEKI, AREN'T YOU CARRYING TOO MANY?
I NEED TO BRING DRINKS FOR THEM, TOO! ♪
SO THEN, MOI'S MEMORIES--
THIS BELONGS TO ME AND NEESAN!
I DON'T NEED YOUR HELP TO DO THIS!

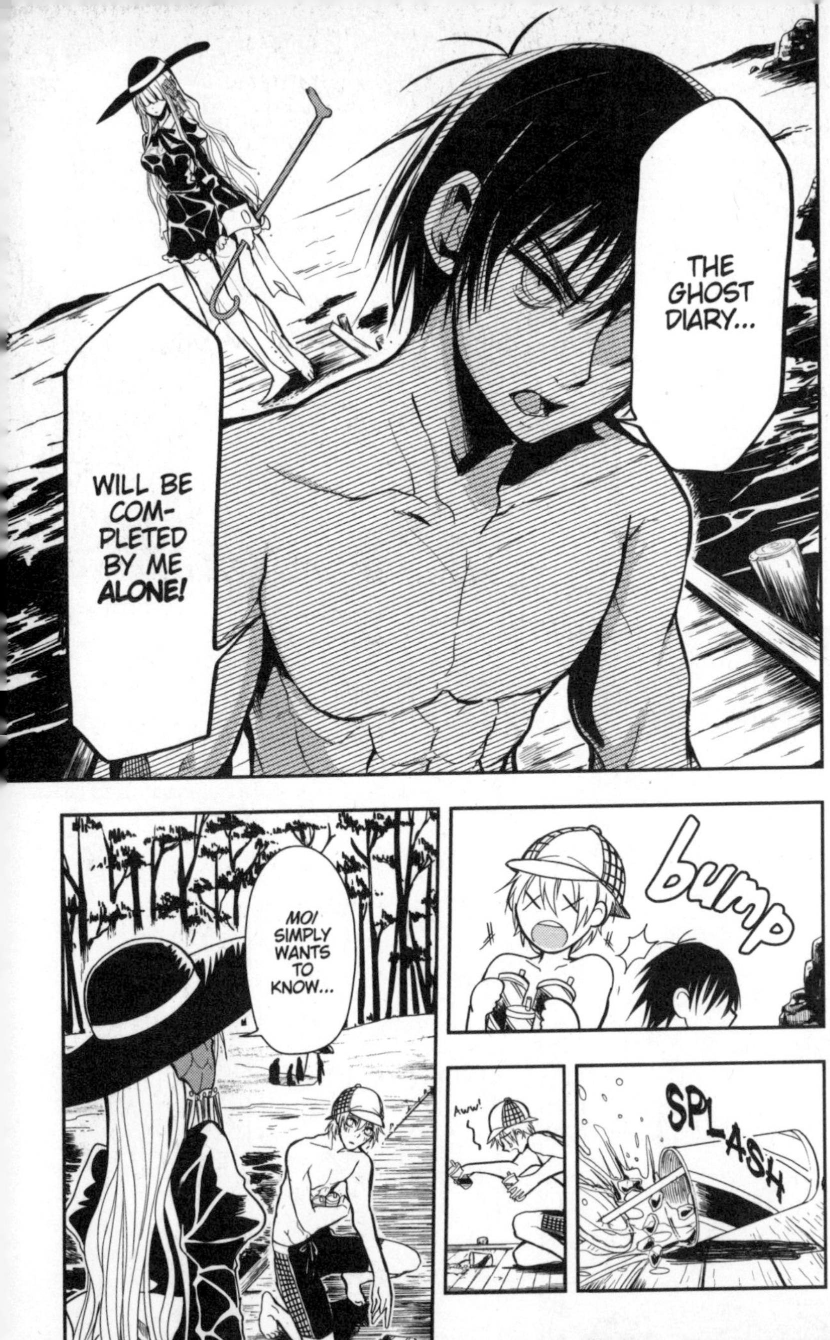
THE GHOST DIARY...
WILL BE COMPLETED BY ME ALONE!
bump
SPLASH
Aww!
MOI SIMPLY WANTS TO KNOW...

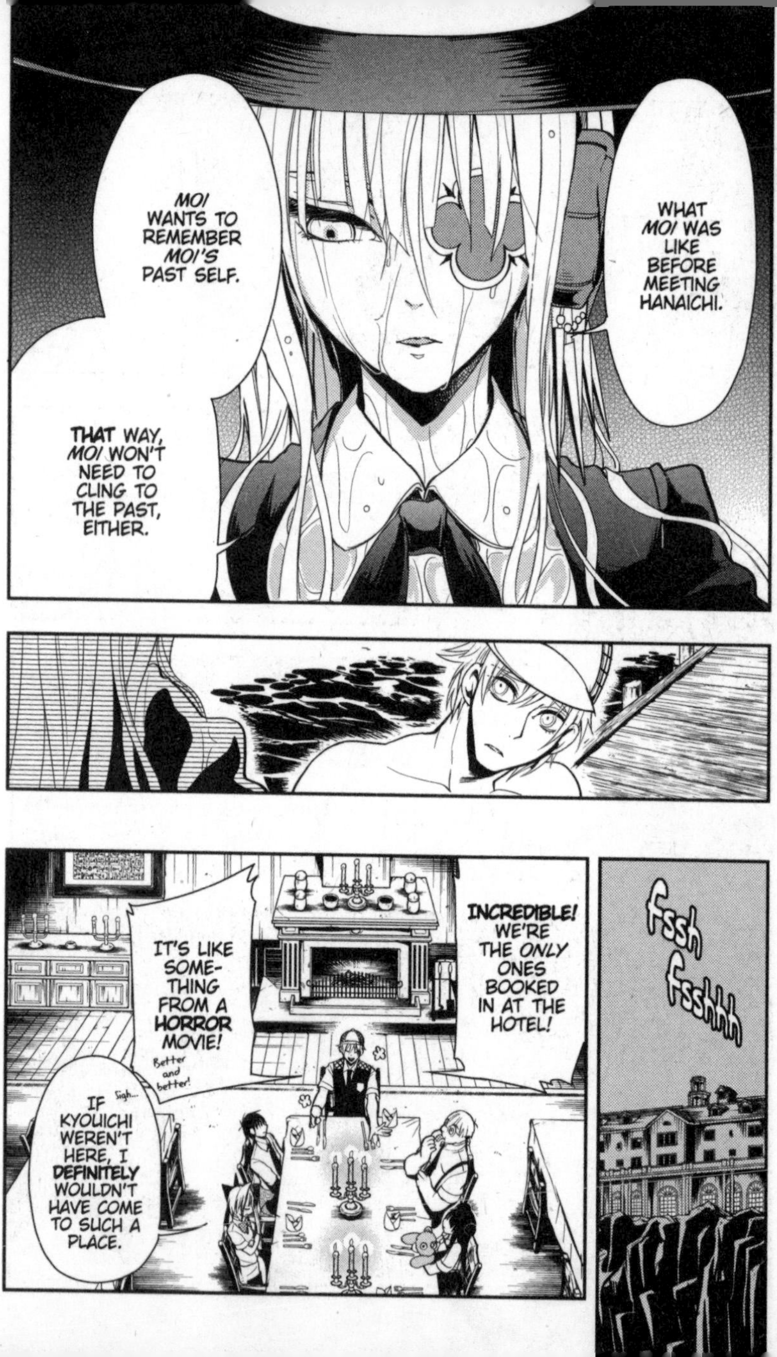
WHAT MOI WAS LIKE BEFORE MEETING HANAICHI.
MOI WANTS TO REMEMBER MOI'S PAST SELF.
THAT WAY, MOI WON'T NEED TO CLING TO THE PAST, EITHER.
fssh fsshhh
INCREDIBLE! WE'RE THE ONLY ONES BOOKED IN AT THE HOTEL!
IT'S LIKE SOME-THING FROM A HORROR MOVIE!
Better and better!
Sigh...
IF KYOUICHI WEREN'T HERE, I DEFINITELY WOULDN'T HAVE COME TO SUCH A PLACE.

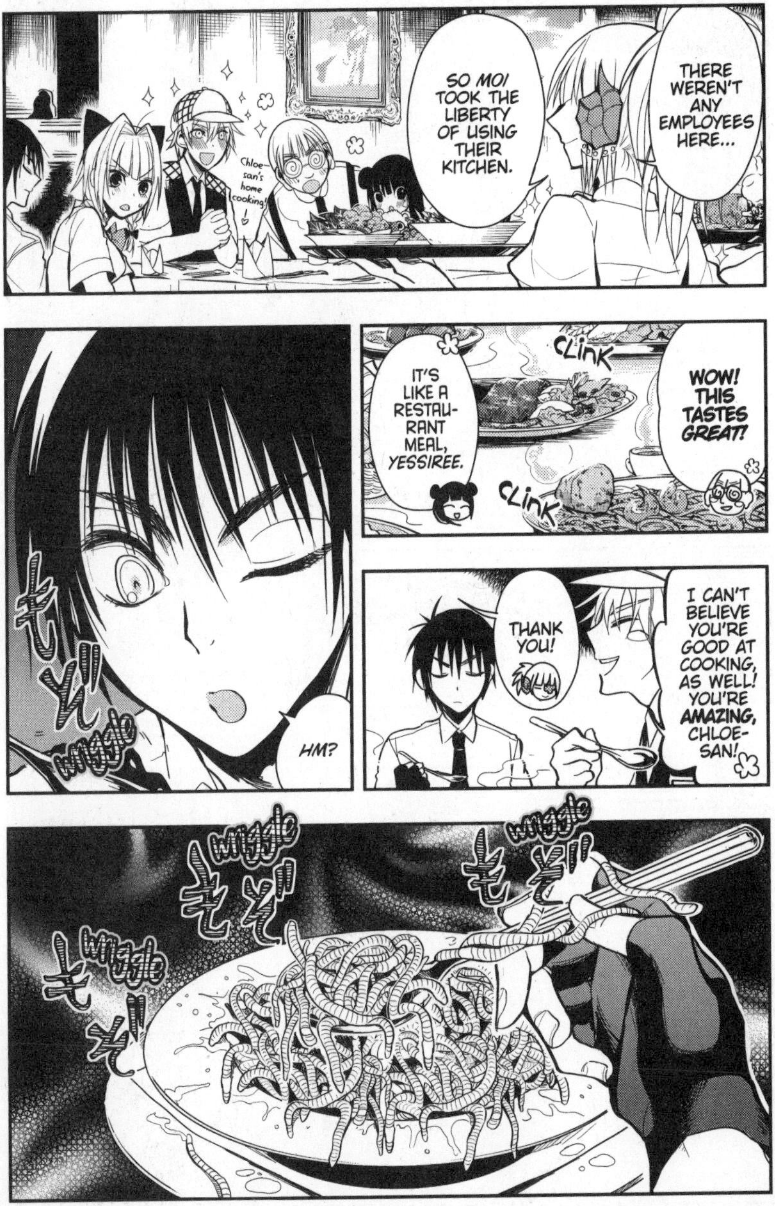
THERE WEREN'T ANY EMPLOYEES HERE...
SO *MOI* TOOK THE LIBERTY OF USING THEIR KITCHEN.
Chloe-san's home cooking!
!
WOW! THIS TASTES *GREAT!*
CLINK
IT'S LIKE A RESTAURANT MEAL, *YESSIREE.*
CLINK
I CAN'T BELIEVE YOU'RE GOOD AT COOKING, AS WELL! YOU'RE **AMAZING,** CHLOE-SAN!
THANK YOU!
HM?
wriggle
wriggle
wriggle
wriggle

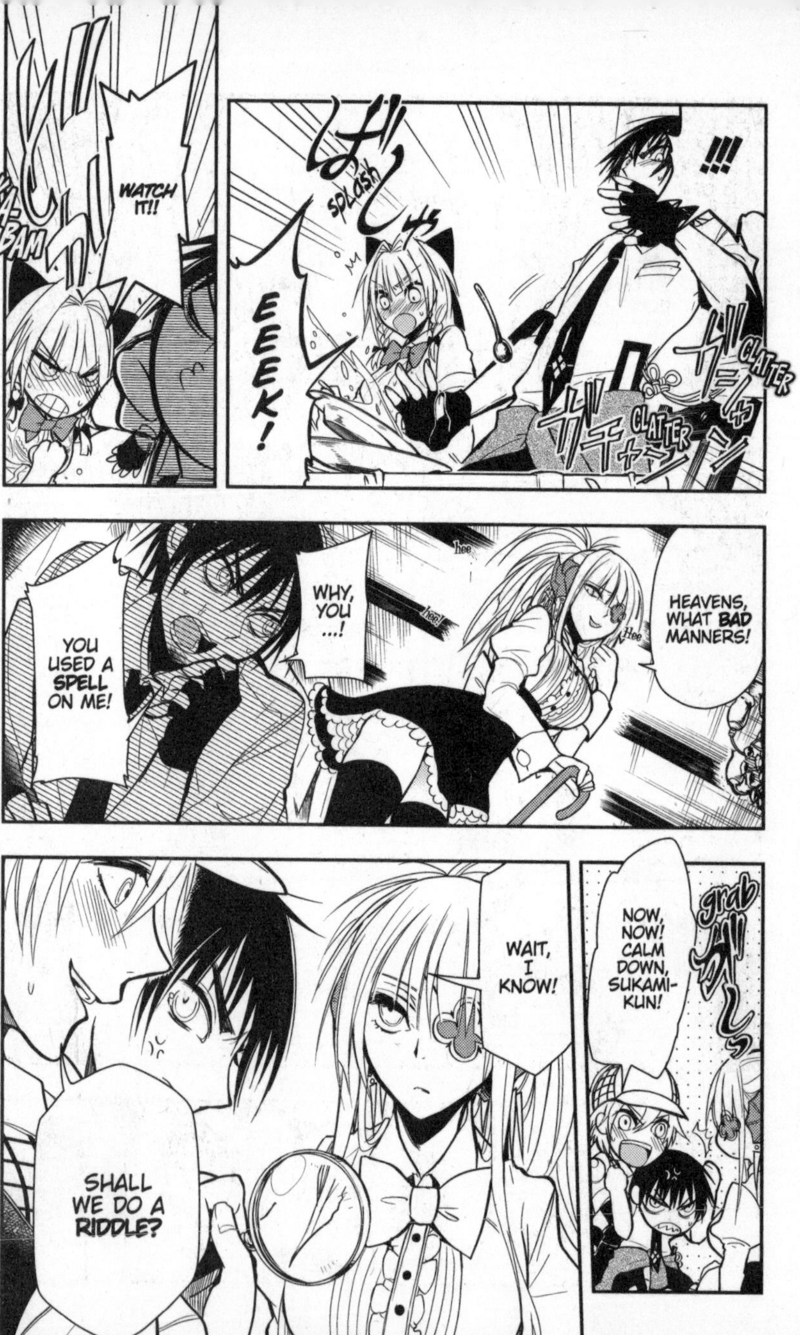
!!!
SPLASH
EEEEK!
CLATTER
CLATTER
KA-BAM
WATCH IT!!
HEAVENS, WHAT BAD MANNERS!
hee
hee!
Hee
WHY, YOU ...!
YOU USED A SPELL ON ME!
grab
NOW, NOW! CALM DOWN, SUKAMI-KUN!
WAIT, I KNOW!
SHALL WE DO A RIDDLE?

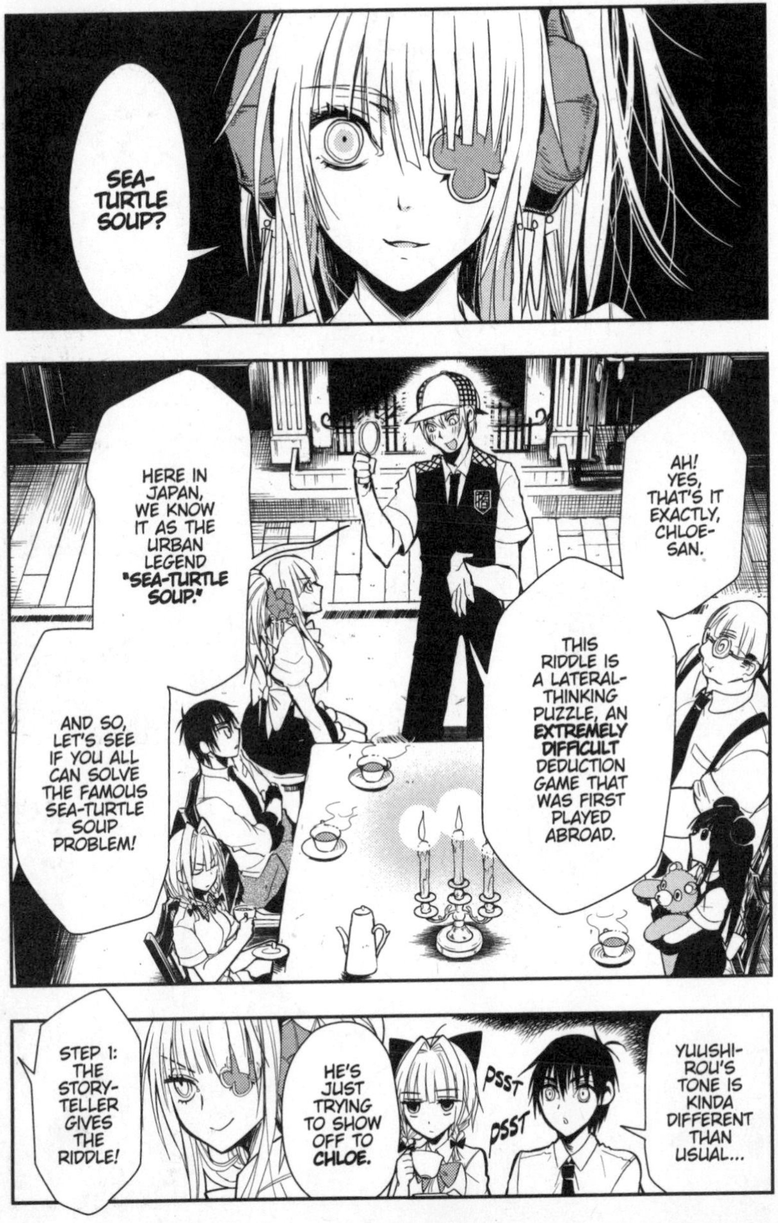
SEA-TURTLE SOUP?
AH! YES, THAT'S IT EXACTLY, CHLOE-SAN.
THIS RIDDLE IS A LATERAL-THINKING PUZZLE, AN **EXTREMELY DIFFICULT** DEDUCTION GAME THAT WAS FIRST PLAYED ABROAD.
HERE IN JAPAN, WE KNOW IT AS THE URBAN LEGEND **"SEA-TURTLE SOUP."**
AND SO, LET'S SEE IF YOU ALL CAN SOLVE THE FAMOUS SEA-TURTLE SOUP PROBLEM!
YUUSHIROU'S TONE IS KINDA DIFFERENT THAN USUAL...
PSST
PSST
HE'S JUST TRYING TO SHOW OFF TO **CHLOE.**
STEP 1: THE STORY-TELLER GIVES THE RIDDLE!

The Sea-Turtle Soup Problem

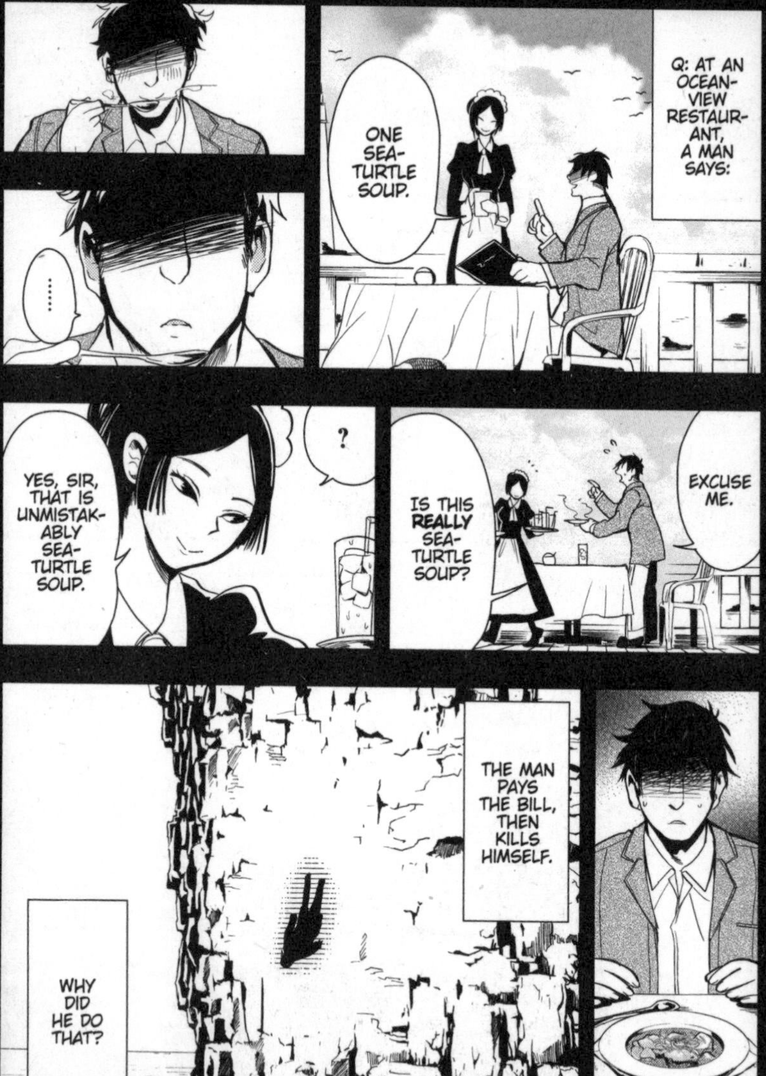
Q: AT AN OCEAN-VIEW RESTAURANT, A MAN SAYS:
ONE SEA-TURTLE SOUP.
......
EXCUSE ME.
IS THIS **REALLY** SEA-TURTLE SOUP?
?
YES, SIR, THAT IS UNMISTAKABLY SEA-TURTLE SOUP.
THE MAN PAYS THE BILL, THEN KILLS HIMSELF.
WHY DID HE DO THAT?

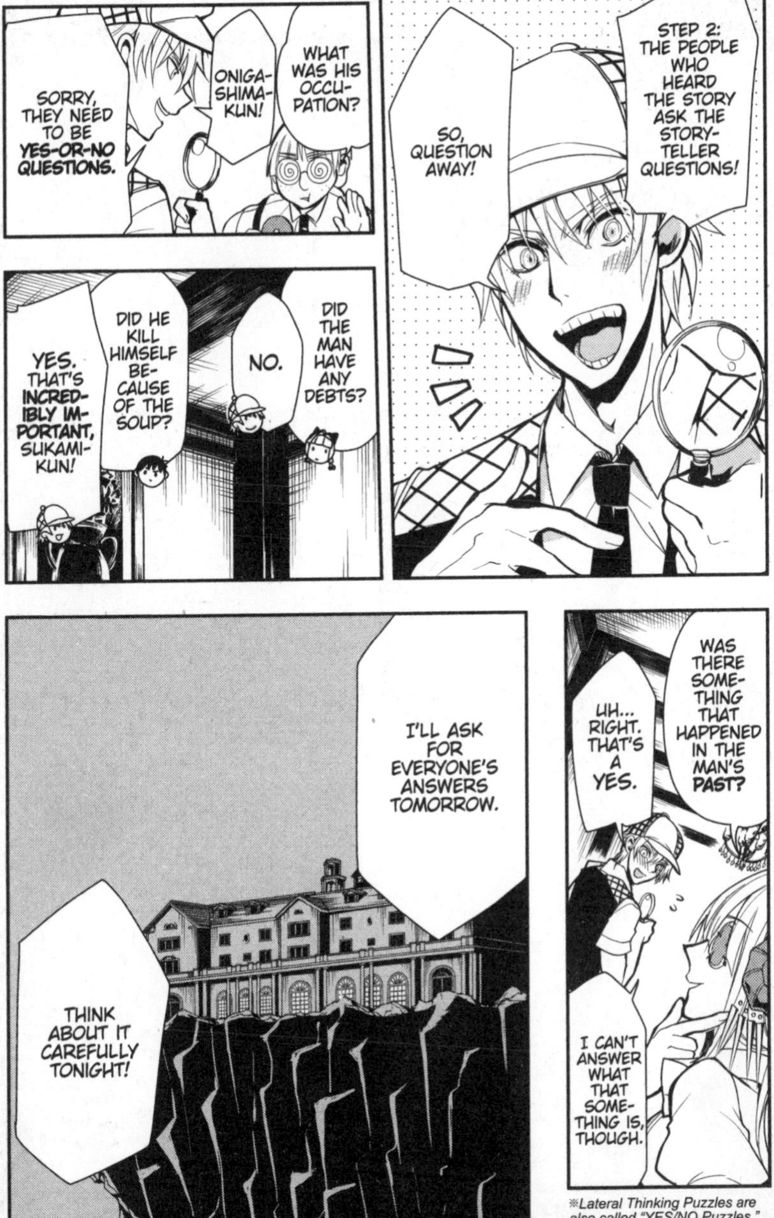
STEP 2: THE PEOPLE WHO HEARD THE STORY ASK THE STORYTELLER QUESTIONS!
SO, QUESTION AWAY!
WHAT WAS HIS OCCUPATION?
ONIGASHIMA-KUN!
SORRY, THEY NEED TO BE **YES-OR-NO QUESTIONS.**
DID THE MAN HAVE ANY DEBTS?
NO.
DID HE KILL HIMSELF BECAUSE OF THE SOUP?
YES. THAT'S **INCREDIBLY IMPORTANT,** SUKAMI-KUN!
WAS THERE SOMETHING THAT HAPPENED IN THE MAN'S **PAST?**
UH... RIGHT. THAT'S A **YES.**
I CAN'T ANSWER WHAT THAT SOMETHING IS, THOUGH.
I'LL ASK FOR EVERYONE'S ANSWERS TOMORROW.
THINK ABOUT IT CAREFULLY TONIGHT!

※Lateral Thinking Puzzles are also called "YES/NO Puzzles."

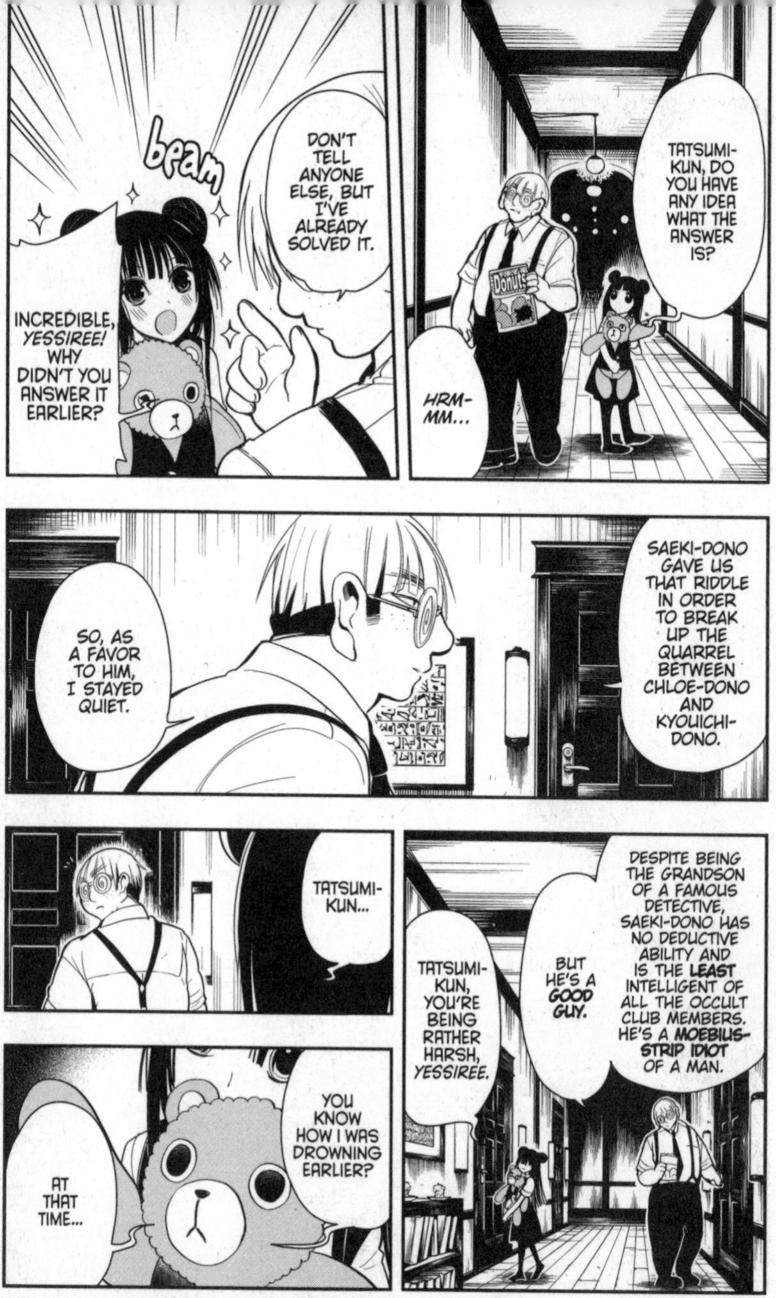

TATSUMI-KUN, DO YOU HAVE ANY IDEA WHAT THE ANSWER IS?
HRMM-MM...
DON'T TELL ANYONE ELSE, BUT I'VE ALREADY SOLVED IT.
beam
INCREDIBLE, YESSIREE! WHY DIDN'T YOU ANSWER IT EARLIER?
SAEKI-DONO GAVE US THAT RIDDLE IN ORDER TO BREAK UP THE QUARREL BETWEEN CHLOE-DONO AND KYOUICHI-DONO.
SO, AS A FAVOR TO HIM, I STAYED QUIET.
DESPITE BEING THE GRANDSON OF A FAMOUS DETECTIVE, SAEKI-DONO HAS NO DEDUCTIVE ABILITY AND IS THE LEAST INTELLIGENT OF ALL THE OCCULT CLUB MEMBERS. HE'S A MOEBIUS-STRIP IDIOT OF A MAN.
BUT HE'S A GOOD GUY.
TATSUMI-KUN, YOU'RE BEING RATHER HARSH, YESSIREE.
TATSUMI-KUN...
YOU KNOW HOW I WAS DROWNING EARLIER?
AT THAT TIME...

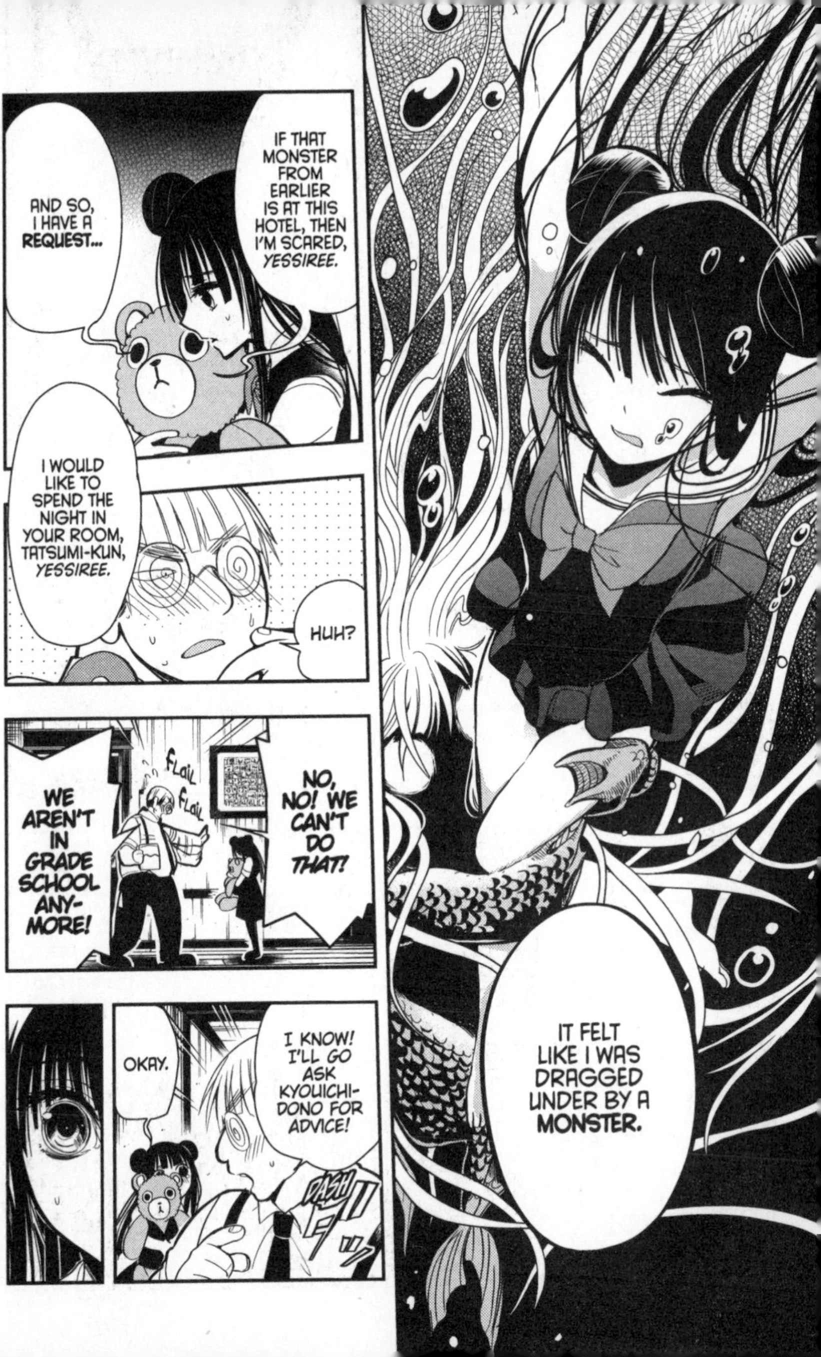
IT FELT LIKE I WAS DRAGGED UNDER BY A **MONSTER.**
IF THAT MONSTER FROM EARLIER IS AT THIS HOTEL, THEN I'M SCARED, *YESSIREE.*
AND SO, I HAVE A **REQUEST...**
I WOULD LIKE TO SPEND THE NIGHT IN YOUR ROOM, TATSUMI-KUN, *YESSIREE.*
HUH?
NO, NO! WE CAN'T DO *THAT!*
FLAIL FLAIL
WE AREN'T IN GRADE SCHOOL ANY-MORE!
I KNOW! I'LL GO ASK KYOUICHI-DONO FOR ADVICE!
OKAY.
DASH

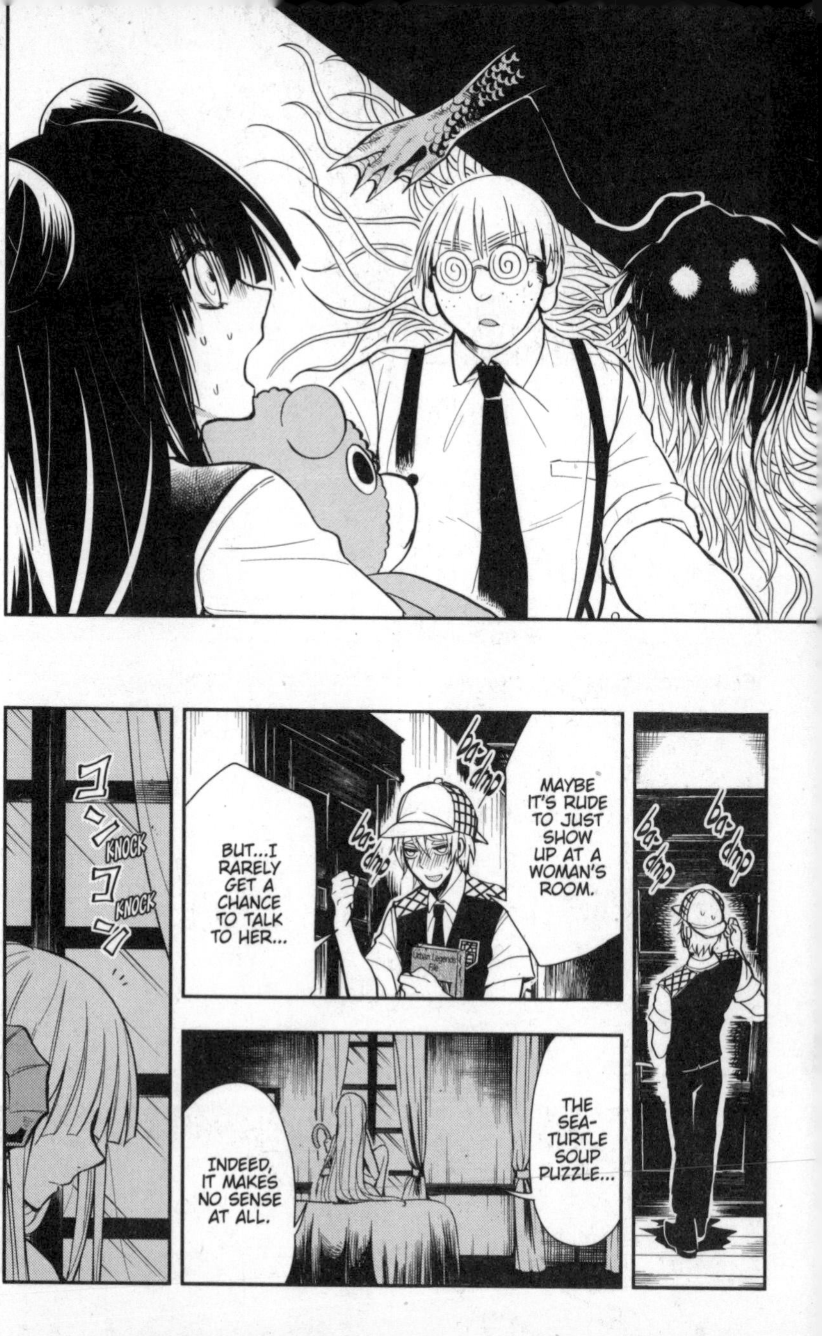
ba-dmp
ba-dmp
MAYBE IT'S RUDE TO JUST SHOW UP AT A WOMAN'S ROOM.
ba-dmp
ba-dmp
BUT...I RARELY GET A CHANCE TO TALK TO HER...
Urban Legends File
THE SEA-TURTLE SOUP PUZZLE...
INDEED, IT MAKES NO SENSE AT ALL.
KNOCK
KNOCK

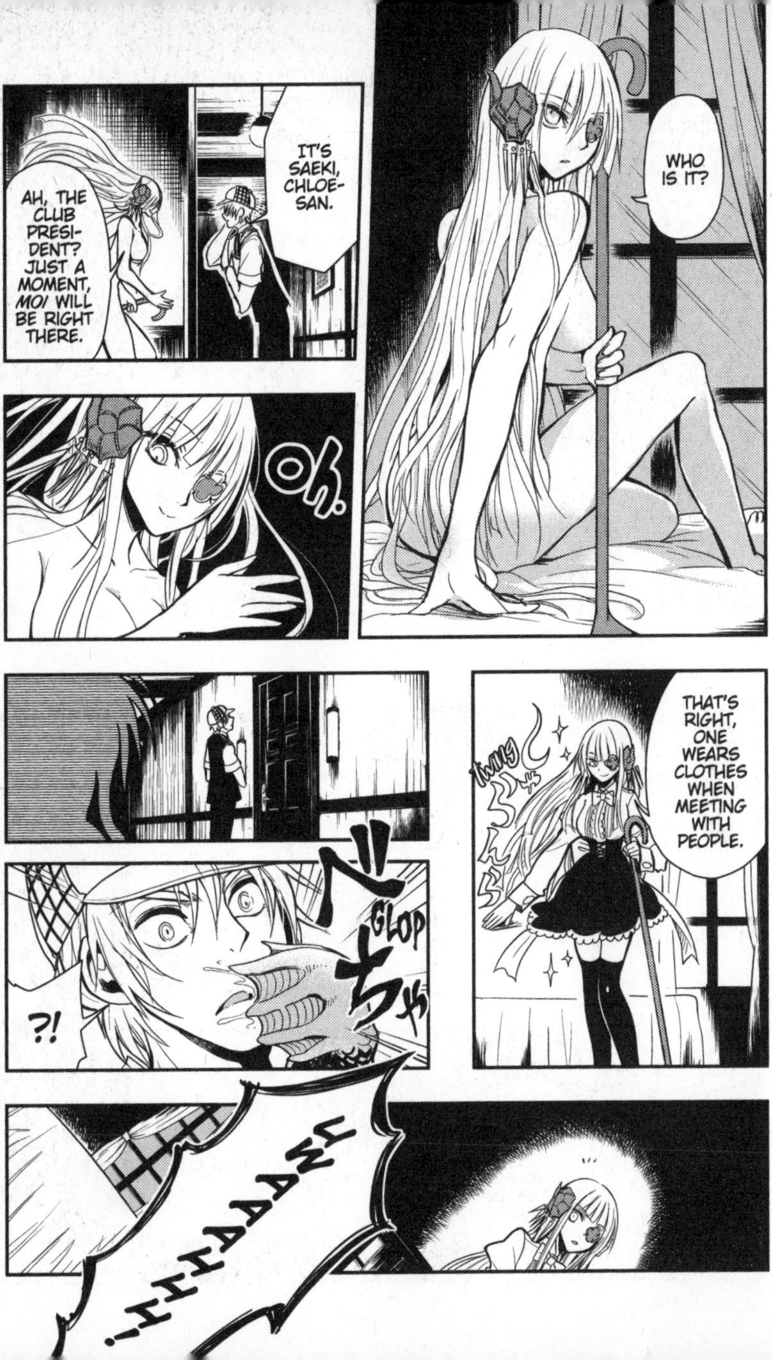
WHO IS IT?
IT'S SAEKI, CHLOE-SAN.
AH, THE CLUB PRESIDENT? JUST A MOMENT, *MOI* WILL BE RIGHT THERE.
oh.
THAT'S RIGHT, ONE WEARS CLOTHES WHEN MEETING WITH PEOPLE.
TWING
GLOP
?!
UWAAAAAHHH!

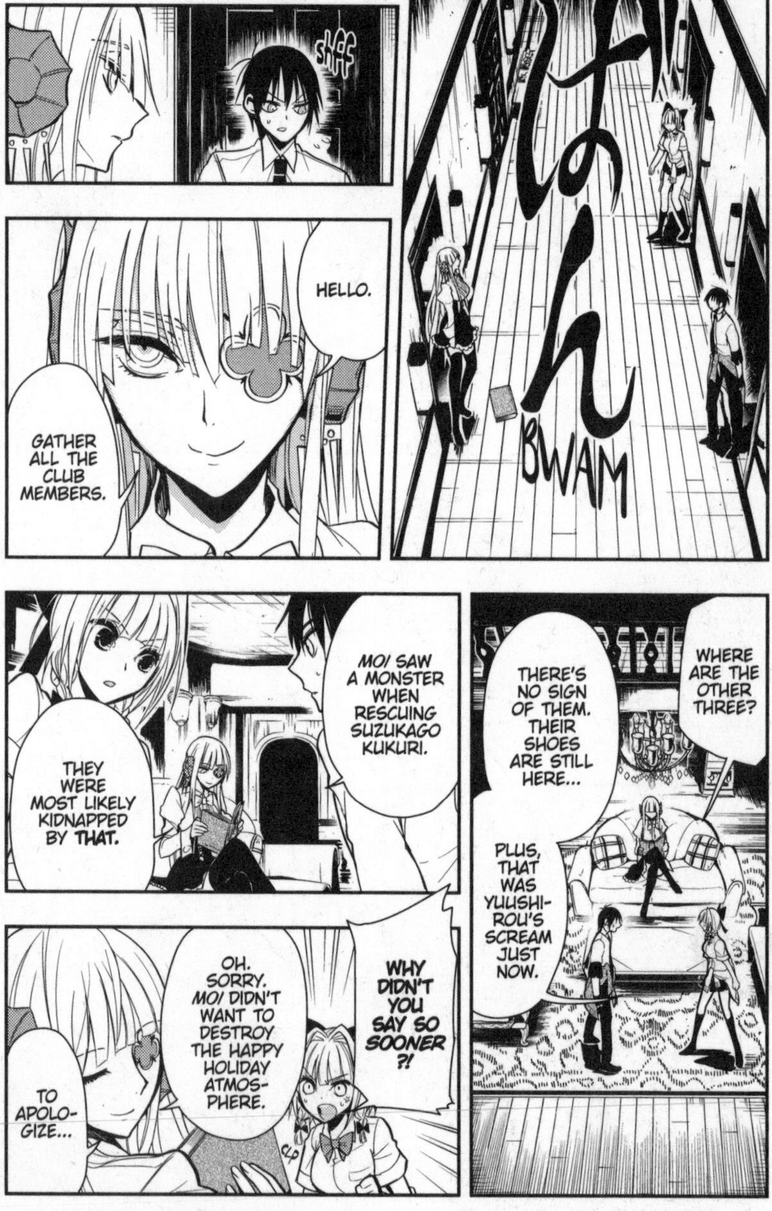
ばん
BWAM
shiff
HELLO.
GATHER ALL THE CLUB MEMBERS.
WHERE ARE THE OTHER THREE?
THERE'S NO SIGN OF THEM. THEIR SHOES ARE STILL HERE...
PLUS, THAT WAS YUUSHIROU'S SCREAM JUST NOW.
MOI SAW A MONSTER WHEN RESCUING SUZUKAGO KUKURI.
THEY WERE MOST LIKELY KIDNAPPED BY **THAT.**
WHY DIDN'T YOU SAY SO *SOONER*?!
OH. SORRY. *MOI* DIDN'T WANT TO DESTROY THE HAPPY HOLIDAY ATMOSPHERE.
TO APOLOGIZE...
CLP

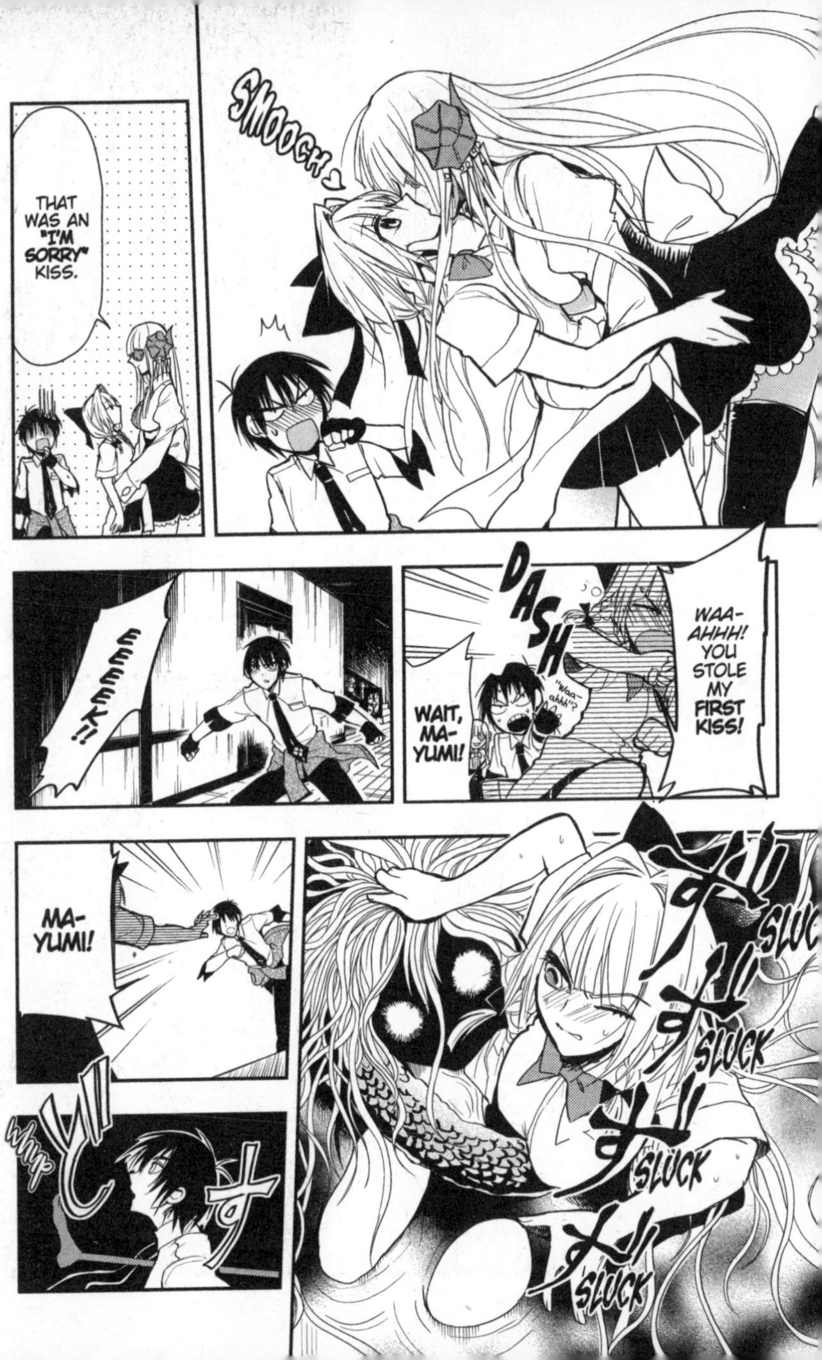
SMOOCH
THAT WAS AN "I'M SORRY" KISS.
DASH
WAA-AHHH! YOU STOLE MY FIRST KISS!
"Waa-ahhh"?
WAIT, MA-YUMI!
EEEEEK!!
SLUCK
SLUCK
SLUCK
SLUCK
MA-YUMI!
whip

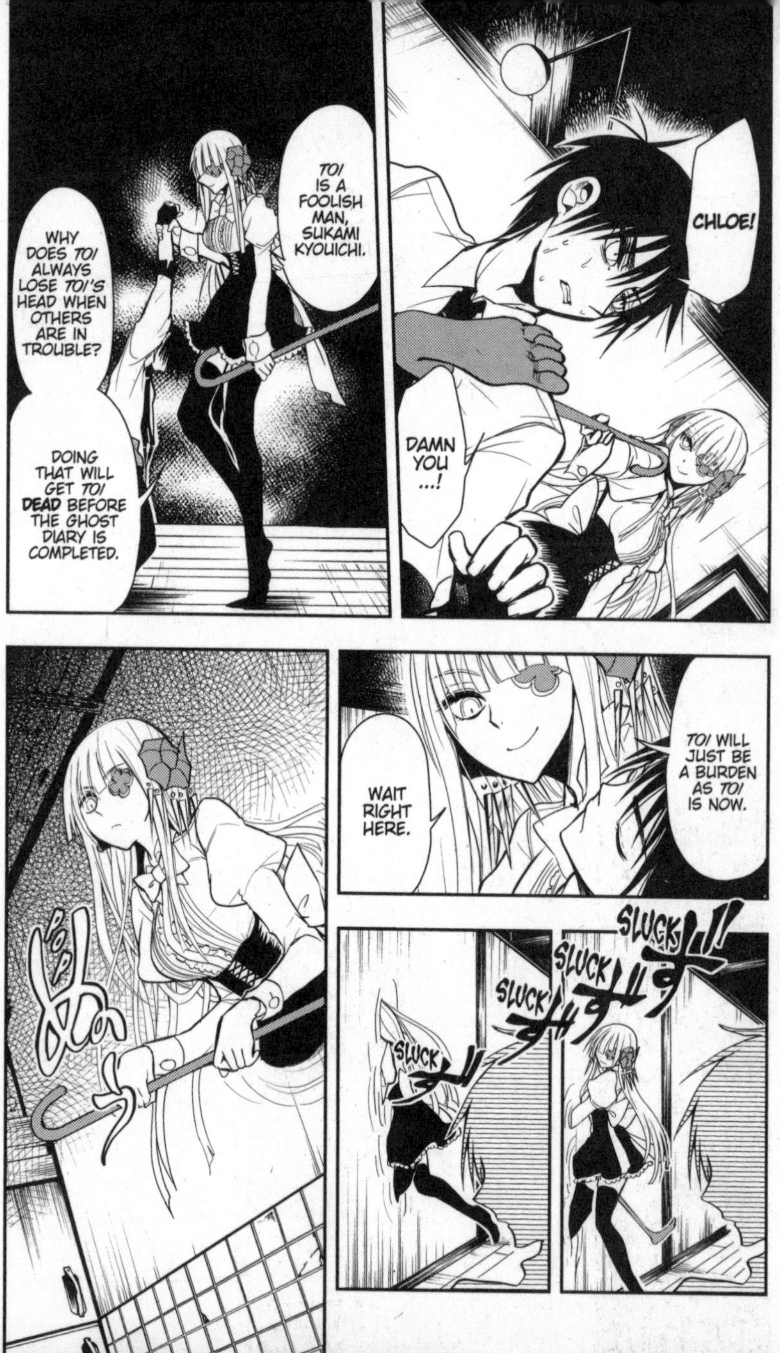

CHLOE!
DAMN YOU ...!
TOI IS A FOOLISH MAN, SUKAMI KYOUICHI.
WHY DOES TOI ALWAYS LOSE TOI'S HEAD WHEN OTHERS ARE IN TROUBLE?
DOING THAT WILL GET TOI DEAD BEFORE THE GHOST DIARY IS COMPLETED.
TOI WILL JUST BE A BURDEN AS TOI IS NOW.
WAIT RIGHT HERE.
SLUCK!!
SLUCK
SLUCK
SLUCK
POP

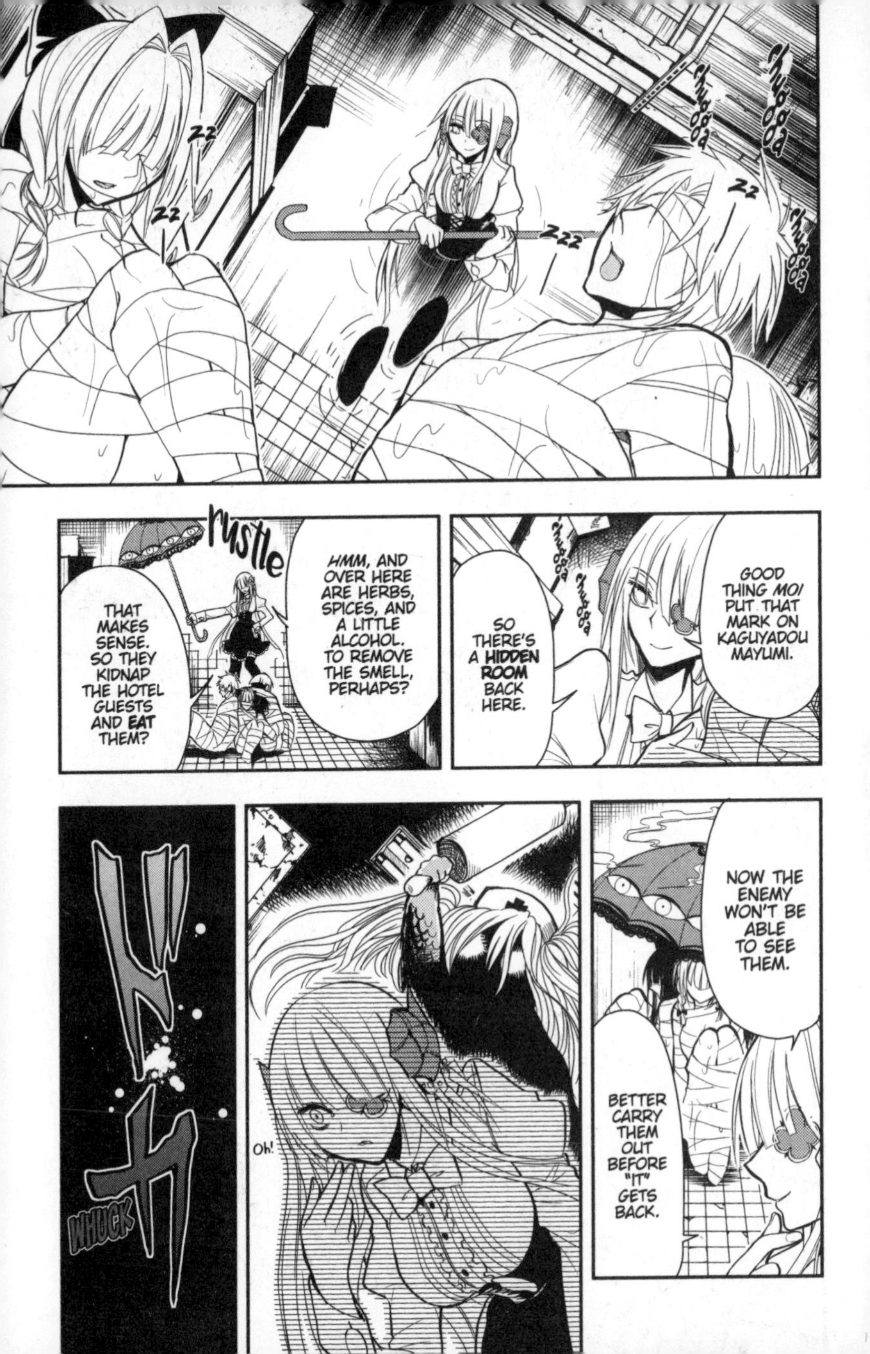
chugga chugga
chugga
zz
zz
zz
zzz
chugga chugga
GOOD THING *MOI* PUT THAT MARK ON KAGUYADOU MAYUMI.
SO THERE'S A **HIDDEN ROOM** BACK HERE.
chugga
rustle
HMM, AND OVER HERE ARE HERBS, SPICES, AND A LITTLE ALCOHOL. TO REMOVE THE SMELL, PERHAPS?
THAT MAKES SENSE. SO THEY KIDNAP THE HOTEL GUESTS AND **EAT** THEM?
NOW THE ENEMY WON'T BE ABLE TO SEE THEM.
BETTER CARRY THEM OUT BEFORE "IT" GETS BACK.
Oh!
WHUCK

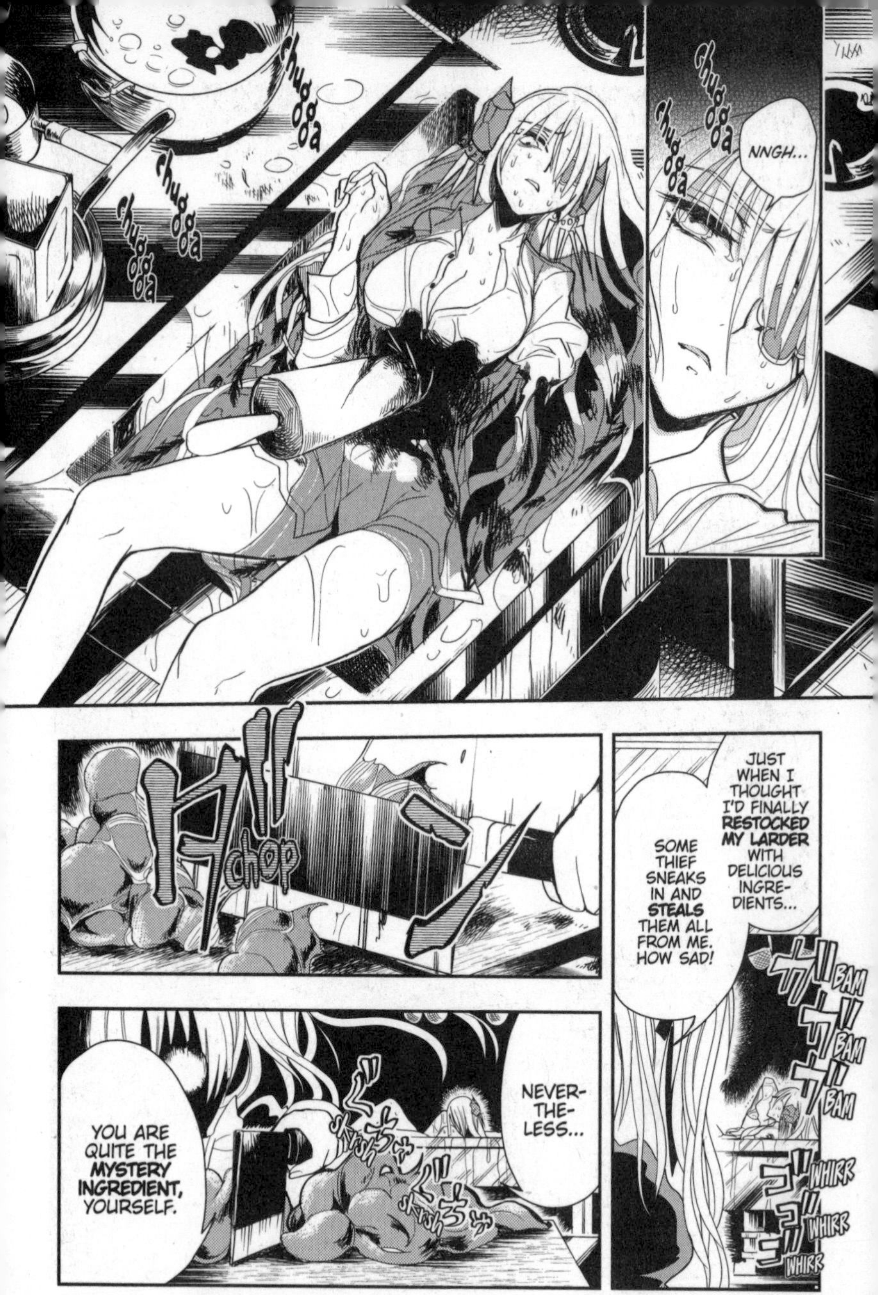
chugga
chugga
chugga
NNGH...
chugga
chugga
chugga
chugga
JUST WHEN I THOUGHT I'D FINALLY **RESTOCKED MY LARDER** WITH DELICIOUS INGREDIENTS...
SOME THIEF SNEAKS IN AND **STEALS** THEM ALL FROM ME. HOW SAD!
BAM
BAM
BAM
WHIRR
WHIRR
WHIRR
chop
NEVER-THE-LESS...
shrsh
shrsh
YOU ARE QUITE THE **MYSTERY INGREDIENT**, YOURSELF.

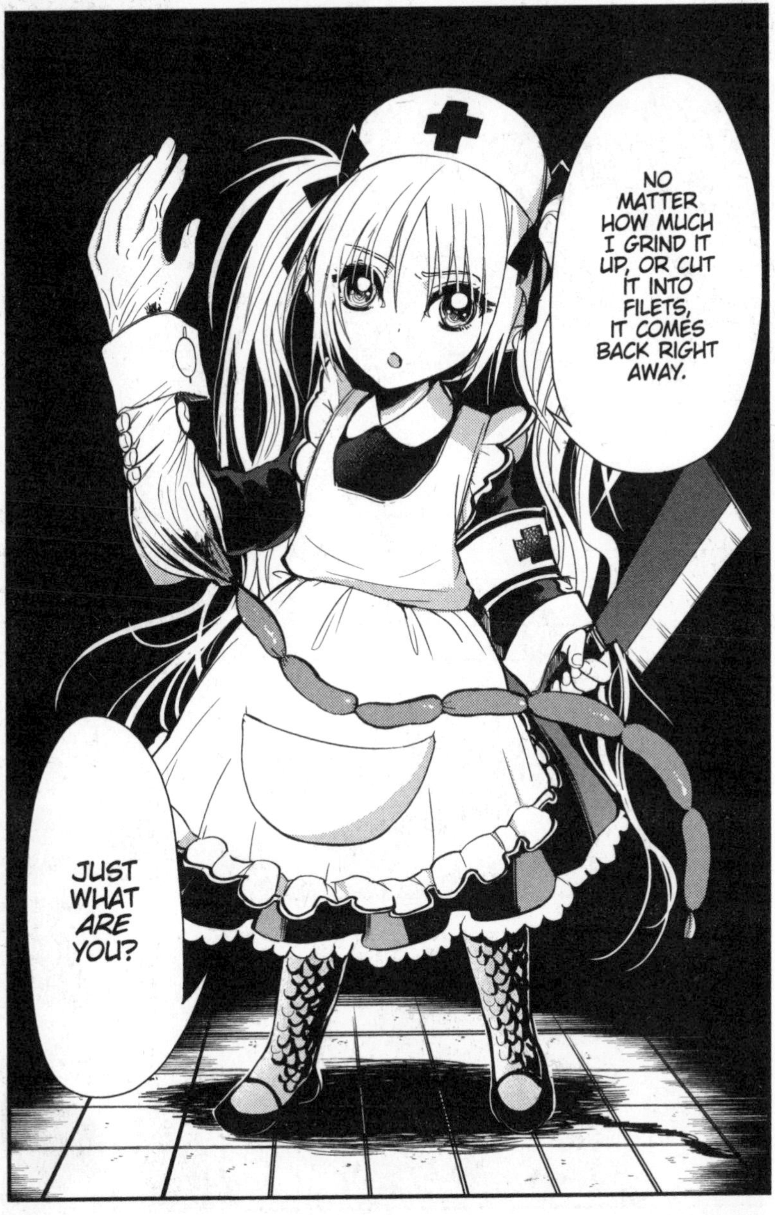
NO MATTER HOW MUCH I GRIND IT UP, OR CUT IT INTO FILETS, IT COMES BACK RIGHT AWAY.
JUST WHAT ARE YOU?

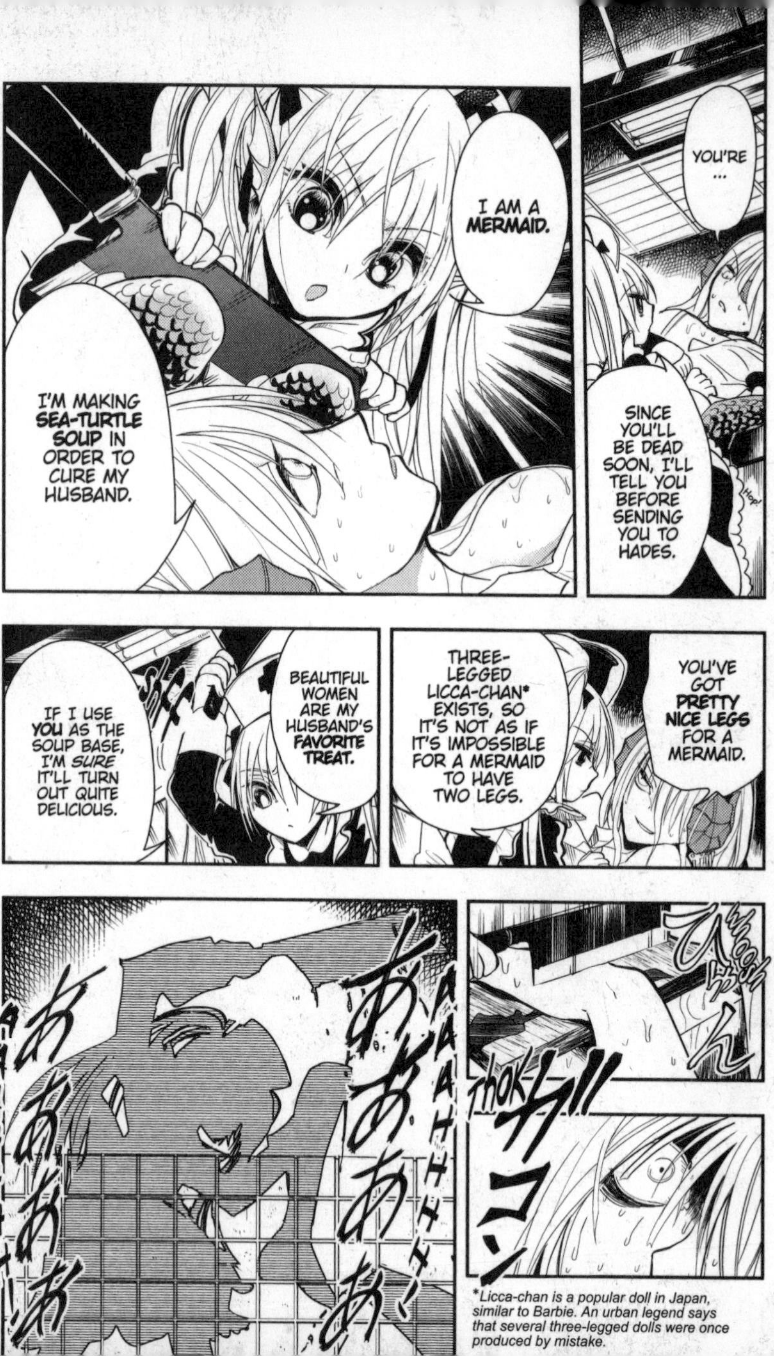

YOU'RE ...
SINCE YOU'LL BE DEAD SOON, I'LL TELL YOU BEFORE SENDING YOU TO HADES.
Hop!
I AM A **MERMAID.**
I'M MAKING **SEA-TURTLE SOUP** IN ORDER TO CURE MY HUSBAND.
YOU'VE GOT **PRETTY NICE LEGS** FOR A MERMAID.
THREE-LEGGED LICCA-CHAN* EXISTS, SO IT'S NOT AS IF IT'S IMPOSSIBLE FOR A MERMAID TO HAVE TWO LEGS.
BEAUTIFUL WOMEN ARE MY HUSBAND'S **FAVORITE TREAT.**
IF I USE **YOU** AS THE SOUP BASE, I'M *SURE* IT'LL TURN OUT QUITE DELICIOUS.
whoosh
ひゅん
THOK
カコン!!
AAAHHHH!
ああああ
AAAHHHH!!
ああああ

*Licca-chan is a popular doll in Japan, similar to Barbie. An urban legend says that several three-legged dolls were once produced by mistake.

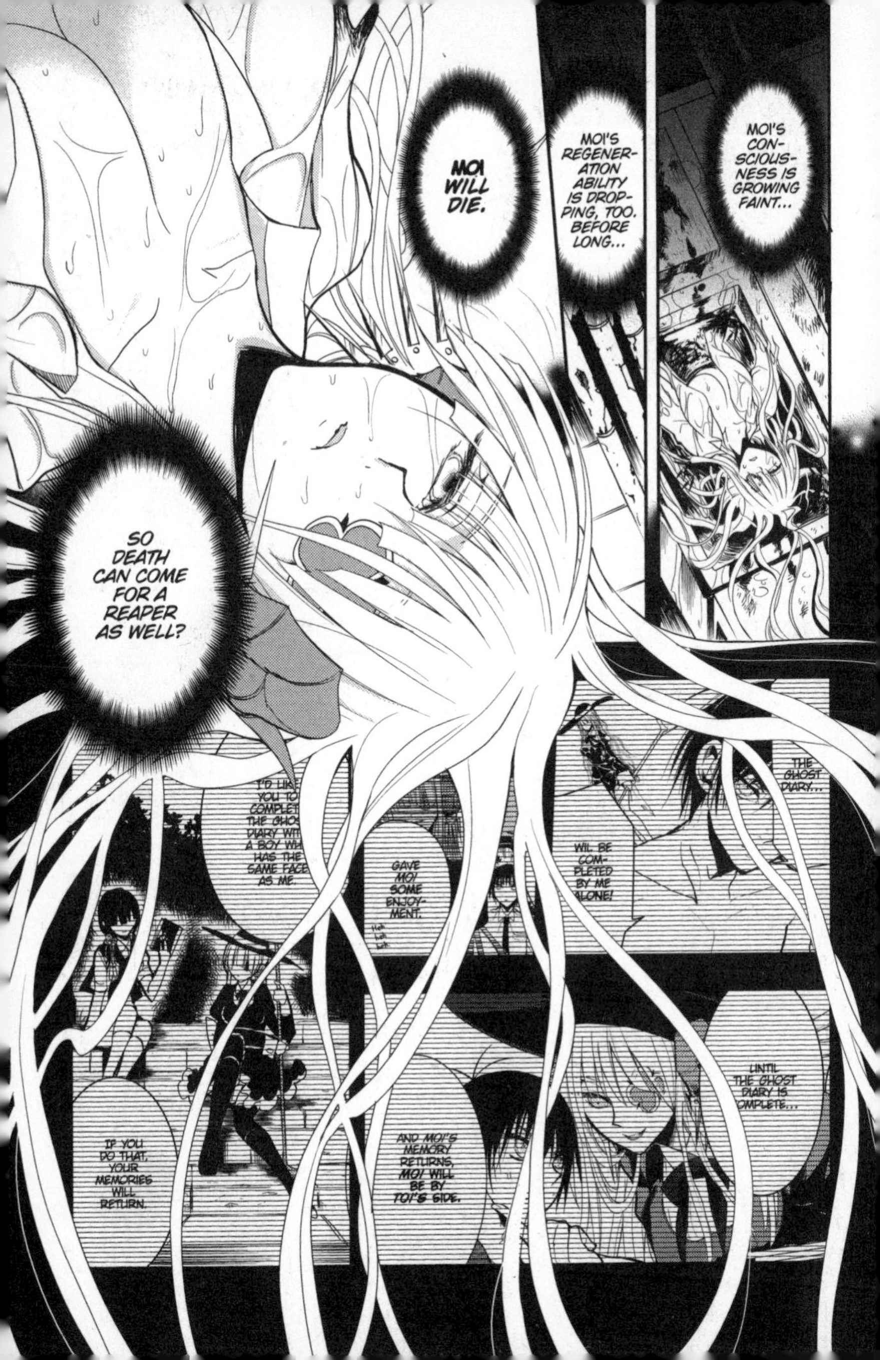

MOI'S CON-SCIOUS-NESS IS GROWING FAINT...
MOI'S REGENER-ATION ABILITY IS DROP-PING, TOO. BEFORE LONG...
MOI WILL DIE.
SO DEATH CAN COME FOR A REAPER AS WELL?
THE GHOST DIARY...
WIL BE COM-PLETED BY ME ALONE!
GAVE MOI SOME ENJOY-MENT.
Heh heh heh
I'D LIKE YOU TO COMPLETE THE GHOST DIARY WITH A BOY WHO HAS THE SAME FACE AS ME.
UNTIL THE GHOST DIARY IS COMPLETE...
AND MOI'S MEMORY RETURNS, MOI WILL BE BY TOI'S SIDE.
IF YOU DO THAT, YOUR MEMORIES WILL RETURN.

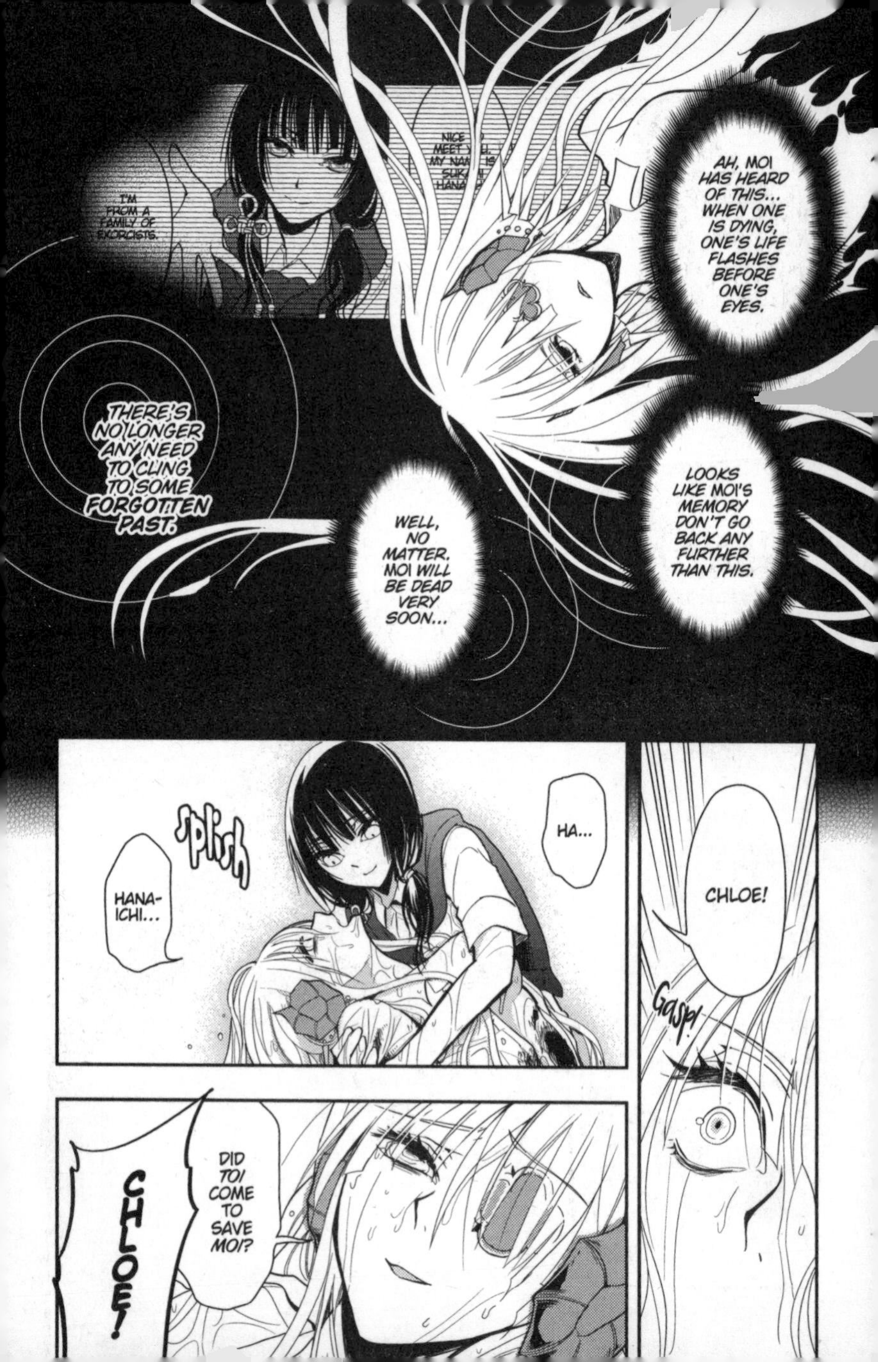
AH, MOI HAS HEARD OF THIS... WHEN ONE IS DYING, ONE'S LIFE FLASHES BEFORE ONE'S EYES.
I'M FROM A FAMILY OF EXORCISTS.
LOOKS LIKE MOI'S MEMORY DON'T GO BACK ANY FURTHER THAN THIS.
WELL, NO MATTER. MOI WILL BE DEAD VERY SOON...
THERE'S NO LONGER ANY NEED TO CLING TO SOME FORGOTTEN PAST.
CHLOE!
GASP!
HA...
HANA-ICHI...
SPLISH
DID TOI COME TO SAVE MOI?
CHLOE!

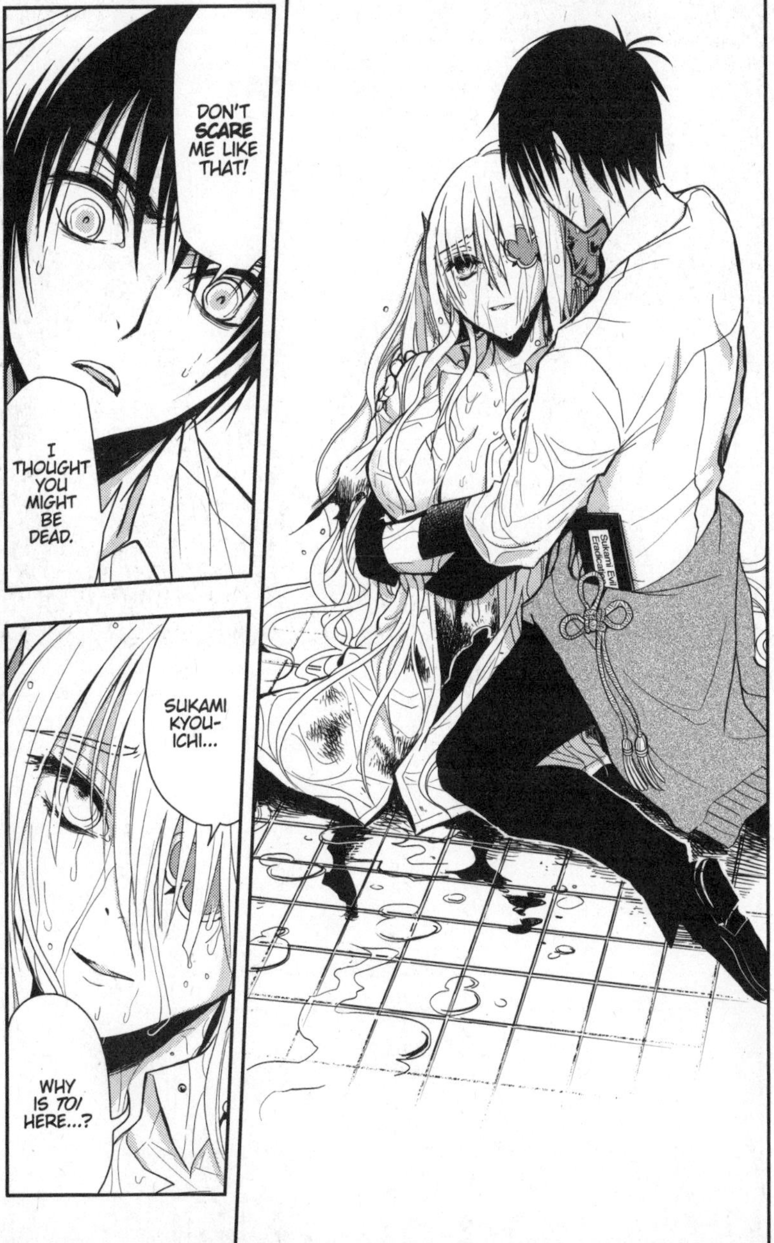
DON'T SCARE ME LIKE THAT!
I THOUGHT YOU MIGHT BE DEAD.
SUKAMI KYOU-ICHI...
WHY IS *TOI* HERE...?

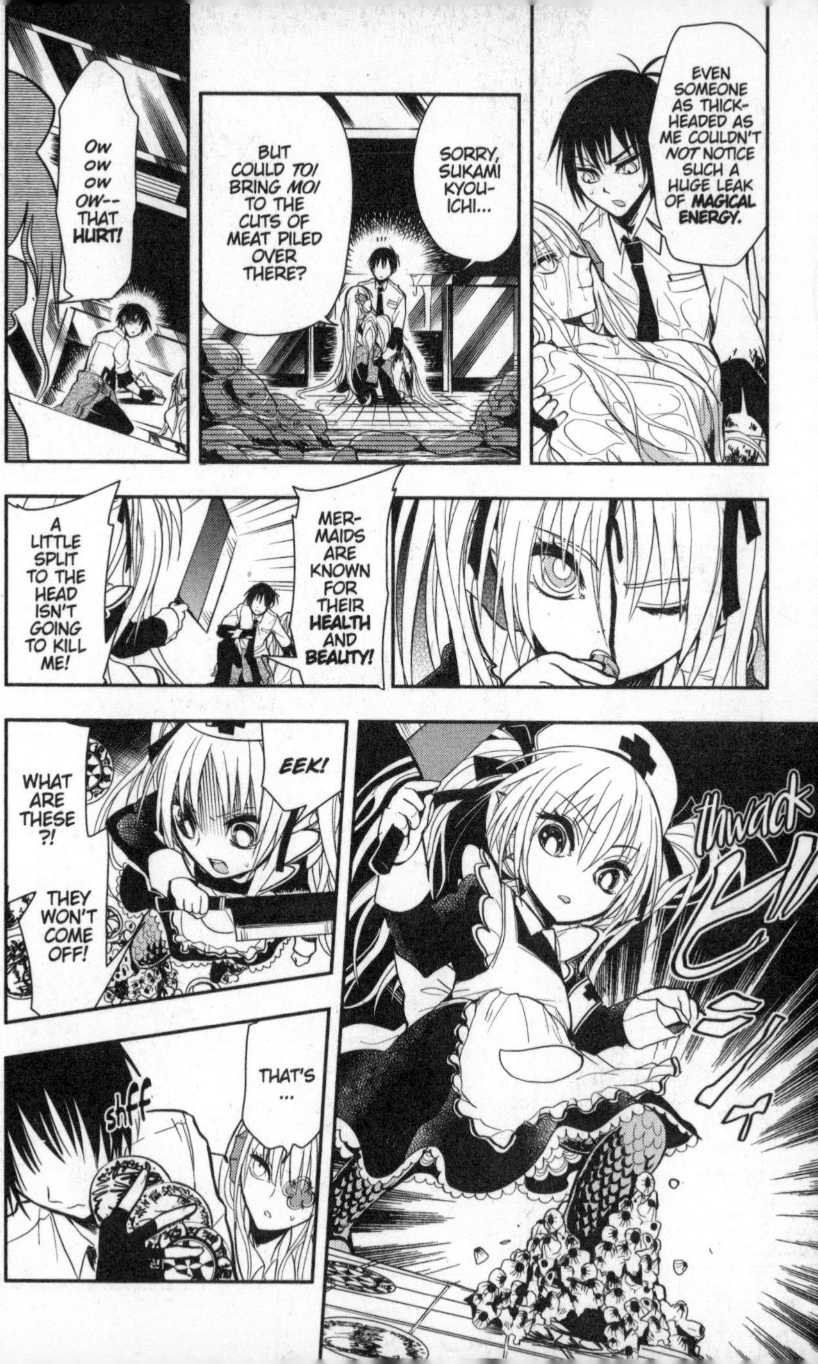
EVEN SOMEONE AS THICK-HEADED AS ME COULDN'T *NOT* NOTICE SUCH A HUGE LEAK OF **MAGICAL ENERGY.**
SORRY, SUKAMI KYOUICHI...
BUT COULD *TOI* BRING *MOI* TO THE CUTS OF MEAT PILED OVER THERE?
OW OW OW OW-- THAT **HURT!**
MERMAIDS ARE KNOWN FOR THEIR **HEALTH** AND **BEAUTY!**
A LITTLE SPLIT TO THE HEAD ISN'T GOING TO KILL ME!
thwack
EEK!
WHAT ARE THESE ?!
THEY WON'T COME OFF!
THAT'S ...
shff

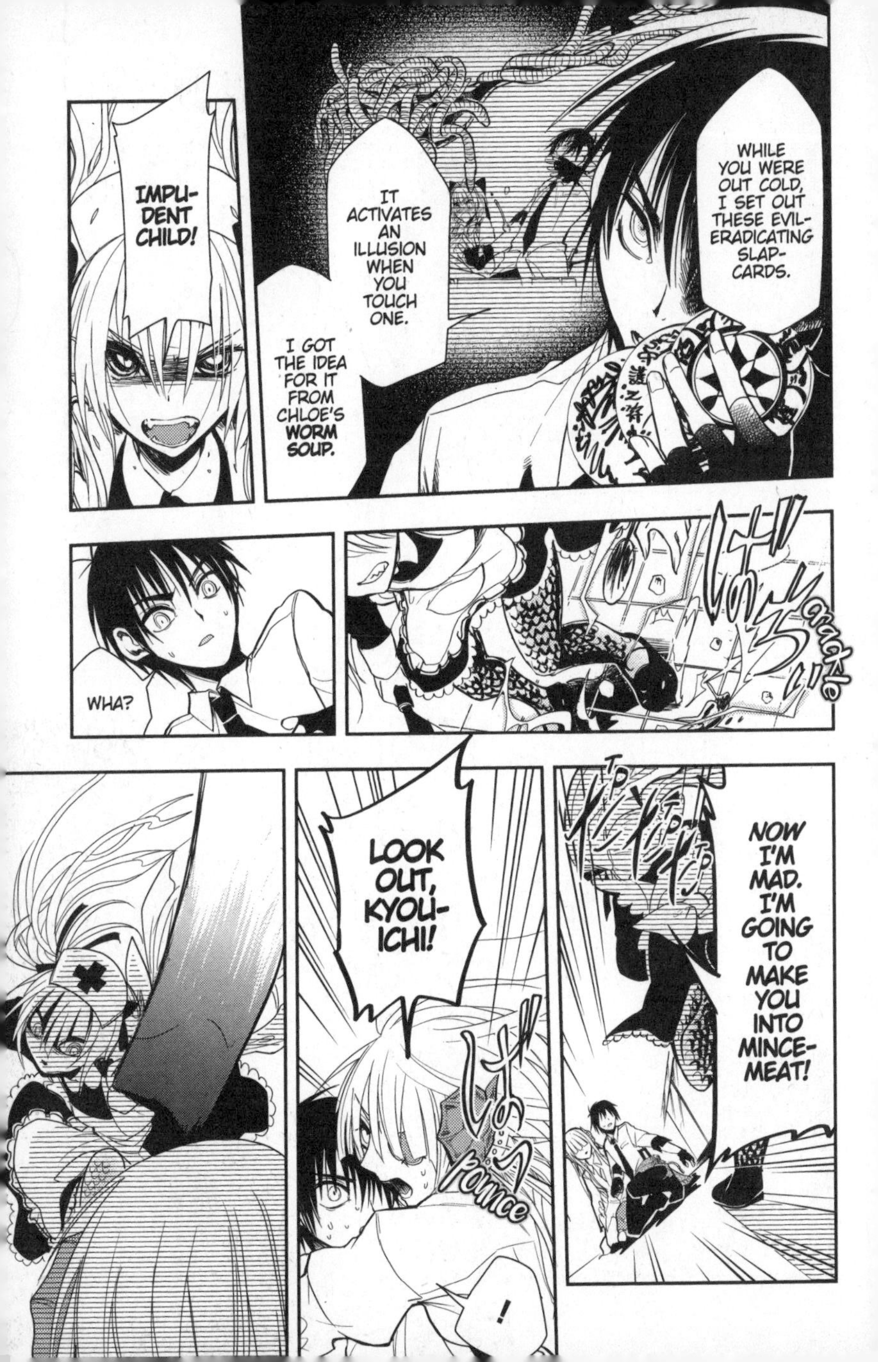
WHILE YOU WERE OUT COLD, I SET OUT THESE EVIL-ERADICATING SLAP-CARDS.
IT ACTIVATES AN ILLUSION WHEN YOU TOUCH ONE.
I GOT THE IDEA FOR IT FROM CHLOE'S WORM SOUP.
IMPU-DENT CHILD!
WHA?
NOW I'M MAD. I'M GOING TO MAKE YOU INTO MINCE-MEAT!
LOOK OUT, KYOUI-ICHI!
pounce
!

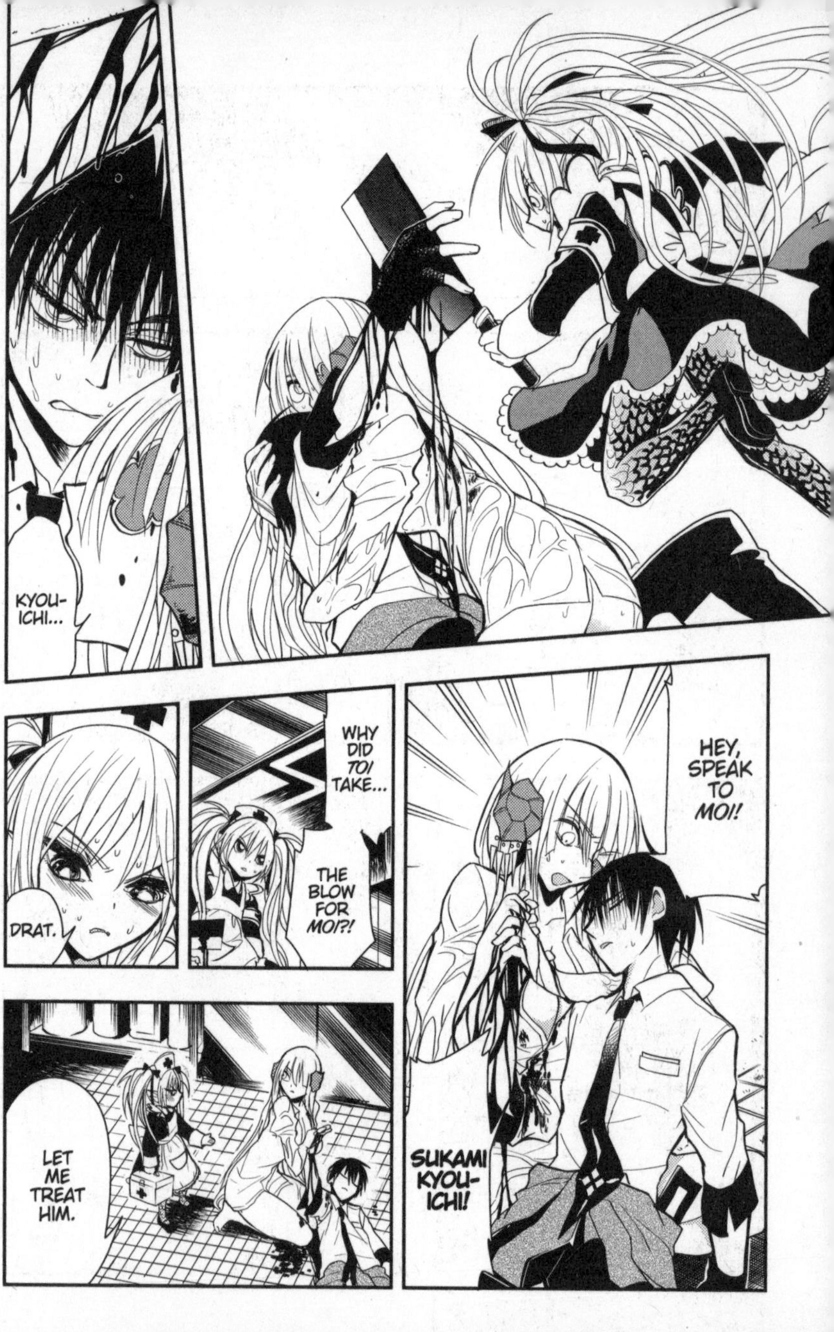
KYOU-ICHI...
HEY, SPEAK TO *MOI*!
SUKAMI KYOU-ICHI!
WHY DID *TOI* TAKE...
THE BLOW FOR *MOI*?!
DRAT.
LET ME TREAT HIM.

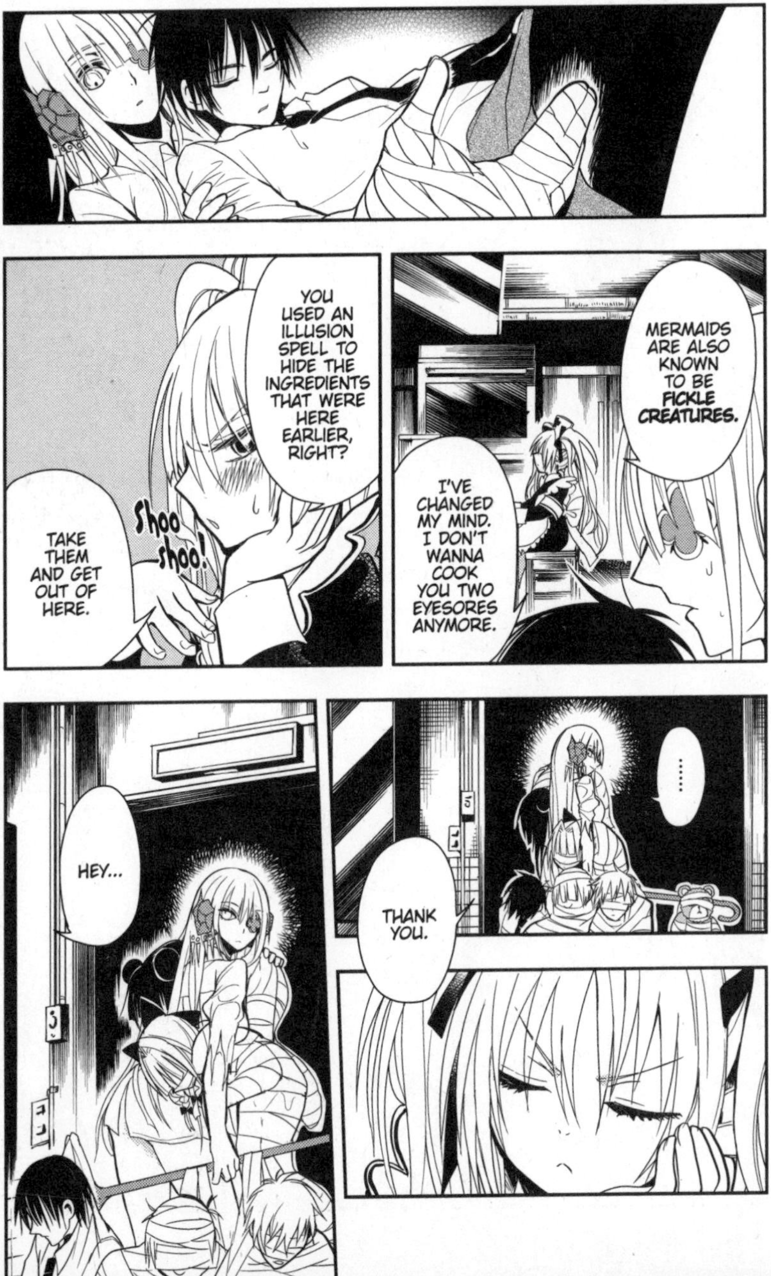
MERMAIDS ARE ALSO KNOWN TO BE FICKLE CREATURES.
I'VE CHANGED MY MIND. I DON'T WANNA COOK YOU TWO EYESORES ANYMORE.
YOU USED AN ILLUSION SPELL TO HIDE THE INGREDIENTS THAT WERE HERE EARLIER, RIGHT?
Shoo shoo!
TAKE THEM AND GET OUT OF HERE.
......
HEY...
THANK YOU.

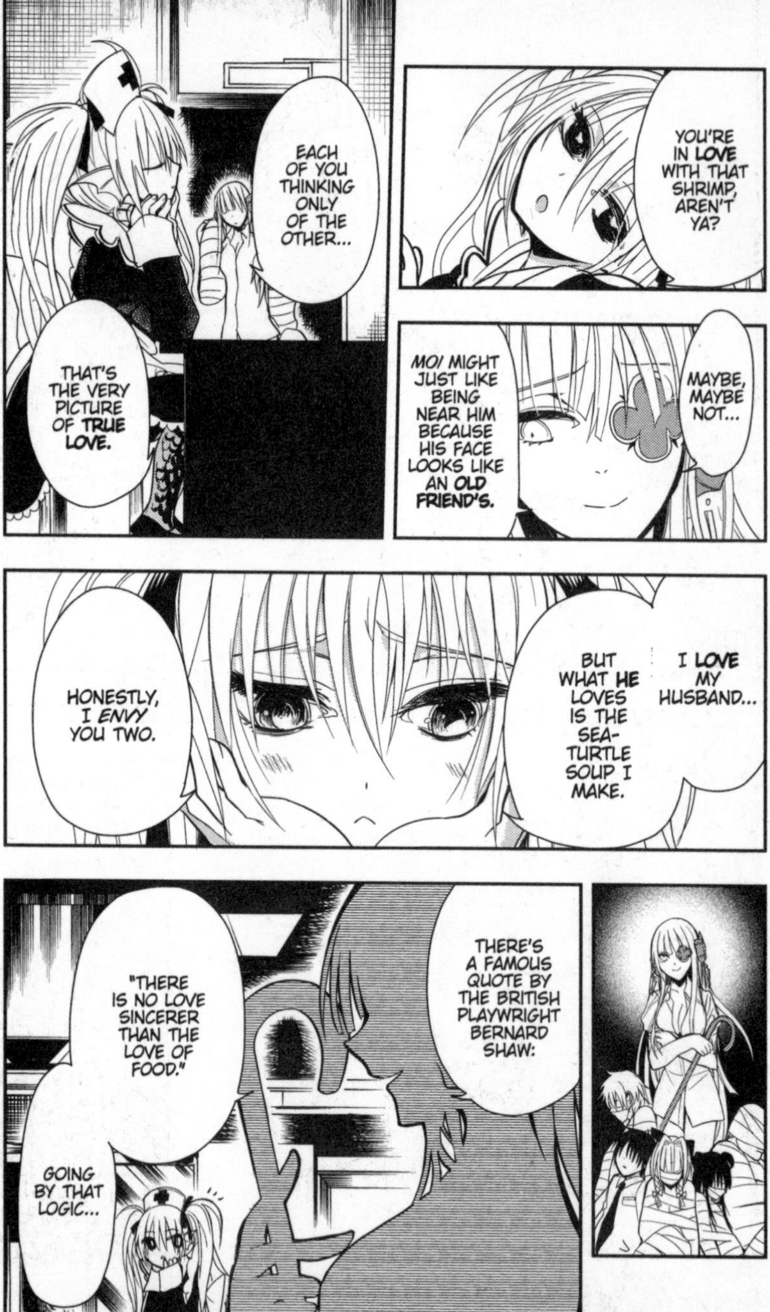
YOU'RE IN LOVE WITH THAT SHRIMP, AREN'T YA?
MAYBE, MAYBE NOT...
MOI MIGHT JUST LIKE BEING NEAR HIM BECAUSE HIS FACE LOOKS LIKE AN OLD FRIEND'S.
EACH OF YOU THINKING ONLY OF THE OTHER...
THAT'S THE VERY PICTURE OF TRUE LOVE.
I LOVE MY HUSBAND...
BUT WHAT HE LOVES IS THE SEA-TURTLE SOUP I MAKE.
HONESTLY, I ENVY YOU TWO.
THERE'S A FAMOUS QUOTE BY THE BRITISH PLAYWRIGHT BERNARD SHAW:
"THERE IS NO LOVE SINCERER THAN THE LOVE OF FOOD."
GOING BY THAT LOGIC...

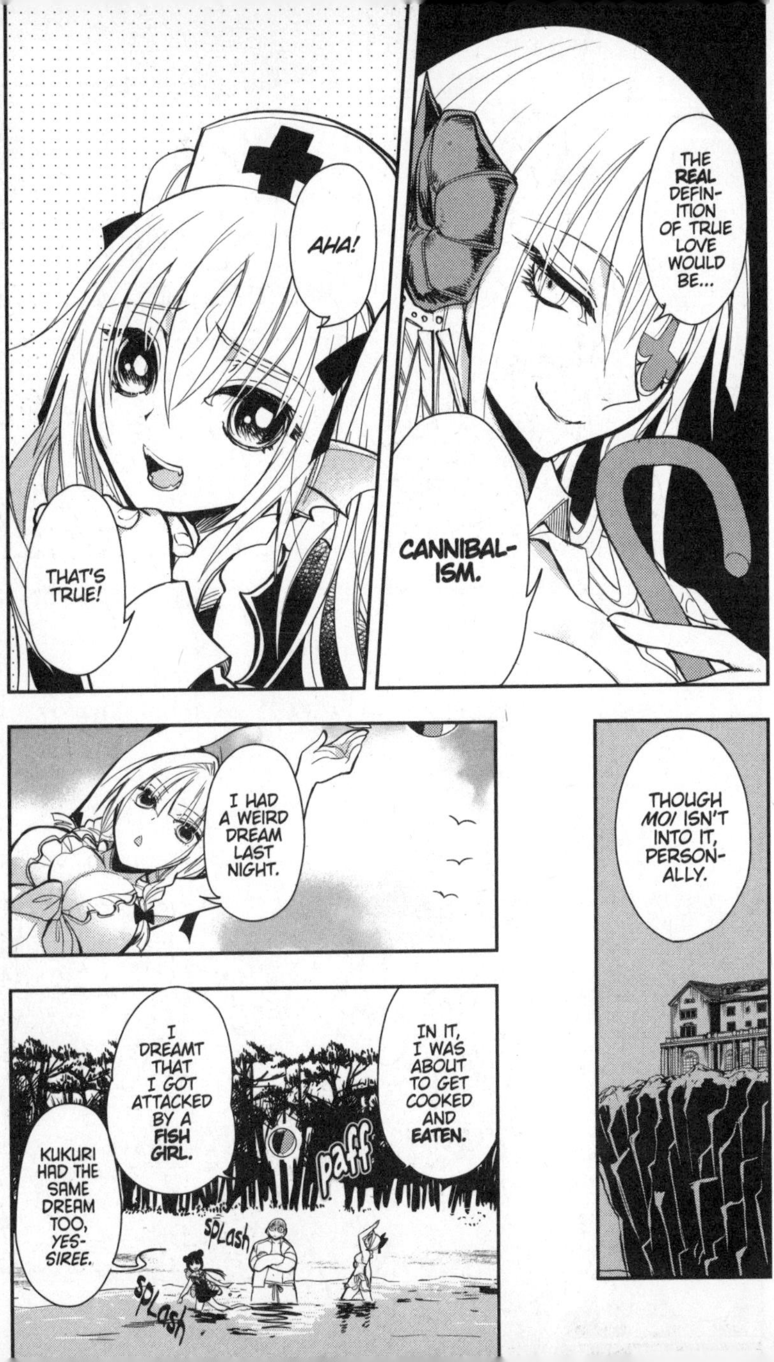
THE REAL DEFINITION OF TRUE LOVE WOULD BE...
CANNIBALISM.
AHA!
THAT'S TRUE!
THOUGH MOI ISN'T INTO IT, PERSONALLY.
I HAD A WEIRD DREAM LAST NIGHT.
IN IT, I WAS ABOUT TO GET COOKED AND EATEN.
I DREAMT THAT I GOT ATTACKED BY A FISH GIRL.
paff
KUKURI HAD THE SAME DREAM TOO, YES-SIREE.
sPLash
sPLash

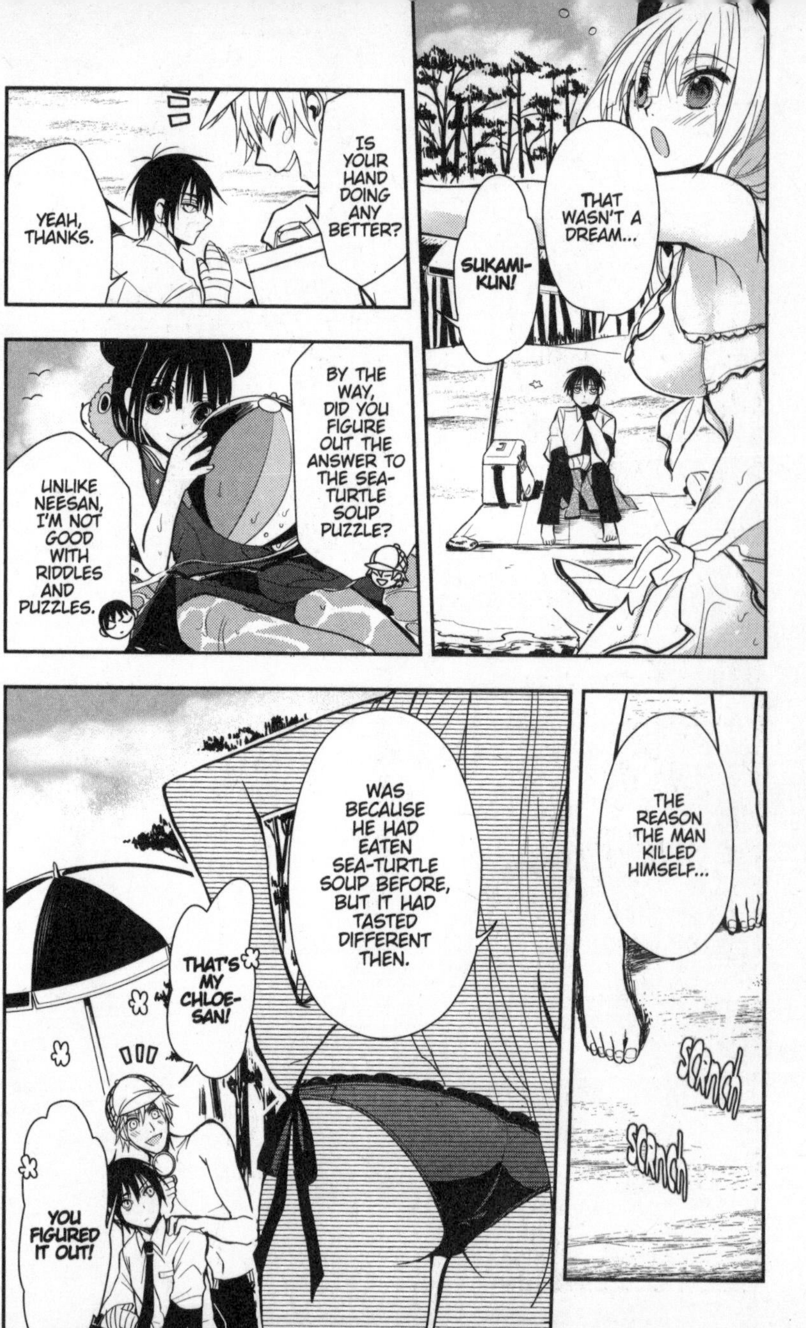
THAT WASN'T A DREAM...
SUKAMI-KUN!
IS YOUR HAND DOING ANY BETTER?
YEAH, THANKS.
BY THE WAY, DID YOU FIGURE OUT THE ANSWER TO THE SEA-TURTLE SOUP PUZZLE?
UNLIKE NEESAN, I'M NOT GOOD WITH RIDDLES AND PUZZLES.
THE REASON THE MAN KILLED HIMSELF...
SCRNCH
SCRNCH
WAS BECAUSE HE HAD EATEN SEA-TURTLE SOUP BEFORE, BUT IT HAD TASTED DIFFERENT THEN.
THAT'S MY CHLOE-SAN!
YOU FIGURED IT OUT!

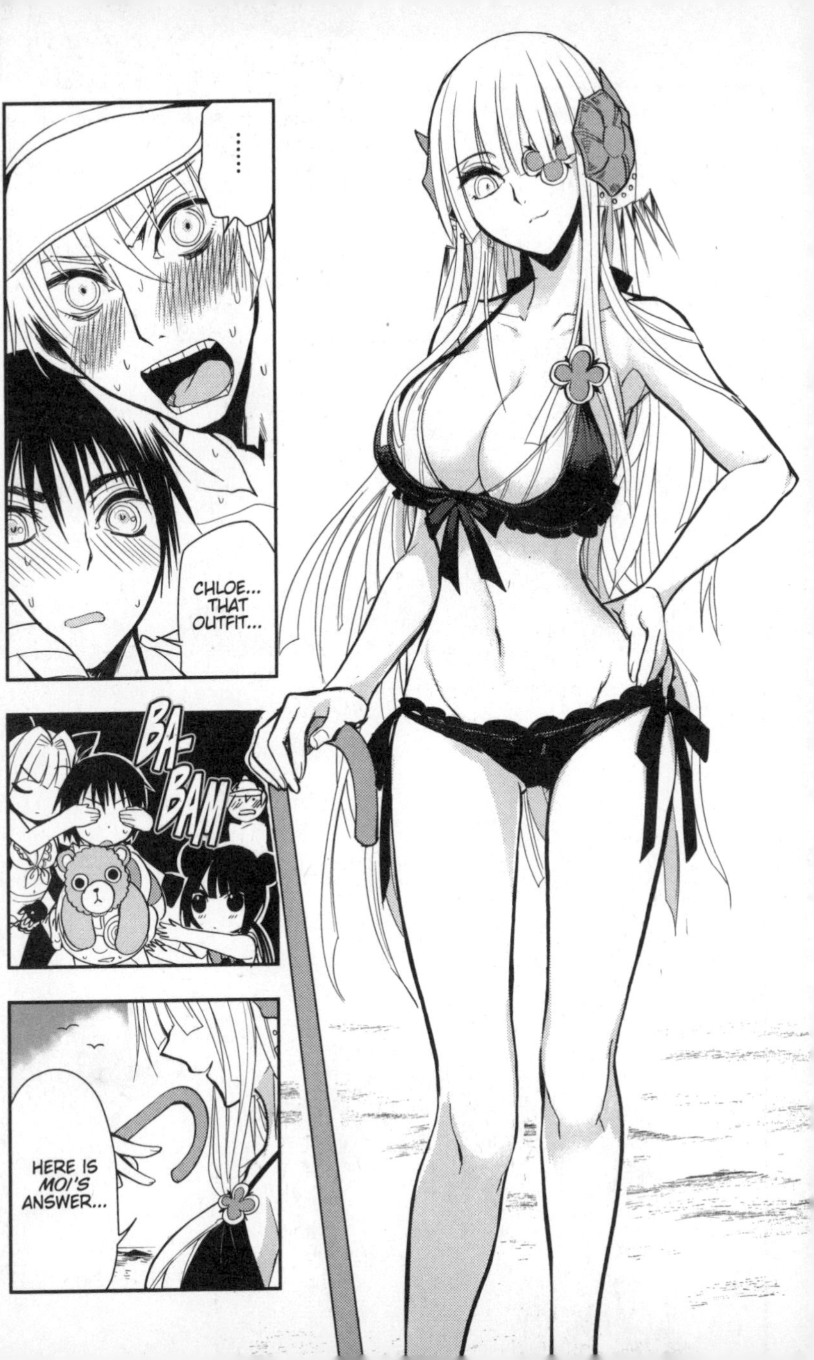
......
CHLOE... THAT OUTFIT...
BA-BAM
HERE IS *MOI'S* ANSWER...

The Sea-Turtle Soup Solution

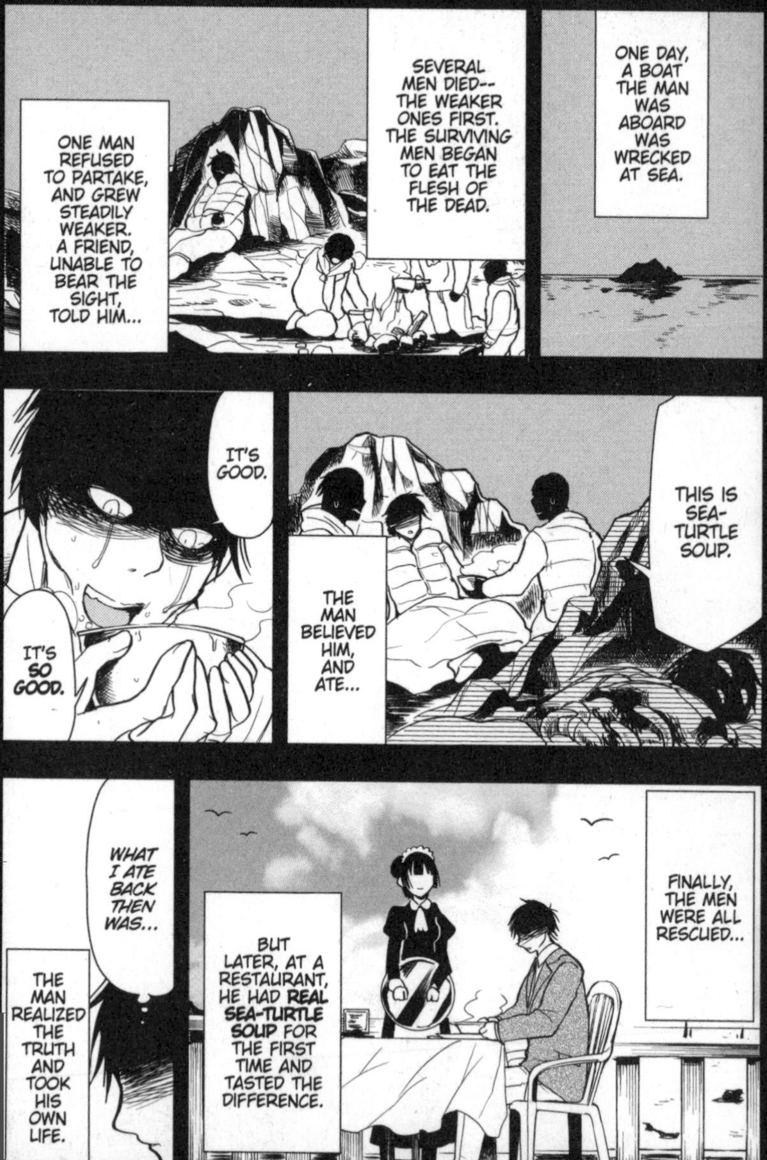
ONE DAY, A BOAT THE MAN WAS ABOARD WAS WRECKED AT SEA.
SEVERAL MEN DIED--THE WEAKER ONES FIRST. THE SURVIVING MEN BEGAN TO EAT THE FLESH OF THE DEAD.
ONE MAN REFUSED TO PARTAKE, AND GREW STEADILY WEAKER. A FRIEND, UNABLE TO BEAR THE SIGHT, TOLD HIM...
THIS IS SEA-TURTLE SOUP.
THE MAN BELIEVED HIM, AND ATE...
IT'S GOOD.
IT'S SO GOOD.
FINALLY, THE MEN WERE ALL RESCUED...
BUT LATER, AT A RESTAURANT, HE HAD REAL SEA-TURTLE SOUP FOR THE FIRST TIME AND TASTED THE DIFFERENCE.
WHAT I ATE BACK THEN WAS...
THE MAN REALIZED THE TRUTH AND TOOK HIS OWN LIFE.

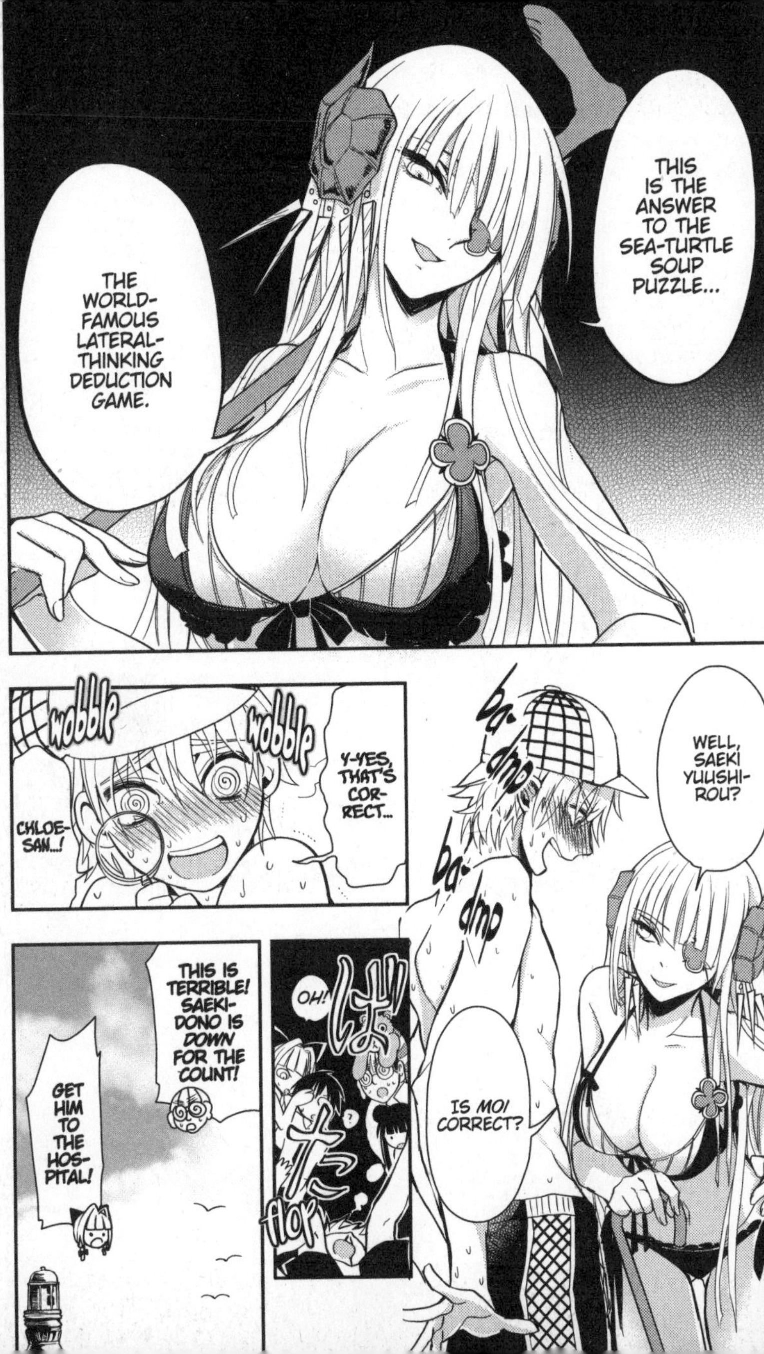
THIS IS THE ANSWER TO THE SEA-TURTLE SOUP PUZZLE...
THE WORLD-FAMOUS LATERAL-THINKING DEDUCTION GAME.
WELL, SAEKI YUUSHIROU?
ba-dmp
ba-dmp
IS *MOI* CORRECT?
wobble
wobble
Y-YES, THAT'S CORRECT...
CHLOE-SAN...!
OH!
flop
THIS IS TERRIBLE! SAEKI-DONO IS *DOWN* FOR THE COUNT!
GET HIM TO THE HOSPITAL!

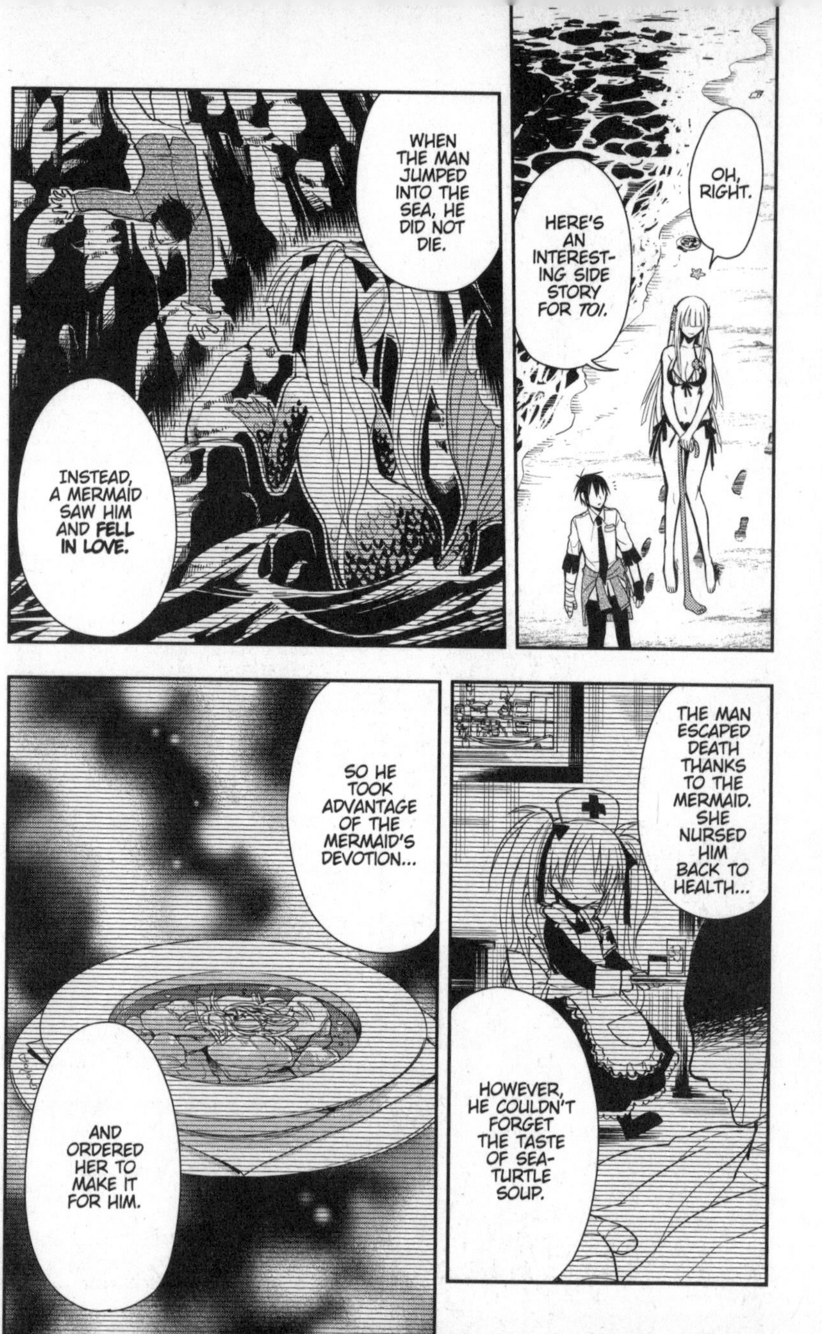
OH, RIGHT.
HERE'S AN INTERESTING SIDE STORY FOR TOI.
WHEN THE MAN JUMPED INTO THE SEA, HE DID NOT DIE.
INSTEAD, A MERMAID SAW HIM AND FELL IN LOVE.
THE MAN ESCAPED DEATH THANKS TO THE MERMAID. SHE NURSED HIM BACK TO HEALTH...
HOWEVER, HE COULDN'T FORGET THE TASTE OF SEA-TURTLE SOUP.
SO HE TOOK ADVANTAGE OF THE MERMAID'S DEVOTION...
AND ORDERED HER TO MAKE IT FOR HIM.

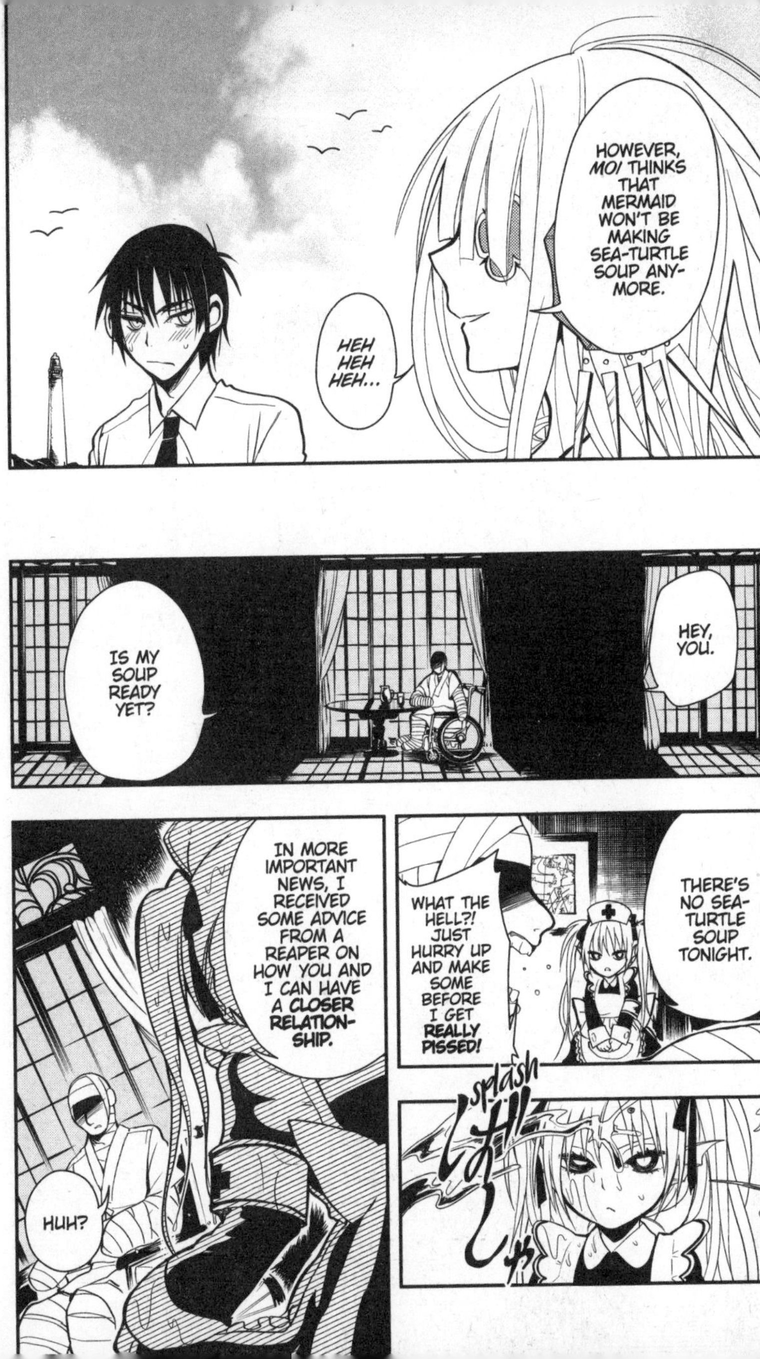
HOWEVER, MOI THINKS THAT MERMAID WON'T BE MAKING SEA-TURTLE SOUP ANY-MORE.
HEH HEH HEH...
HEY, YOU.
IS MY SOUP READY YET?
THERE'S NO SEA-TURTLE SOUP TONIGHT.
WHAT THE HELL?! JUST HURRY UP AND MAKE SOME BEFORE I GET REALLY PISSED!
splash
IN MORE IMPORTANT NEWS, I RECEIVED SOME ADVICE FROM A REAPER ON HOW YOU AND I CAN HAVE A CLOSER RELATION-SHIP.
HUH?

SHE SAID THAT CANNIBALISM IS\THE ULTIMATE FORM OF LOVE.

THEREFORE, I'VE DECIDED TO PARTAKE OF YOU, MY DEAR, DEAR HUSBAND.

NO DON'T!

NO...

GLUP

BECAUSE I LOVE YOU THAT MUCH, DARLING! ♡

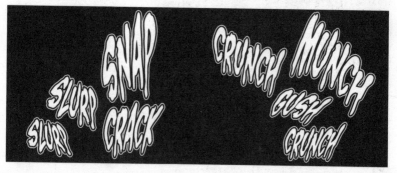

SNAP
SLURP
SLURP
CRACK
CRUNCH MUNCH
GUSH
CRUNCH

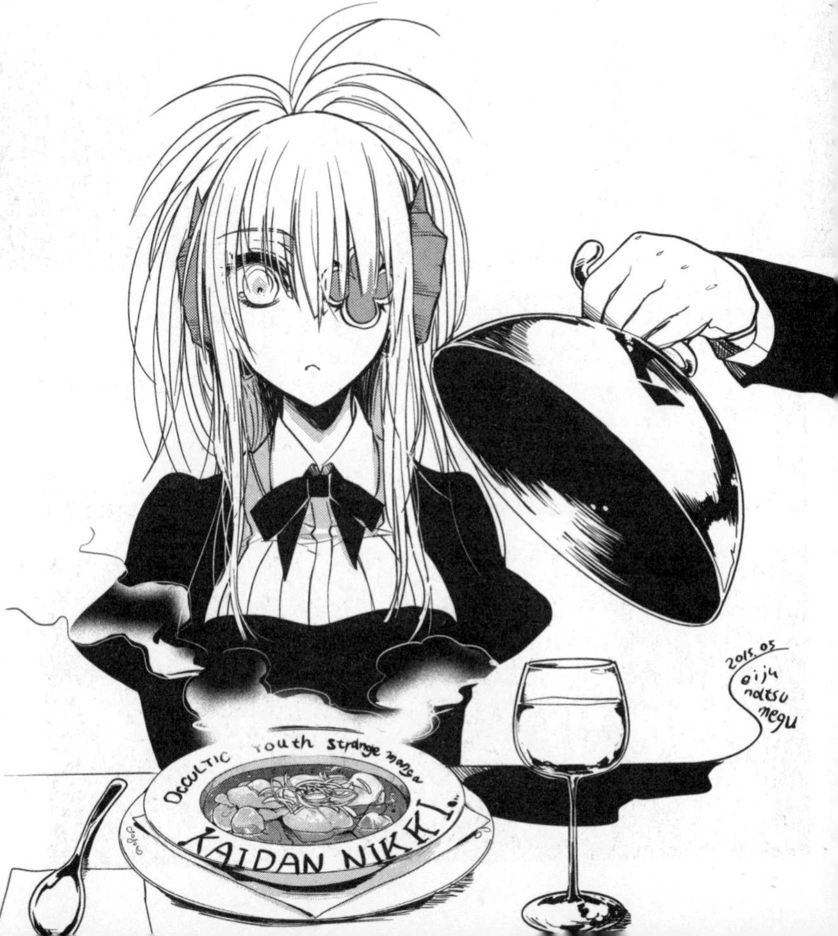
2015.05
oiju
natsu
megu
OCCULTIC Youth strange manga
KAIDAN NIKKI...

Greetings
Pedestrians

Nice to meet you. I am Seiju Natsumegu.

Thank you for picking up volume two of my strange, occultic young-adult manga, *Ghost Diary*.

As I type this, Volume 2 is still in production. The cover and retouching are not even done yet, but surely it all came out all right if you're reading this. They say practice makes perfect, and it must be true because I've been having a lot more fun with this volume.

In this volume, I got to talk about the Occult Club's weird designs and Reaper Chloe's mental state. And I also got to work one of my favorite urban legends into the story! (I've long aspired to make a story like the *Hyakki-Yakou* series, or *Hayarigami*) I also packed in disgusting things and all kinds of dirty jokes (lol).

In Volume 1, I drew an original urban legend based on an anecdote, but... I thought, since I'm drawing an urban legend manga, "From Volume 2 onward I'll use existing urban legends!" and drew this volume enthusiastically.

I referenced all sorts of things when drawing this-- from things passed down from time immemorial to relatively modern urban legends. The more you read it, the more you'll acquire occultic knowledge, for sure. I get to say whatever I want in these author's notes, and I plan to use it to introduce different concepts and ideas. I would be happy if you looked at these pages as a little breather after you've finished reading this volume of *Ghost Diary*.

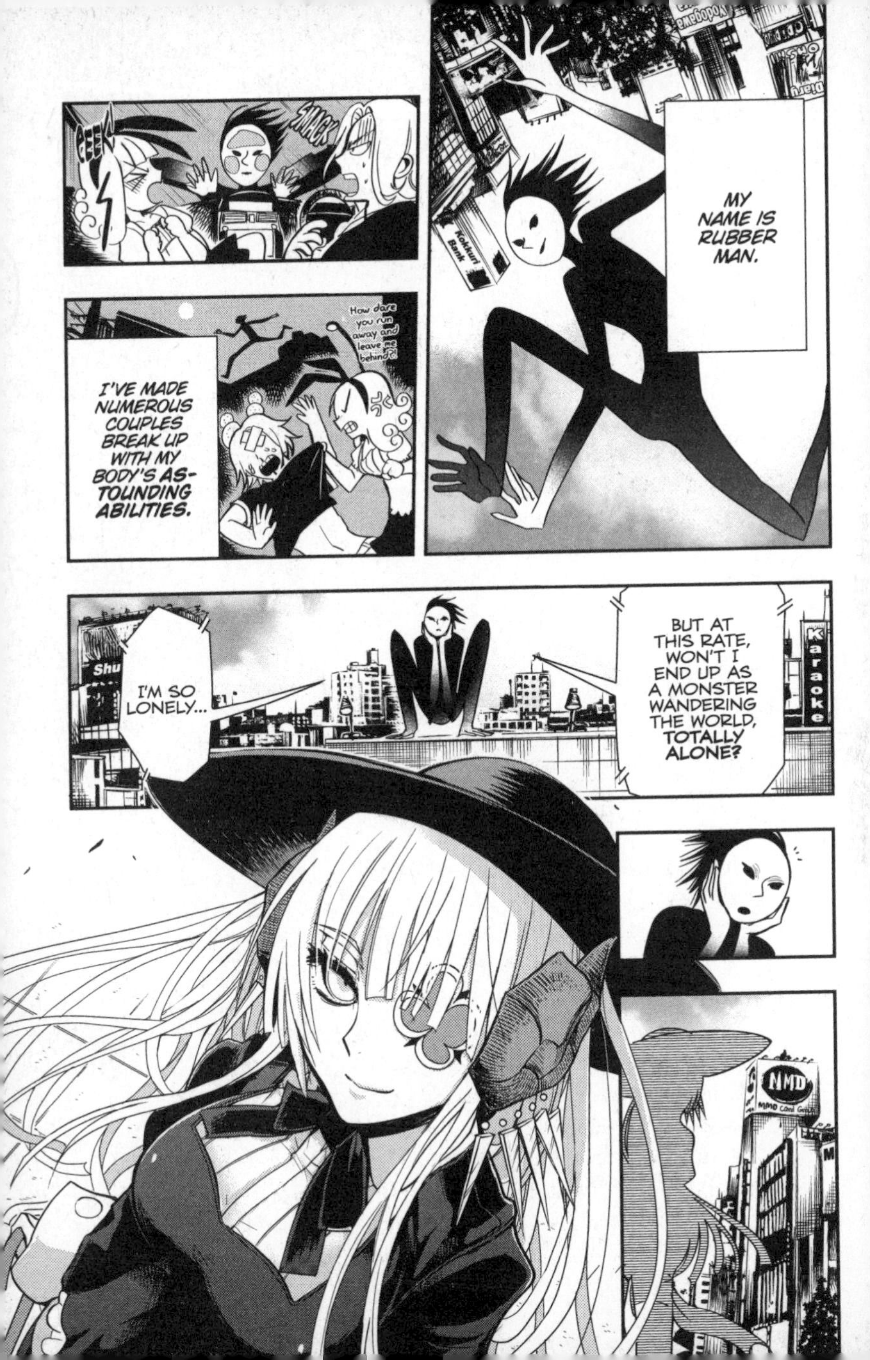
MY NAME IS RUBBER MAN.
Kokkuri Bank
SMACK
EEEK!
How dare you run away and leave me behind?!
I'VE MADE NUMEROUS COUPLES BREAK UP WITH MY BODY'S AS-TOUNDING ABILITIES.
Karaoke
BUT AT THIS RATE, WON'T I END UP AS A MONSTER WANDERING THE WORLD, TOTALLY ALONE?
I'M SO LONELY...
NMD

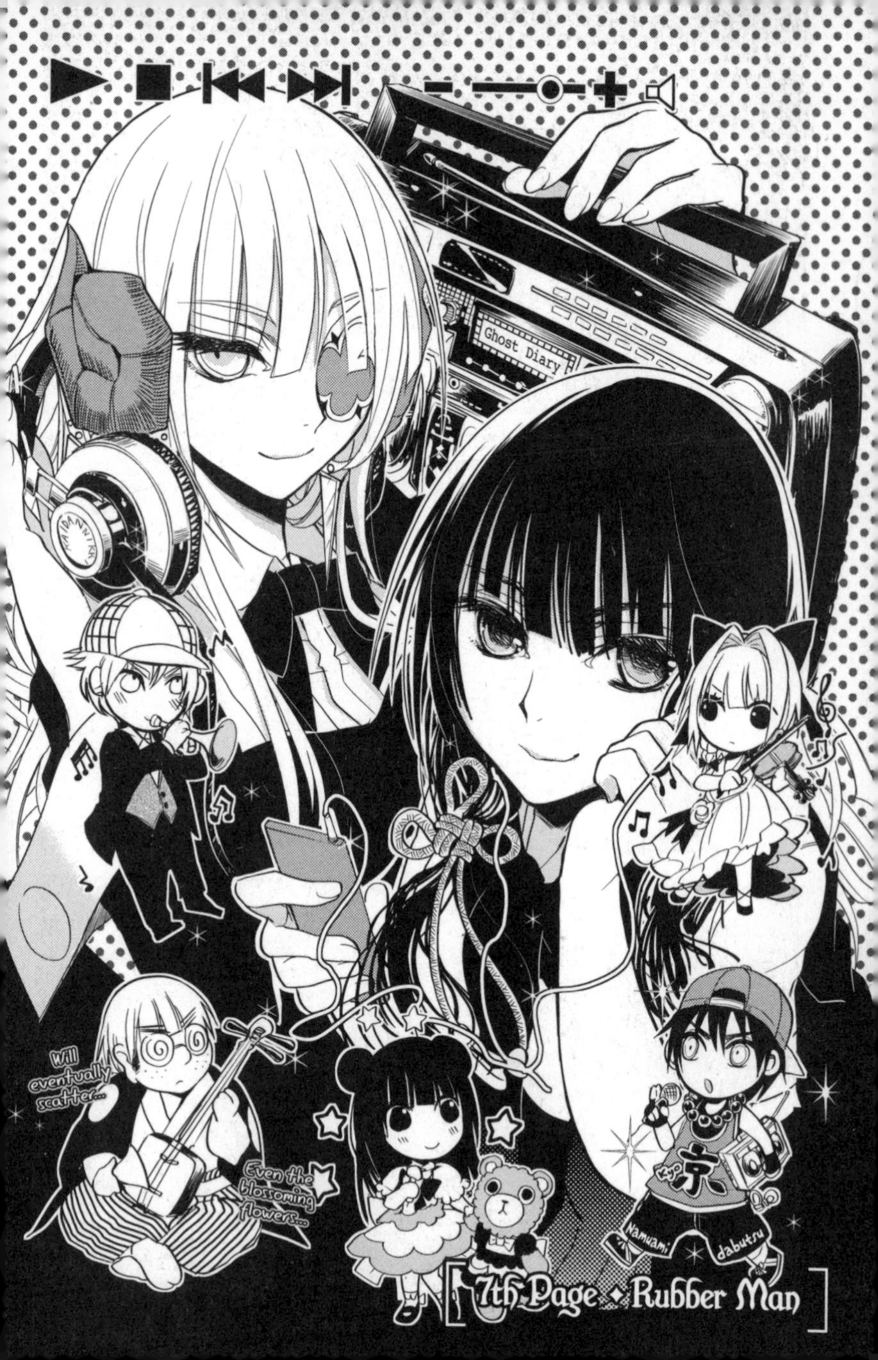
Ghost Diary
Will eventually scatter...
Even the blossoming flowers...
Kyo 京
Namuami dabutsu
7th Page ◆ Rubber Man

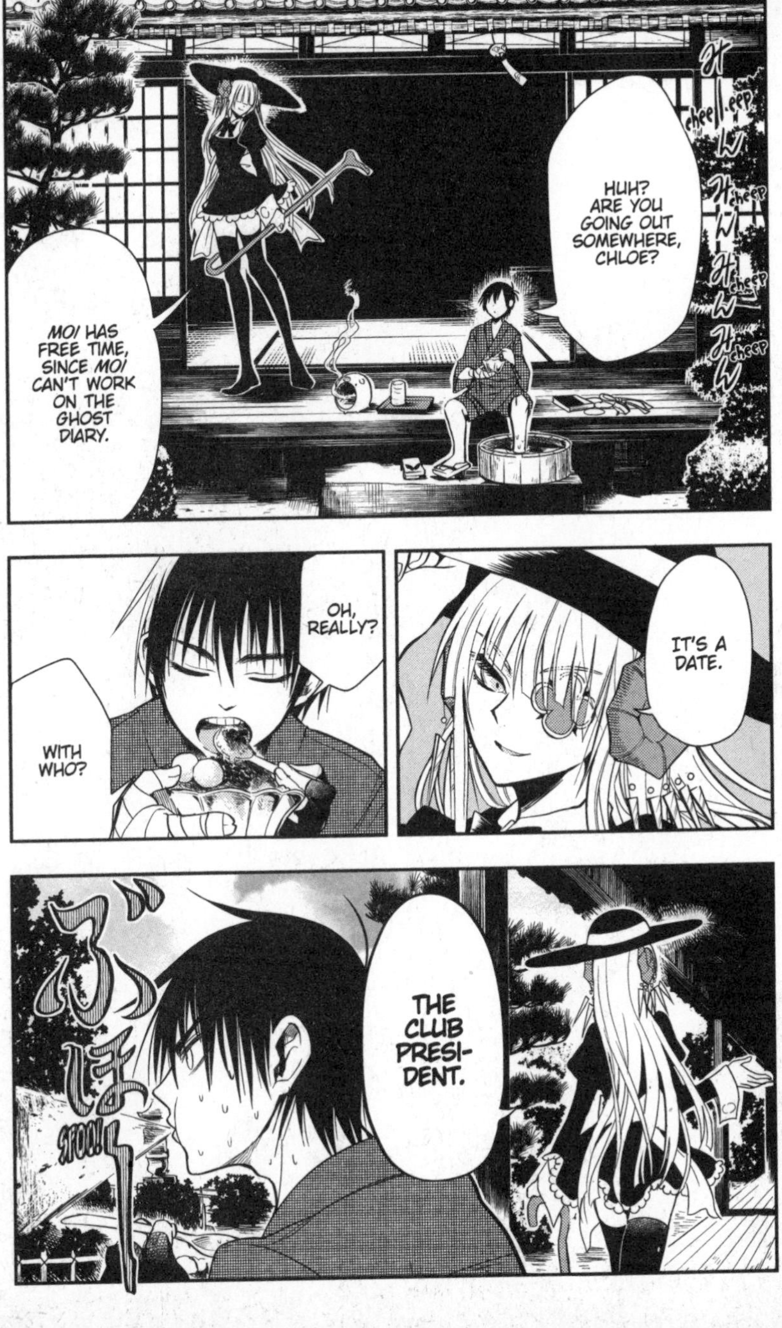
cheep
cheep
cheep
cheep
HUH? ARE YOU GOING OUT SOMEWHERE, CHLOE?
MOI HAS FREE TIME, SINCE *MOI* CAN'T WORK ON THE GHOST DIARY.
IT'S A DATE.
OH, REALLY?
WITH WHO?
THE CLUB PRESI-DENT.

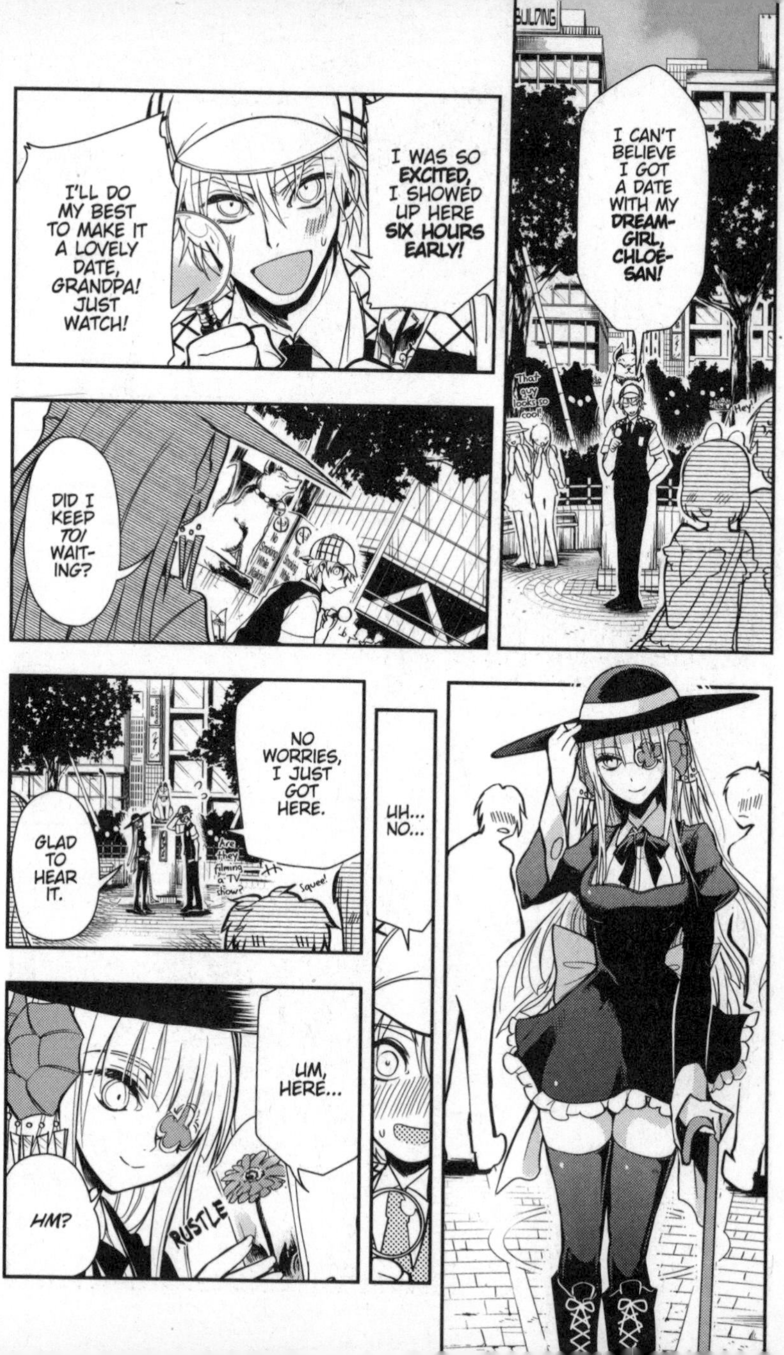
BUILDING
I CAN'T BELIEVE I GOT A DATE WITH MY DREAM-GIRL, CHLOÉ-SAN!
That guy looks so cool!
Hey!
I WAS SO EXCITED, I SHOWED UP HERE SIX HOURS EARLY!
I'LL DO MY BEST TO MAKE IT A LOVELY DATE, GRANDPA! JUST WATCH!
DID I KEEP TO/ WAITING?
UH... NO...
NO WORRIES, I JUST GOT HERE.
GLAD TO HEAR IT.
Are they filming a TV show?
Squee!
UM, HERE...
HM?
RUSTLE

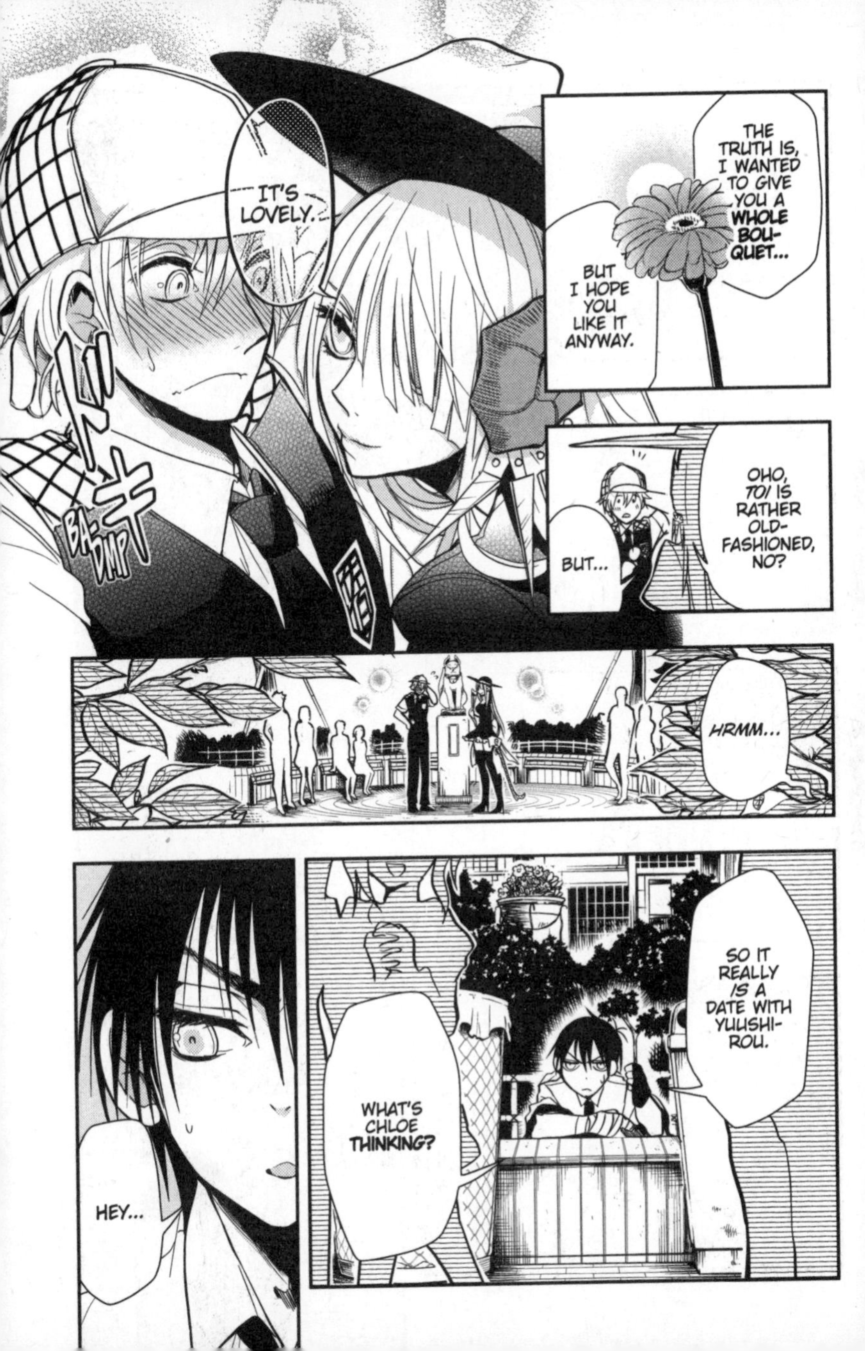
THE TRUTH IS, I WANTED TO GIVE YOU A **WHOLE BOUQUET...**
BUT I HOPE YOU LIKE IT ANYWAY.
OHO, *TOI* IS RATHER OLD-FASHIONED, NO?
BUT...
IT'S LOVELY.
BA-DMP
HRMM...
SO IT REALLY *IS* A DATE WITH YUUSHIROU.
WHAT'S CHLOE **THINKING?**
HEY...

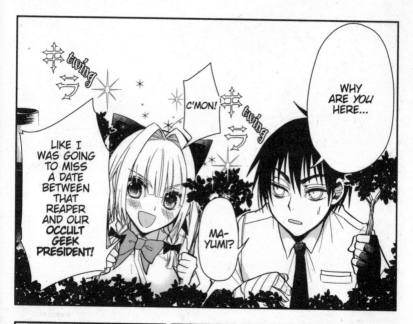

WHY ARE *YOU* HERE...
C'MON!
twing
twing
MA-YUMI?
LIKE I WAS GOING TO MISS A DATE BETWEEN THAT REAPER AND OUR OCCULT GEEK PRESIDENT!
ANYWAY, WHY ARE *YOU* TAILING THEM, KYOUICHI?
I'M JUST WATCHING OUT TO MAKE SURE CHLOE DOESN'T GET YUUSHIROU **HURT.**
sneak
sneak
STARE
HMMM.
WHAT'S WITH **THAT** LOOK?
LIAR. THE ONE YOU'RE WORRIED ABOUT IS **CHLOE.**
WHY WOULD I BE WORRIED ABOUT *HER?!*

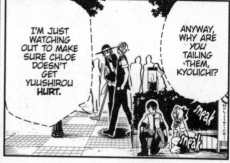

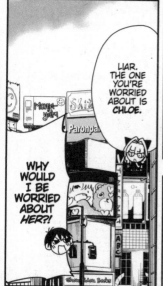

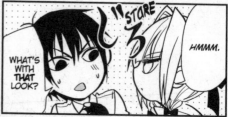

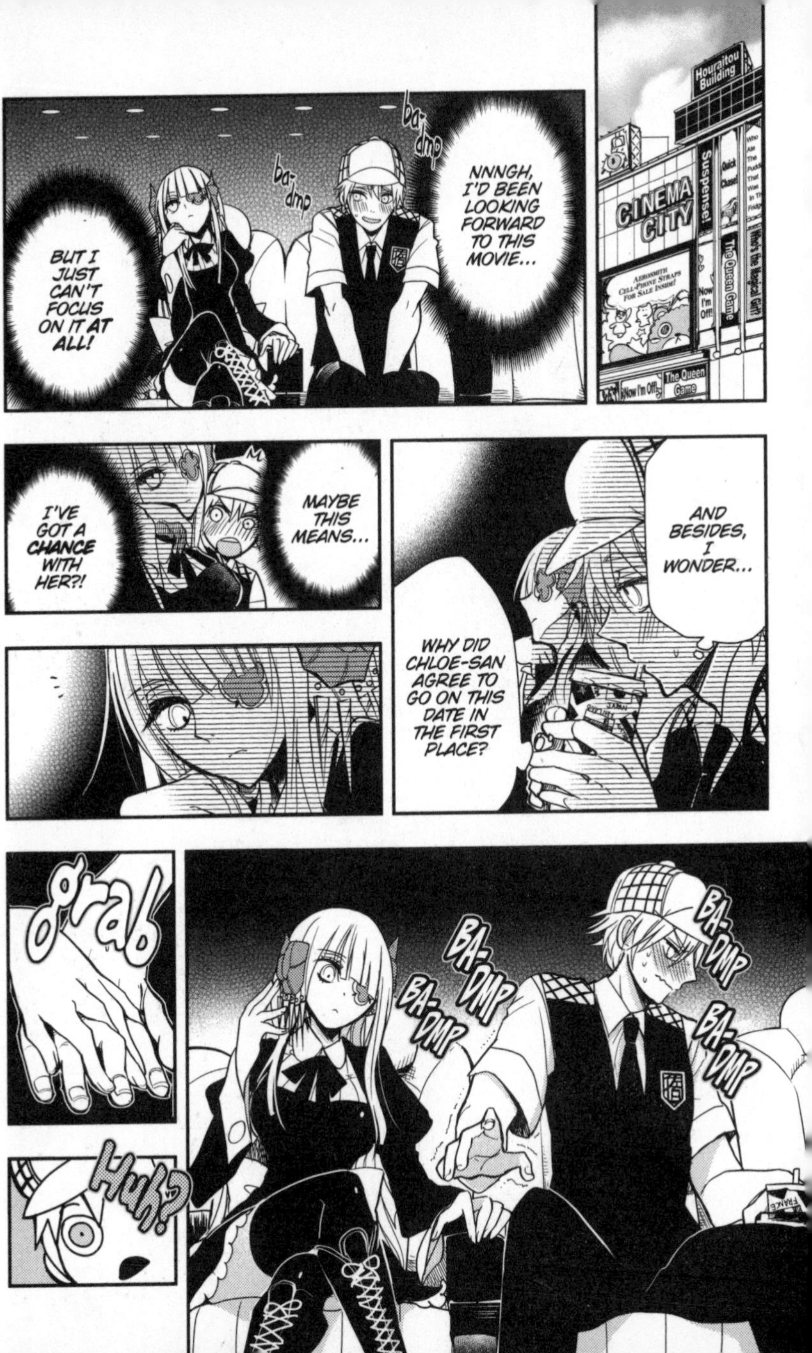
Houraitou Building
CINEMA CITY
Suspense!
Quick Chase!
The Queen Game
AEROSMITH CELL-PHONE STRAPS FOR SALE INSIDE!
Now I'm Off!
Now I'm Off!
The Queen Game
ba-dmp
ba-dmp
NNNGH, I'D BEEN LOOKING FORWARD TO THIS MOVIE...
BUT I JUST CAN'T FOCUS ON IT AT ALL!
AND BESIDES, I WONDER...
WHY DID CHLOE-SAN AGREE TO GO ON THIS DATE IN THE FIRST PLACE?
MAYBE THIS MEANS...
I'VE GOT A CHANCE WITH HER?!
BA-DMP
BA-DMP
BA-DMP
BA-DMP
grab
Huh?

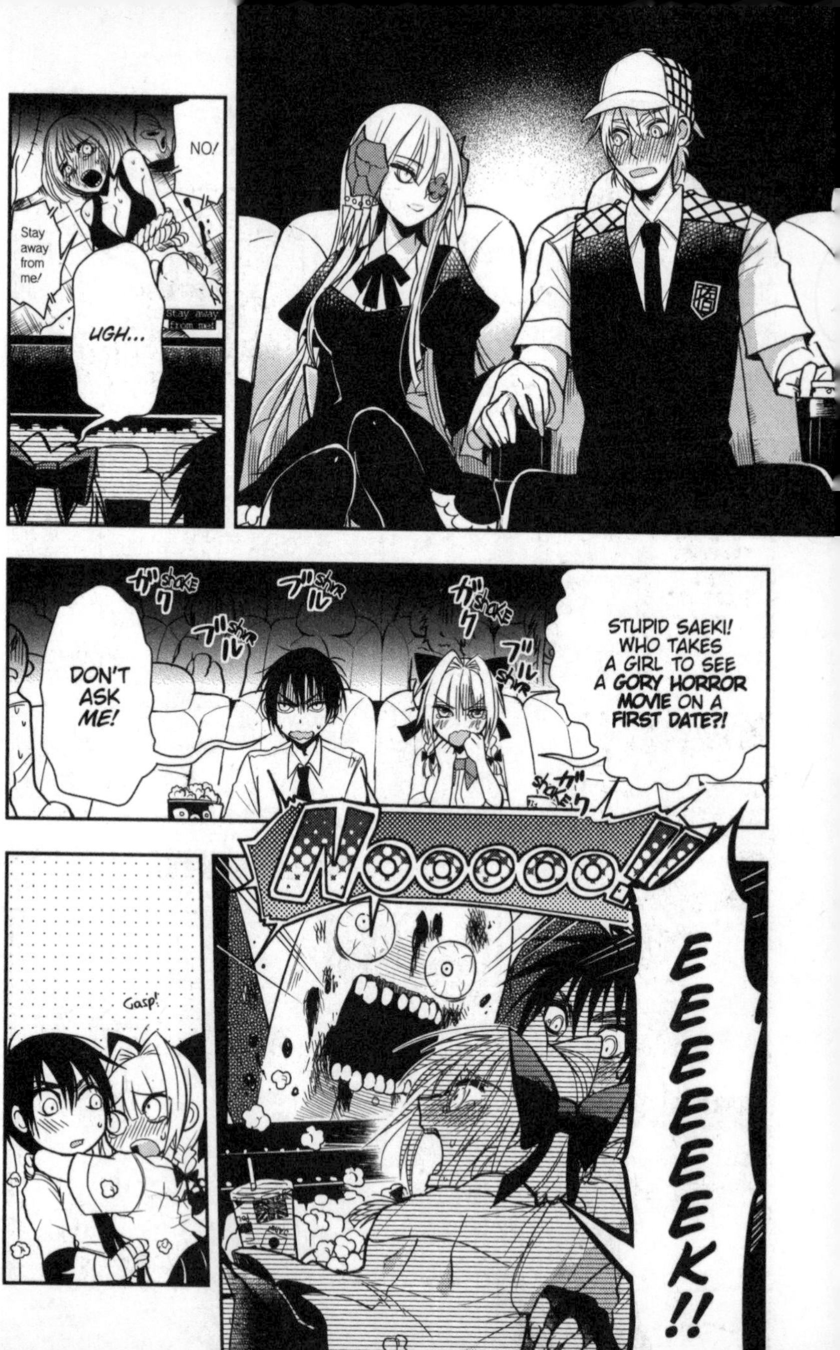
NO!
Stay away from me!
Stay away from me!
UGH...
STUPID SAEKI! WHO TAKES A GIRL TO SEE A GORY HORROR MOVIE ON A FIRST DATE?!
ガク SHAKE
ブル SHVR
ブル SHVR
ガク SHAKE
ブル SHVR
ガク SHAKE
DON'T ASK ME!
NOOOOOO!!
EEEEEEEK!!
Gasp!

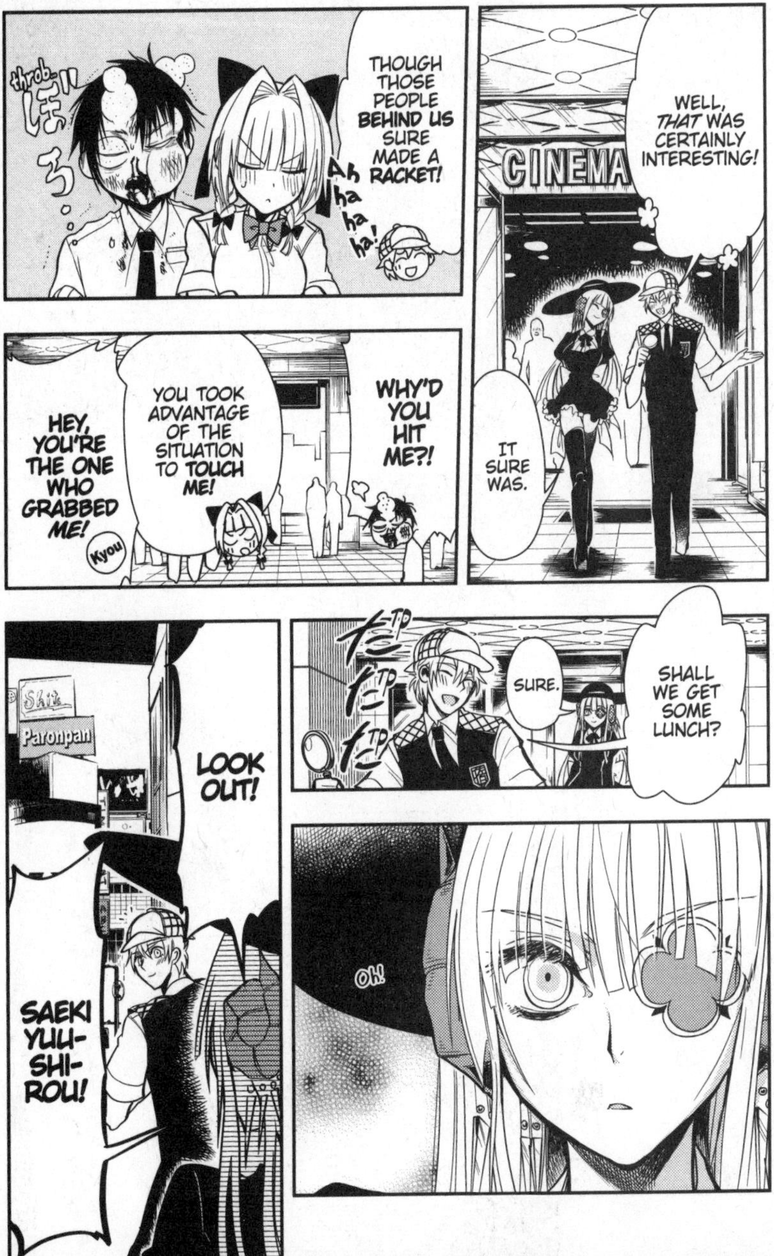
CINEMA
WELL, *THAT* WAS CERTAINLY INTERESTING!
IT SURE WAS.
THOUGH THOSE PEOPLE **BEHIND US** SURE MADE A **RACKET!**
Ah ha ha ha!
throb
WHY'D YOU HIT ME?!
YOU TOOK ADVANTAGE OF THE SITUATION TO **TOUCH** ME!
HEY, YOU'RE THE ONE WHO GRABBED *ME!*
Kyou
SHALL WE GET SOME LUNCH?
SURE.
TP
TP
TP
OH!
Paronpan
LOOK OUT!
SAEKI YUU-SHI-ROU!

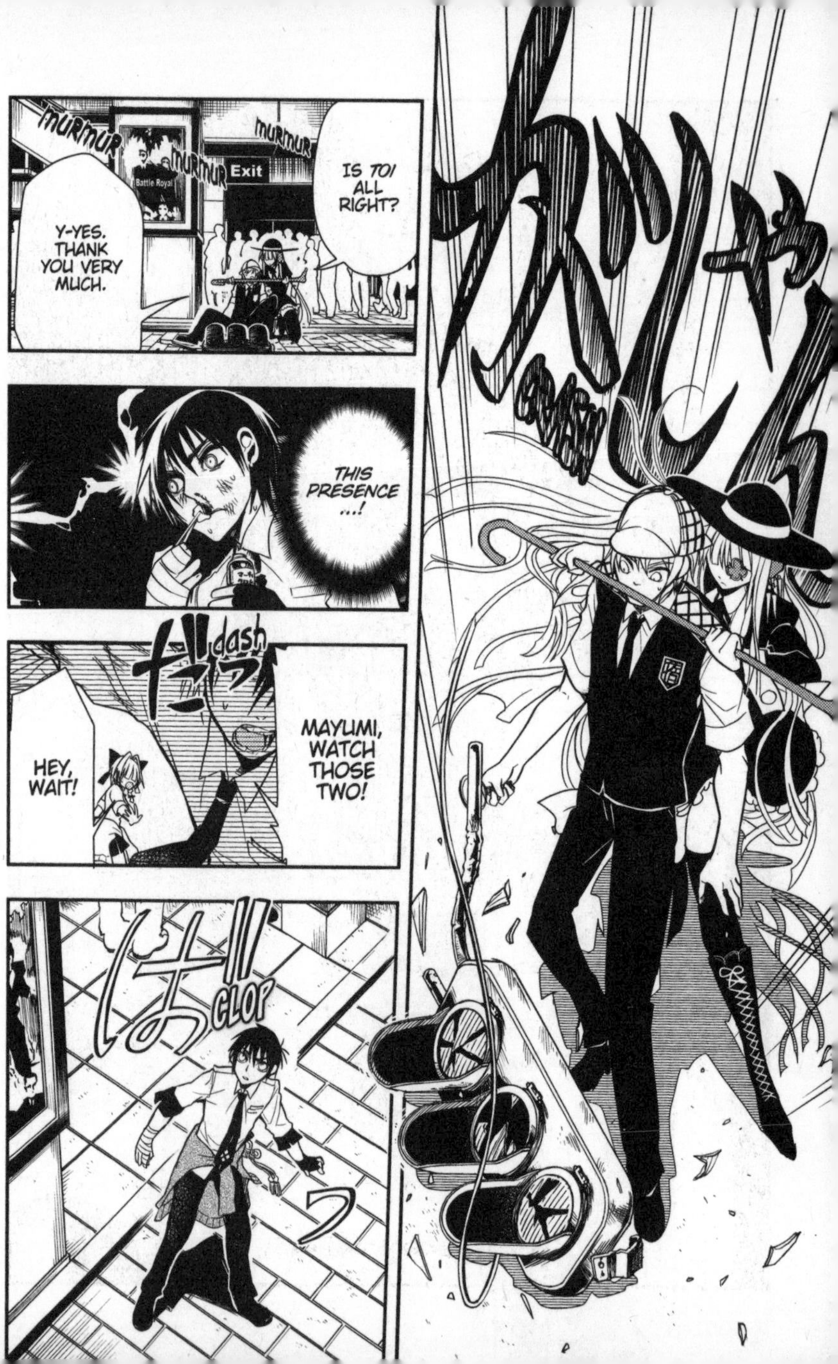
CRASH
murmur
murmur
murmur
murmur
Exit
Battle Royal
IS TOI ALL RIGHT?
Y-YES. THANK YOU VERY MUCH.
THIS PRESENCE ...!
dash
MAYUMI, WATCH THOSE TWO!
HEY, WAIT!
CLOP

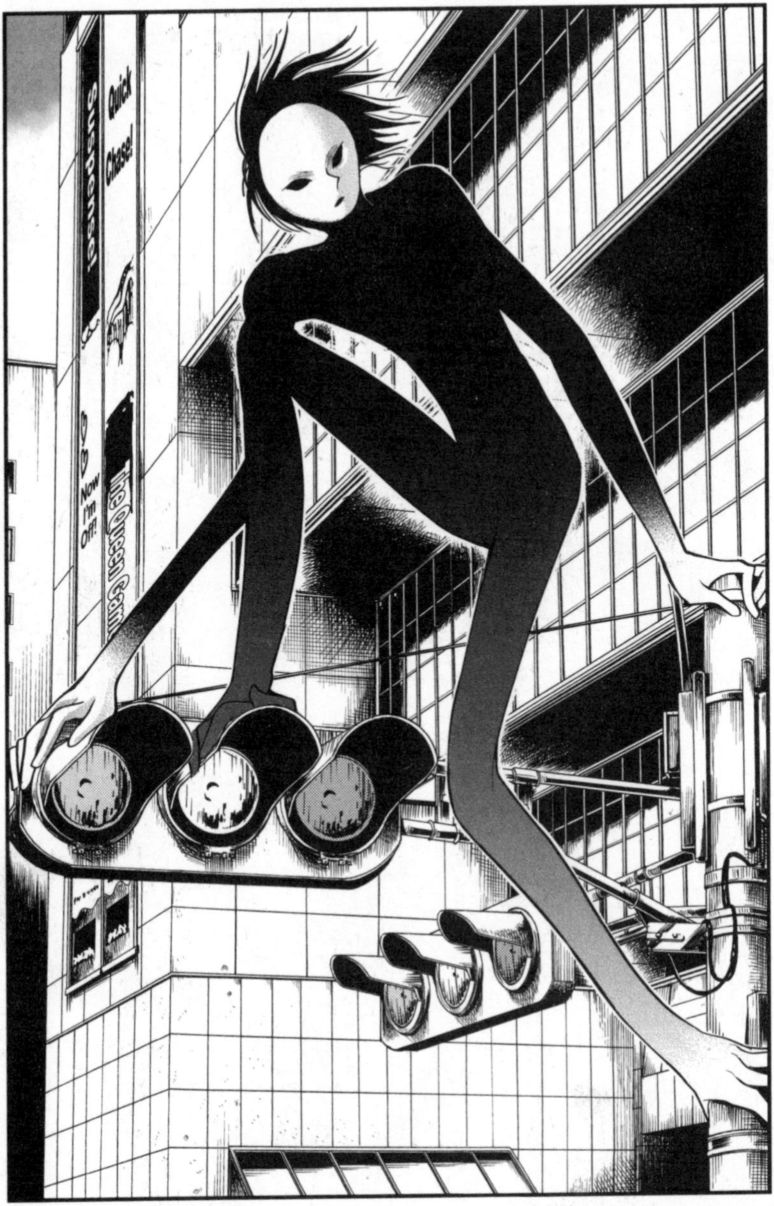
Suspense!
Quick Chase!
Now I'm Off!
The Queen Gam

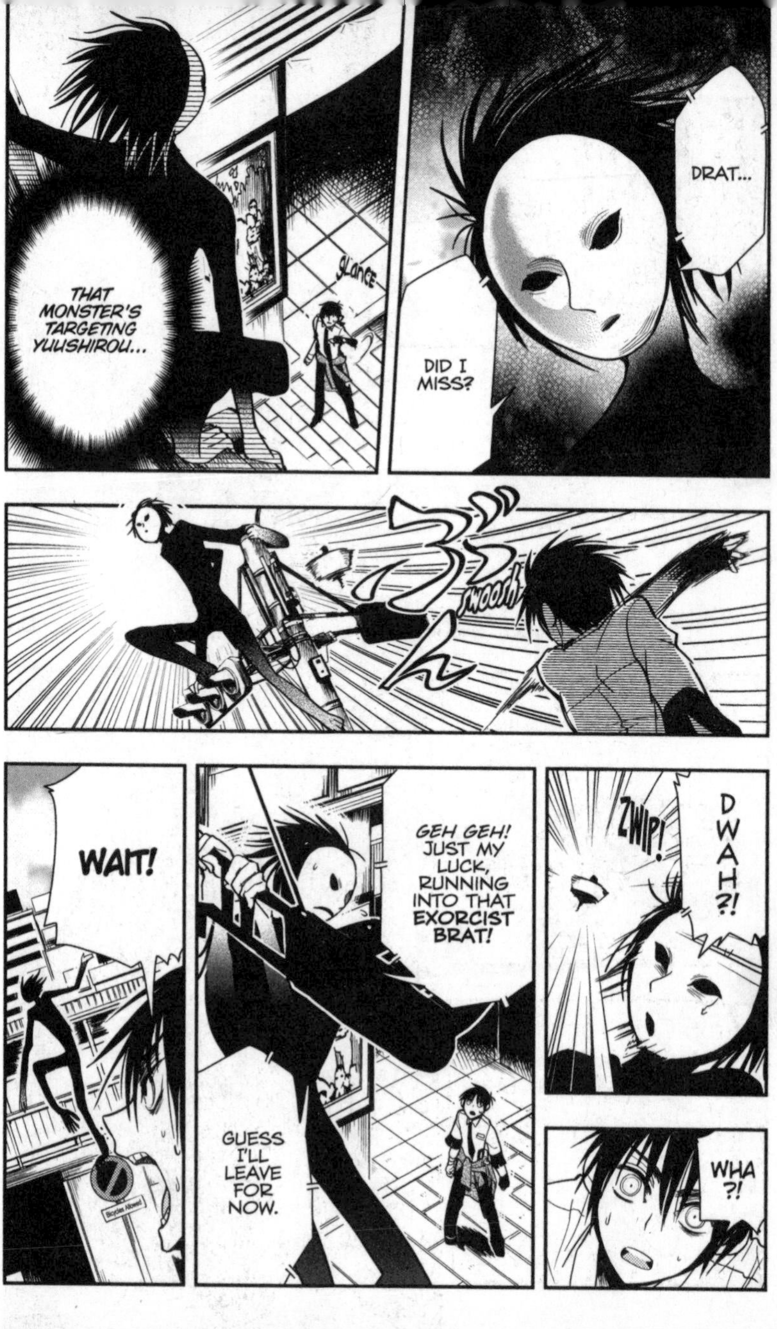
DRAT...
DID I MISS?
GLANCE
THAT MONSTER'S TARGETING YUUSHIROU...
SWOOSH
ZWIP!
DWAH?!
WHA?!
GEH GEH! JUST MY LUCK, RUNNING INTO THAT EXORCIST BRAT!
GUESS I'LL LEAVE FOR NOW.
WAIT!

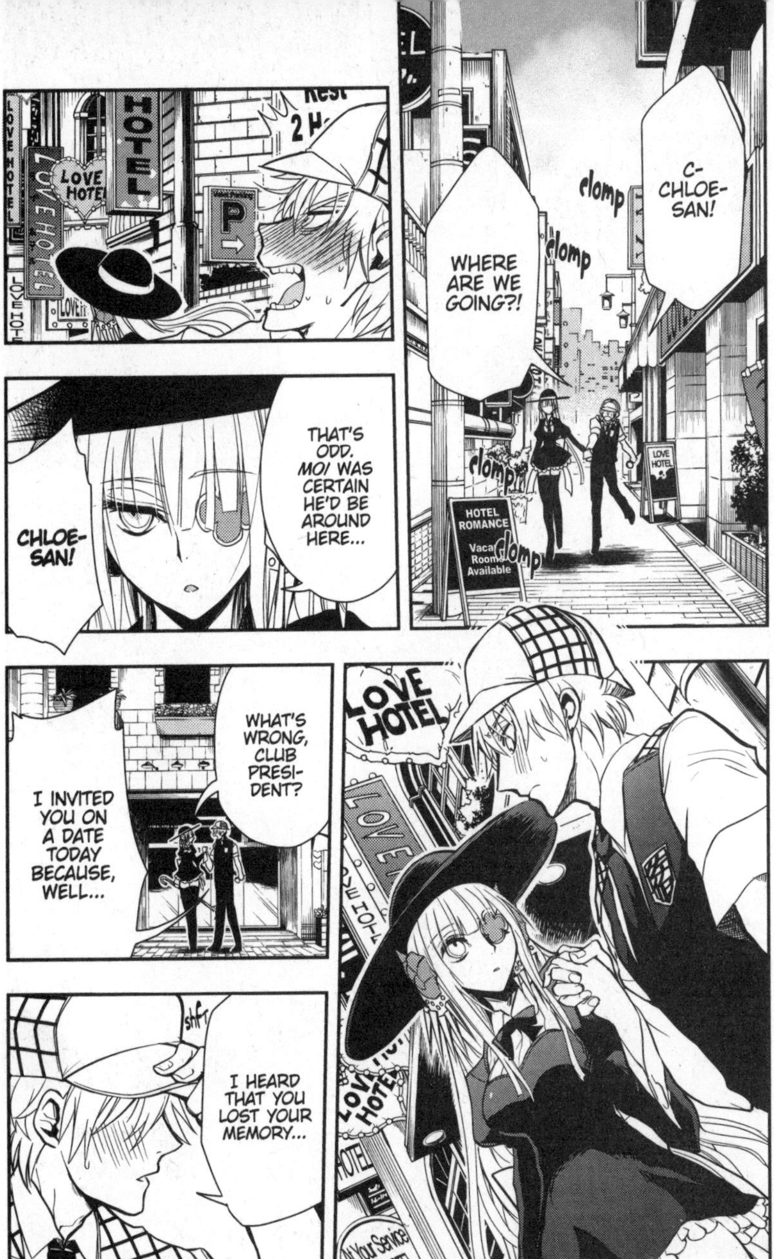
C-CHLOE-SAN!
clomp
clomp
WHERE ARE WE GOING?!
clomp
clomp
HOTEL ROMANCE Vaca Room Available
LOVE HOTEL
Rest 2 H
HOTEL
LOVE HOTEL
LOVE HOTEL
LOVE HOTEL
THAT'S ODD. MOI WAS CERTAIN HE'D BE AROUND HERE...
CHLOE-SAN!
LOVE HOTEL
At Your Service LOVE HOTEL
WHAT'S WRONG, CLUB PRESIDENT?
I INVITED YOU ON A DATE TODAY BECAUSE, WELL...
shff
I HEARD THAT YOU LOST YOUR MEMORY...

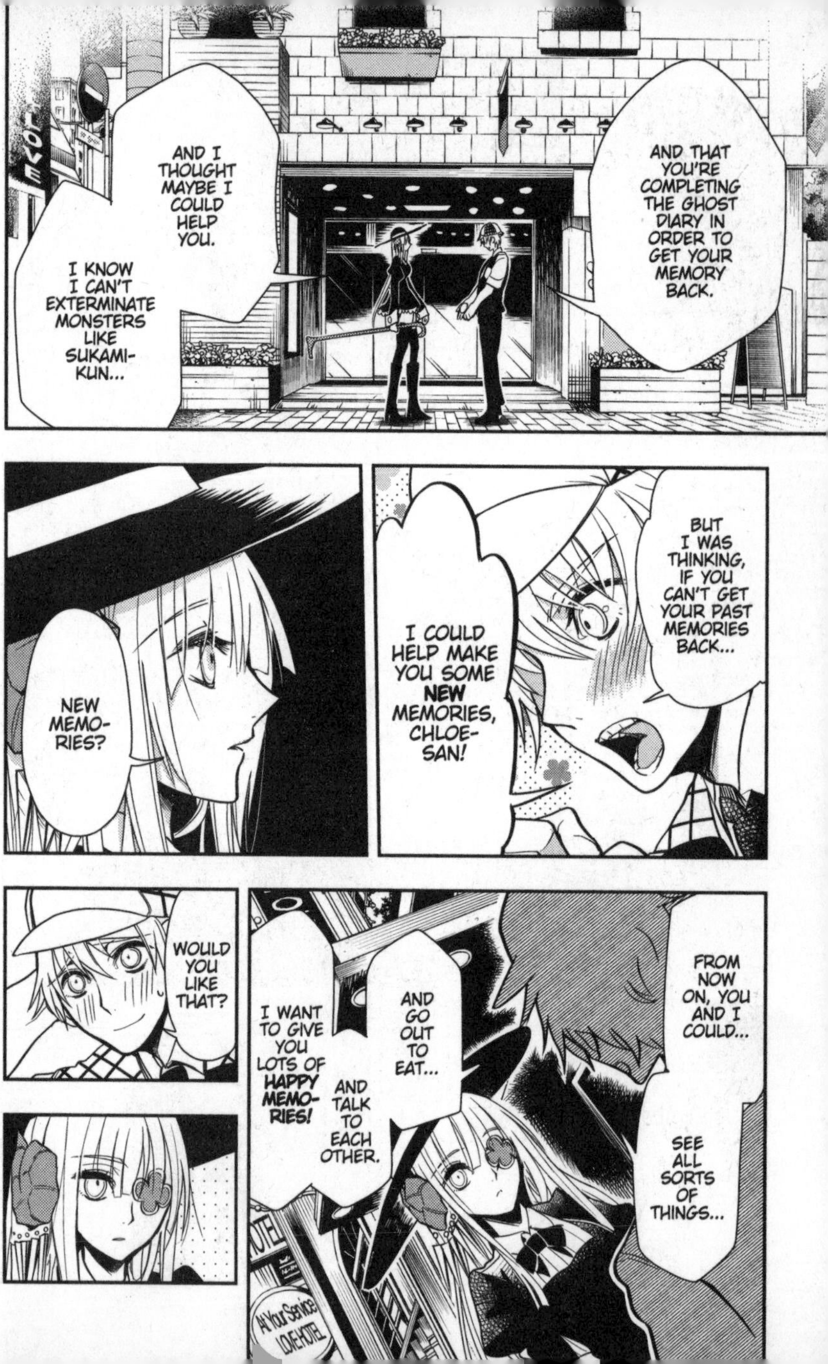
LOVE
I KNOW I CAN'T EXTERMINATE MONSTERS LIKE SUKAMI-KUN...
AND THAT YOU'RE COMPLETING THE GHOST DIARY IN ORDER TO GET YOUR MEMORY BACK.
AND I THOUGHT MAYBE I COULD HELP YOU.
BUT I WAS THINKING, IF YOU CAN'T GET YOUR PAST MEMORIES BACK...
I COULD HELP MAKE YOU SOME **NEW** MEMORIES, CHLOE-SAN!
NEW MEMO-RIES?
FROM NOW ON, YOU AND I COULD...
SEE ALL SORTS OF THINGS...
AND GO OUT TO EAT...
AND TALK TO EACH OTHER.
I WANT TO GIVE YOU LOTS OF **HAPPY MEMO-RIES!**
HOTEL
At Your Service LOVE HOTEL
WOULD YOU LIKE THAT?

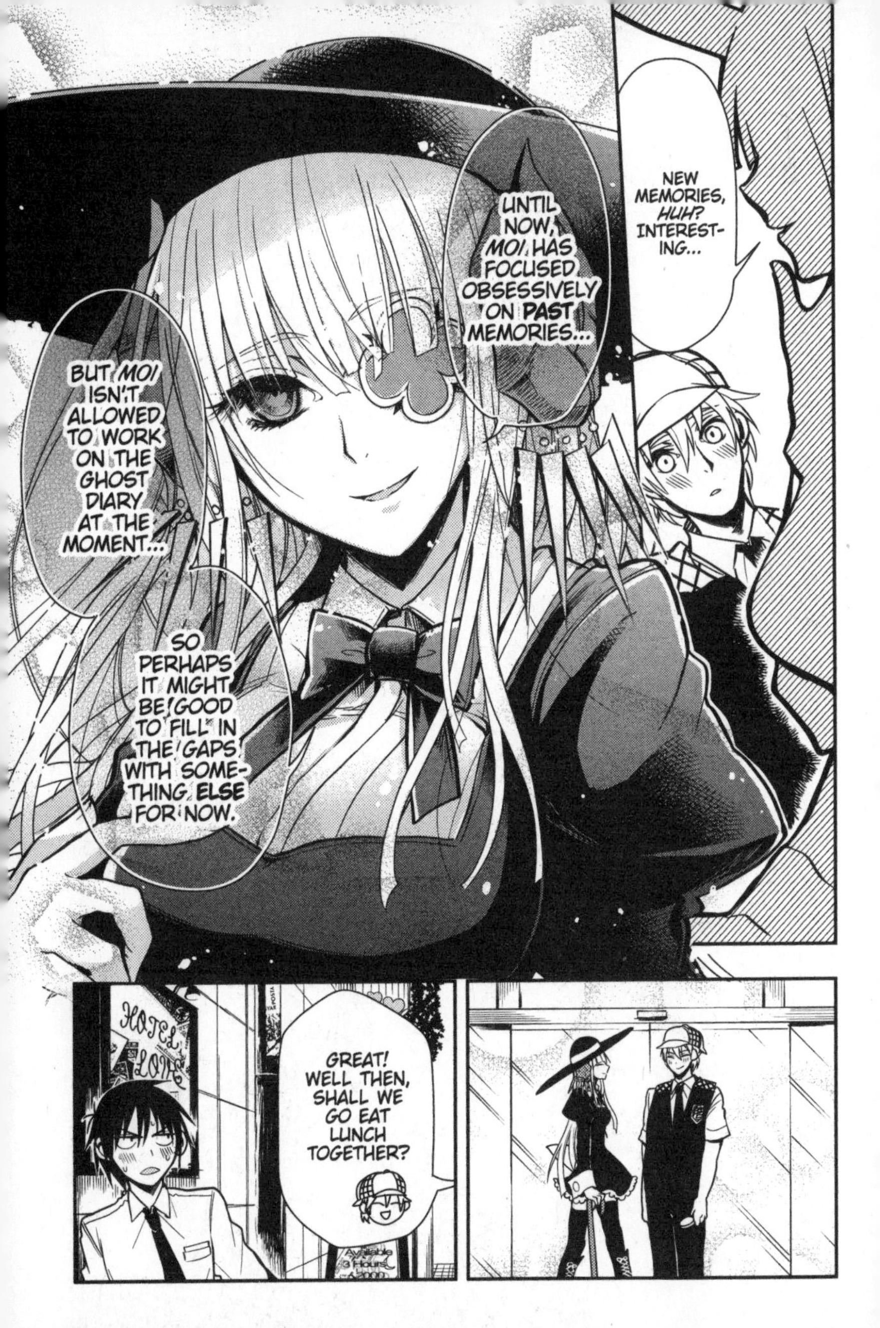
NEW MEMORIES, *HUH?* INTEREST-ING...
UNTIL NOW, *MOI* HAS FOCUSED OBSESSIVELY ON **PAST** MEMORIES...
BUT *MOI* ISN'T ALLOWED TO WORK ON THE GHOST DIARY AT THE MOMENT...
SO PERHAPS IT MIGHT BE GOOD TO FILL IN THE GAPS WITH SOME-THING **ELSE** FOR NOW.
GREAT! WELL THEN, SHALL WE GO EAT LUNCH TOGETHER?

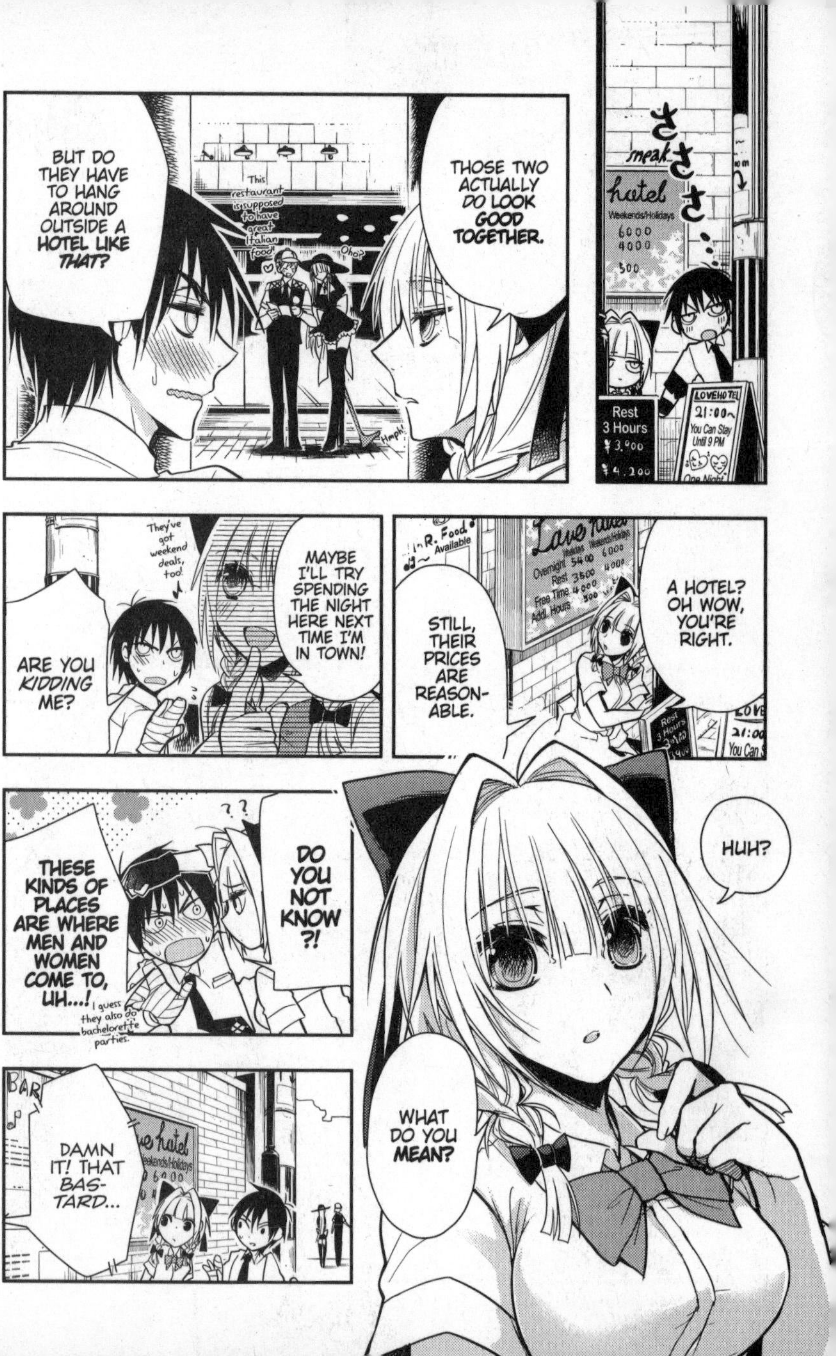

hotel
Weekends/Holidays
6000
4000
500
Rest
3 Hours
¥3,900
¥4,200
LOVEHOTEL
21:00~
You Can Stay Until 9 PM
One Night
THOSE TWO ACTUALLY DO LOOK GOOD TOGETHER.
This restaurant is supposed to have great Italian food!
Oho?
Hmph!
BUT DO THEY HAVE TO HANG AROUND OUTSIDE A HOTEL LIKE THAT?
A HOTEL? OH WOW, YOU'RE RIGHT.
R. Food Available
Overnight 5400 6000
Rest 3500 4000
Free Time 4000
Addl. Hours 500
STILL, THEIR PRICES ARE REASONABLE.
MAYBE I'LL TRY SPENDING THE NIGHT HERE NEXT TIME I'M IN TOWN!
They've got weekend deals, too!
ARE YOU KIDDING ME?
HUH?
WHAT DO YOU MEAN?
DO YOU NOT KNOW?!
THESE KINDS OF PLACES ARE WHERE MEN AND WOMEN COME TO, UH...!
I guess they also do bachelorette parties.
BAR
DAMN IT! THAT BASTARD...

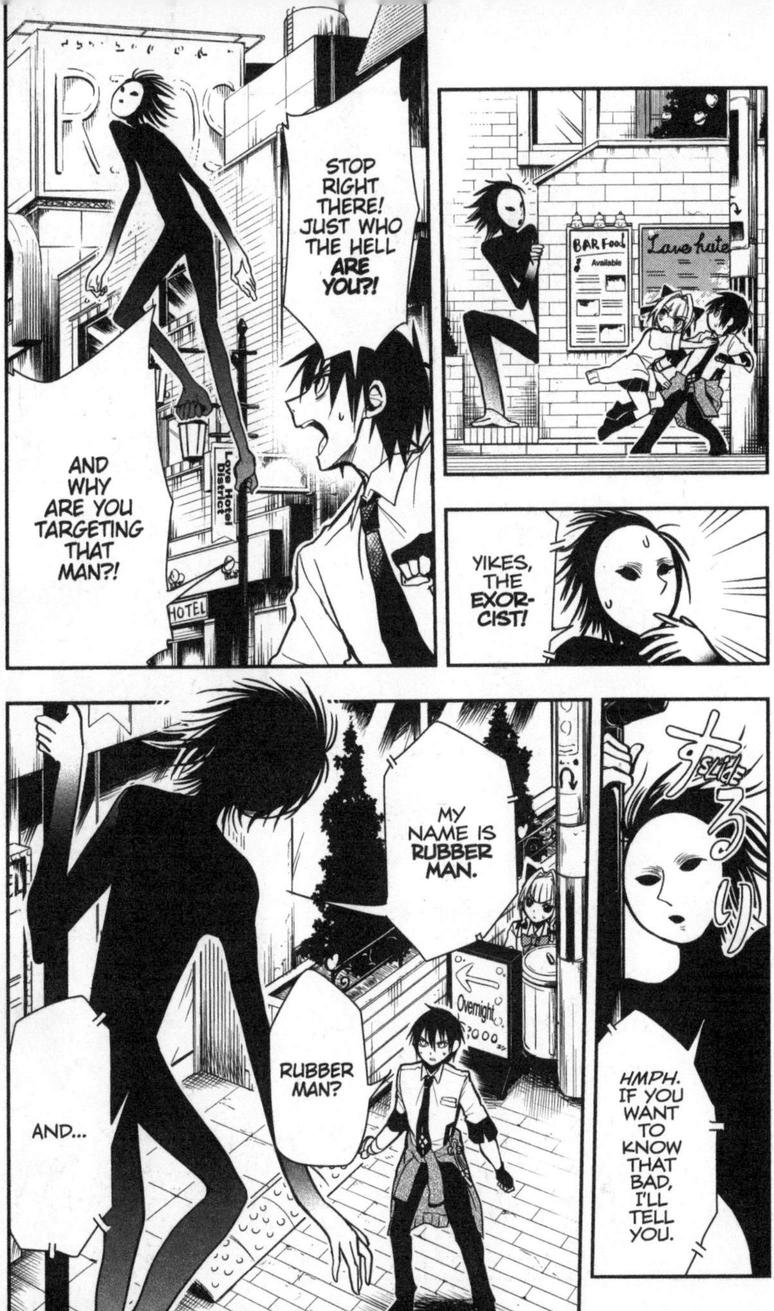
BAR Food
Available
YIKES, THE EXORCIST!
STOP RIGHT THERE! JUST WHO THE HELL **ARE YOU?!**
Love Hotel District
HOTEL
AND WHY ARE YOU TARGETING THAT MAN?!
HMPH. IF YOU WANT TO KNOW THAT BAD, I'LL TELL YOU.
MY NAME IS **RUBBER MAN.**
Overnight
RUBBER MAN?
AND...

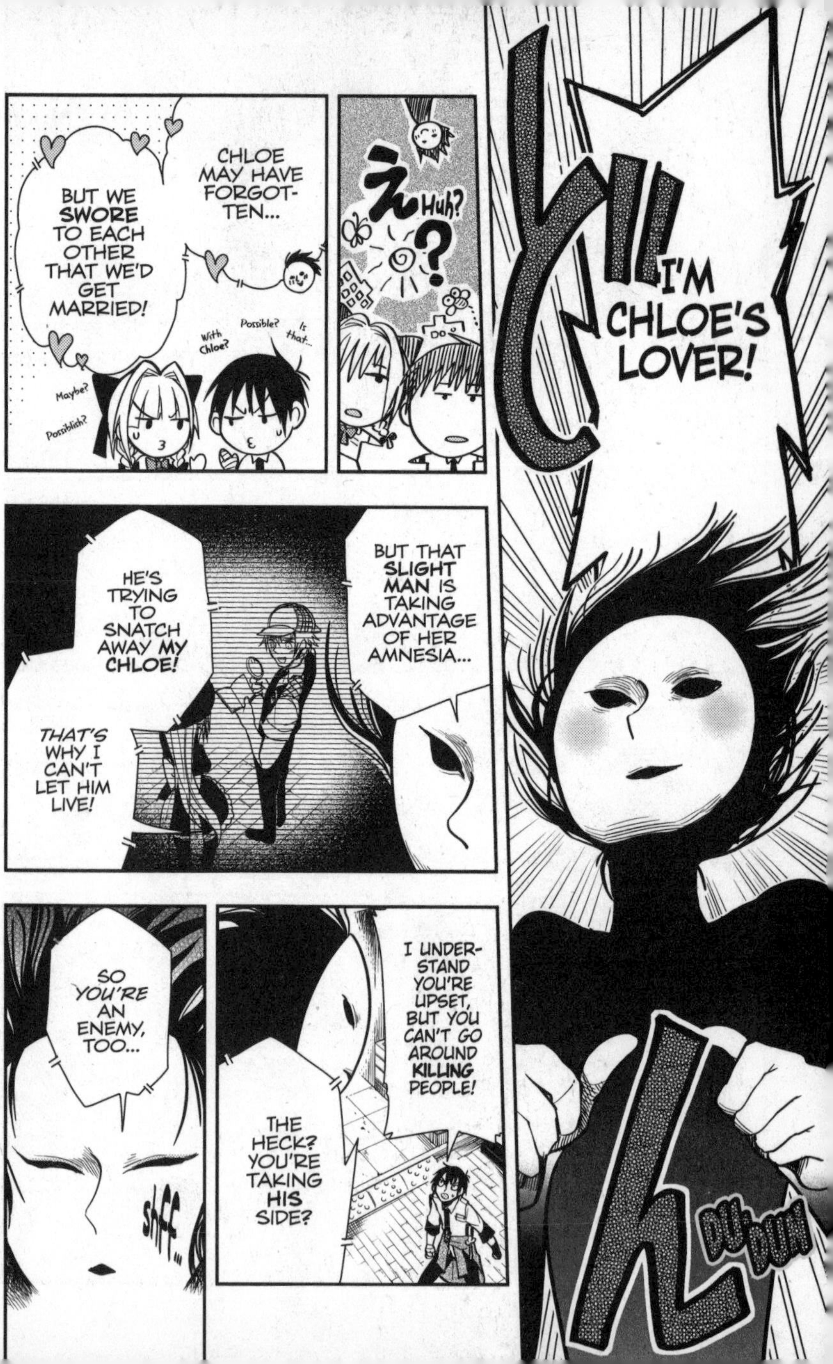
I'M CHLOE'S LOVER!
DU-DUN
え
Huh?
Do
CHLOE MAY HAVE FORGOT-TEN...
BUT WE SWORE TO EACH OTHER THAT WE'D GET MARRIED!
Is that...
Possible?
With Chloe?
Maybe?
Possiblish?
BUT THAT SLIGHT MAN IS TAKING ADVANTAGE OF HER AMNESIA...
HE'S TRYING TO SNATCH AWAY MY CHLOE!
THAT'S WHY I CAN'T LET HIM LIVE!
I UNDER-STAND YOU'RE UPSET, BUT YOU CAN'T GO AROUND KILLING PEOPLE!
THE HECK? YOU'RE TAKING HIS SIDE?
SO YOU'RE AN ENEMY, TOO...
shff...

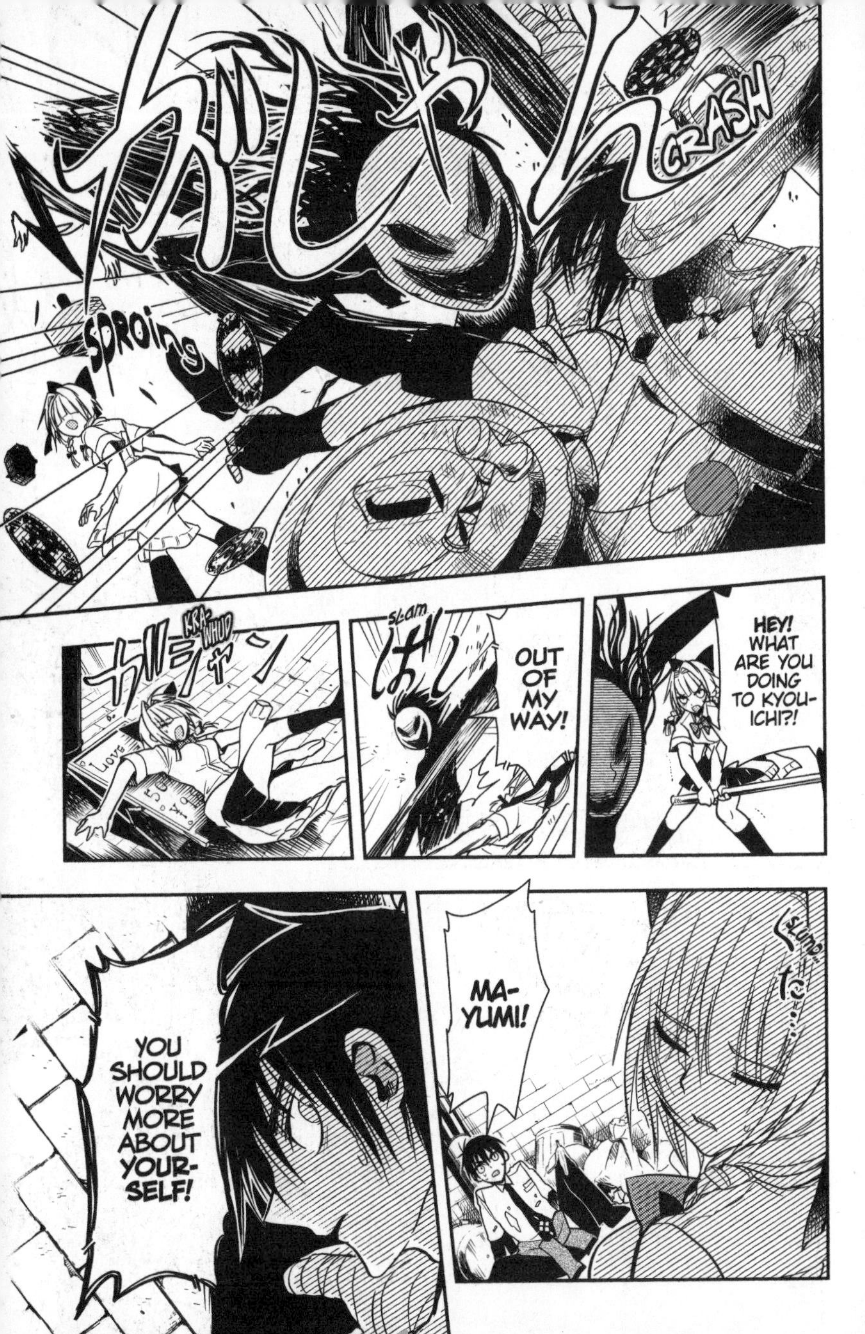
CRASH
SPROING
HEY! WHAT ARE YOU DOING TO KYOU-ICHI?!
SLAM
OUT OF MY WAY!
KRA-WHUD
SLUMP
MA-YUMI!
YOU SHOULD WORRY MORE ABOUT YOUR-SELF!

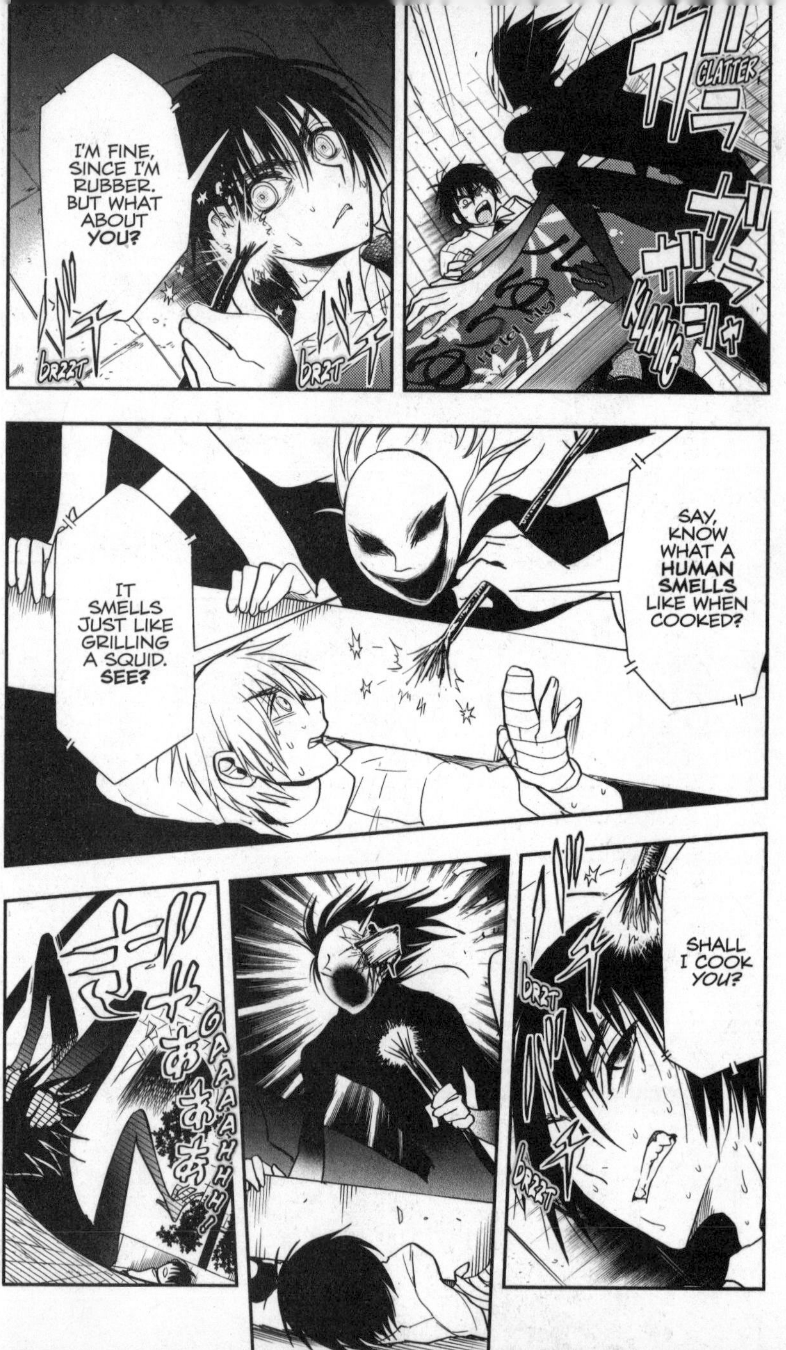
CLATTER
KLAANG
I'M FINE, SINCE I'M RUBBER. BUT WHAT ABOUT YOU?
brzzt
brzt
SAY, KNOW WHAT A HUMAN SMELLS LIKE WHEN COOKED?
IT SMELLS JUST LIKE GRILLING A SQUID. SEE?
SHALL I COOK YOU?
brzt
brzzt
GAAAAHHH!

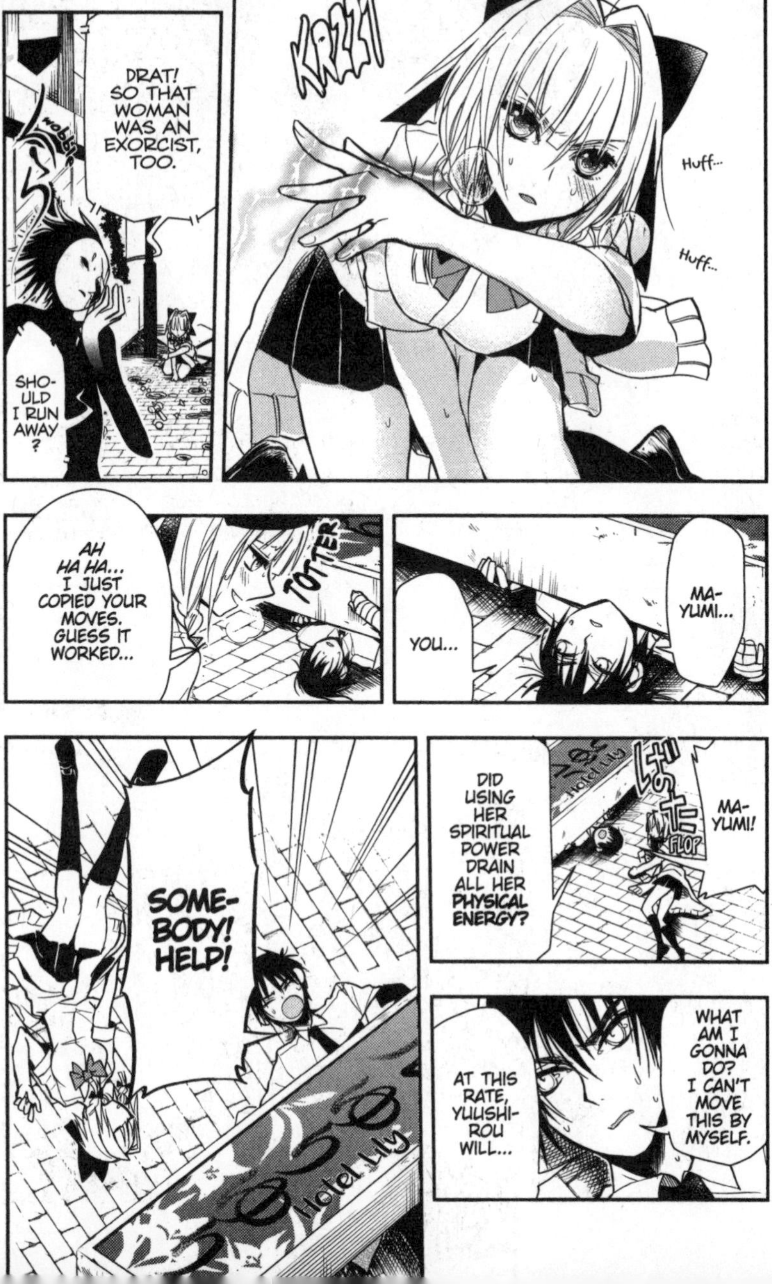
KRZZZT
Huff...
Huff...
DRAT! SO THAT WOMAN WAS AN EXORCIST, TOO.
wobble
SHOULD I RUN AWAY?
MAYUMI...
YOU...
AH HA HA... I JUST COPIED YOUR MOVES. GUESS IT WORKED...
TOTTER
Hotel Lily
MAYUMI!
FLOP
DID USING HER SPIRITUAL POWER DRAIN ALL HER PHYSICAL ENERGY?
WHAT AM I GONNA DO? I CAN'T MOVE THIS BY MYSELF.
AT THIS RATE, YUUSHIROU WILL...
SOMEBODY! HELP!
Hotel Lily

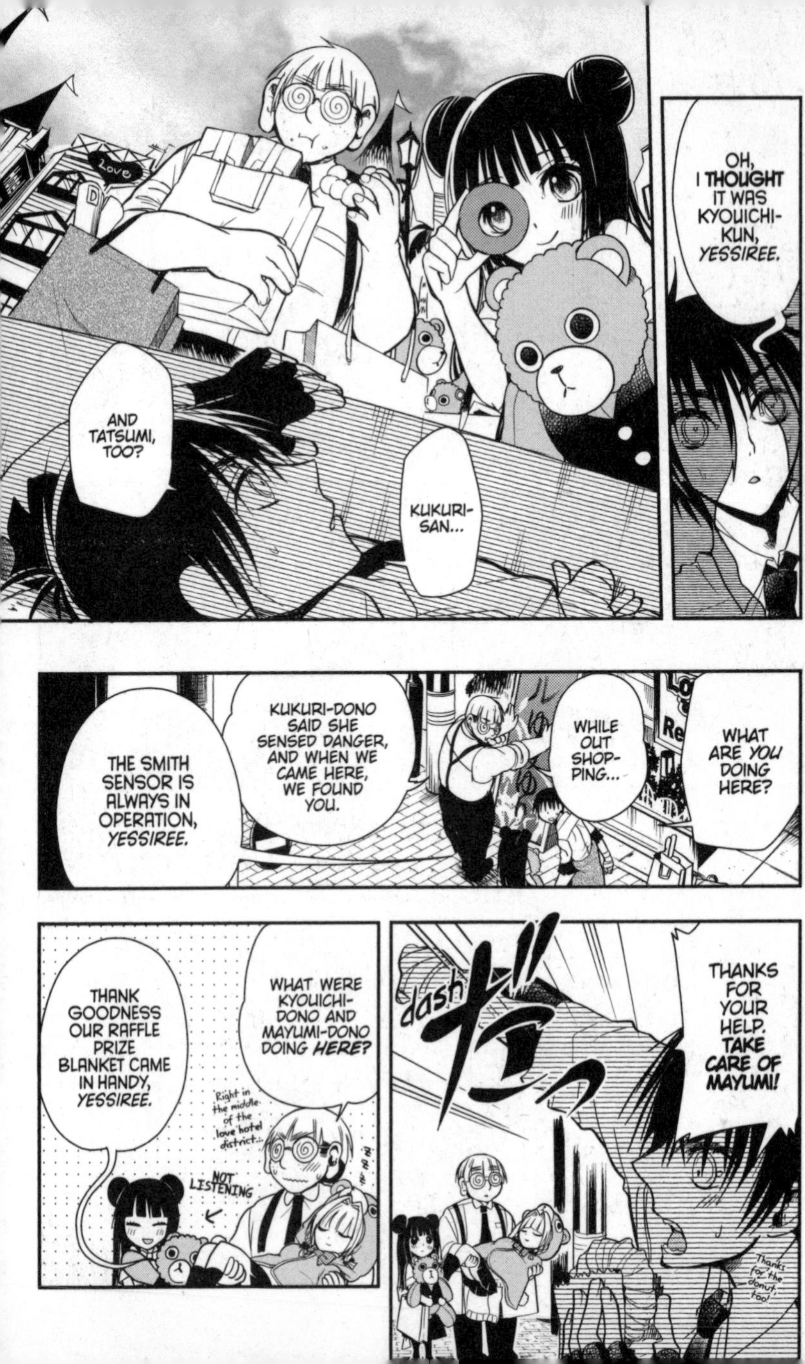
OH, I THOUGHT IT WAS KYOUICHI-KUN, YESSIREE.
Love
KUKURI-SAN...
AND TATSUMI, TOO?
WHAT ARE YOU DOING HERE?
WHILE OUT SHOP-PING...
KUKURI-DONO SAID SHE SENSED DANGER, AND WHEN WE CAME HERE, WE FOUND YOU.
THE SMITH SENSOR IS ALWAYS IN OPERATION, YESSIREE.
THANKS FOR YOUR HELP. TAKE CARE OF MAYUMI!
dash
Thanks for the donut, too!
WHAT WERE KYOUICHI-DONO AND MAYUMI-DONO DOING HERE?
Right in the middle of the love hotel district...
NOT LISTENING
THANK GOODNESS OUR RAFFLE PRIZE BLANKET CAME IN HANDY, YESSIREE.

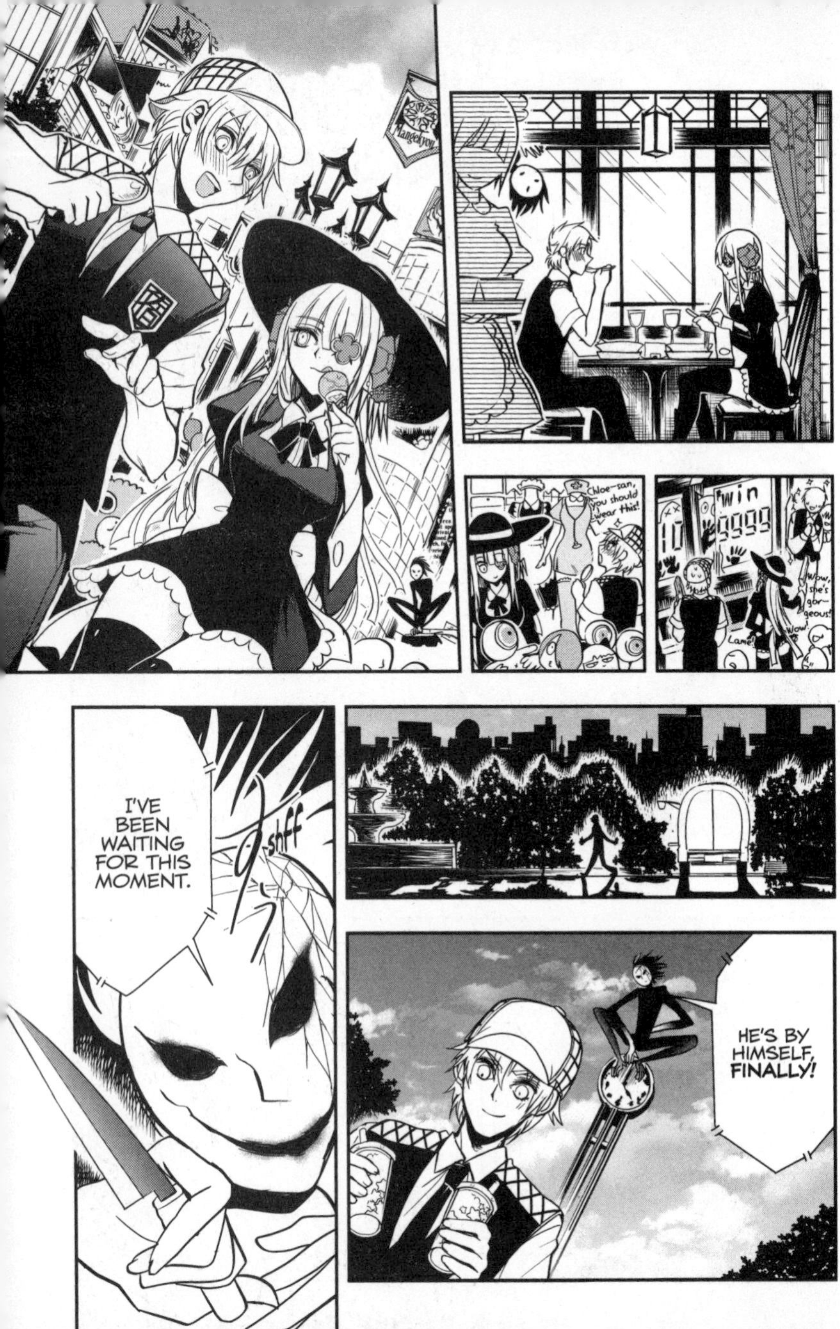
win
9999
Wow, she's gorgeous!
Wow!
Lame!
Chloe-san, you should wear this!
Mangekyou
HE'S BY HIMSELF, FINALLY!
I'VE BEEN WAITING FOR THIS MOMENT.
shff

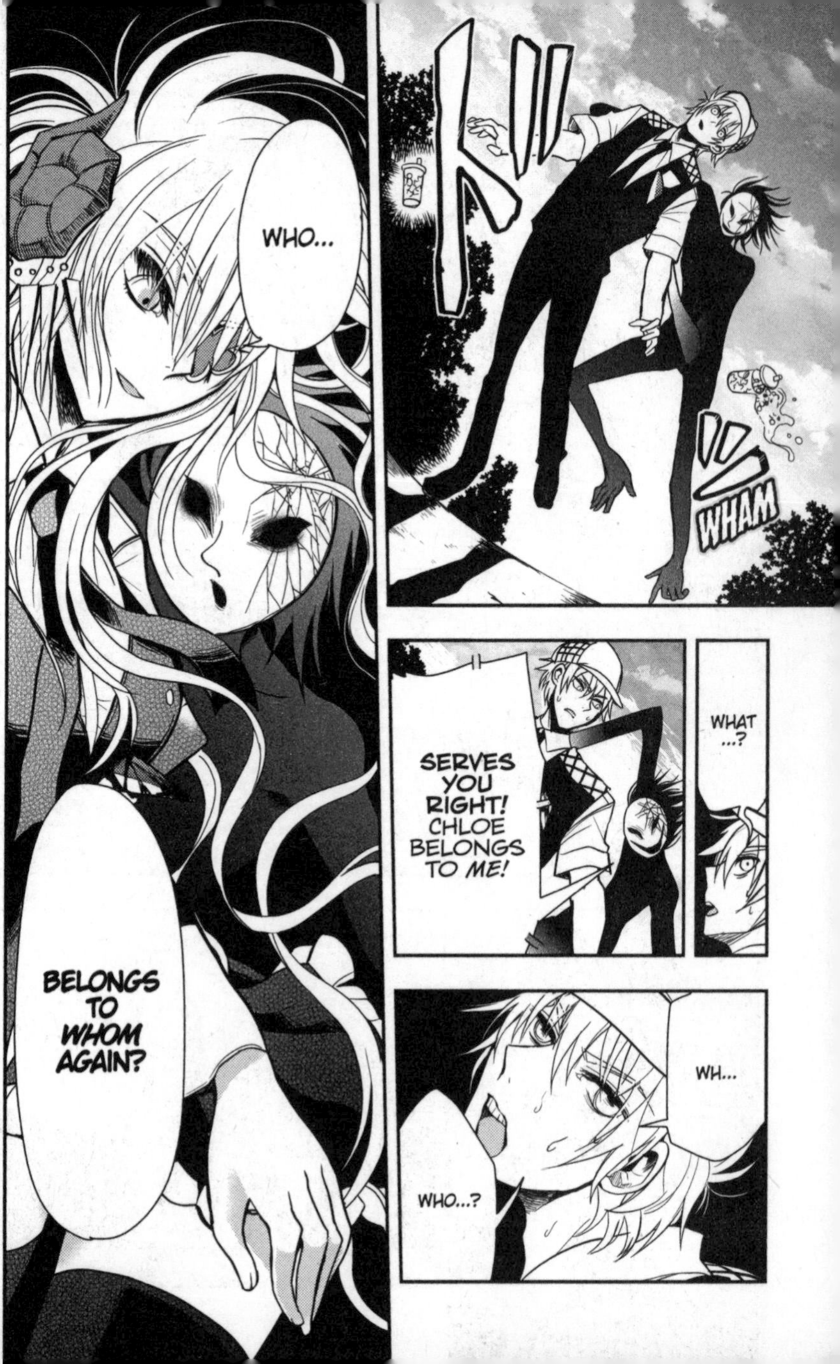
WHAM
WHAT ...?
SERVES YOU RIGHT! CHLOE BELONGS TO *ME!*
WH...
WHO...?
WHO...
BELONGS TO *WHOM* AGAIN?

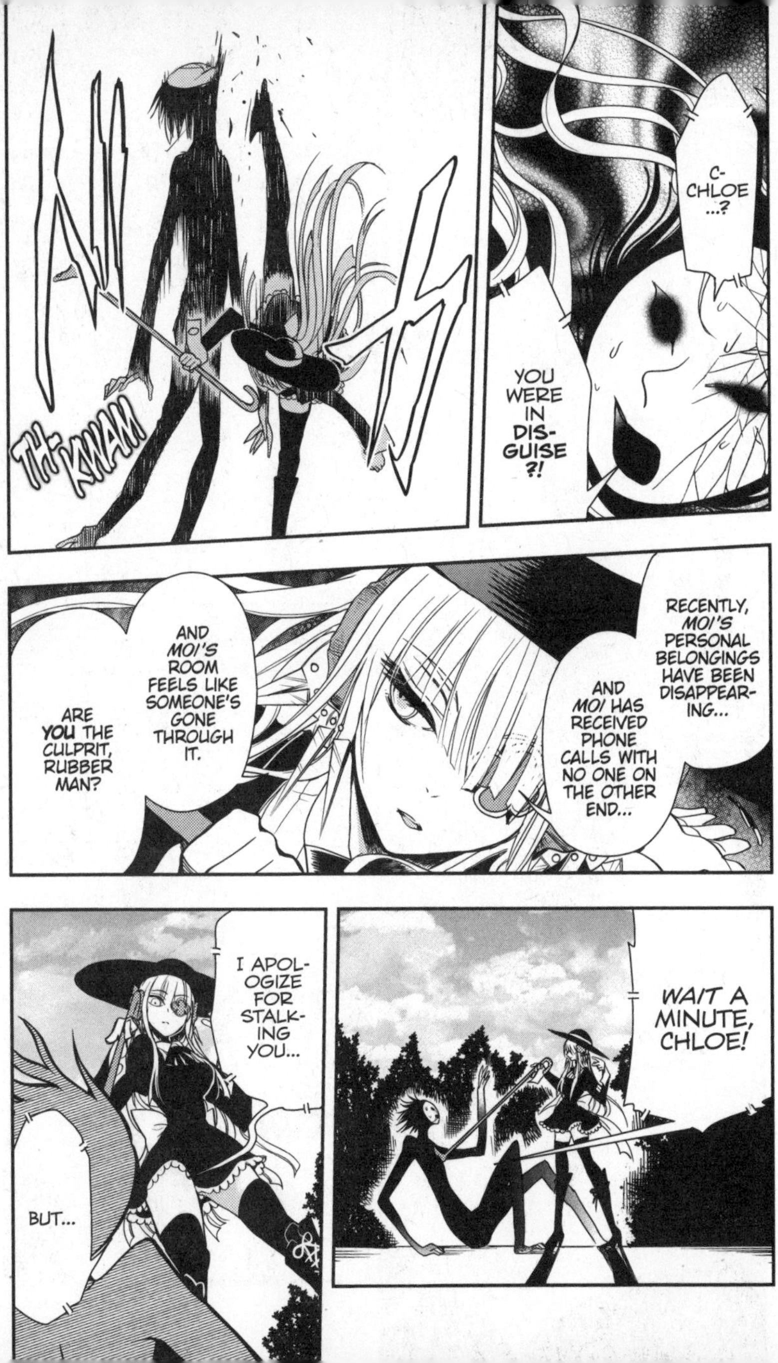
C-CHLOE...?
YOU WERE IN DISGUISE?!
TH-KWAM
RECENTLY, *MOI'S* PERSONAL BELONGINGS HAVE BEEN DISAPPEARING...
AND *MOI* HAS RECEIVED PHONE CALLS WITH NO ONE ON THE OTHER END...
AND *MOI'S* ROOM FEELS LIKE SOMEONE'S GONE THROUGH IT.
ARE **YOU** THE CULPRIT, RUBBER MAN?
WAIT A MINUTE, CHLOE!
I APOLOGIZE FOR STALKING YOU...
BUT...

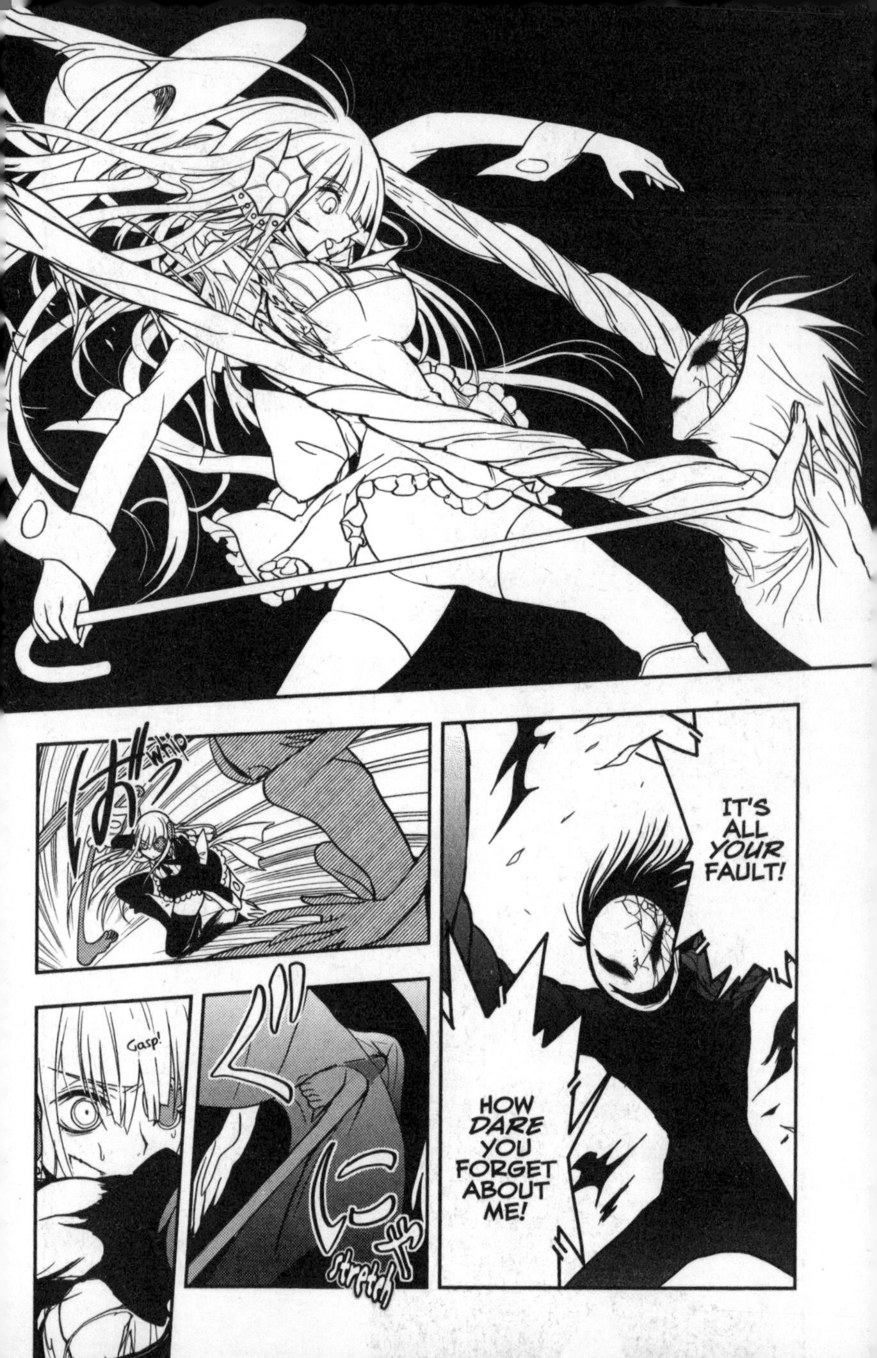
IT'S ALL YOUR FAULT!
HOW DARE YOU FORGET ABOUT ME!
whip
stretch
Gasp!

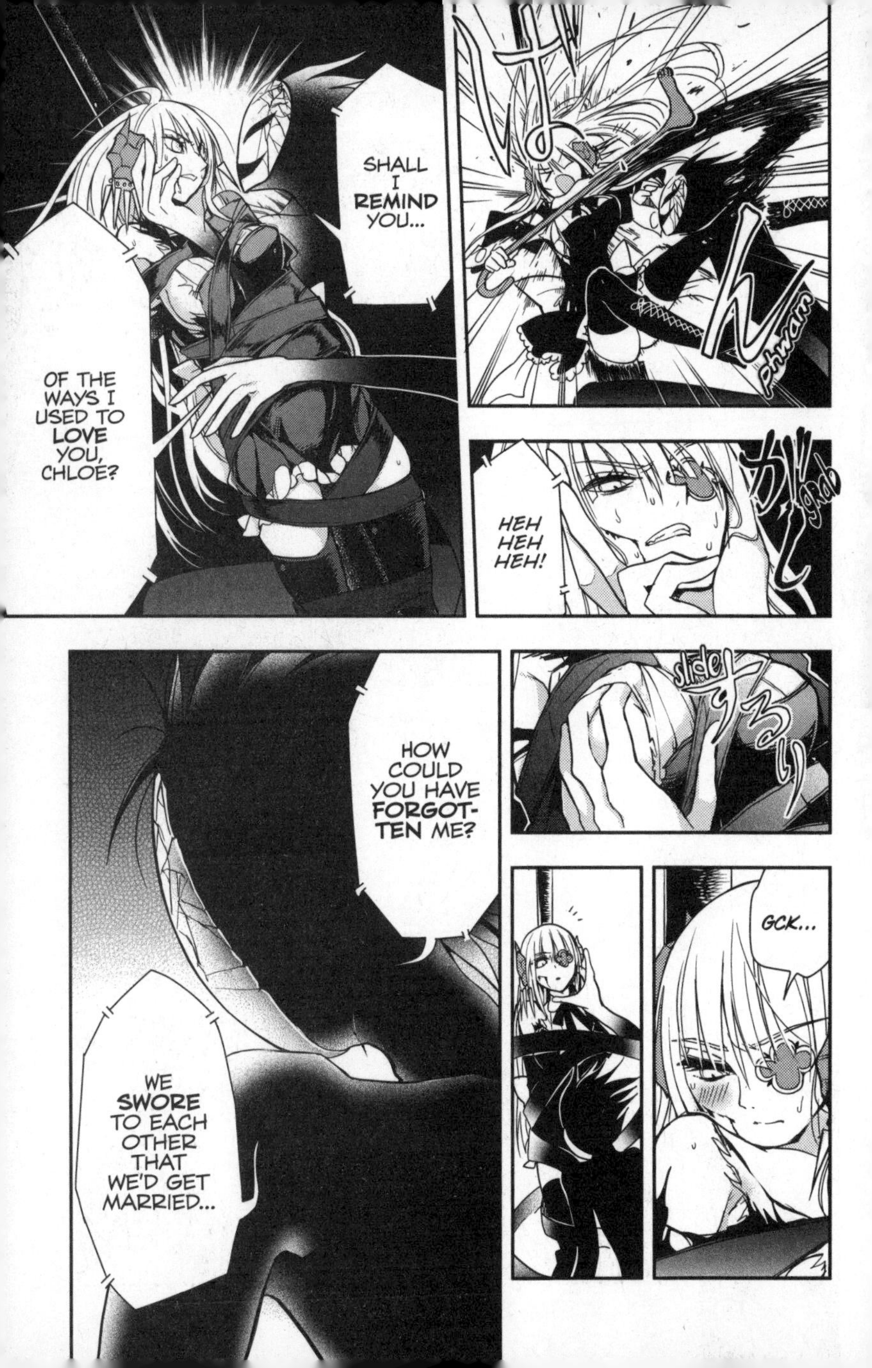
phwam
HEH HEH HEH!
grab
SHALL I REMIND YOU...
OF THE WAYS I USED TO LOVE YOU, CHLOE?
slide
GCK...
HOW COULD YOU HAVE FORGOT-TEN ME?
WE SWORE TO EACH OTHER THAT WE'D GET MARRIED...

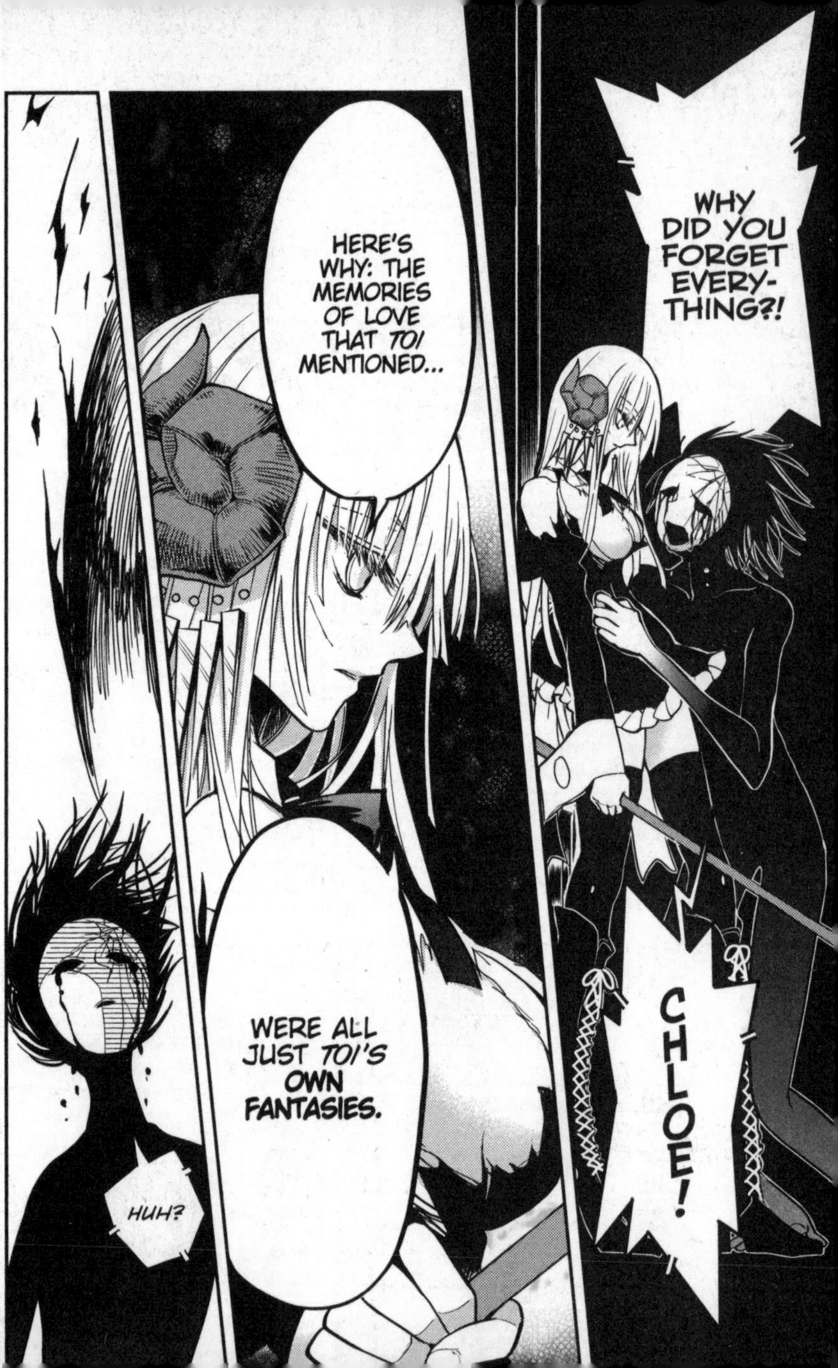
WHY DID YOU FORGET EVERY-THING?!
CHLOE!
HERE'S WHY: THE MEMORIES OF LOVE THAT *TOI* MENTIONED...
WERE ALL JUST *TOI'S* OWN FANTASIES.
HUH?

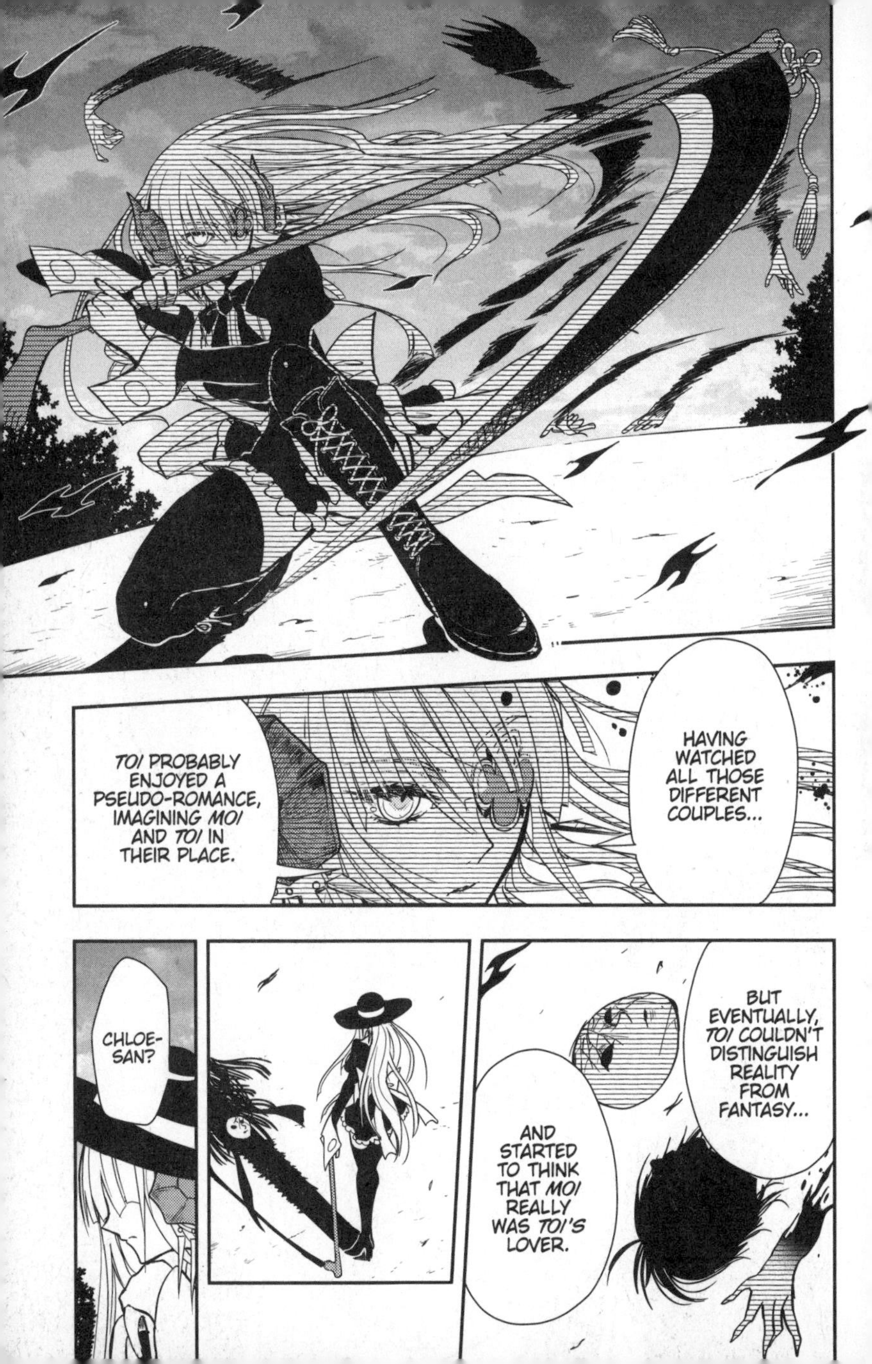
HAVING WATCHED ALL THOSE DIFFERENT COUPLES...
TOI PROBABLY ENJOYED A PSEUDO-ROMANCE, IMAGINING *MOI* AND *TOI* IN THEIR PLACE.
BUT EVENTUALLY, *TOI* COULDN'T DISTINGUISH REALITY FROM FANTASY...
AND STARTED TO THINK THAT *MOI* REALLY WAS *TOI*'S LOVER.
CHLOE-SAN?

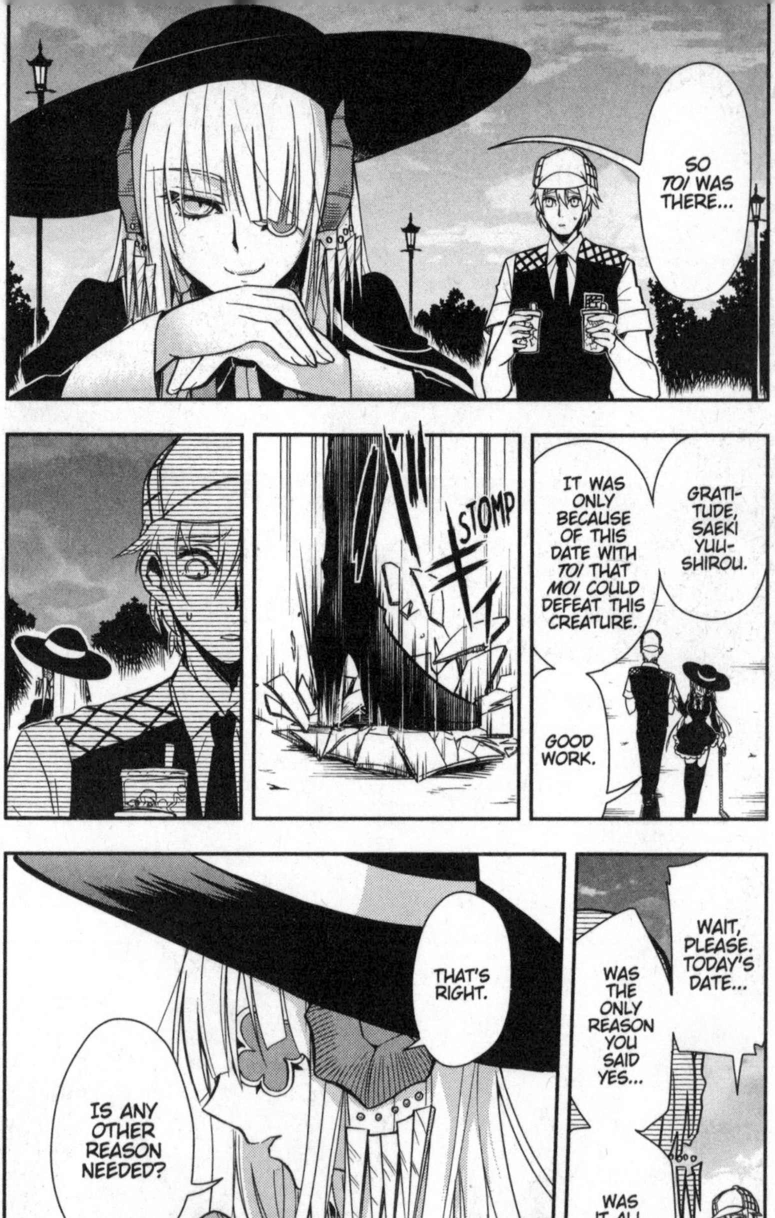
SO *TOI* WAS THERE...
GRATITUDE, SAEKI YUUSHIROU.
IT WAS ONLY BECAUSE OF THIS DATE WITH *TOI* THAT *MOI* COULD DEFEAT THIS CREATURE.
GOOD WORK.
STOMP
WAIT, PLEASE. TODAY'S DATE...
WAS THE ONLY REASON YOU SAID YES...
WAS IT ALL JUST TO DEFEAT **THIS MONSTER?**
THAT'S RIGHT.
IS ANY OTHER REASON NEEDED?

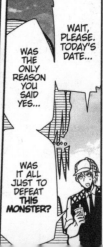

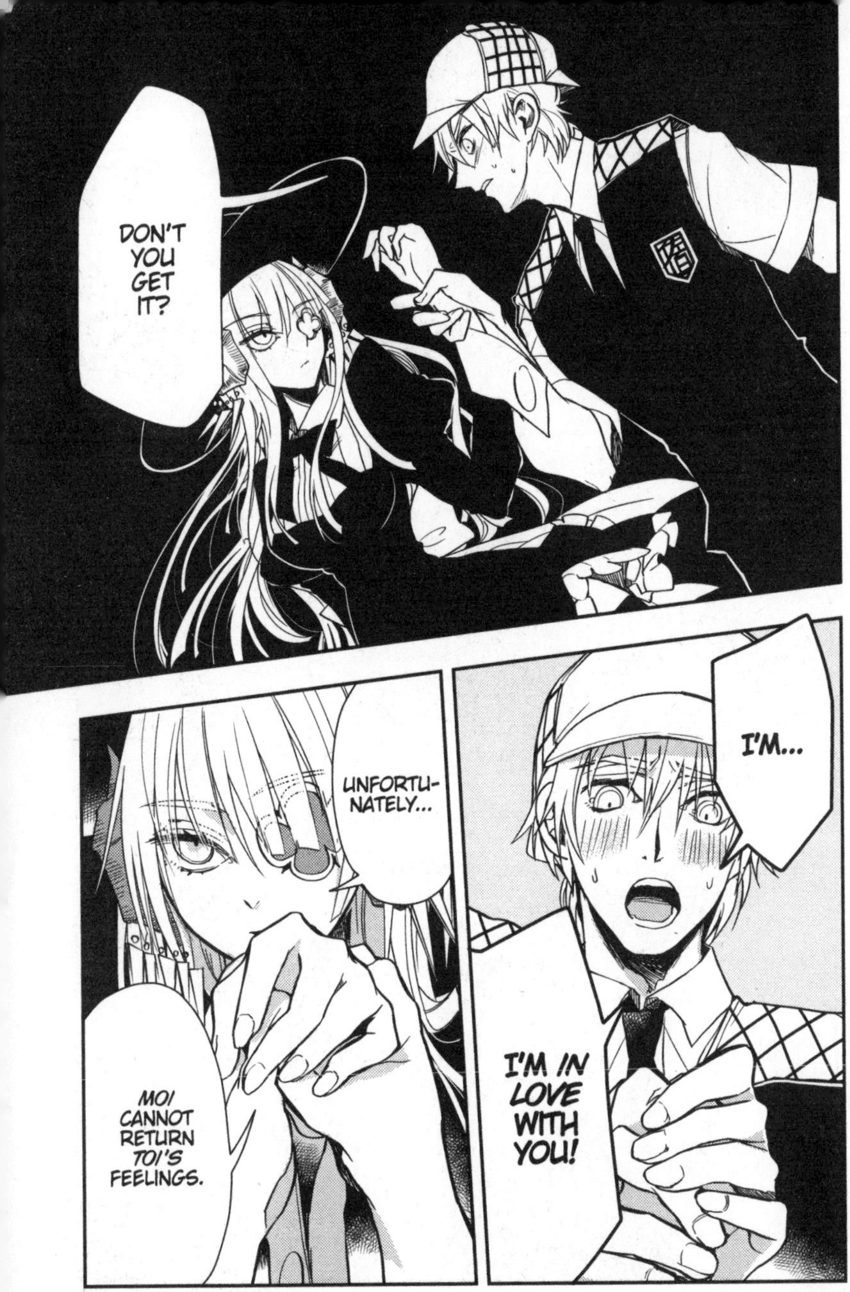
DON'T YOU GET IT?
I'M...
I'M *IN LOVE* WITH YOU!
UNFORTUNATELY...
MOI CANNOT RETURN *TOI'S* FEELINGS.

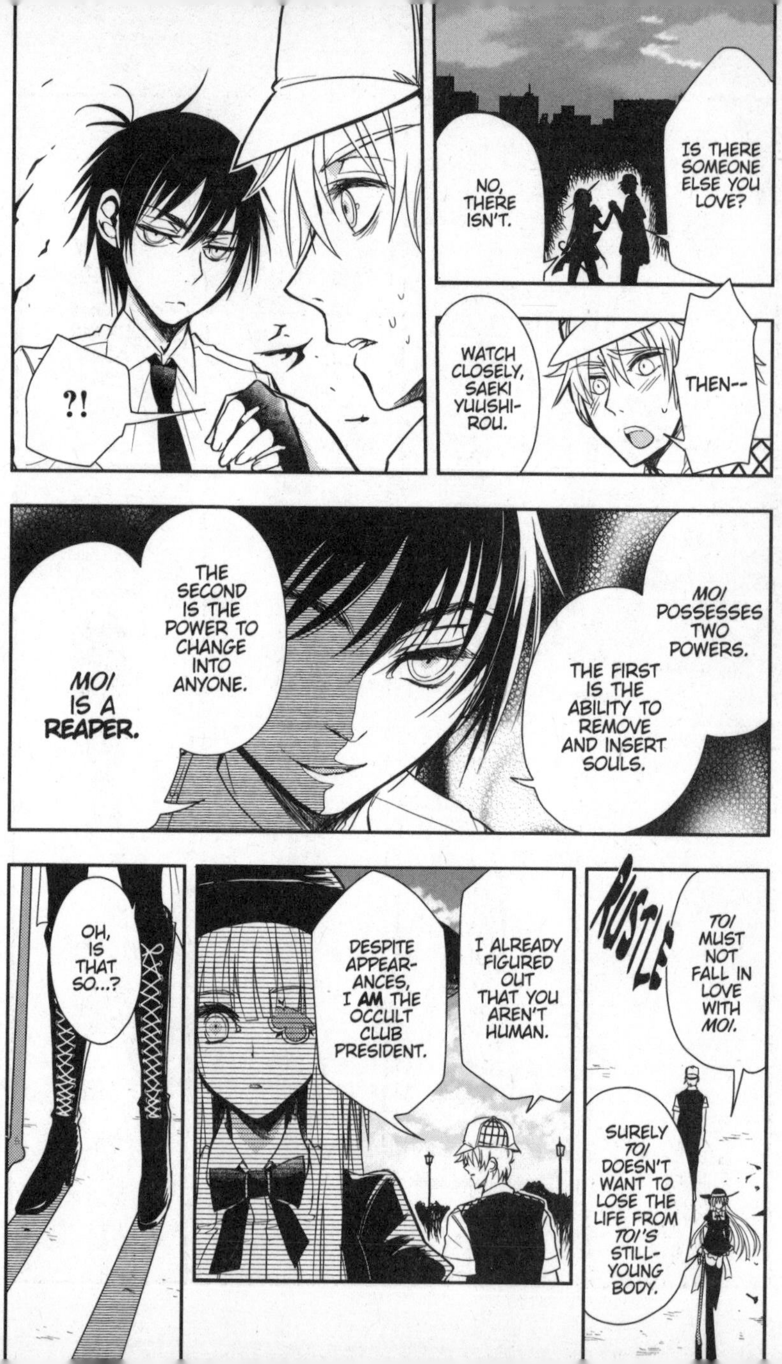
IS THERE SOMEONE ELSE YOU LOVE?
NO, THERE ISN'T.
THEN--
WATCH CLOSELY, SAEKI YUUSHIROU.
?!
MOI POSSESSES TWO POWERS.
THE FIRST IS THE ABILITY TO REMOVE AND INSERT SOULS.
THE SECOND IS THE POWER TO CHANGE INTO ANYONE.
MOI IS A **REAPER.**
RUSTLE
TOI MUST NOT FALL IN LOVE WITH *MOI*.
SURELY *TOI* DOESN'T WANT TO LOSE THE LIFE FROM *TOI'S* STILL-YOUNG BODY.
I ALREADY FIGURED OUT THAT YOU AREN'T HUMAN.
DESPITE APPEARANCES, I **AM** THE OCCULT CLUB PRESIDENT.
OH, IS THAT SO...?

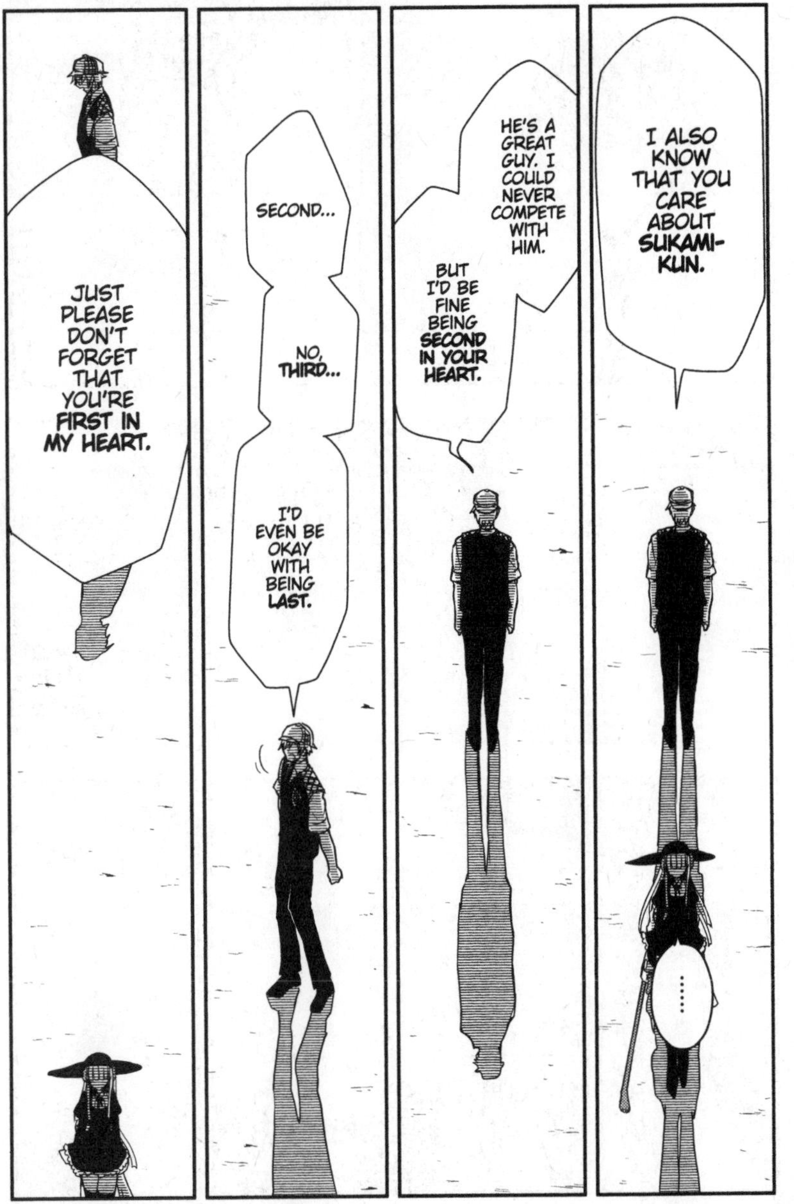
I ALSO KNOW THAT YOU CARE ABOUT SUKAMI-KUN.
......
HE'S A GREAT GUY. I COULD NEVER COMPETE WITH HIM.
BUT I'D BE FINE BEING SECOND IN YOUR HEART.
SECOND...
NO, THIRD...
I'D EVEN BE OKAY WITH BEING LAST.
JUST PLEASE DON'T FORGET THAT YOU'RE FIRST IN MY HEART.

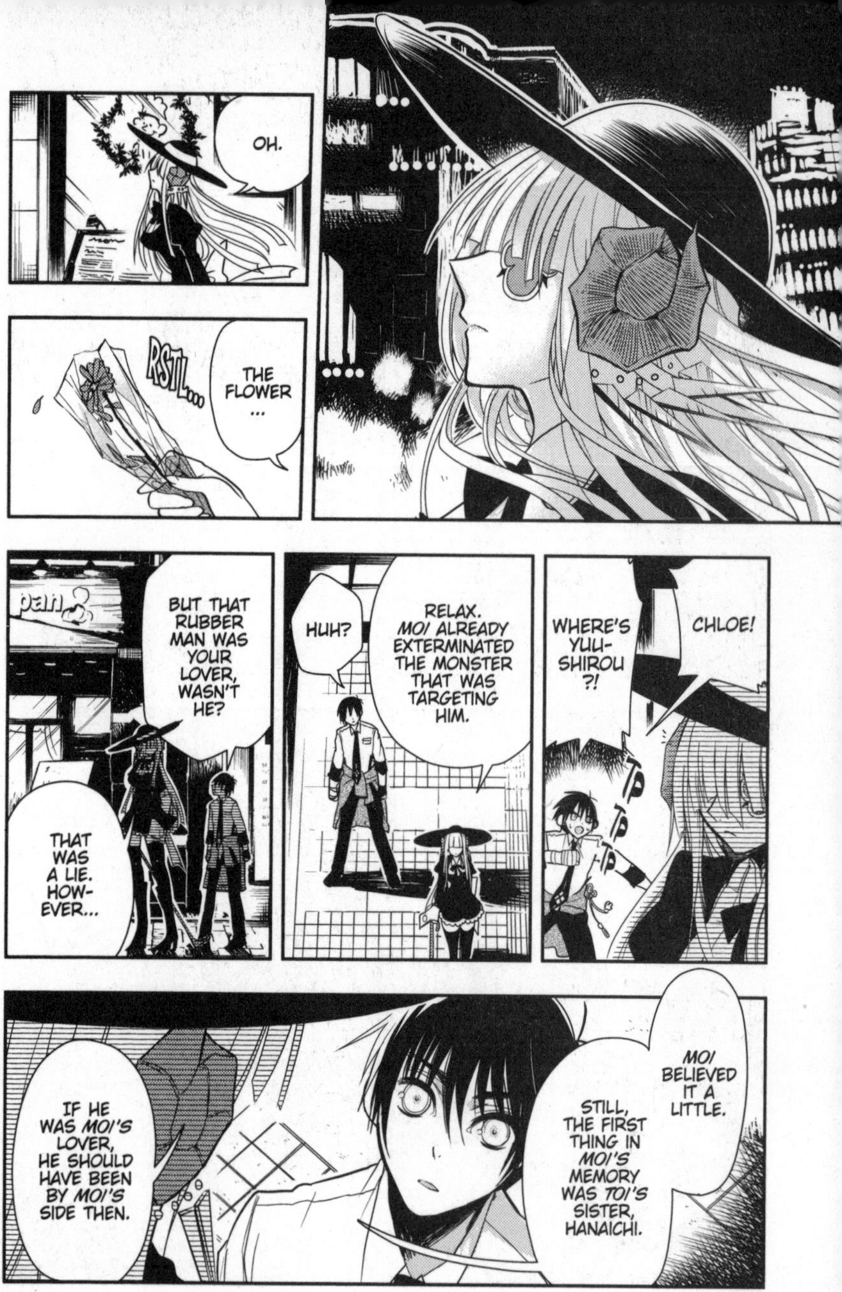
OH.
RSTL...
THE FLOWER ...
CHLOE!
WHERE'S YUU-SHIROU?!
TP TP TP TP
RELAX. *MOI* ALREADY EXTERMINATED THE MONSTER THAT WAS TARGETING HIM.
HUH?
pan
BUT THAT RUBBER MAN WAS YOUR LOVER, WASN'T HE?
THAT WAS A LIE. HOW-EVER...
MOI BELIEVED IT A LITTLE.
STILL, THE FIRST THING IN *MOI'S* MEMORY WAS *TOI'S* SISTER, HANAICHI.
IF HE WAS *MOI'S* LOVER, HE SHOULD HAVE BEEN BY *MOI'S* SIDE THEN.

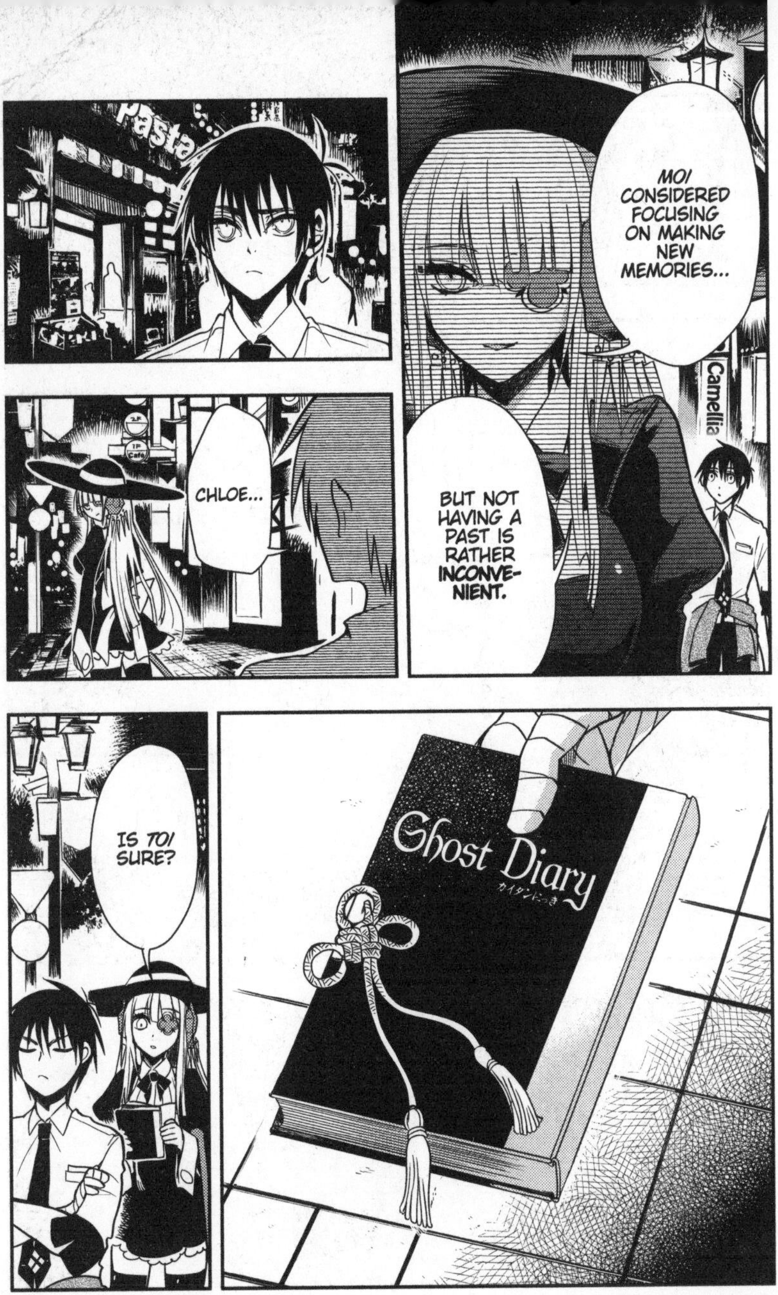
MOI CONSIDERED FOCUSING ON MAKING NEW MEMORIES...
BUT NOT HAVING A PAST IS RATHER INCONVENIENT.
Camellia
Pasta
CHLOE...
Ghost Diary
IS TOI SURE?

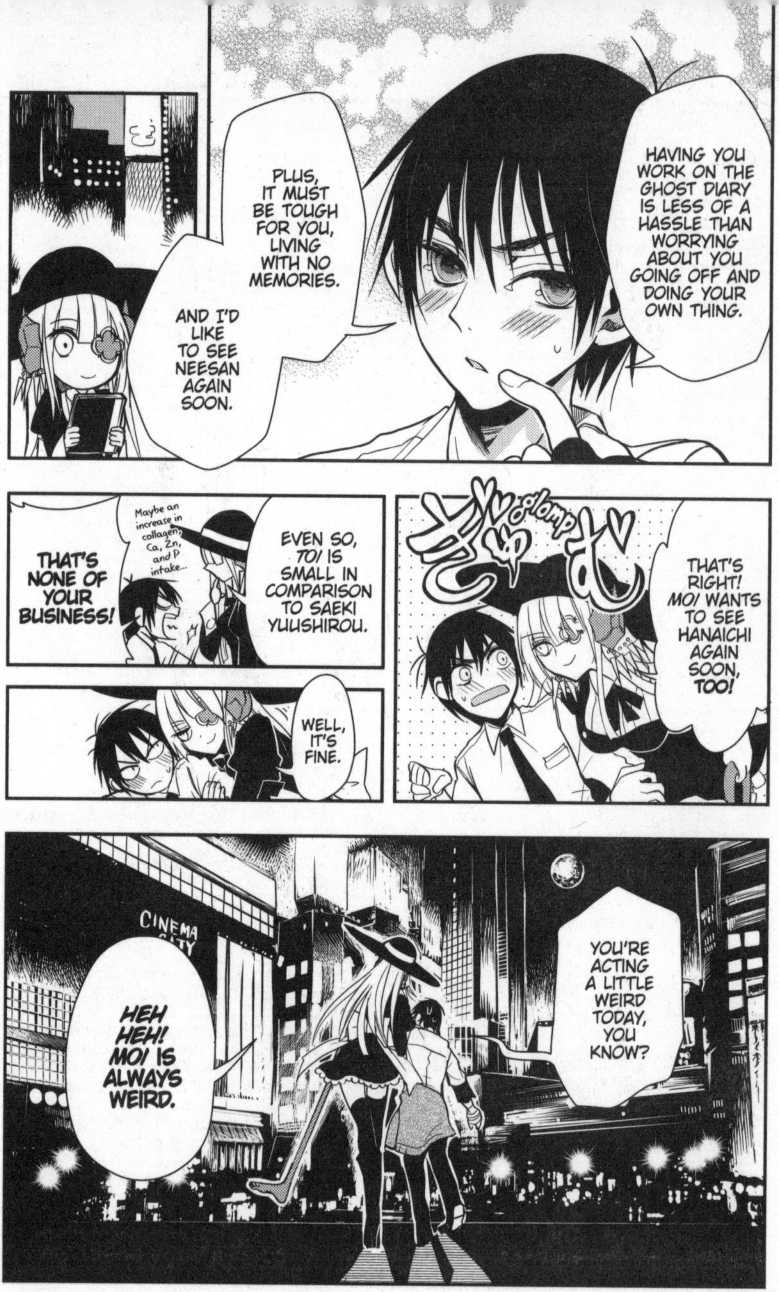
HAVING YOU WORK ON THE GHOST DIARY IS LESS OF A HASSLE THAN WORRYING ABOUT YOU GOING OFF AND DOING YOUR OWN THING.
PLUS, IT MUST BE TOUGH FOR YOU, LIVING WITH NO MEMORIES.
AND I'D LIKE TO SEE NEESAN AGAIN SOON.
glomp
THAT'S RIGHT! *MOI* WANTS TO SEE HANAICHI AGAIN SOON, TOO!
EVEN SO, *TOI* IS SMALL IN COMPARISON TO SAEKI YUUSHIROU.
Maybe an increase in collagen, Ca, Zn, and P intake...
THAT'S NONE OF YOUR BUSINESS!
WELL, IT'S FINE.
YOU'RE ACTING A LITTLE WEIRD TODAY, YOU KNOW?
CINEMA
HEH HEH! *MOI* IS ALWAYS WEIRD.

K a i d a n n i k k i

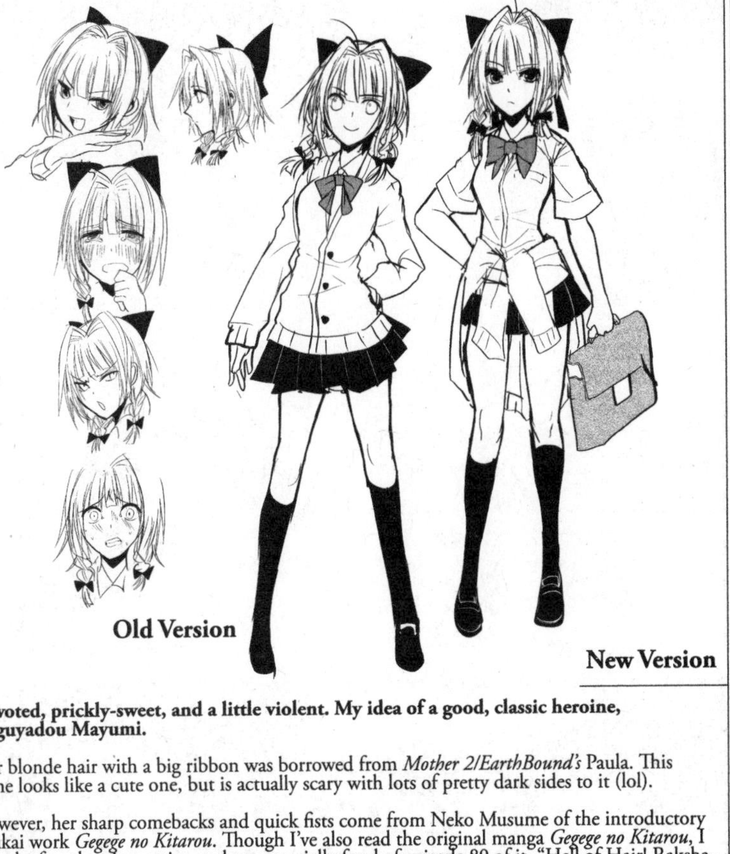
Old Version
New Version

Devoted, prickly-sweet, and a little violent. My idea of a good, classic heroine, Kaguyadou Mayumi.

Her blonde hair with a big ribbon was borrowed from *Mother 2/EarthBound's* Paula. This game looks like a cute one, but is actually scary with lots of pretty dark sides to it (lol).

However, her sharp comebacks and quick fists come from Neko Musume of the introductory youkai work *Gegege no Kitarou*. Though I've also read the original manga *Gegege no Kitarou*, I love the fourth anime series, and am especially fond of episode 89 of it, "Hell of Hair! Raksha-sa." It's the one where Neko Musume, who feels down about having to remain a child forever, becomes a beautiful adult woman through a youkai scheme. With her strange expressions and voluptuous beauty, it's a wonderful episode packed with plenty of Neko Musume drama. At the very end, Kitarou and Neko Musume smile pleasantly at each other. It's worth a watch.

What I'd like to say is that I'd like Kyouichi and Mayumi to have a relationship like Kitarou and Neko Musume's. Looking at her with that in mind, she *is* a little cat-like (lol).

By the way, during character design, the one I had the toughest time with was Mayumi-chan. At the very start, I'd decided that she'd be a girl with braided hair, but just that was a little lacking... I was hooked on a sad ero-game at the time, so I then added her layered bangs. Thanks to that, I was able to create a girl who seems like she could appear in a cute, stylish game, I think.

Today's Theme: Kaguyadou Mayumi

Chapter 6 Cover Line Drawing

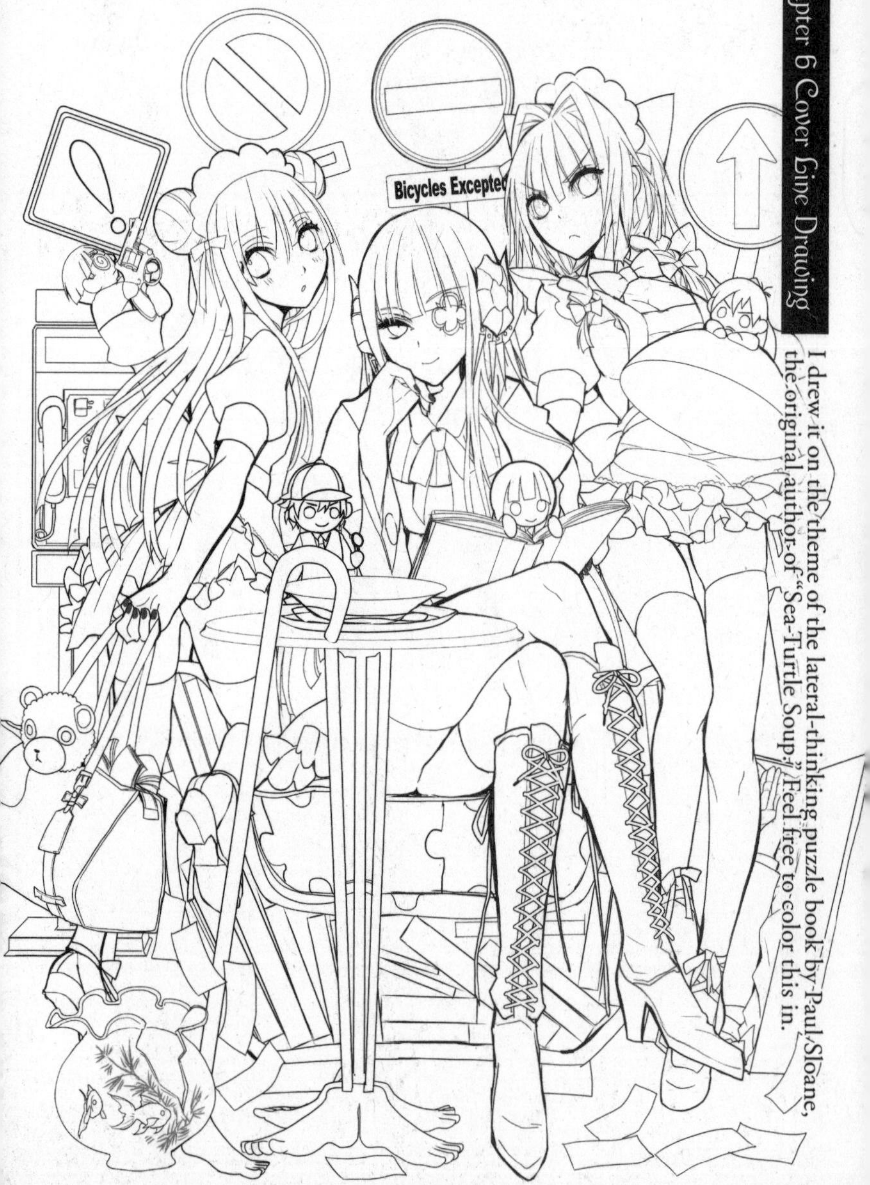

Bicycles Excepte

I drew it on the theme of the lateral-thinking puzzle book by Paul Sloane, the original author of "Sea-Turtle Soup." Feel free to color this in.

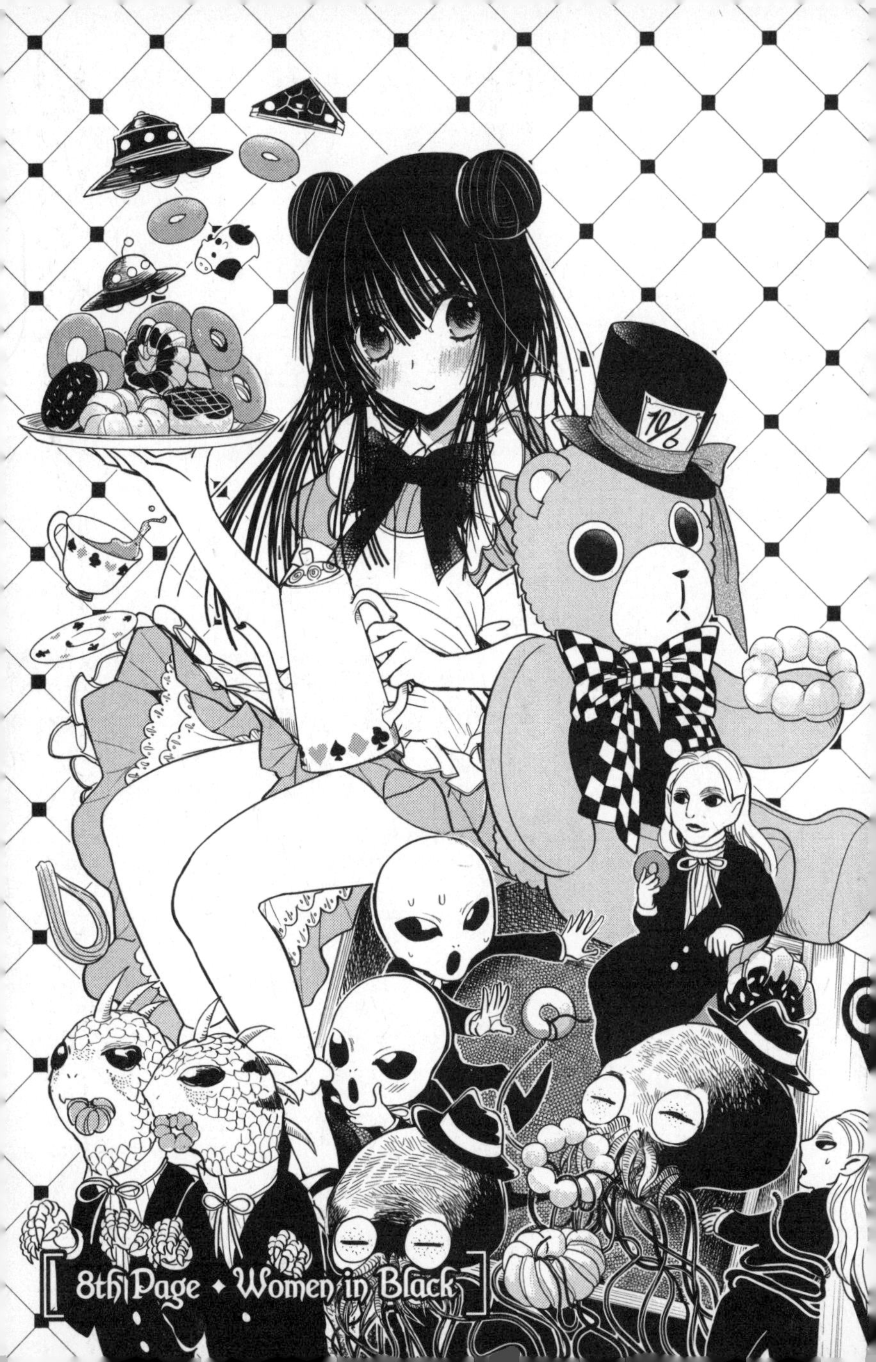
10/6
8th Page ✦ Women in Black

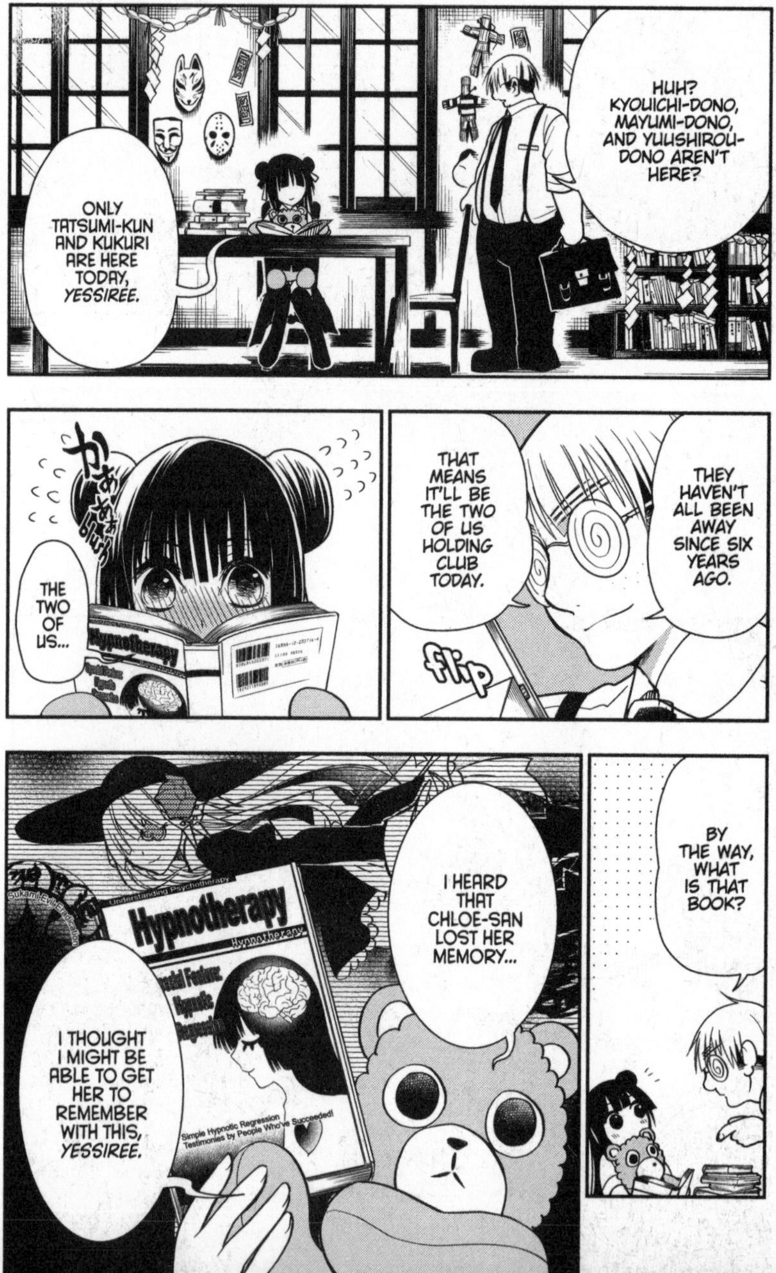
HUH? KYOUICHI-DONO, MAYUMI-DONO, AND YUUSHIROU-DONO AREN'T HERE?
ONLY TATSUMI-KUN AND KUKURI ARE HERE TODAY, YESSIREE.
THEY HAVEN'T ALL BEEN AWAY SINCE SIX YEARS AGO.
THAT MEANS IT'LL BE THE TWO OF US HOLDING CLUB TODAY.
flip
blush
THE TWO OF US...
BY THE WAY, WHAT IS THAT BOOK?
I HEARD THAT CHLOE-SAN LOST HER MEMORY...
Understanding Psychotherapy
Hypnotherapy
Hypnotherapy
Simple Hypnotic Regression
Testimonies by People Who've Succeeded!
I THOUGHT I MIGHT BE ABLE TO GET HER TO REMEMBER WITH THIS, YESSIREE.

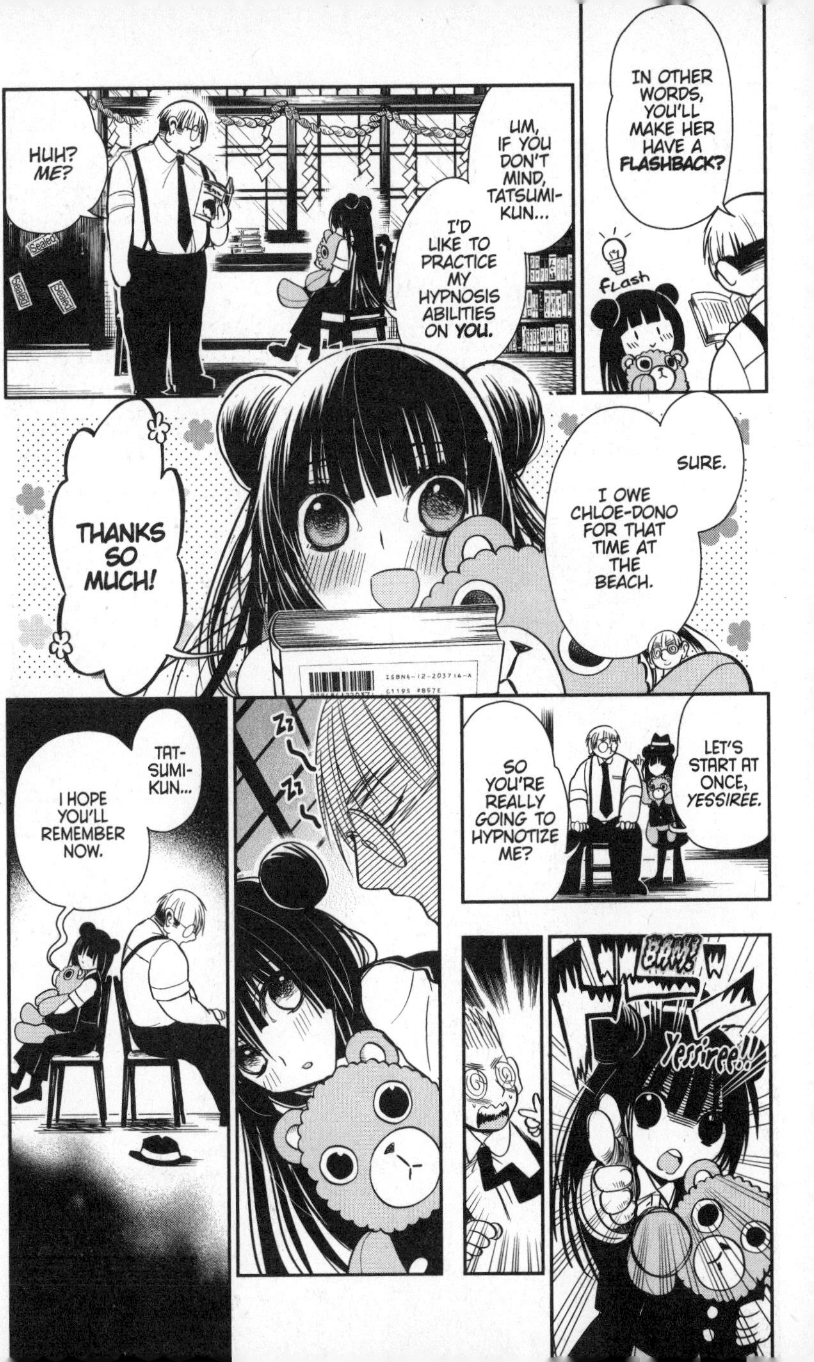
IN OTHER WORDS, YOU'LL MAKE HER HAVE A FLASHBACK?
Flash
UM, IF YOU DON'T MIND, TATSUMI-KUN...
I'D LIKE TO PRACTICE MY HYPNOSIS ABILITIES ON YOU.
HUH? ME?
Sealed
Sealed
Sealed
SURE.
I OWE CHLOE-DONO FOR THAT TIME AT THE BEACH.
THANKS SO MUCH!
ISBN4-12-203714-A
LET'S START AT ONCE, YESSIREE.
SO YOU'RE REALLY GOING TO HYPNOTIZE ME?
BAM!
Yessiree!!
Zz
Zz
TAT-SUMI-KUN...
I HOPE YOU'LL REMEMBER NOW.

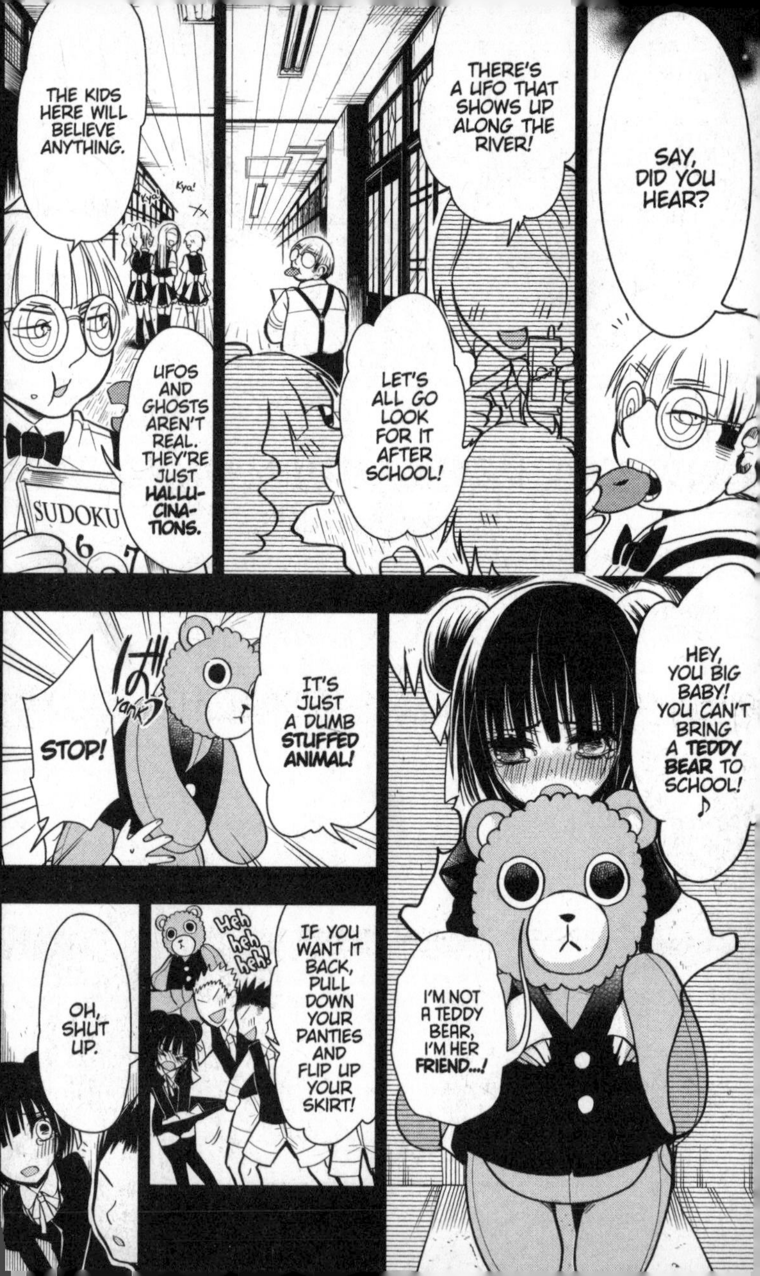
SAY, DID YOU HEAR?
THERE'S A UFO THAT SHOWS UP ALONG THE RIVER!
LET'S ALL GO LOOK FOR IT AFTER SCHOOL!
THE KIDS HERE WILL BELIEVE ANYTHING.
Kya!
Kya!
UFOS AND GHOSTS AREN'T REAL. THEY'RE JUST HALLUCINATIONS.
SUDOKU
HEY, YOU BIG BABY! YOU CAN'T BRING A TEDDY BEAR TO SCHOOL! ♪
I'M NOT A TEDDY BEAR, I'M HER FRIEND...!
IT'S JUST A DUMB STUFFED ANIMAL!
Yank
STOP!
IF YOU WANT IT BACK, PULL DOWN YOUR PANTIES AND FLIP UP YOUR SKIRT!
Heh heh heh!
OH, SHUT UP.

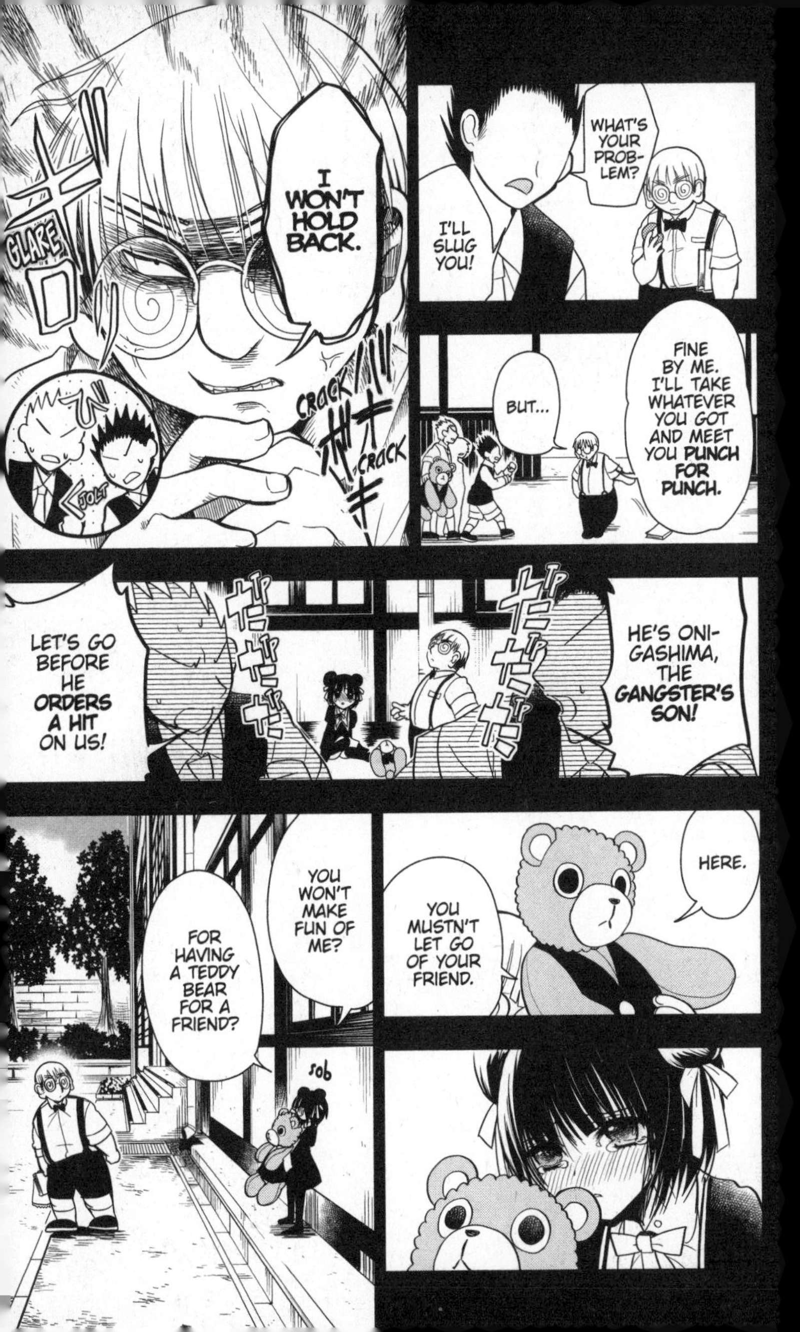
WHAT'S YOUR PROB-LEM?
I'LL SLUG YOU!
FINE BY ME. I'LL TAKE WHATEVER YOU GOT AND MEET YOU PUNCH FOR PUNCH.
BUT...
I WON'T HOLD BACK.
GLARE
CRACK
CRACK
JOLT
HE'S ONI-GASHIMA, THE GANGSTER'S SON!
TP
TP
TP
TP
TP
LET'S GO BEFORE HE ORDERS A HIT ON US!
HERE.
YOU MUSTN'T LET GO OF YOUR FRIEND.
YOU WON'T MAKE FUN OF ME?
FOR HAVING A TEDDY BEAR FOR A FRIEND?
sob

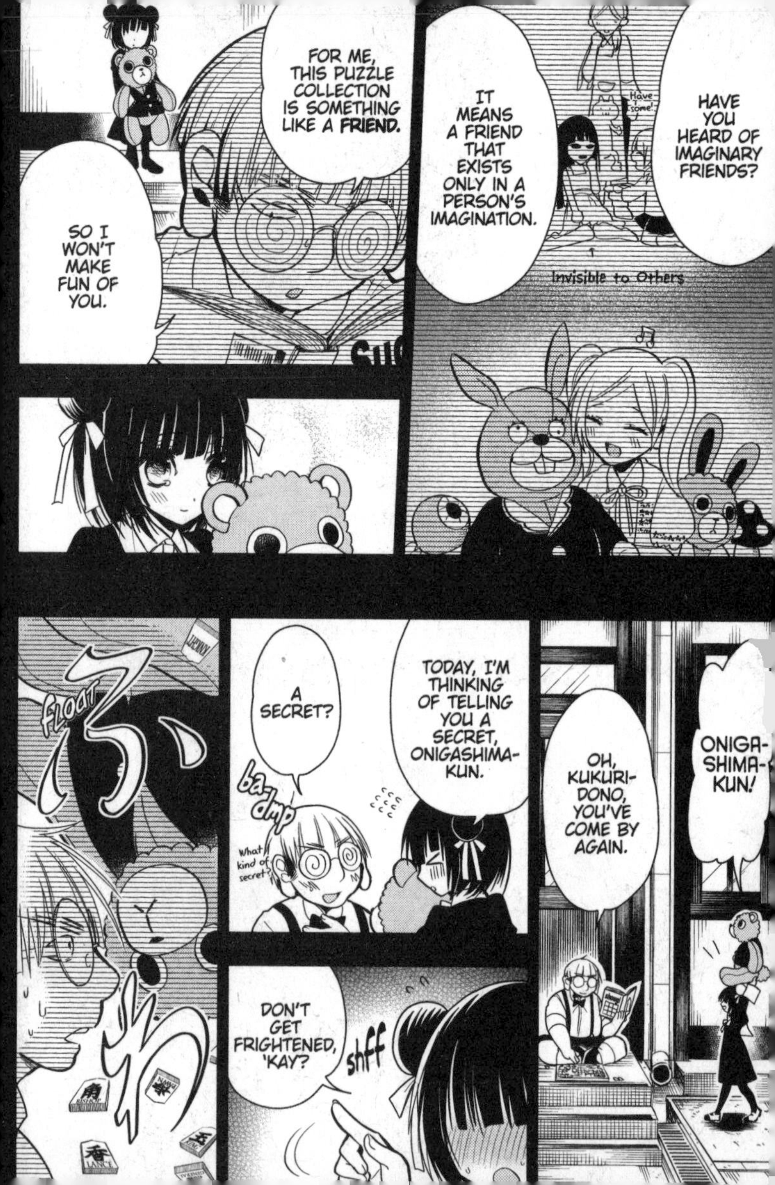
HAVE YOU HEARD OF IMAGINARY FRIENDS?
Have some!
IT MEANS A FRIEND THAT EXISTS ONLY IN A PERSON'S IMAGINATION.
Invisible to Others
FOR ME, THIS PUZZLE COLLECTION IS SOMETHING LIKE A **FRIEND.**
SO I WON'T MAKE FUN OF YOU.
ONIGA-SHIMA-KUN!
OH, KUKURI-DONO, YOU'VE COME BY AGAIN.
TODAY, I'M THINKING OF TELLING YOU A SECRET, ONIGASHIMA-KUN.
A SECRET?
ba-dmp
What kind of secret?
DON'T GET FRIGHTENED, 'KAY?
shff
FLOAT
LANCE

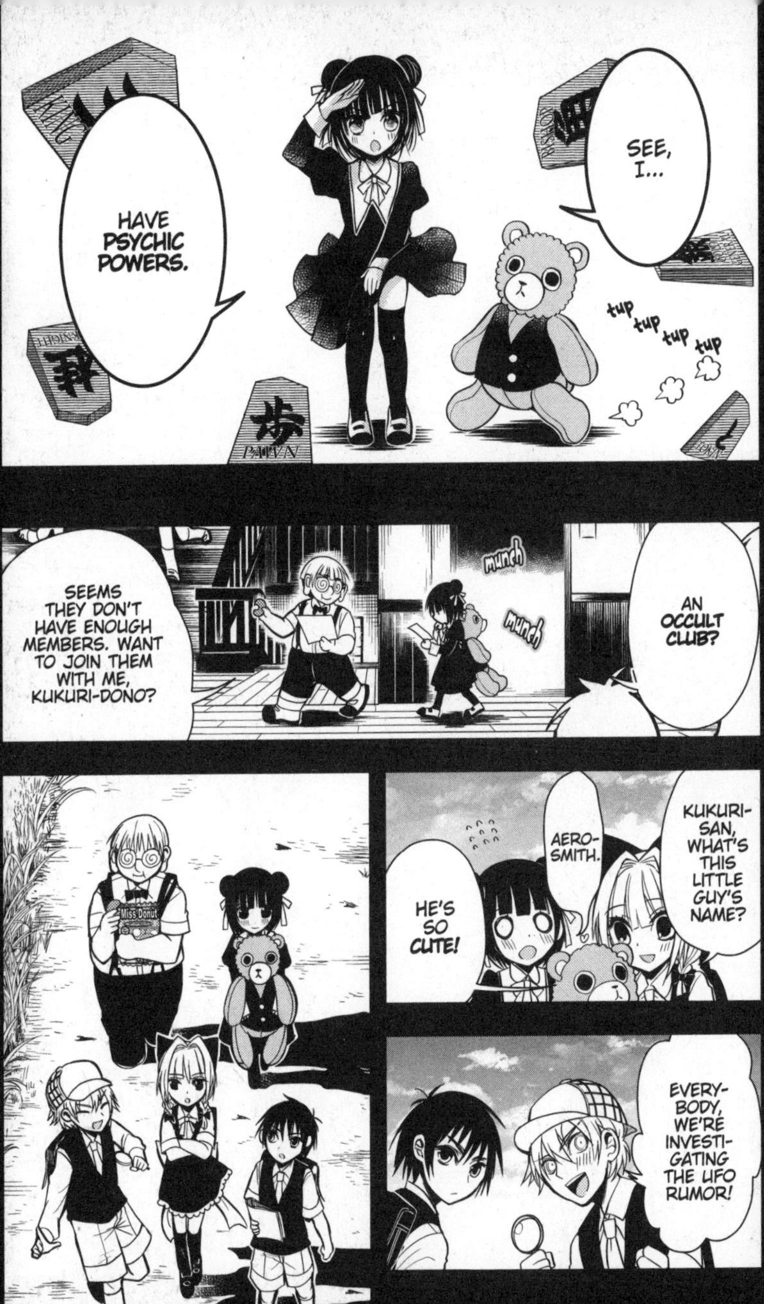
KING
SEE, I...
HAVE PSYCHIC POWERS.
KNIGHT
PAWN
tup tup tup tup
AN OCCULT CLUB?
munch
munch
SEEMS THEY DON'T HAVE ENOUGH MEMBERS. WANT TO JOIN THEM WITH ME, KUKURI-DONO?
KUKURI-SAN, WHAT'S THIS LITTLE GUY'S NAME?
AERO-SMITH.
HE'S SO CUTE!
EVERY-BODY, WE'RE INVESTI-GATING THE UFO RUMOR!
Miss Donut

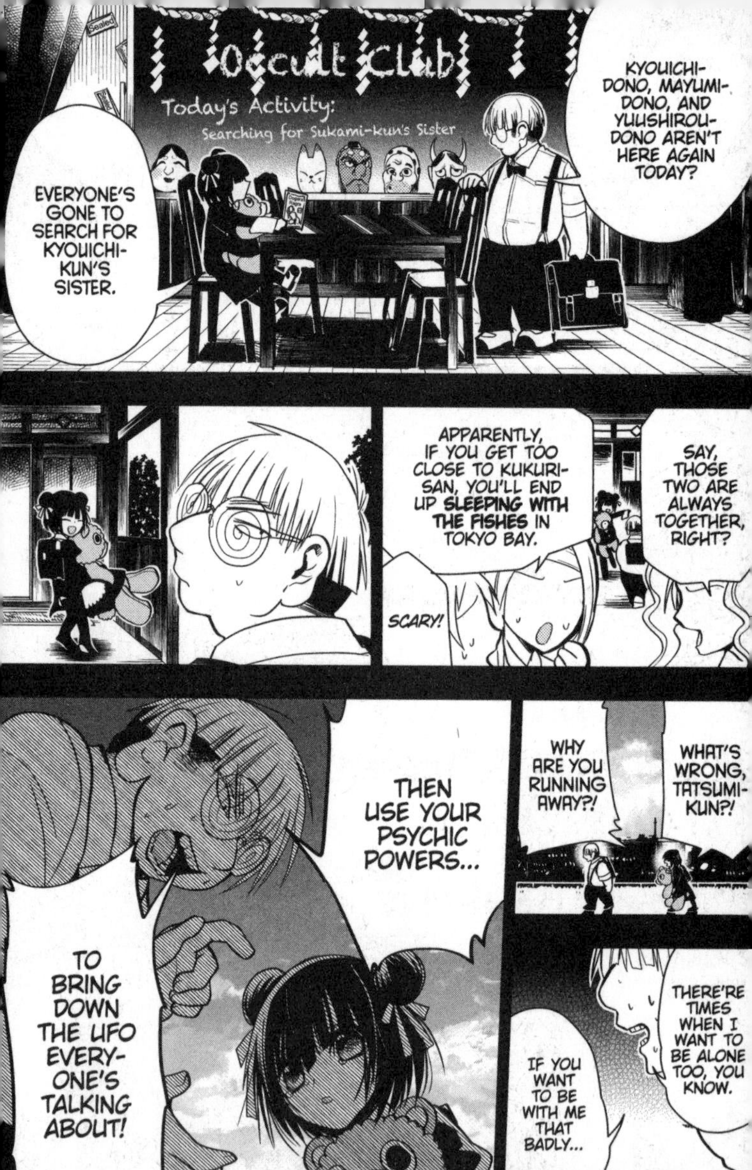
Sealed
Occult Club
Today's Activity:
Searching for Sukami-kun's Sister
KYOUICHI-DONO, MAYUMI-DONO, AND YUUSHIROU-DONO AREN'T HERE AGAIN TODAY?
EVERYONE'S GONE TO SEARCH FOR KYOUICHI-KUN'S SISTER.
SAY, THOSE TWO ARE ALWAYS TOGETHER, RIGHT?
APPARENTLY, IF YOU GET TOO CLOSE TO KUKURI-SAN, YOU'LL END UP **SLEEPING WITH THE FISHES** IN TOKYO BAY.
SCARY!
WHAT'S WRONG, TATSUMI-KUN?!
WHY ARE YOU RUNNING AWAY?!
THERE'RE TIMES WHEN I WANT TO BE ALONE TOO, YOU KNOW.
IF YOU WANT TO BE WITH ME THAT BADLY...
THEN USE YOUR PSYCHIC POWERS...
TO BRING DOWN THE UFO EVERYONE'S TALKING ABOUT!

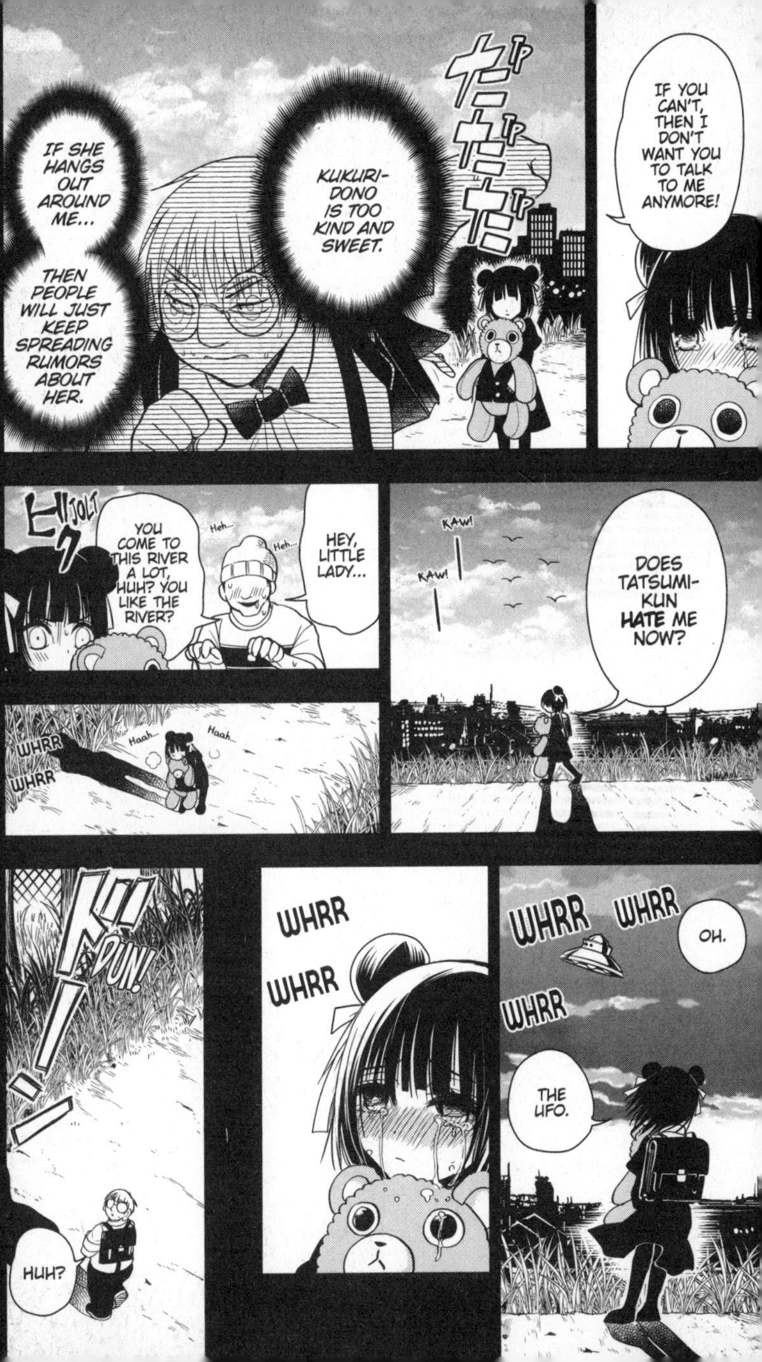
IF YOU CAN'T, THEN I DON'T WANT YOU TO TALK TO ME ANYMORE!
TP TP TP
KUKURI-DONO IS TOO KIND AND SWEET.
IF SHE HANGS OUT AROUND ME...
THEN PEOPLE WILL JUST KEEP SPREADING RUMORS ABOUT HER.
KAW!
KAW!
DOES TATSUMI-KUN HATE ME NOW?
HEY, LITTLE LADY...
Heh...
Heh...
YOU COME TO THIS RIVER A LOT, HUH? YOU LIKE THE RIVER?
JOLT
Haah...
Haah...
WHRR
WHRR
WHRR
WHRR
OH.
WHRR
THE UFO.
WHRR
WHRR
DUN!
HUH?

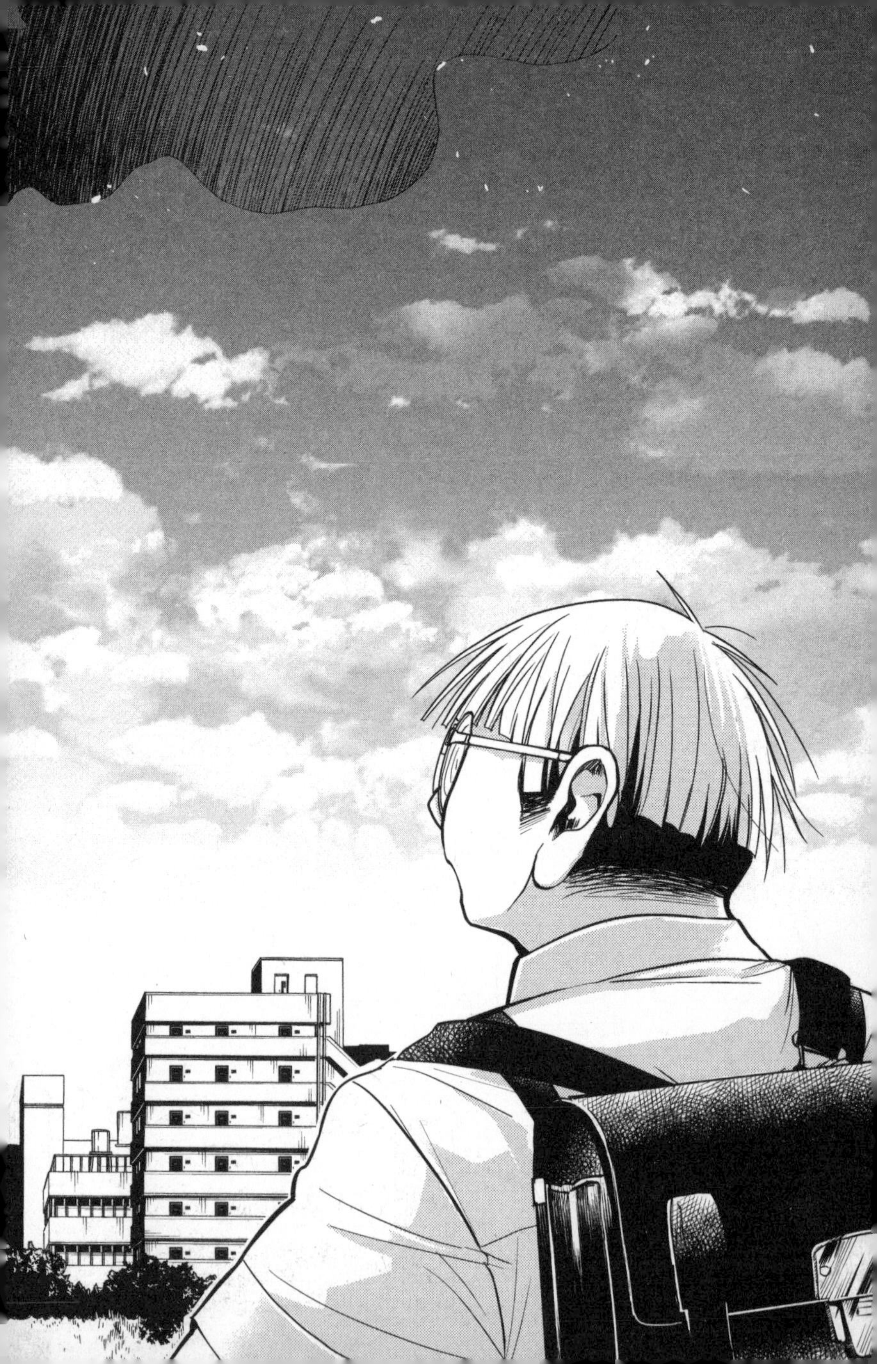

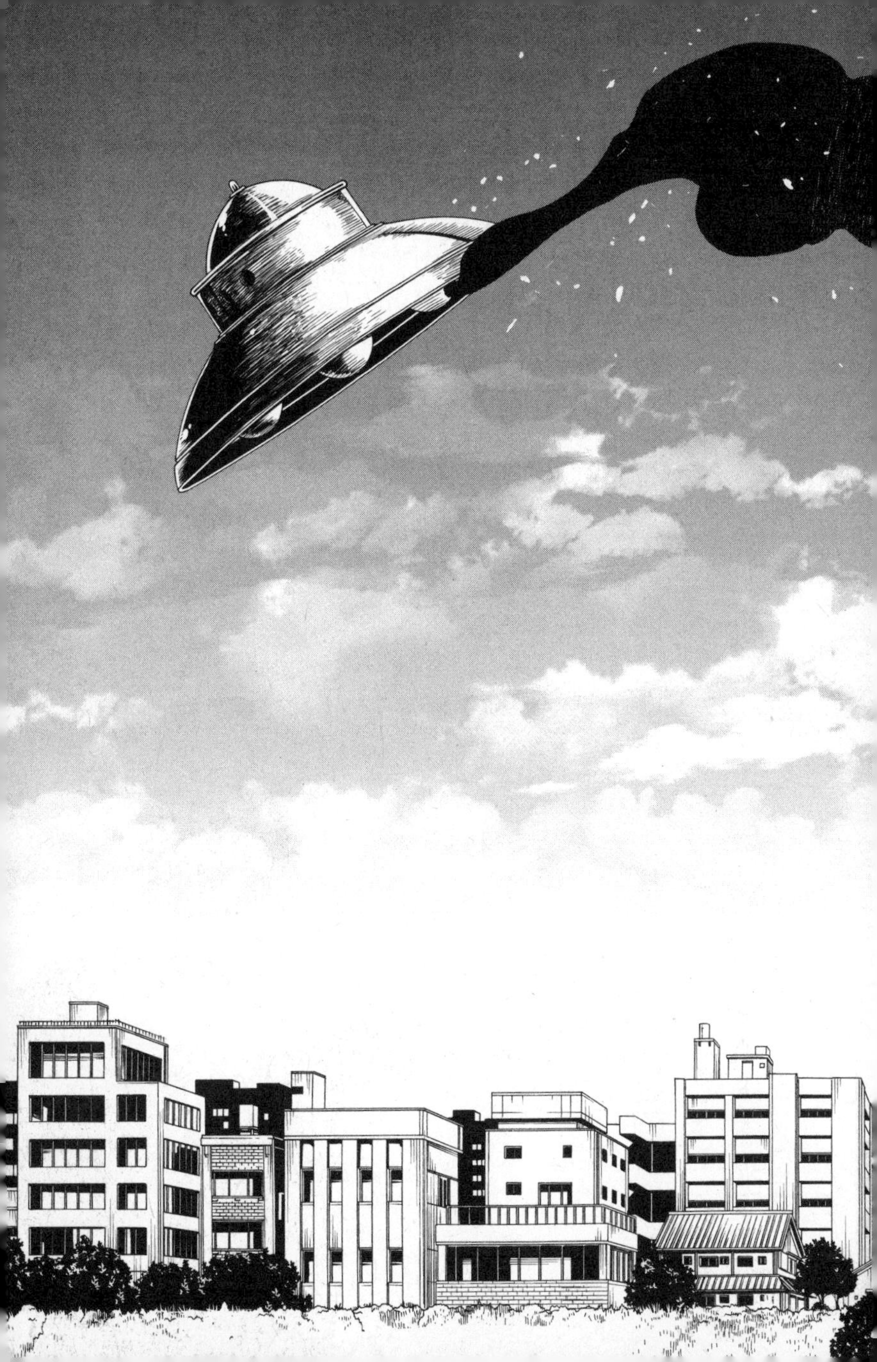

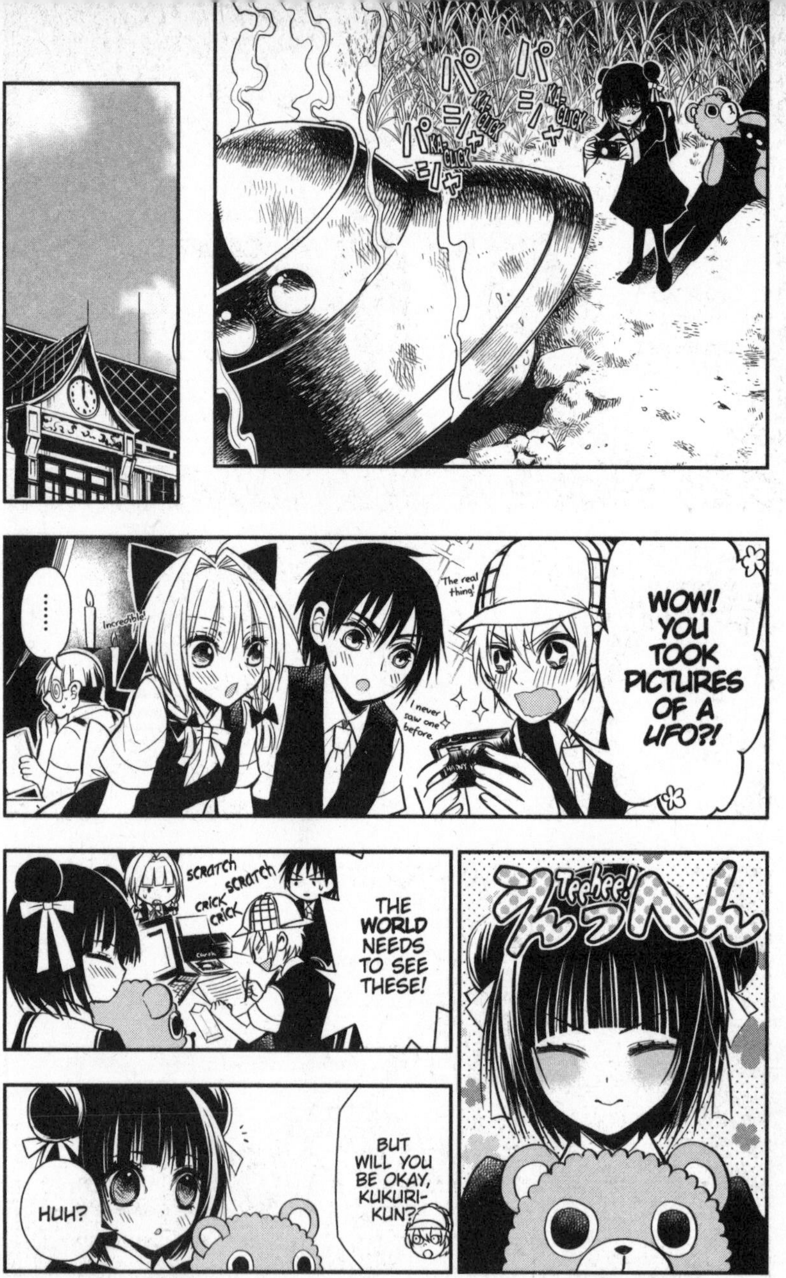

パシャ
KA-CLICK
パシャ
KA-CLICK
パシャ
KA-CLICK
WOW! YOU TOOK PICTURES OF A UFO?!
The real thing!
I never saw one before.
Incredible!
......
えっへん
Teehee!
THE WORLD NEEDS TO SEE THESE!
SCRATCH SCRATCH
CRICK CRICK
BUT WILL YOU BE OKAY, KUKURI-KUN?
HUH?

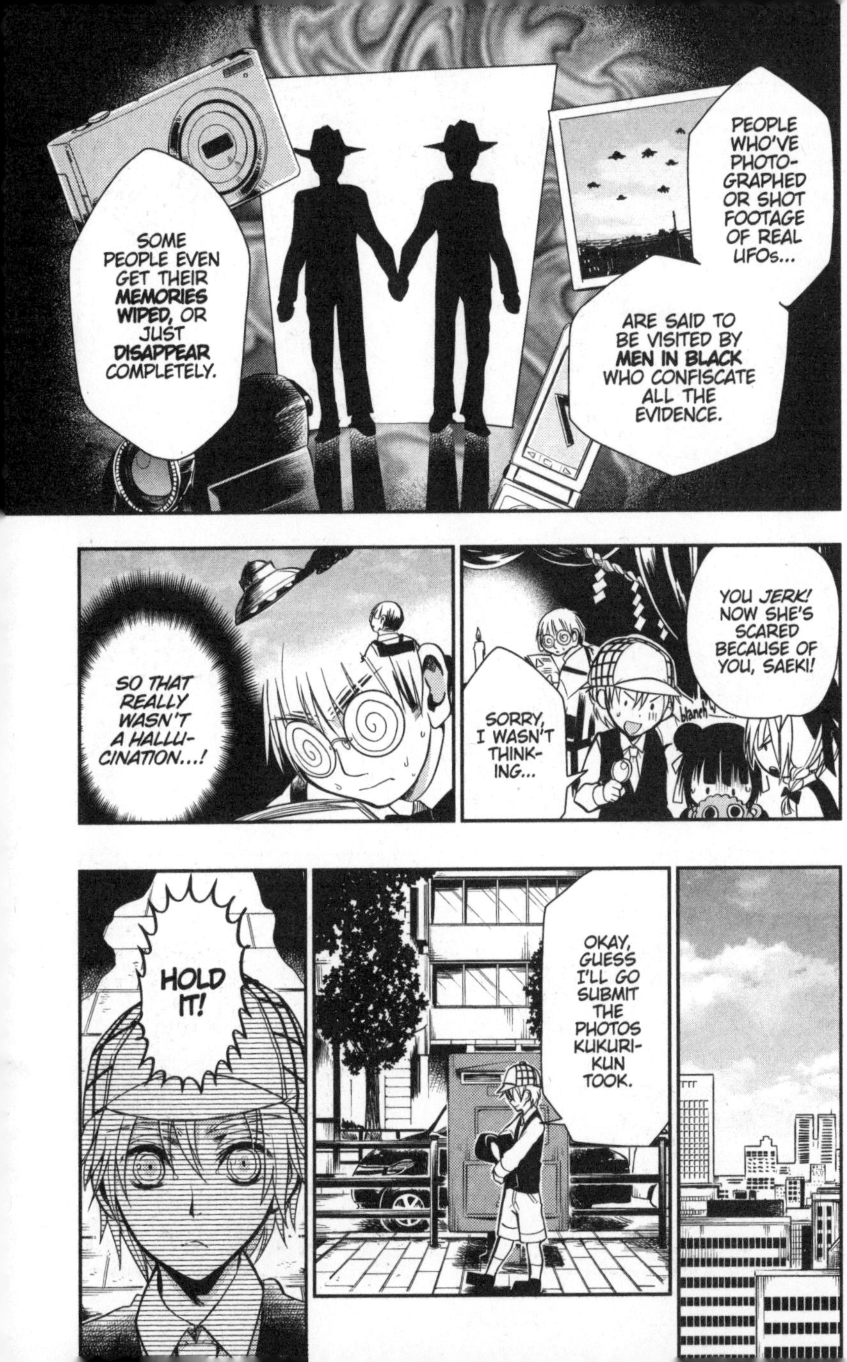
PEOPLE WHO'VE PHOTO-GRAPHED OR SHOT FOOTAGE OF REAL UFOs...
ARE SAID TO BE VISITED BY MEN IN BLACK WHO CONFISCATE ALL THE EVIDENCE.
SOME PEOPLE EVEN GET THEIR MEMORIES WIPED, OR JUST DISAPPEAR COMPLETELY.
YOU JERK! NOW SHE'S SCARED BECAUSE OF YOU, SAEKI!
blanch
SORRY, I WASN'T THINK-ING...
SO THAT REALLY WASN'T A HALLU-CINATION...!
OKAY, GUESS I'LL GO SUBMIT THE PHOTOS KUKURI-KUN TOOK.
HOLD IT!

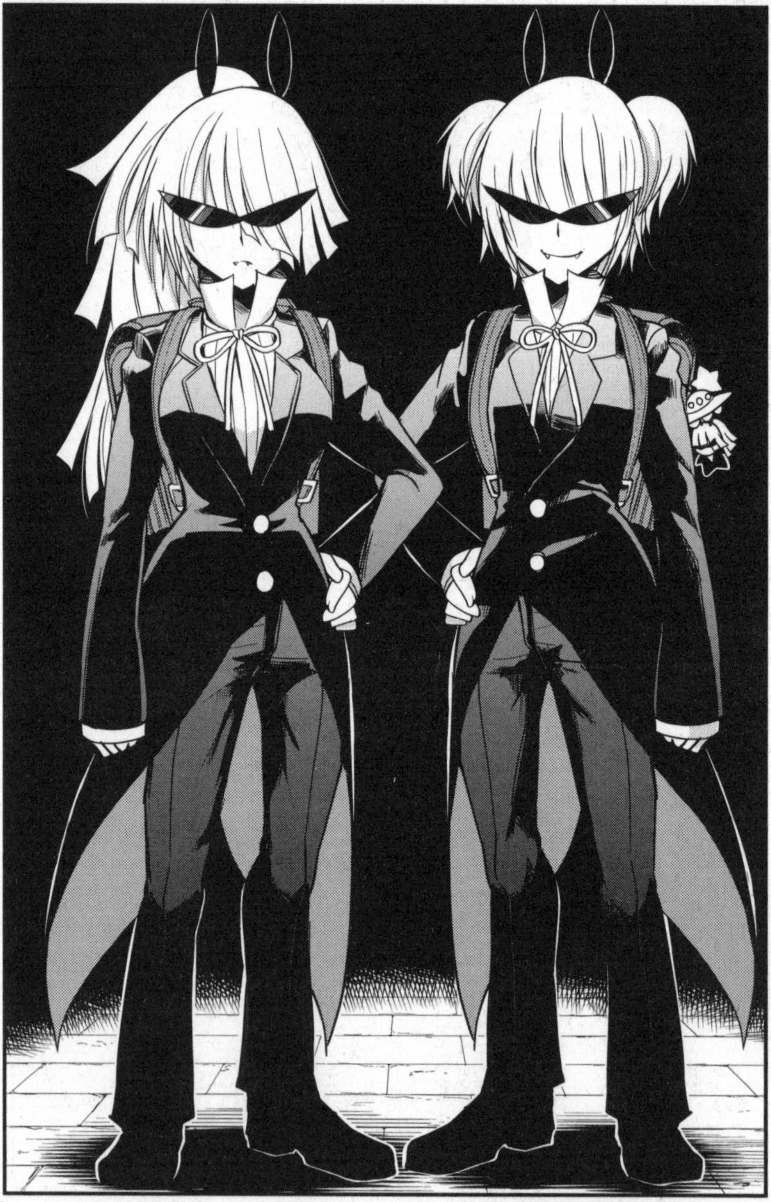

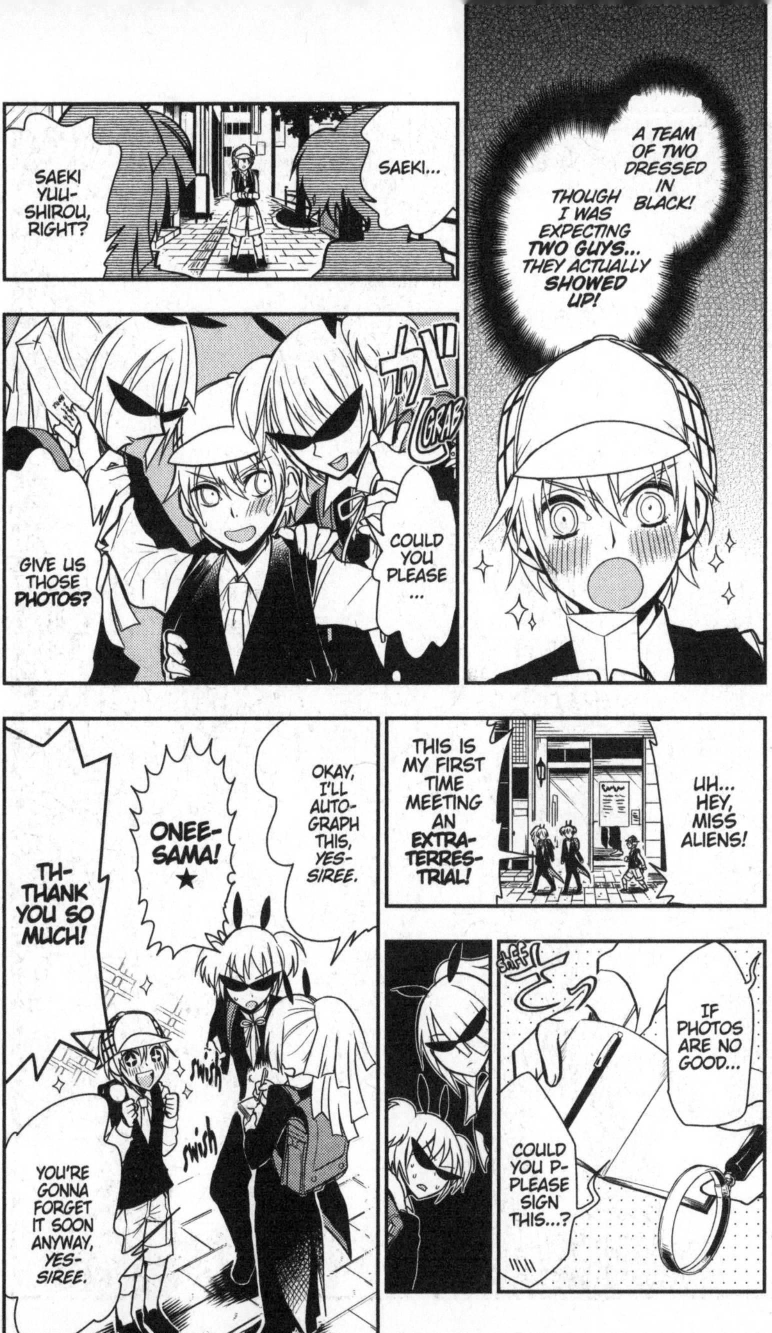
A TEAM OF TWO DRESSED IN BLACK!
THOUGH I WAS EXPECTING TWO GUYS... THEY ACTUALLY SHOWED UP!
SAEKI...
SAEKI YUU-SHIROU, RIGHT?
GRAB
COULD YOU PLEASE ...
GIVE US THOSE PHOTOS?
UH... HEY, MISS ALIENS!
THIS IS MY FIRST TIME MEETING AN EXTRA-TERRES-TRIAL!
IF PHOTOS ARE NO GOOD...
COULD YOU P-PLEASE SIGN THIS...?
OKAY, I'LL AUTO-GRAPH THIS, YES-SIREE.
ONEE-SAMA! ★
TH-THANK YOU SO MUCH!
swish
swish
YOU'RE GONNA FORGET IT SOON ANYWAY, YES-SIREE.

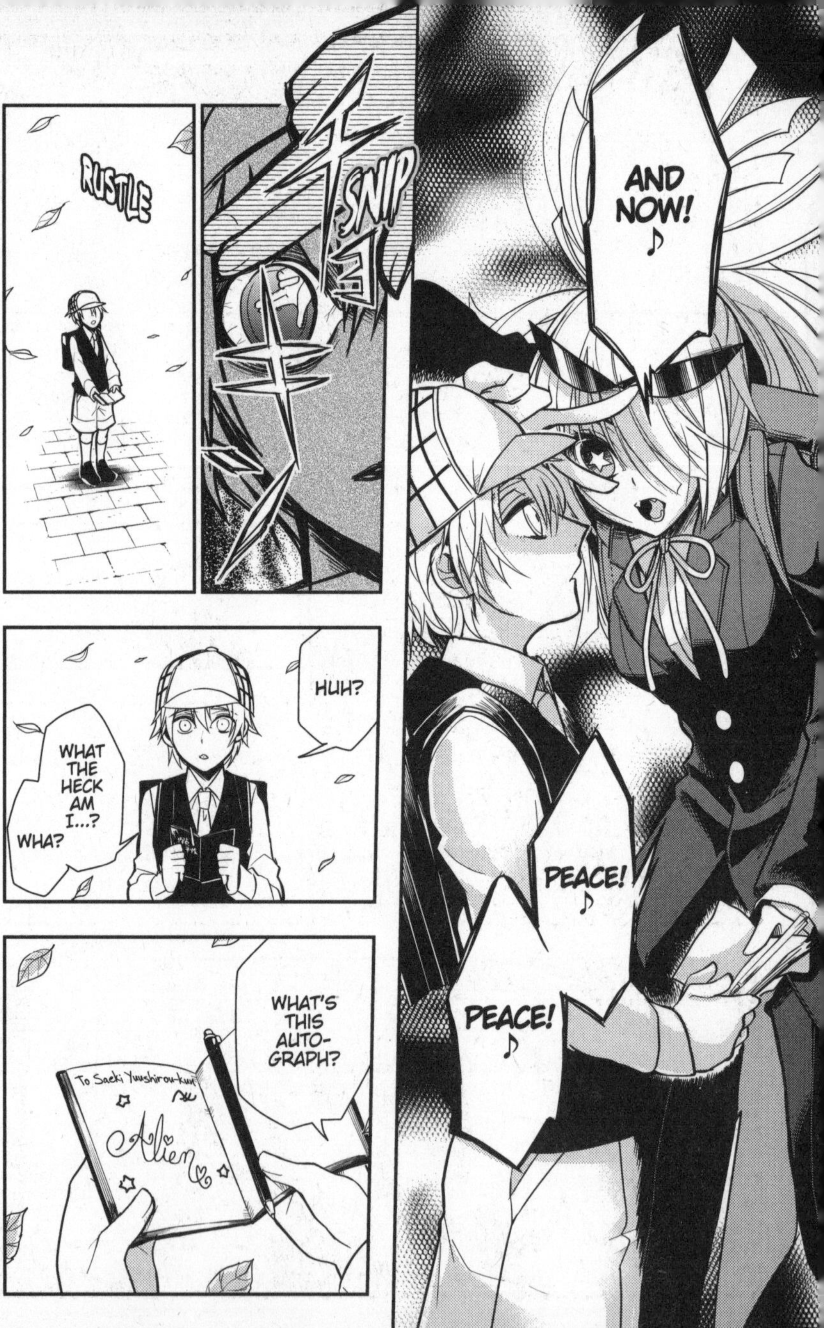
AND NOW! ♪
PEACE! ♪
PEACE! ♪
SNIP
RUSTLE
HUH?
WHAT THE HECK AM I...? WHA?
WHAT'S THIS AUTOGRAPH?
To Saeki Yuushirou-kun
Alien

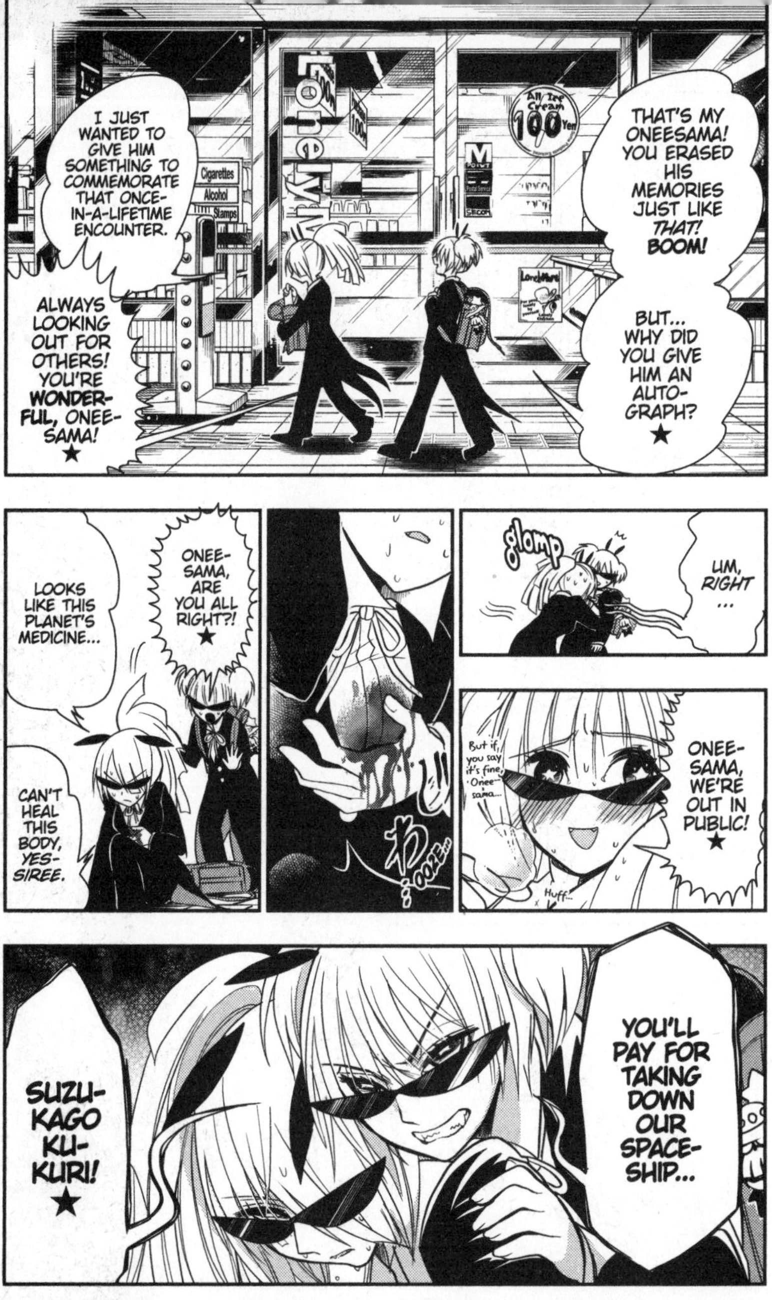
THAT'S MY ONEESAMA! YOU ERASED HIS MEMORIES JUST LIKE *THAT!* **BOOM!**
BUT... WHY DID YOU GIVE HIM AN AUTO-GRAPH? ★
All Ice Cream 100 Yen
Postal Service
SECOM
Cigarettes
Alcohol
Stamps
I JUST WANTED TO GIVE HIM SOMETHING TO COMMEMORATE THAT ONCE-IN-A-LIFETIME ENCOUNTER.
ALWAYS LOOKING OUT FOR OTHERS! YOU'RE **WONDER-FUL**, ONEE-SAMA! ★
UM, *RIGHT* ...
glomp
ONEE-SAMA, WE'RE OUT IN PUBLIC! ★
But if, you say it's fine, Onee-sama...
Huff...
OOZE...
ONEE-SAMA, ARE YOU ALL RIGHT?! ★
LOOKS LIKE THIS PLANET'S MEDICINE...
CAN'T HEAL THIS BODY, YES-SIREE.
YOU'LL PAY FOR TAKING DOWN OUR SPACE-SHIP...
SUZU-KAGO KU-KURI! ★

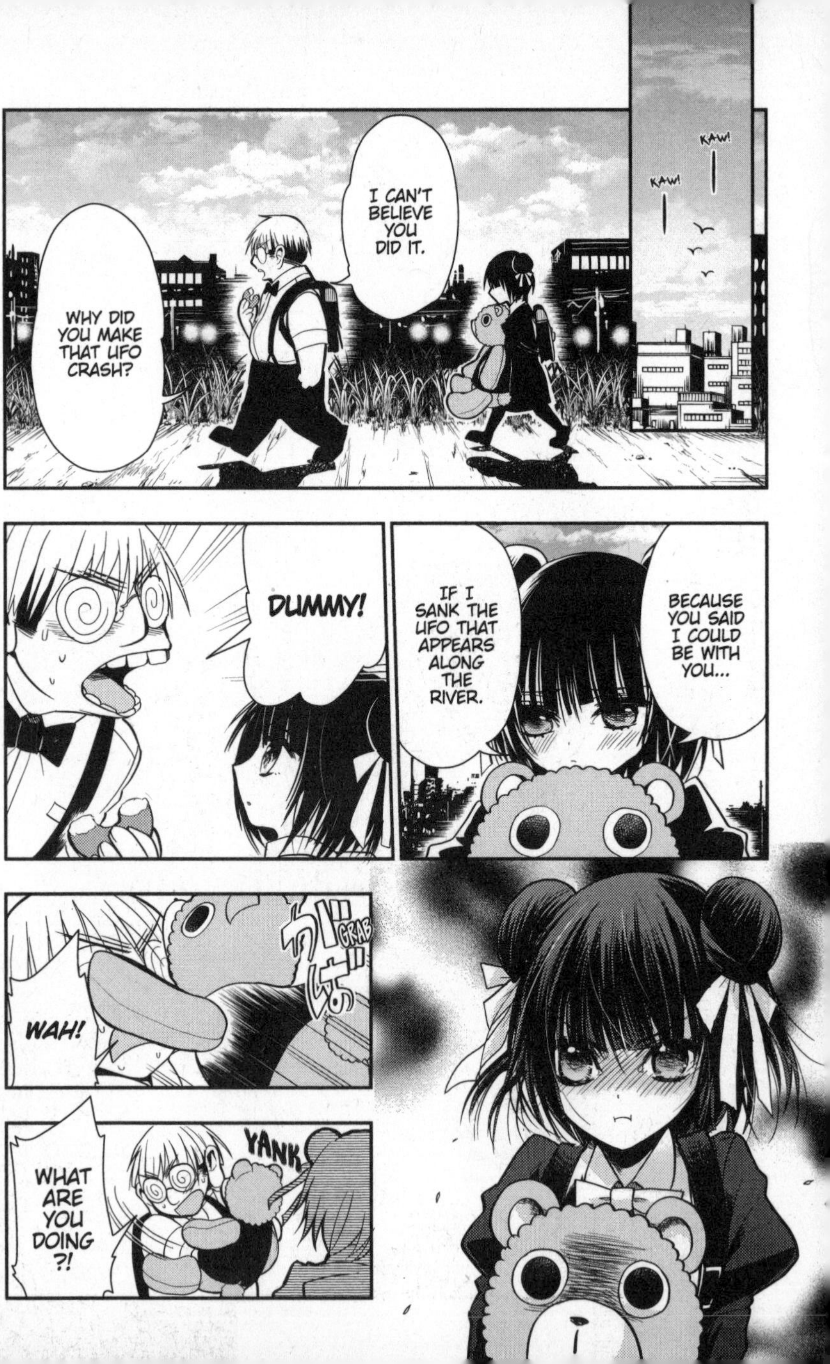
KAW!
KAW!
I CAN'T BELIEVE YOU DID IT.
WHY DID YOU MAKE THAT UFO CRASH?
BECAUSE YOU SAID I COULD BE WITH YOU...
IF I SANK THE UFO THAT APPEARS ALONG THE RIVER.
DUMMY!
GRAB
WAH!
YANK
WHAT ARE YOU DOING ?!

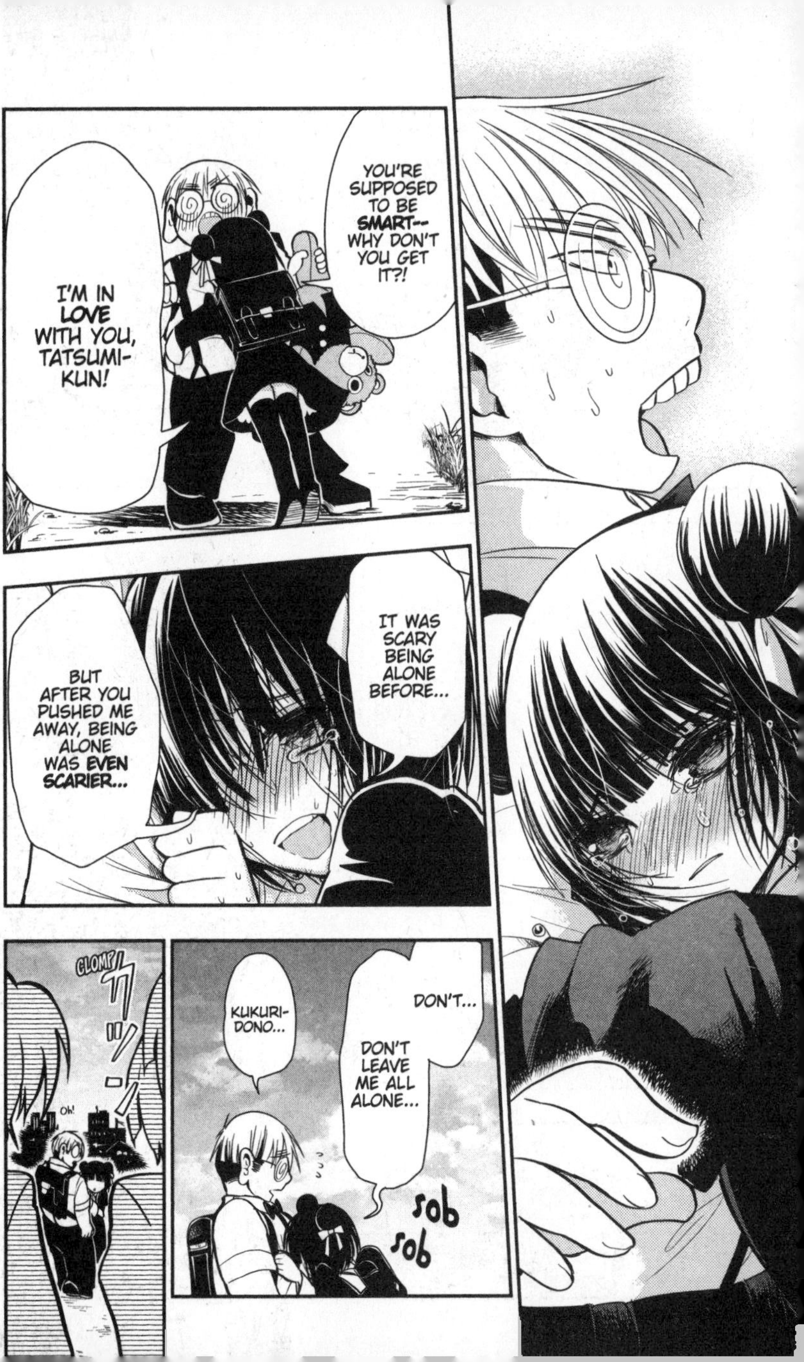
YOU'RE SUPPOSED TO BE SMART-- WHY DON'T YOU GET IT?!
I'M IN LOVE WITH YOU, TATSUMI-KUN!
IT WAS SCARY BEING ALONE BEFORE...
BUT AFTER YOU PUSHED ME AWAY, BEING ALONE WAS EVEN SCARIER...
DON'T...
DON'T LEAVE ME ALL ALONE...
KUKURI-DONO...
sob
sob
GLOMP
Oh!

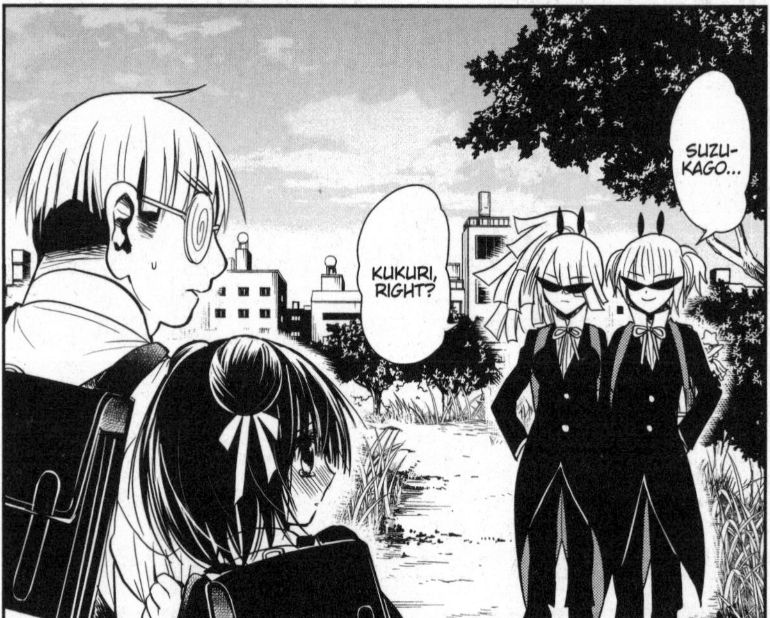
SUZU-KAGO...
KUKURI, RIGHT?

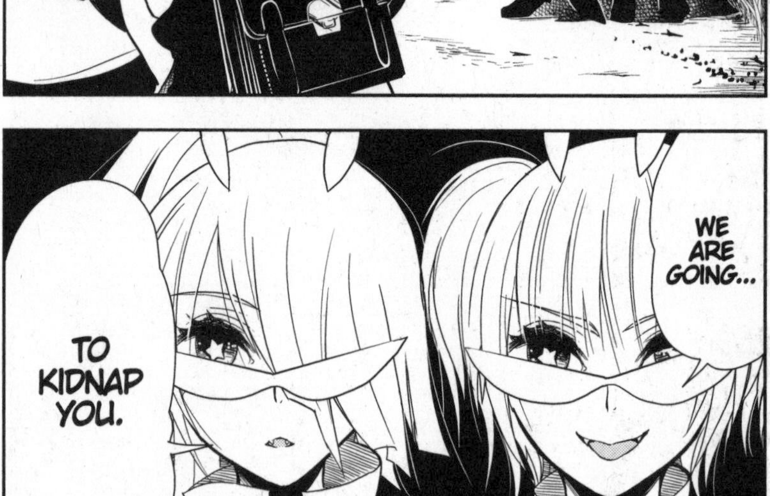
WE ARE GOING...
TO KIDNAP YOU.
Yessiree.

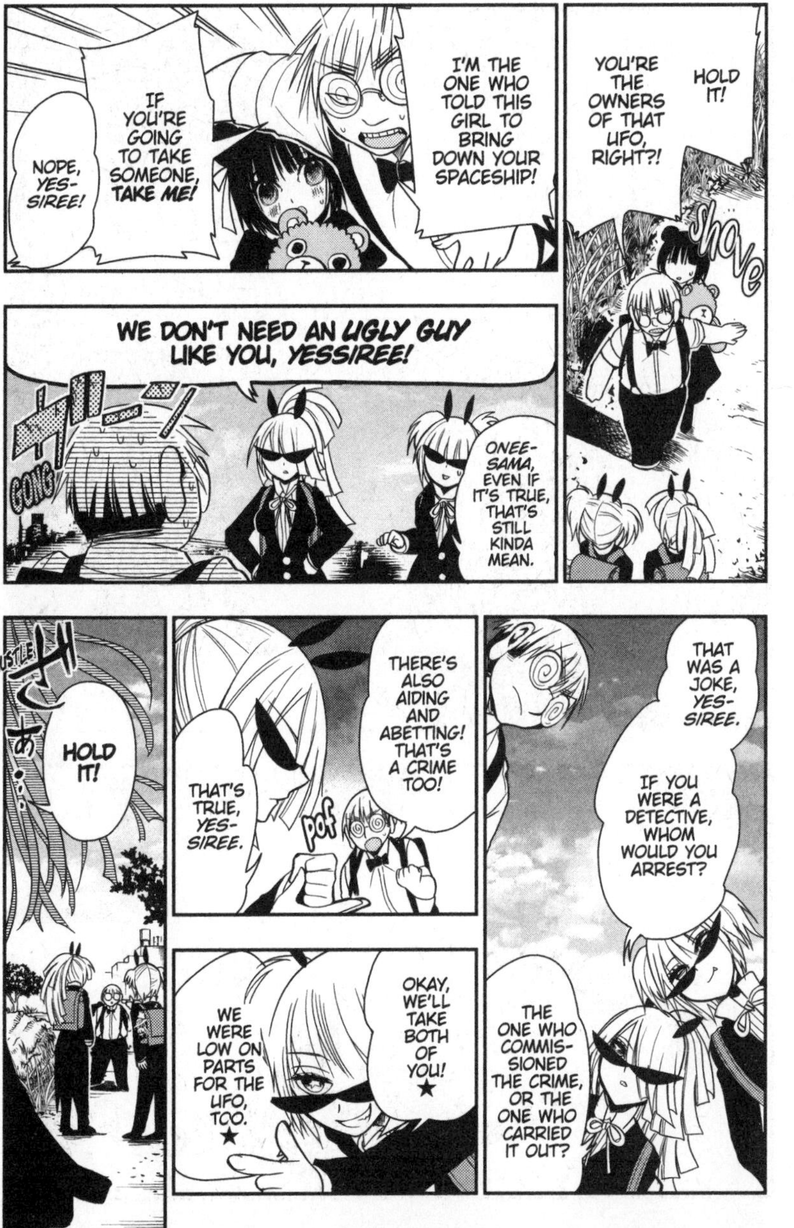
HOLD IT!
YOU'RE THE OWNERS OF THAT UFO, RIGHT?!
SHOVE
I'M THE ONE WHO TOLD THIS GIRL TO BRING DOWN YOUR SPACESHIP!
IF YOU'RE GOING TO TAKE SOMEONE, TAKE *ME!*
NOPE, YES-SIREE!
WE DON'T NEED AN *UGLY GUY* LIKE YOU, *YESSIREE!*
ONEE-SAMA, EVEN IF IT'S TRUE, THAT'S STILL KINDA MEAN.
GONG
THAT WAS A JOKE, YES-SIREE.
IF YOU WERE A DETECTIVE, WHOM WOULD YOU ARREST?
THE ONE WHO COMMISSIONED THE CRIME, OR THE ONE WHO CARRIED IT OUT?
THERE'S ALSO AIDING AND ABETTING! THAT'S A CRIME TOO!
THAT'S TRUE, YES-SIREE.
POF
OKAY, WE'LL TAKE BOTH OF YOU! ★
WE WERE LOW ON PARTS FOR THE UFO, TOO. ★
RUSTLE
HOLD IT!

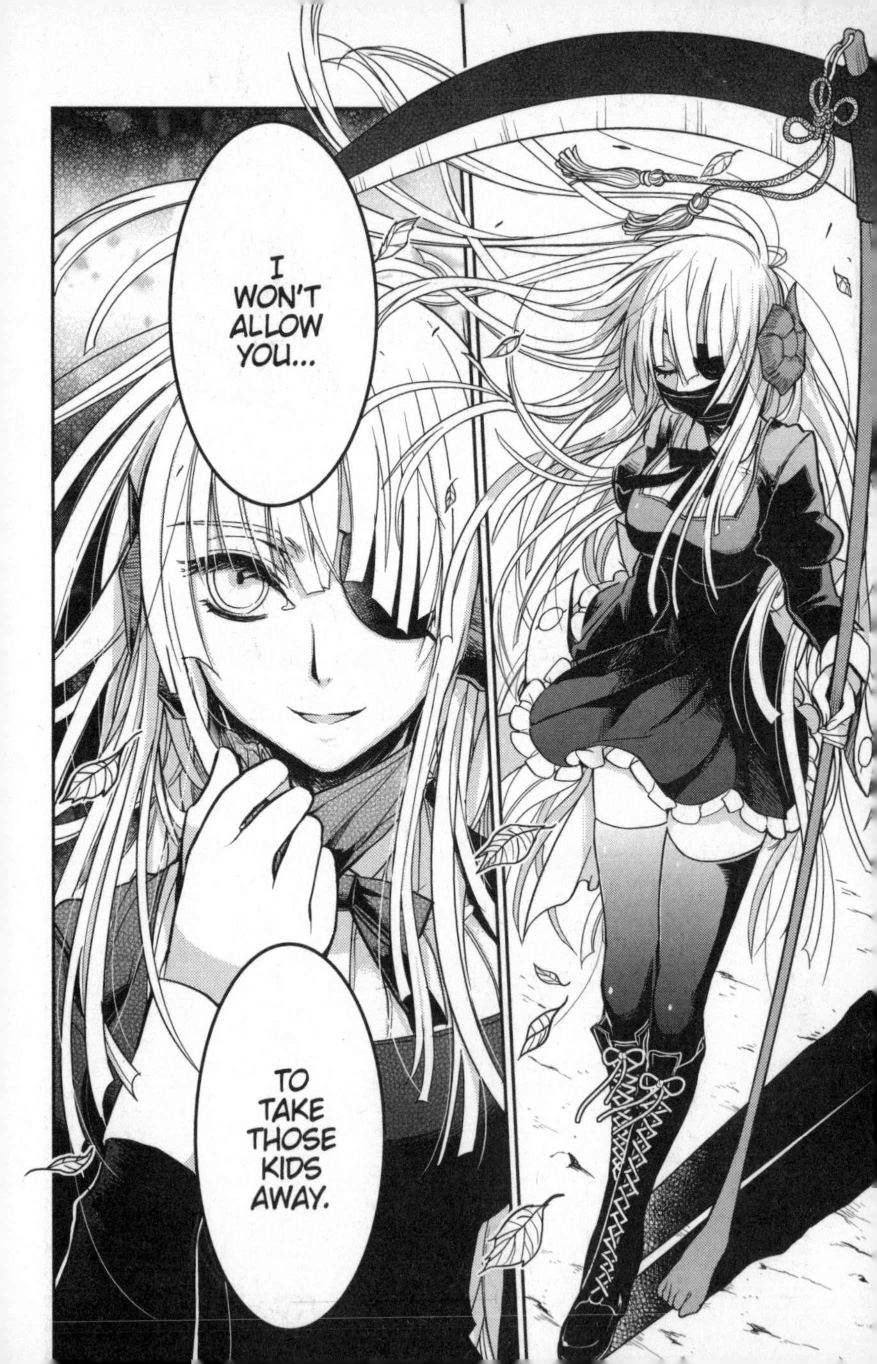
I WON'T ALLOW YOU...
TO TAKE THOSE KIDS AWAY.

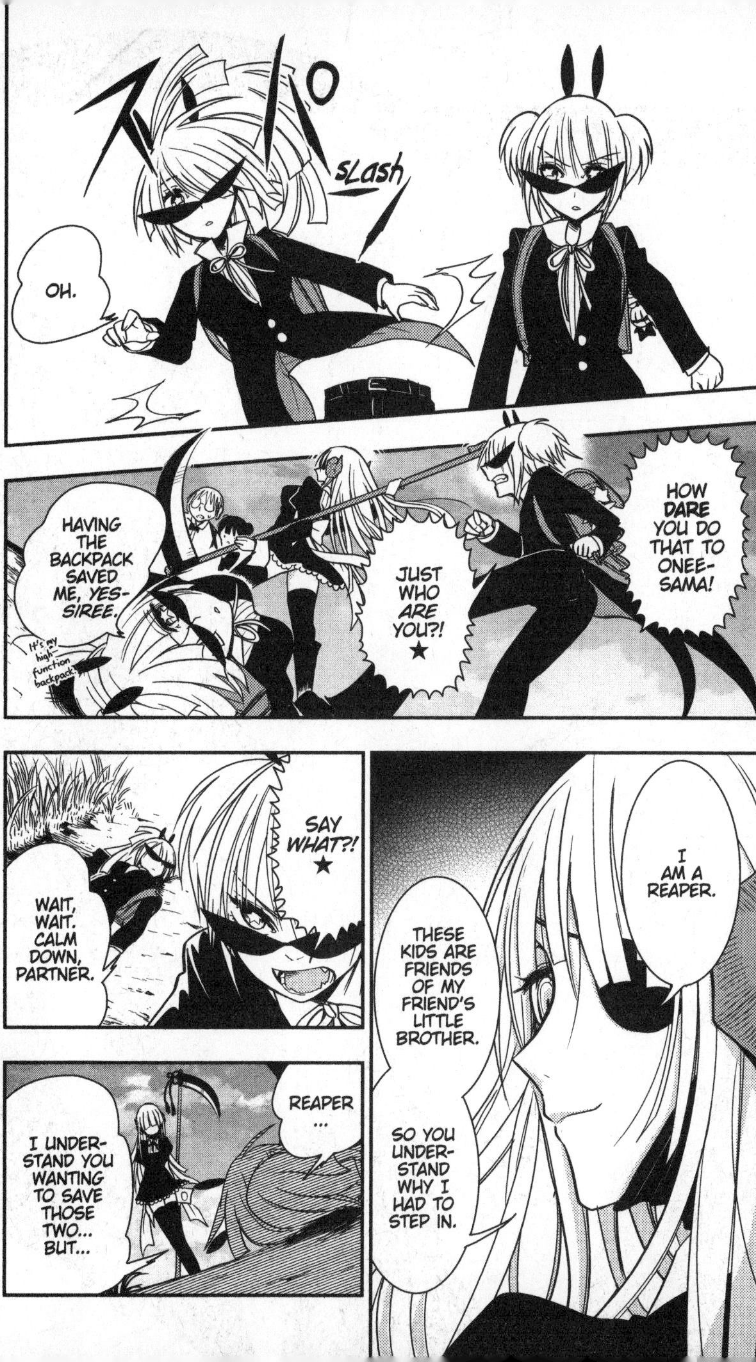
SLASH
OH.
HOW DARE YOU DO THAT TO ONEE-SAMA!
JUST WHO ARE YOU?! ★
HAVING THE BACKPACK SAVED ME, YES-SIREE.
It's my high-function backpack.
I AM A REAPER.
THESE KIDS ARE FRIENDS OF MY FRIEND'S LITTLE BROTHER.
SO YOU UNDERSTAND WHY I HAD TO STEP IN.
SAY WHAT?! ★
WAIT, WAIT. CALM DOWN, PARTNER.
REAPER ...
I UNDER-STAND YOU WANTING TO SAVE THOSE TWO... BUT...

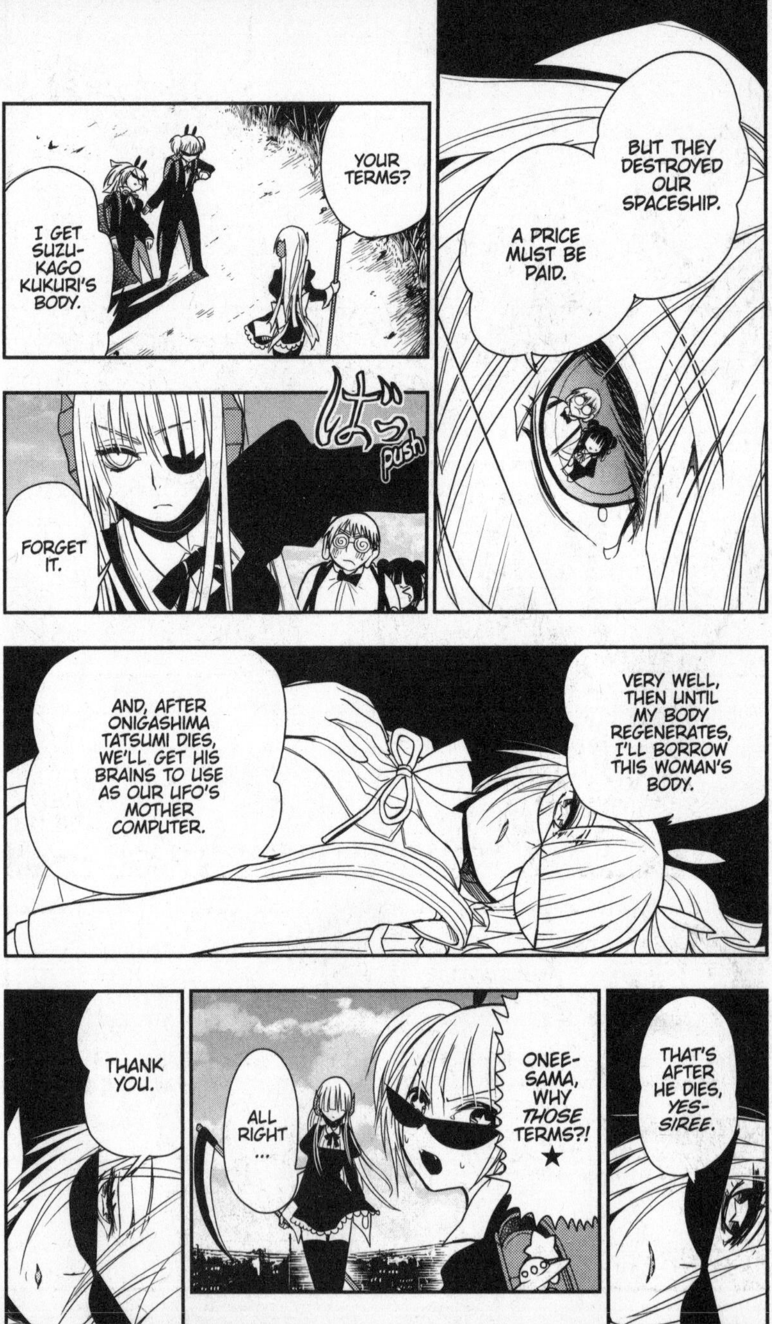
BUT THEY DESTROYED OUR SPACESHIP.
A PRICE MUST BE PAID.
YOUR TERMS?
I GET SUZU-KAGO KUKURI'S BODY.
はっ
push
FORGET IT.
VERY WELL, THEN UNTIL MY BODY REGENERATES, I'LL BORROW THIS WOMAN'S BODY.
AND, AFTER ONIGASHIMA TATSUMI DIES, WE'LL GET HIS BRAINS TO USE AS OUR UFO'S MOTHER COMPUTER.
THAT'S AFTER HE DIES, YES-SIREE.
ONEE-SAMA, WHY THOSE TERMS?! ★
ALL RIGHT ...
THANK YOU.

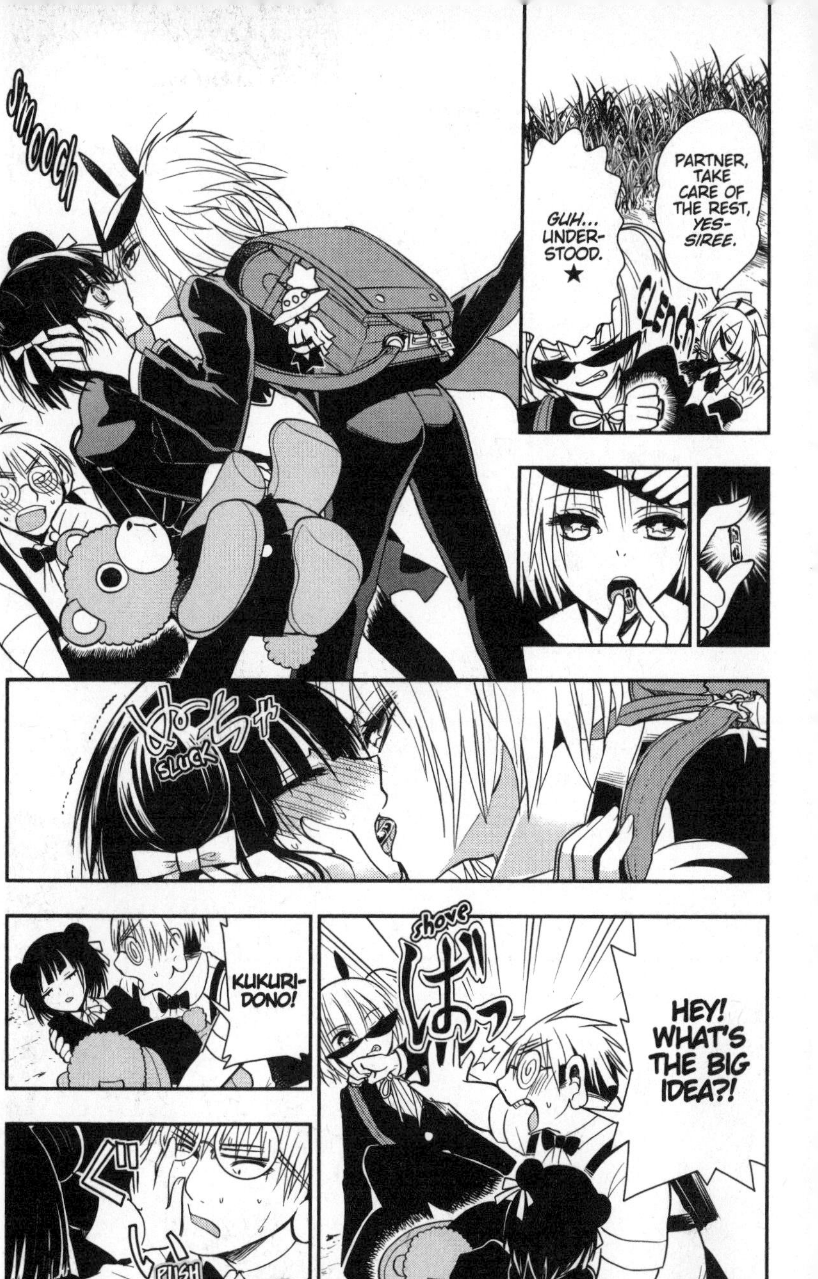
PARTNER, TAKE CARE OF THE REST, YES-SIREE.
GUH... UNDER-STOOD. ★
CLENCH
smooch
ぬちゃ
SLUCK
ばっ
shove
HEY! WHAT'S THE BIG IDEA?!
KUKURI-DONO!
ぐい
PUSH

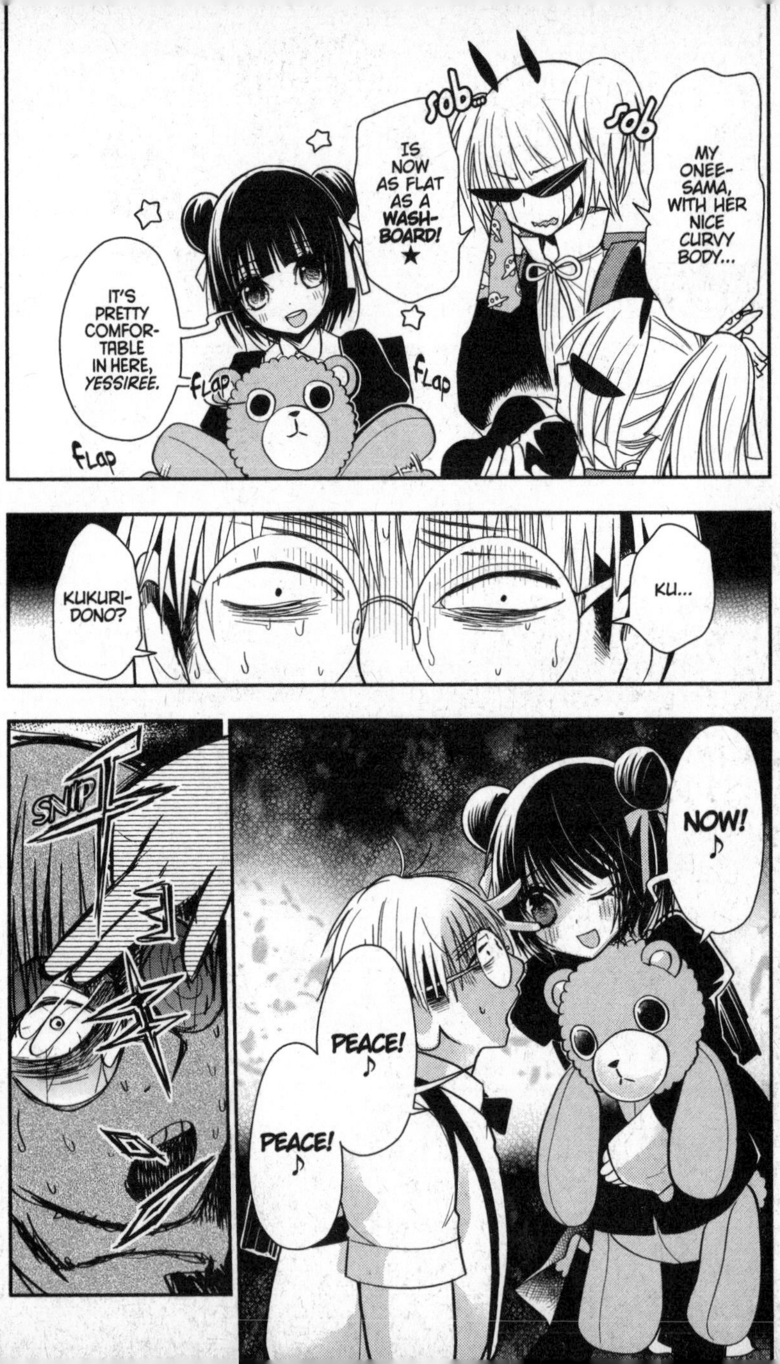
MY ONEE-SAMA, WITH HER NICE CURVY BODY...
sob
sob...
IS NOW AS FLAT AS A WASHBOARD! ★
IT'S PRETTY COMFORTABLE IN HERE, YESSIREE.
FLAP
FLAP
FLAP
KU...
KUKURI-DONO?
NOW! ♪
PEACE! ♪
PEACE! ♪
SNIP

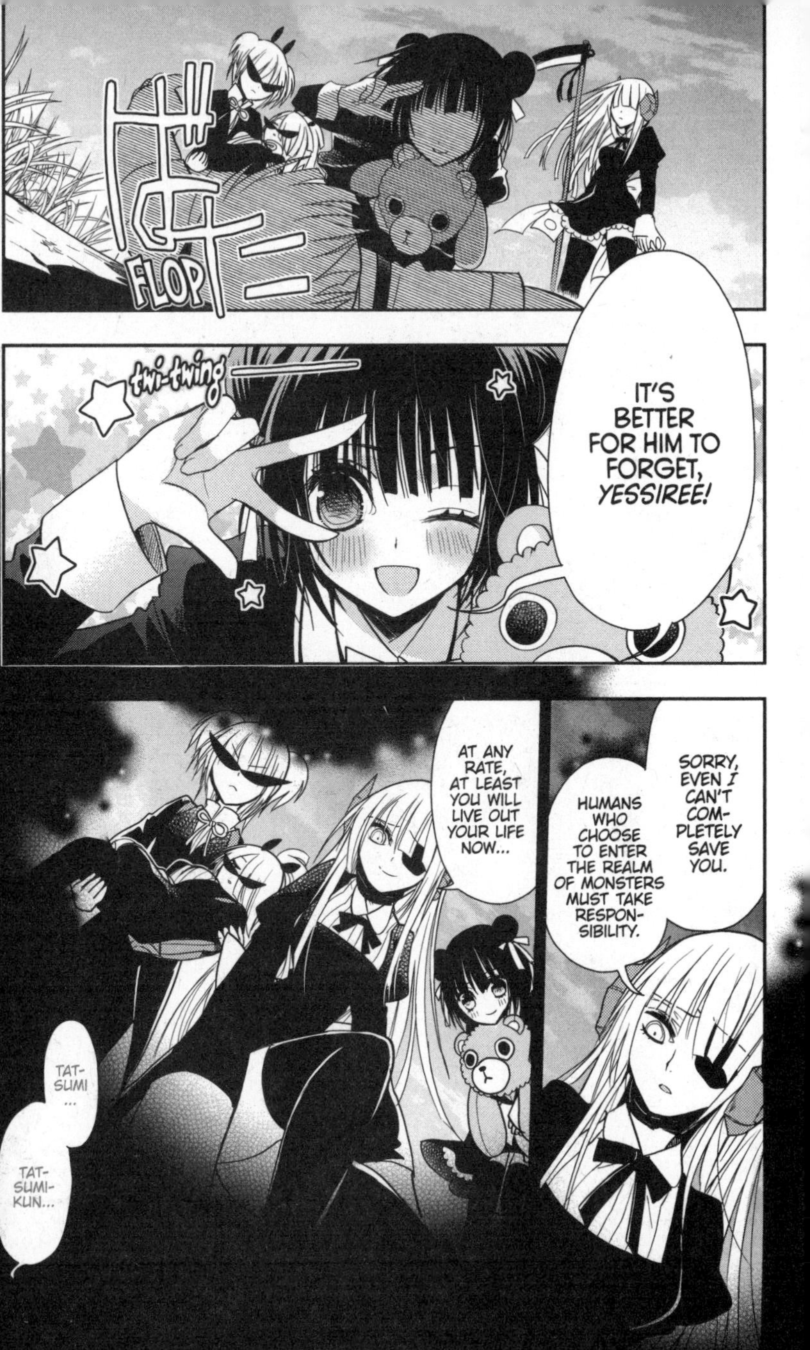

FLOP
twi-twing
IT'S BETTER FOR HIM TO FORGET, *YESSIREE!*
SORRY, EVEN *I* CAN'T COMPLETELY SAVE YOU.
HUMANS WHO CHOOSE TO ENTER THE REALM OF MONSTERS MUST TAKE RESPONSIBILITY.
AT ANY RATE, AT LEAST YOU WILL LIVE OUT YOUR LIFE NOW...
TATSUMI...
TATSUMI-KUN...

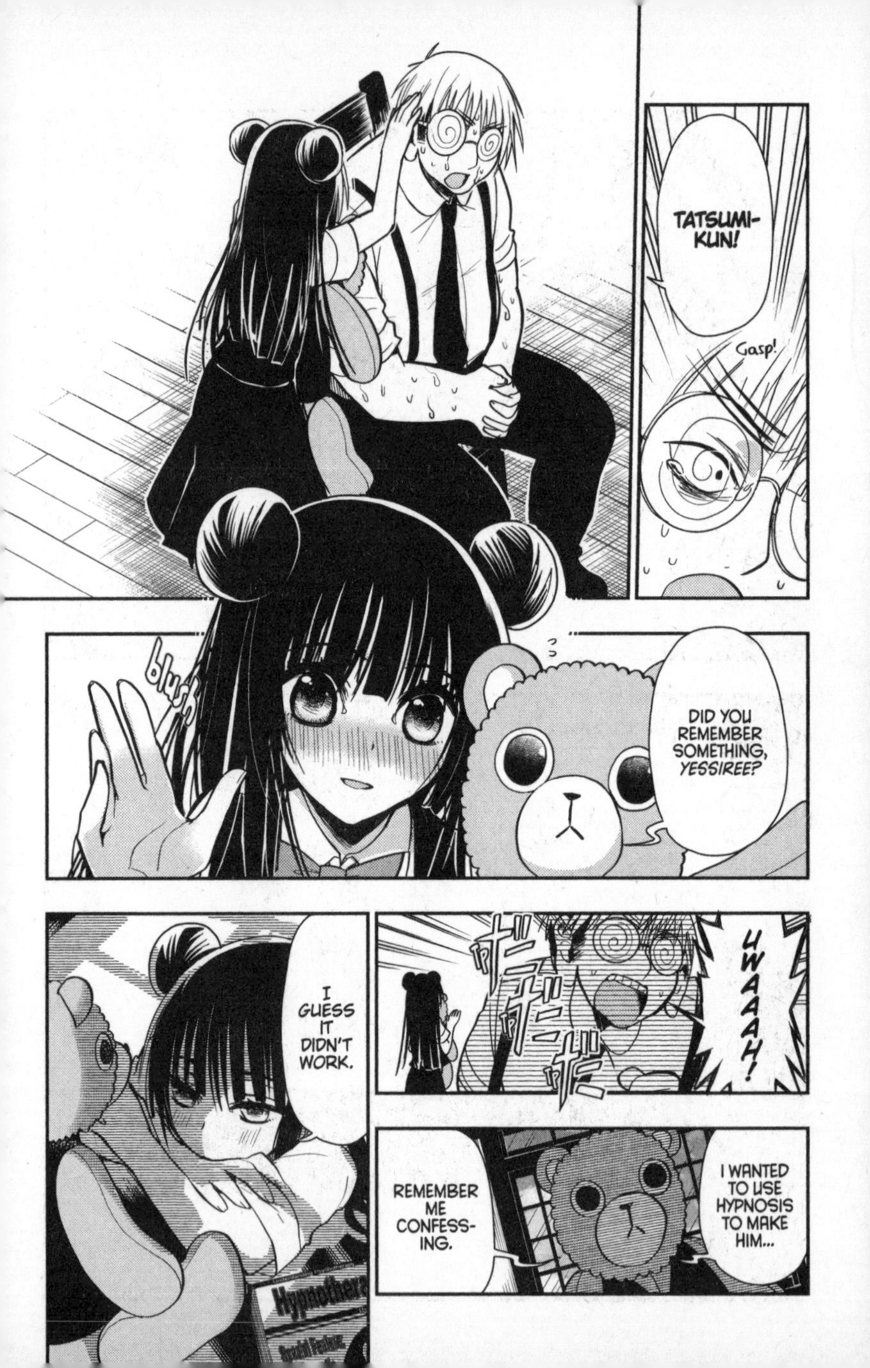
TATSUMI-KUN!
Gasp!
blush
DID YOU REMEMBER SOMETHING, YESSIREE?
UWAAAH!
I WANTED TO USE HYPNOSIS TO MAKE HIM...
REMEMBER ME CONFESSING.
I GUESS IT DIDN'T WORK.

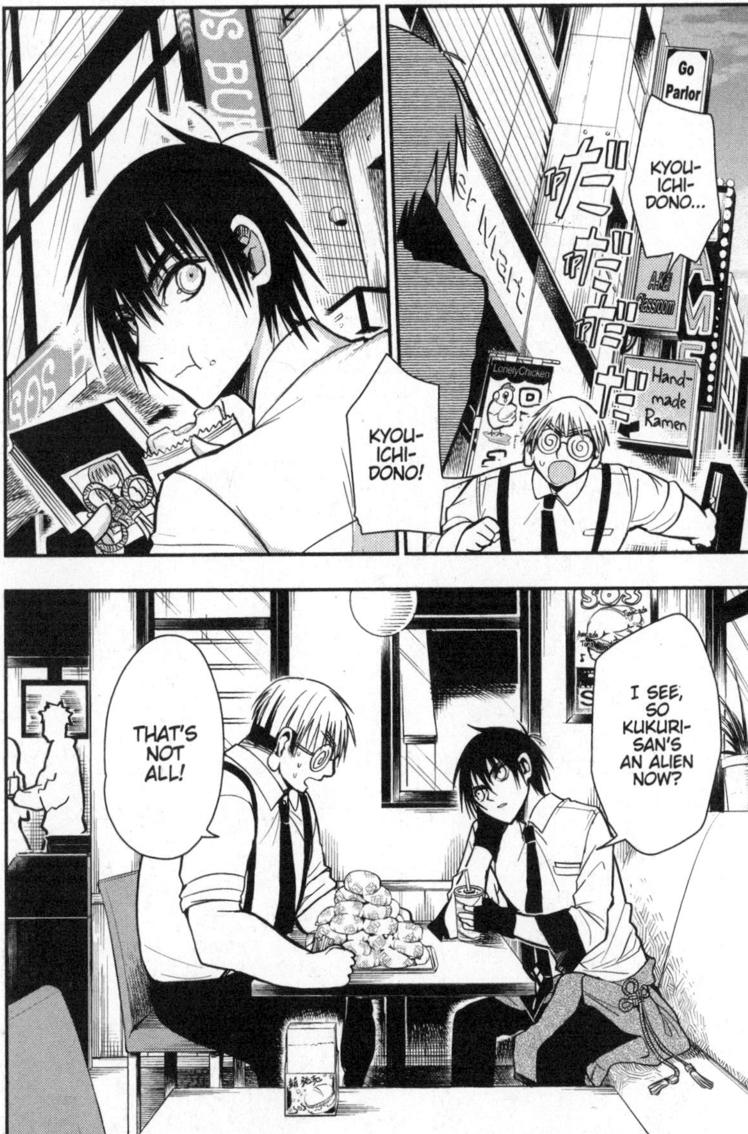
Go Parlor
KYOU-ICHI-DONO...
A-Kai Classroom
LonelyChicken
Hand-made Ramen
KYOU-ICHI-DONO!
I SEE, SO KUKURI-SAN'S AN ALIEN NOW?
THAT'S NOT ALL!

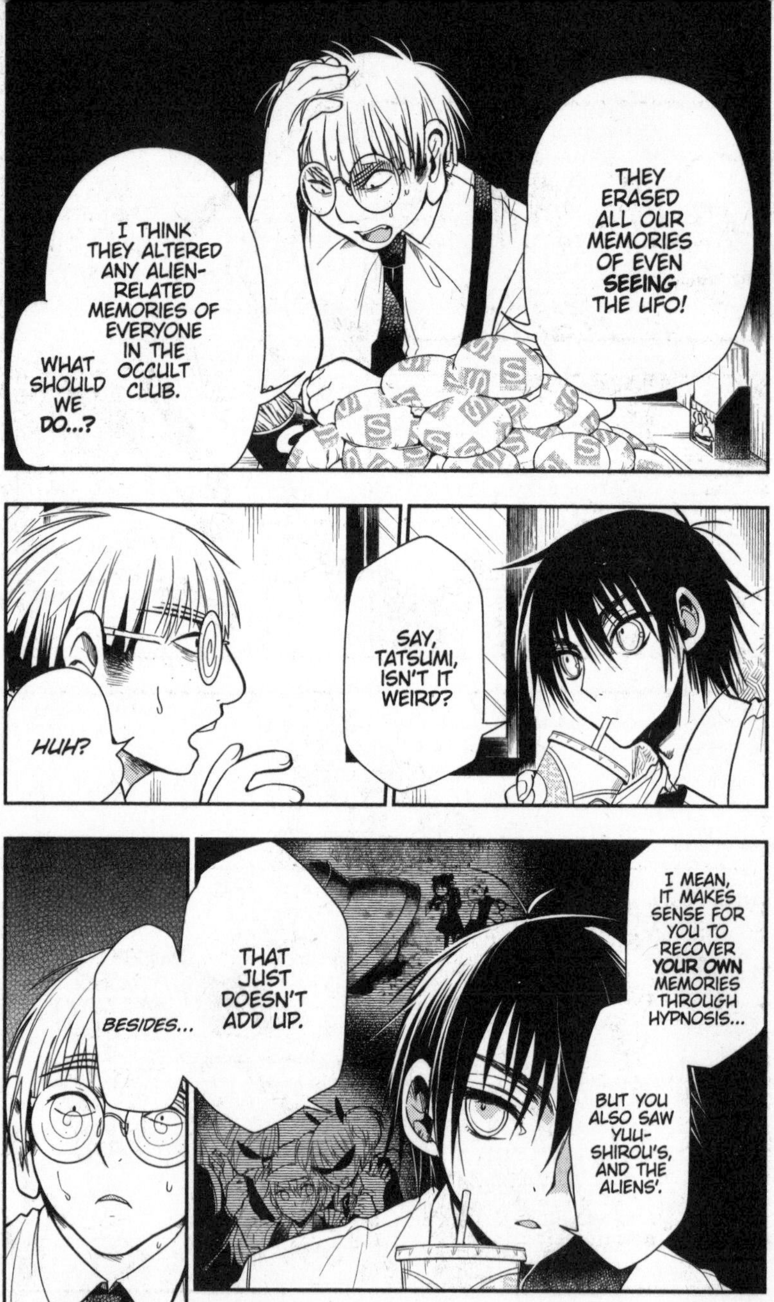
THEY ERASED ALL OUR MEMORIES OF EVEN SEEING THE UFO!
I THINK THEY ALTERED ANY ALIEN-RELATED MEMORIES OF EVERYONE IN THE OCCULT CLUB.
WHAT SHOULD WE DO...?
SAY, TATSUMI, ISN'T IT WEIRD?
HUH?
I MEAN, IT MAKES SENSE FOR YOU TO RECOVER YOUR OWN MEMORIES THROUGH HYPNOSIS...
BUT YOU ALSO SAW YUU-SHIROU'S, AND THE ALIENS'.
THAT JUST DOESN'T ADD UP.
BESIDES...

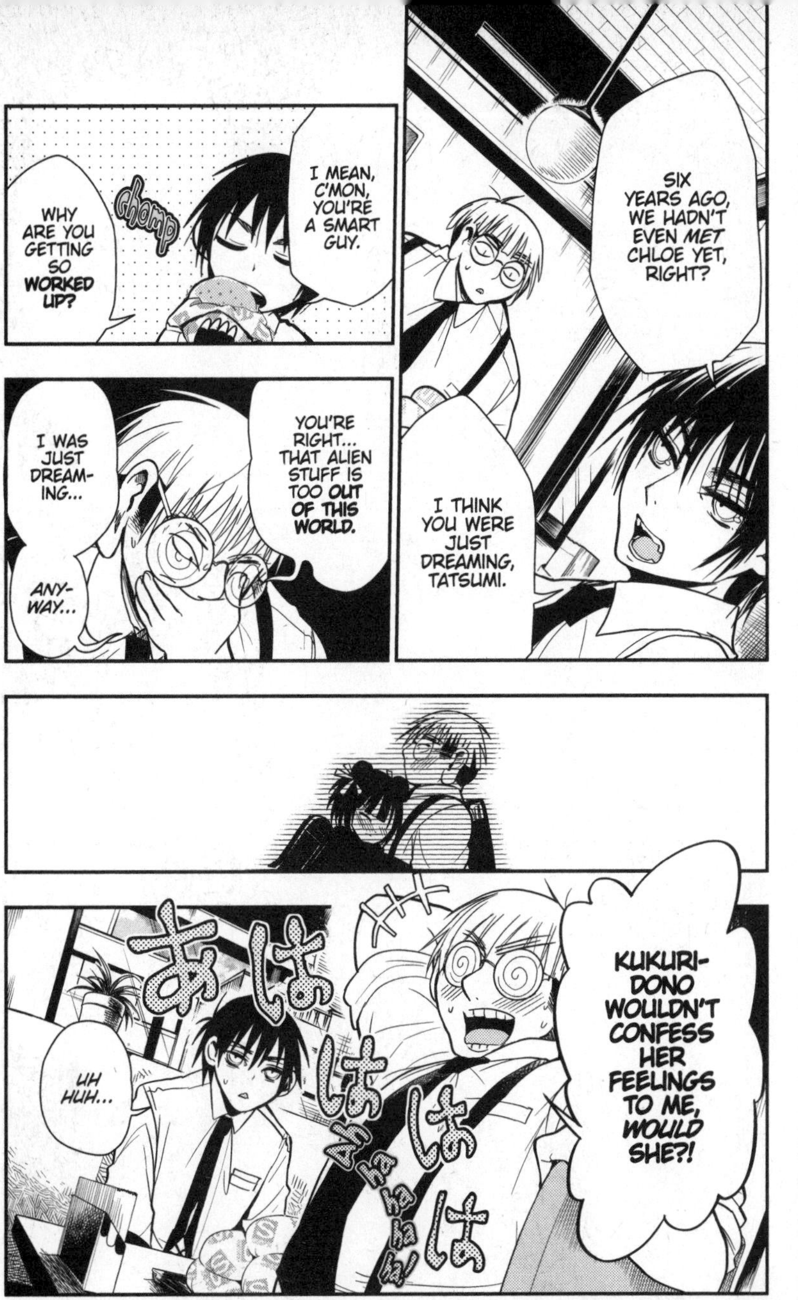
SIX YEARS AGO, WE HADN'T EVEN *MET* CHLOE YET, RIGHT?
I THINK YOU WERE JUST DREAMING, TATSUMI.
I MEAN, C'MON, YOU'RE A SMART GUY.
champ
WHY ARE YOU GETTING SO **WORKED UP?**
YOU'RE RIGHT... THAT ALIEN STUFF IS TOO **OUT OF THIS WORLD.**
I WAS JUST DREAMING...
ANYWAY...
KUKURI-DONO WOULDN'T CONFESS HER FEELINGS TO ME, *WOULD* SHE?!
あははは
aha ha ha ha!
UH HUH...

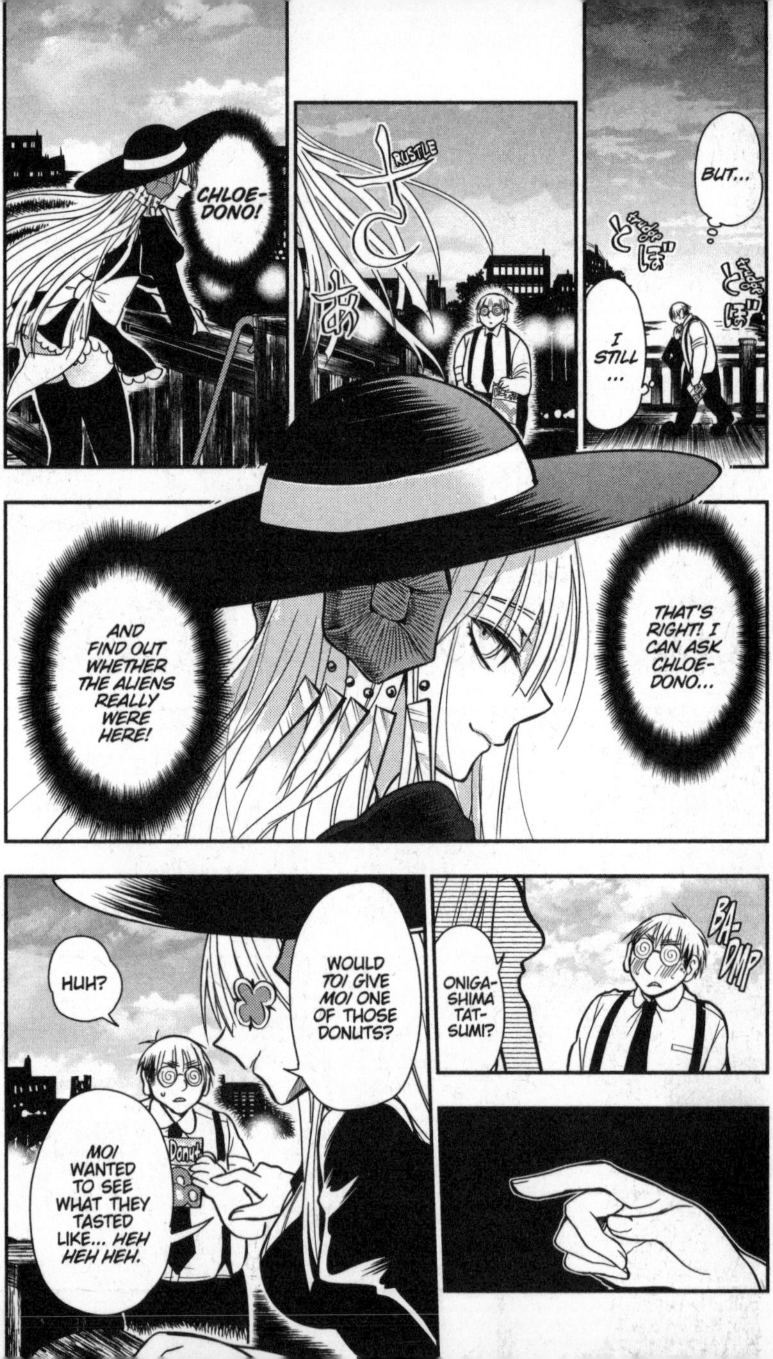
BUT...
I STILL...
RUSTLE
CHLOE-DONO!
THAT'S RIGHT! I CAN ASK CHLOE-DONO...
AND FIND OUT WHETHER THE ALIENS REALLY WERE HERE!
ONIGA-SHIMA TAT-SUMI?
BA-DMP
WOULD TOI GIVE MOI ONE OF THOSE DONUTS?
HUH?
MOI WANTED TO SEE WHAT THEY TASTED LIKE... HEH HEH HEH.
Donut

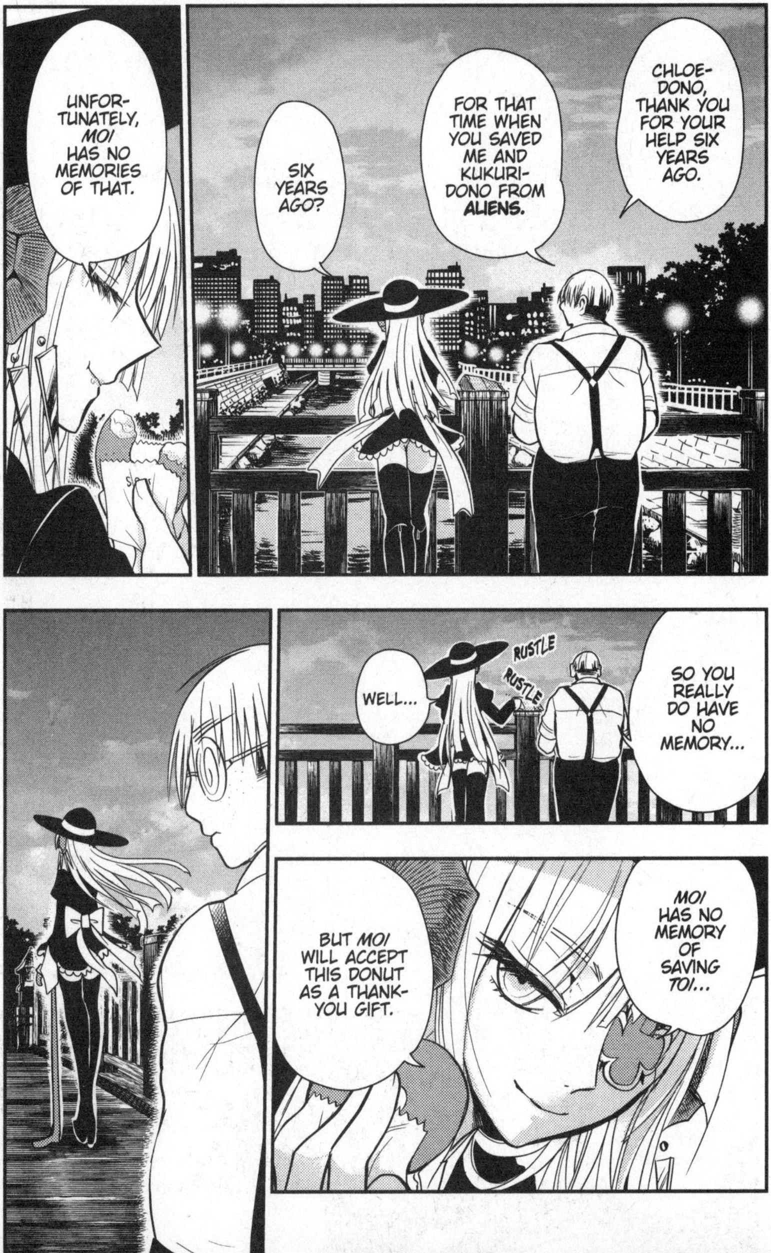
CHLOE-DONO, THANK YOU FOR YOUR HELP SIX YEARS AGO.
FOR THAT TIME WHEN YOU SAVED ME AND KUKURI-DONO FROM **ALIENS.**
SIX YEARS AGO?
UNFOR-TUNATELY, *MOI* HAS NO MEMORIES OF THAT.
SO YOU REALLY DO HAVE NO MEMORY...
RUSTLE
RUSTLE
WELL...
MOI HAS NO MEMORY OF SAVING *TOI*...
BUT *MOI* WILL ACCEPT THIS DONUT AS A THANK-YOU GIFT.

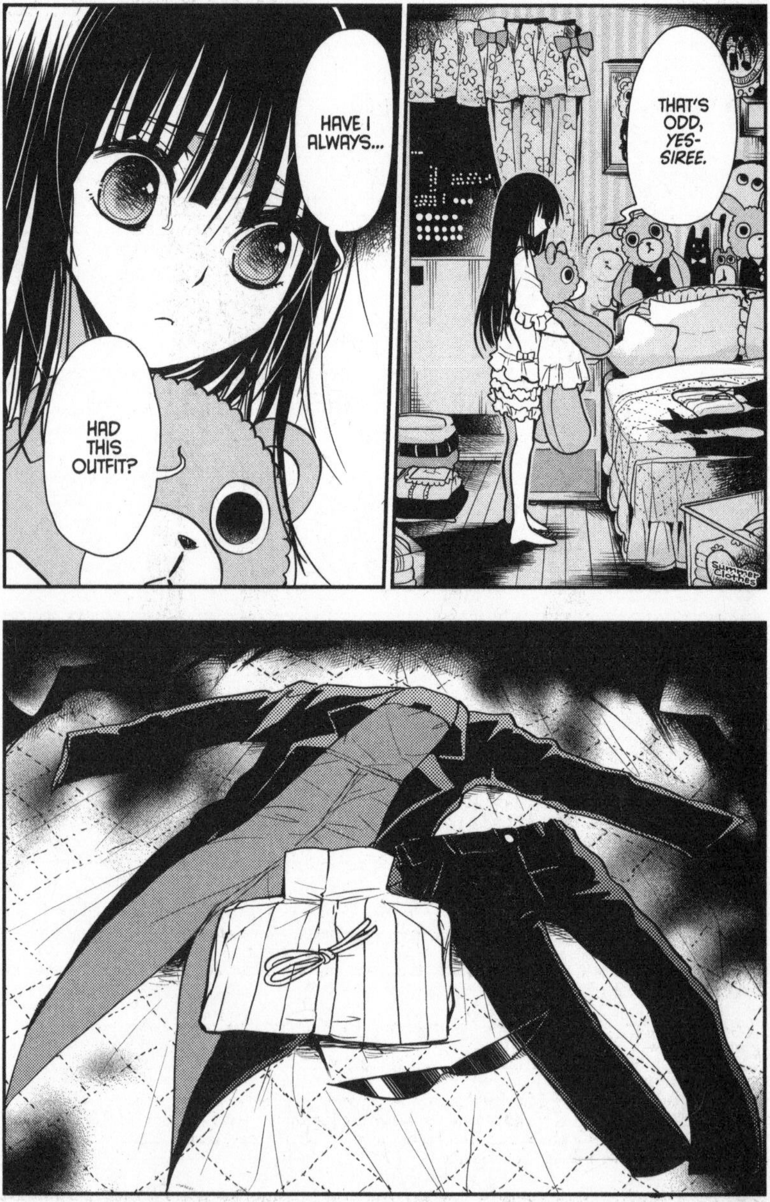
THAT'S ODD, YES-SIREE.
Summer Clothes
HAVE I ALWAYS...
HAD THIS OUTFIT?

K   a   i   d   a   n   n   i   k   i

Old Version   **New Version**

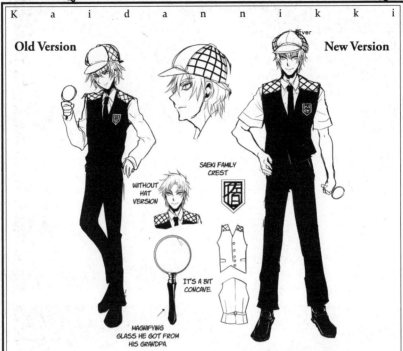

ver

SAEKI FAMILY
CREST

WITHOUT
HAT
VERSION

IT'S A BIT
CONCAVE.

MAGNIFYING
GLASS HE GOT FROM
HIS GRANDPA.

Occult Club President and Grandson of a Great Detective, Saeki Yuushirou-kun

For the image of a handsome young man with frizzy blonde hair, I referenced the detective Enokizu Reijirou, who appears in the *Hyakki Yakou* novel series. I only faintly recalled him when I designed Yuushirou, but when I checked later, I'd made the names sound pretty similar too... I feel kinda bad about that. I like works like the *Hyakki Yakou* series, which entangle rumors and strangeness with human drama. I've read and watched a good number of them by now.

Lately, I've been really into the *Shishou* series. The *Shishou* series is a series of occult short stories that were originally posted on online message boards, which features two people: the storyteller, and "Shishou," whom he met at club during university. I've read them all at sites that collect the stories, or in comics form, but I was impressed, thinking, "So here's another way to use weirdness!"

I also highly recommend the game *Hayarigami*. It entwines occult elements into a detective drama, and since I love both those things, I was hooked on it. Since *Hayarigami* deals with urban legends, it and *Ghost Diary* share similar concepts.

And last, here's something I finally noticed just recently. The *Ju-On* series reached its final chapter in 2015. The ghost who appears in it has the last name "Saeki"... I'd used this last name without knowing about that, but I have a strong feeling that I'd been influenced by an invisible something. Oh no, I'm so scared (lol)!

Sukami Family Album

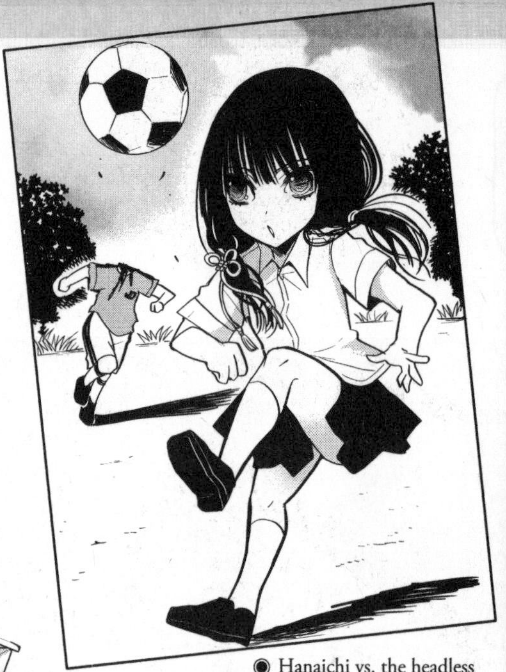

◉ Hanaichi vs. the headless soccer boy!

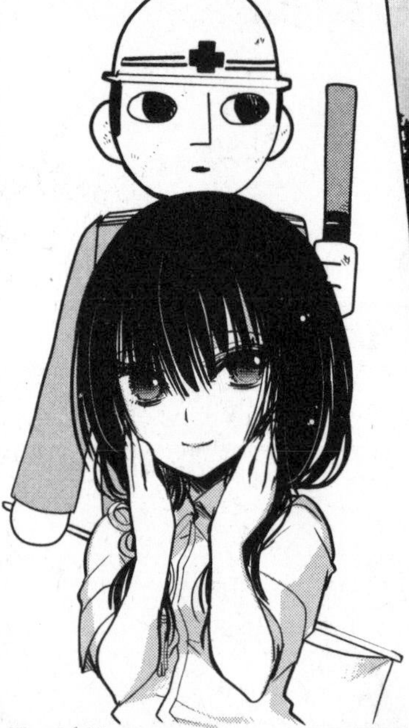

◉ Hanaichi in a commemorative photo with a board doll. She's looking more and more like her mother.

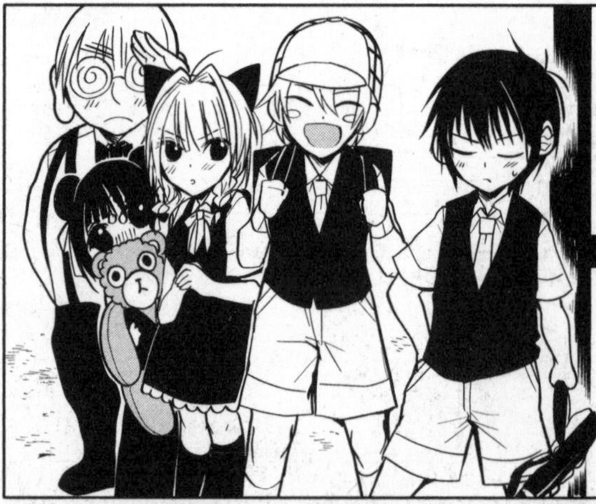

◉ Kyouichi brings his friends over for the first time! What a unique bunch!

◉ H-HEY! WHAT ARE YOU DOING WITH MY DAUGHTER?!

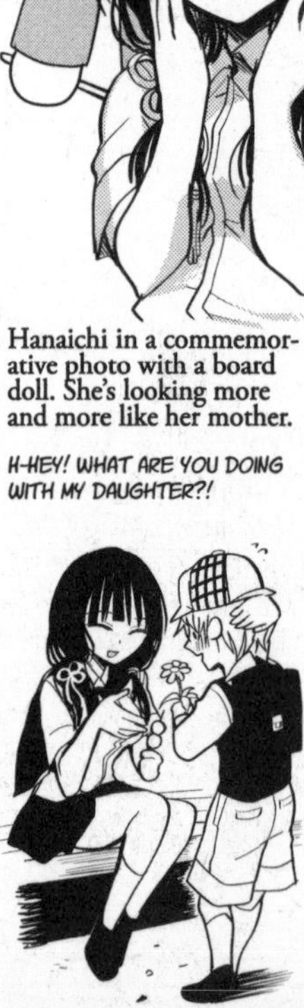

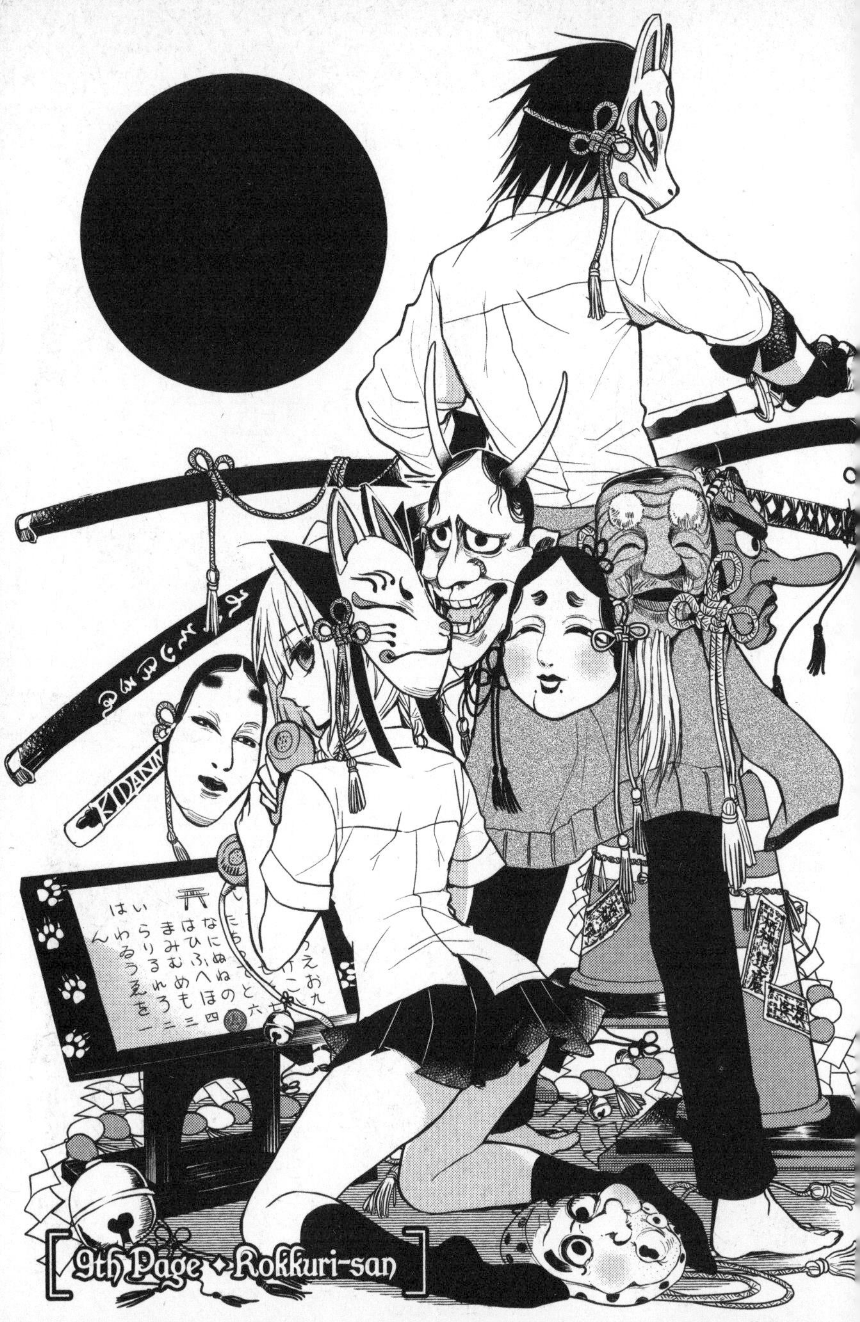
9th Page ◆ Rokkuri-san

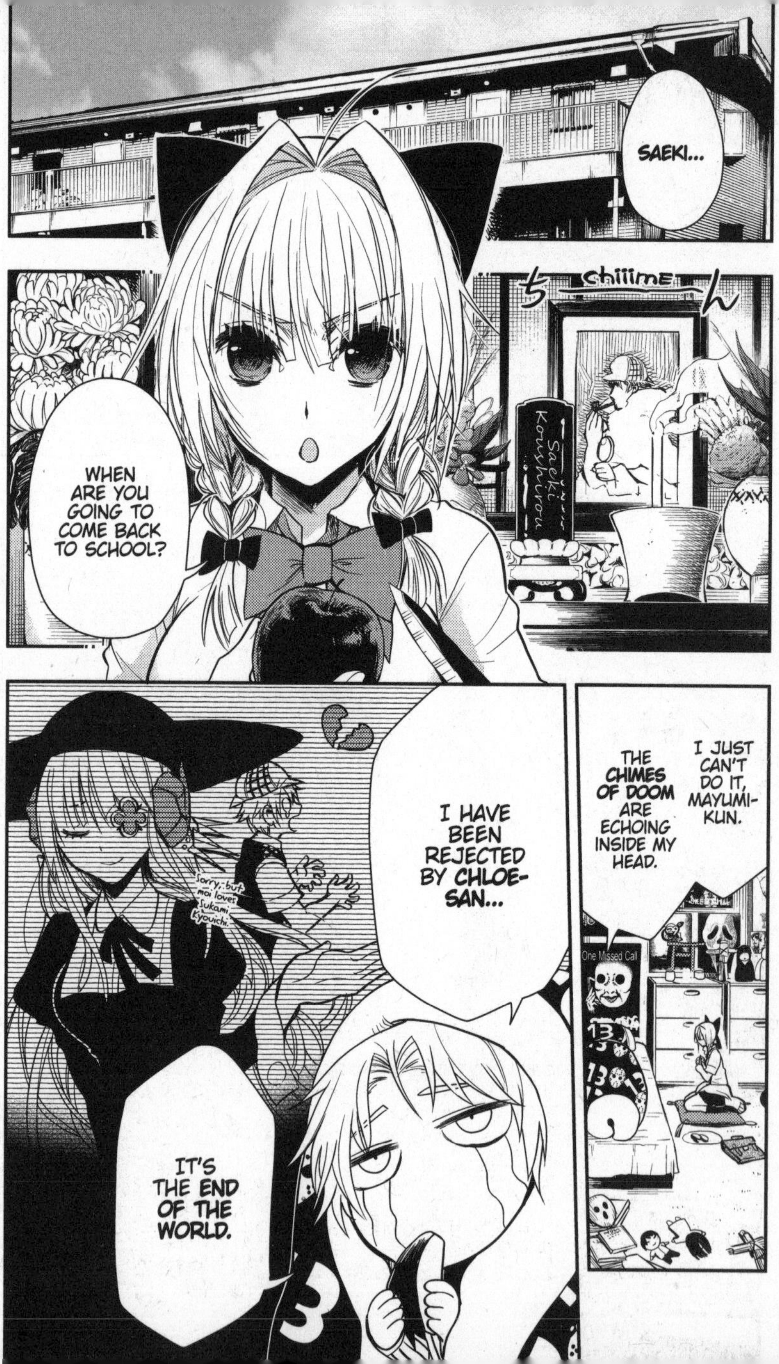
SAEKI...
ち chiiimE ん
Saeki Koushirou
WHEN ARE YOU GOING TO COME BACK TO SCHOOL?
I JUST CAN'T DO IT, MAYUMI-KUN.
THE CHIMES OF DOOM ARE ECHOING INSIDE MY HEAD.
One Missed Call
I HAVE BEEN REJECTED BY CHLOE-SAN...
Sorry, but moi loves Sukami Kyouichi.
IT'S THE END OF THE WORLD.

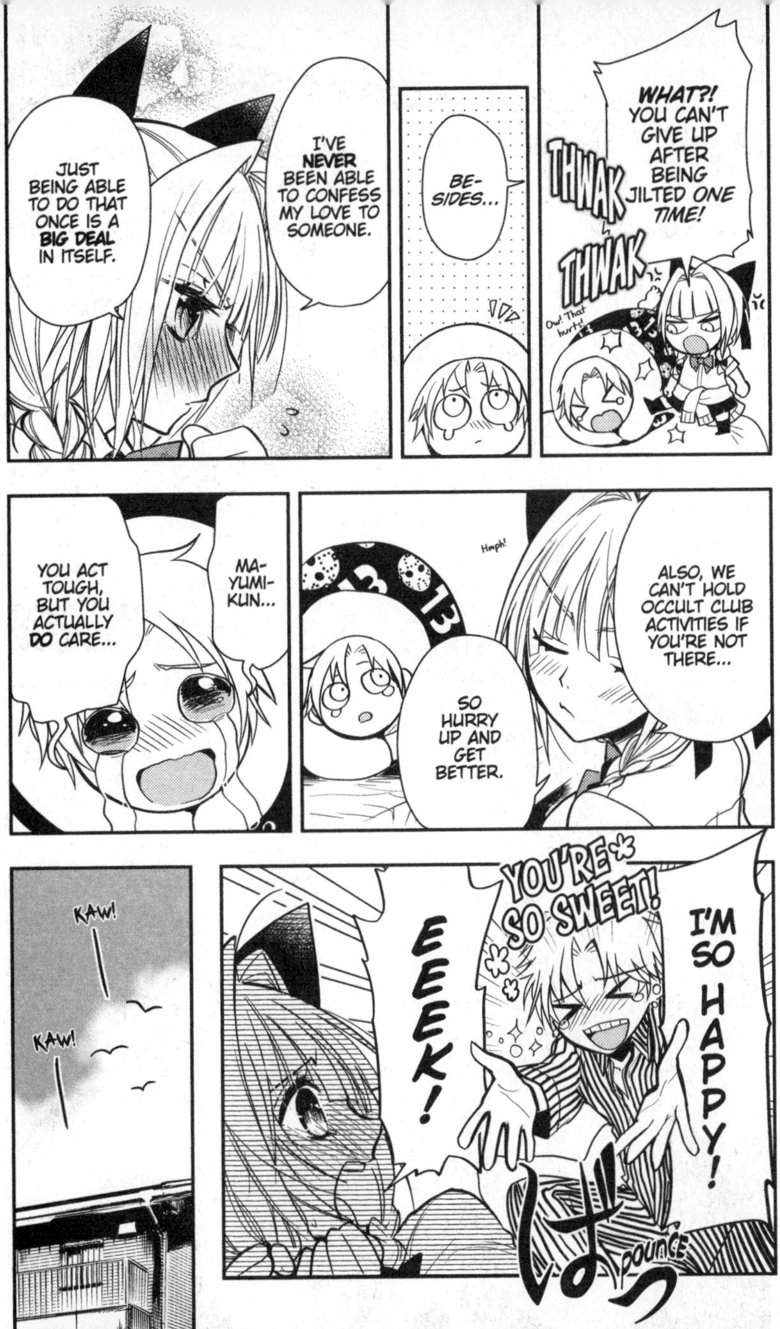
WHAT?! YOU CAN'T GIVE UP AFTER BEING JILTED ONE TIME!
THWAK
THWAK
Ow! That hurts!
BE-SIDES...
I'VE NEVER BEEN ABLE TO CONFESS MY LOVE TO SOMEONE.
JUST BEING ABLE TO DO THAT ONCE IS A BIG DEAL IN ITSELF.
ALSO, WE CAN'T HOLD OCCULT CLUB ACTIVITIES IF YOU'RE NOT THERE...
Hmph!
SO HURRY UP AND GET BETTER.
MA-YUMI-KUN...
YOU ACT TOUGH, BUT YOU ACTUALLY DO CARE...
I'M SO HAPPY!
YOU'RE SO SWEET!
EEEK!
pounce
KAW!
KAW!

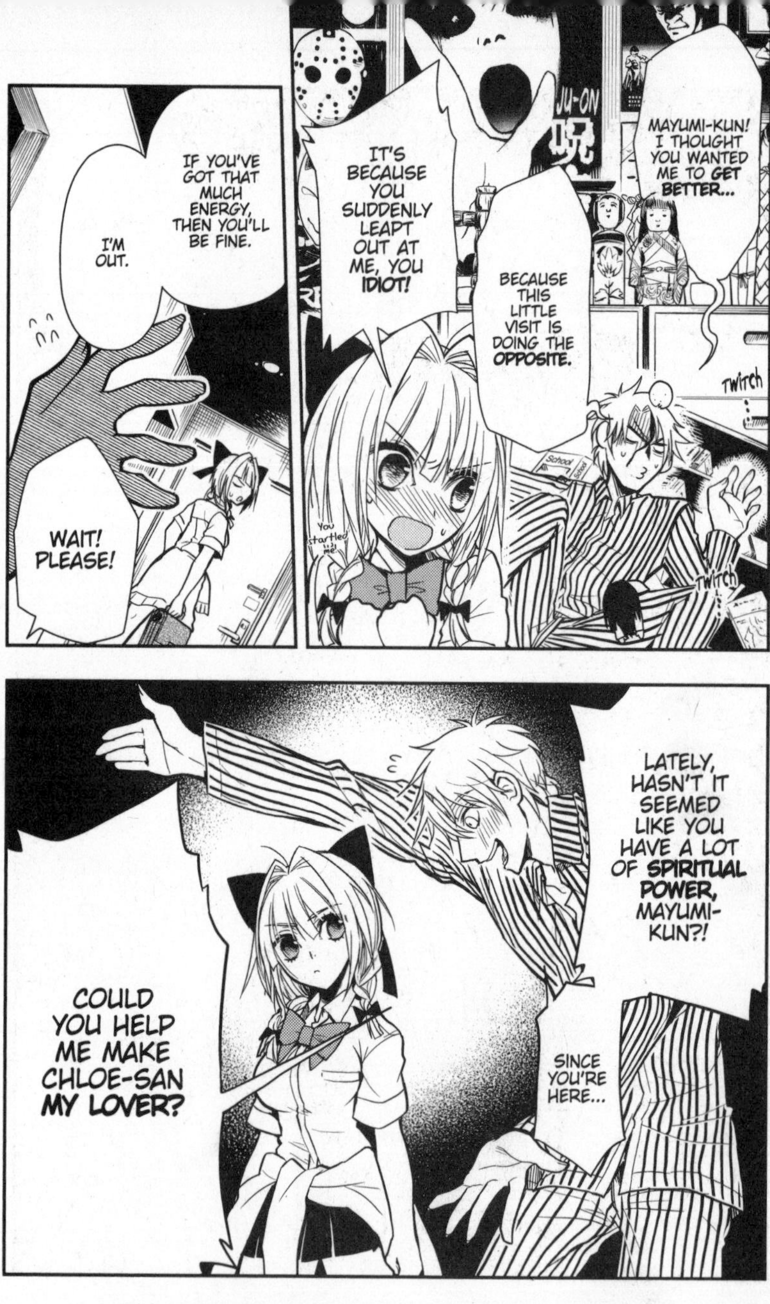

JU-ON 呪
MAYUMI-KUN! I THOUGHT YOU WANTED ME TO GET BETTER...
BECAUSE THIS LITTLE VISIT IS DOING THE OPPOSITE.
TWITCH
IT'S BECAUSE YOU SUDDENLY LEAPT OUT AT ME, YOU IDIOT!
You startled me!
TWITCH
IF YOU'VE GOT THAT MUCH ENERGY, THEN YOU'LL BE FINE.
I'M OUT.
WAIT! PLEASE!
LATELY, HASN'T IT SEEMED LIKE YOU HAVE A LOT OF SPIRITUAL POWER, MAYUMI-KUN?!
SINCE YOU'RE HERE...
COULD YOU HELP ME MAKE CHLOE-SAN MY LOVER?

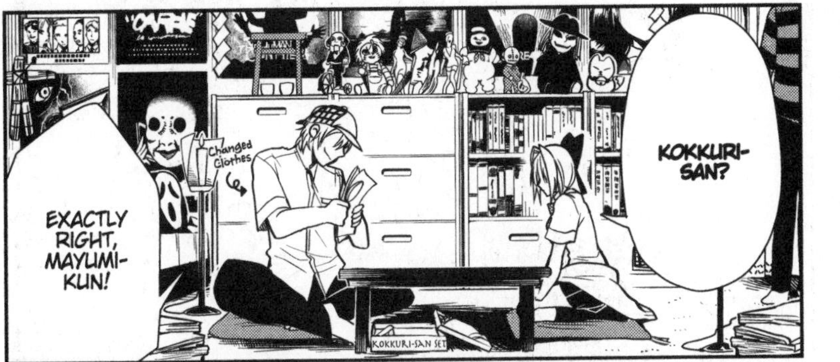
KOKKURI-SAN?
EXACTLY RIGHT, MAYUMI-KUN!
Changed Clothes
KOKKURI-SAN SET

※The prototype for Kokkuri-san was the Western spiritualist technique of "Table-Turning." A wester equivalent would be a Ouija board.

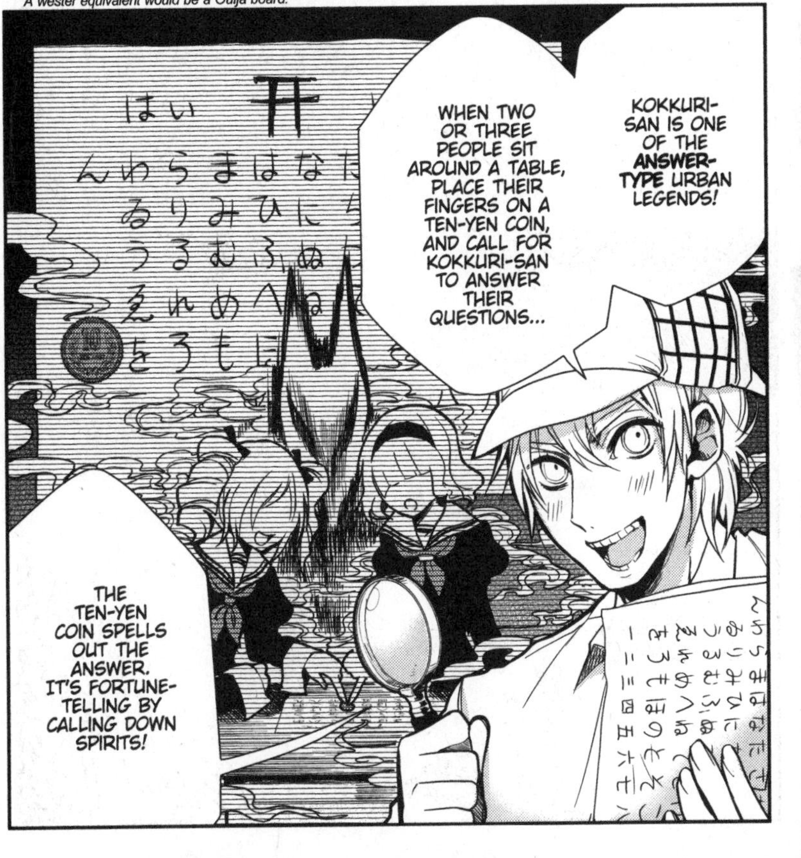
KOKKURI-SAN IS ONE OF THE **ANSWER-TYPE** URBAN LEGENDS!
WHEN TWO OR THREE PEOPLE SIT AROUND A TABLE, PLACE THEIR FINGERS ON A TEN-YEN COIN, AND CALL FOR KOKKURI-SAN TO ANSWER THEIR QUESTIONS...
THE TEN-YEN COIN SPELLS OUT THE ANSWER. IT'S FORTUNE-TELLING BY CALLING DOWN SPIRITS!

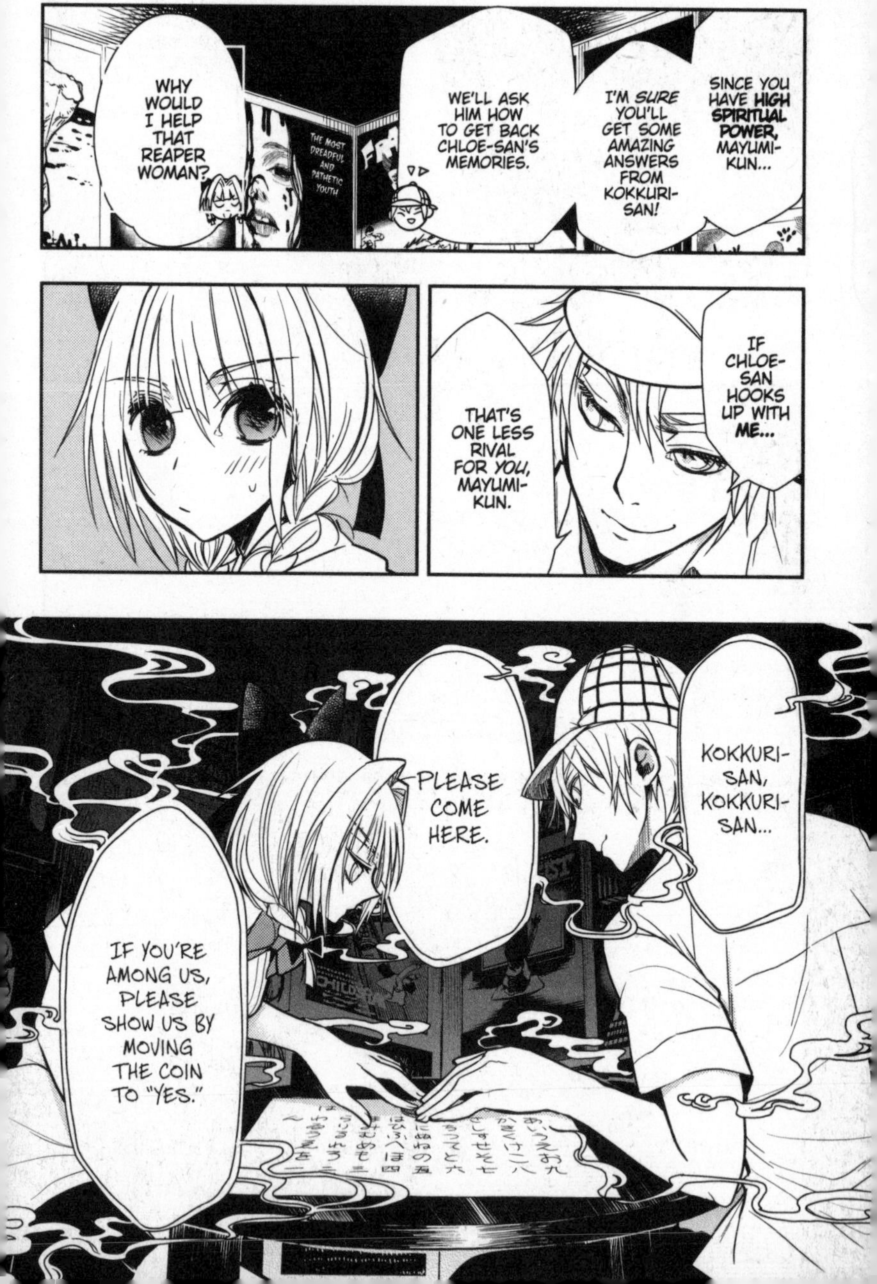
SINCE YOU HAVE **HIGH SPIRITUAL POWER,** MAYUMI-KUN...
I'M *SURE* YOU'LL GET SOME AMAZING ANSWERS FROM KOKKURI-SAN!
WE'LL ASK HIM HOW TO GET BACK CHLOE-SAN'S MEMORIES.
THE MOST DREADFUL AND PATHETIC YOUTH
WHY WOULD I HELP THAT REAPER WOMAN?
IF CHLOE-SAN HOOKS UP WITH **ME...**
THAT'S ONE LESS RIVAL FOR *YOU,* MAYUMI-KUN.
KOKKURI-SAN, KOKKURI-SAN...
PLEASE COME HERE.
IF YOU'RE AMONG US, PLEASE SHOW US BY MOVING THE COIN TO "YES."

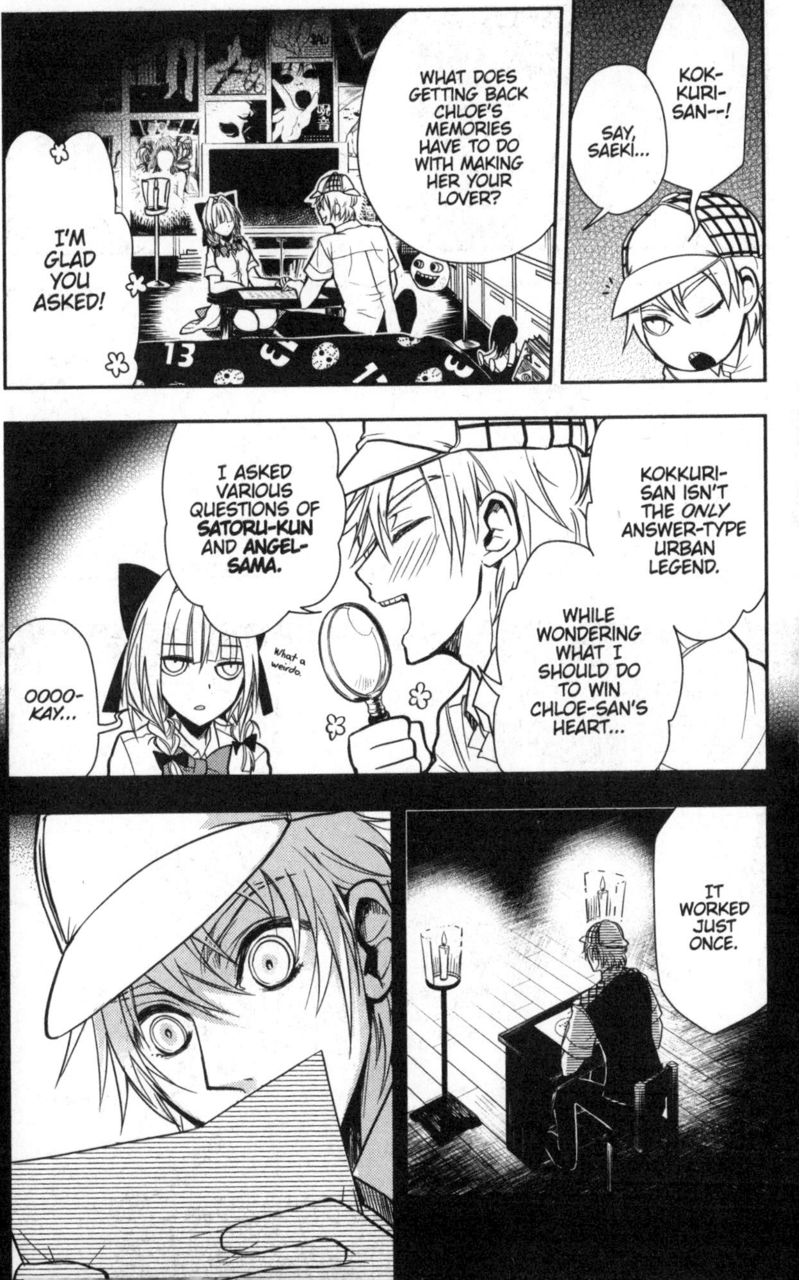
KOK-KURI-SAN--!
SAY, SAEKI...
WHAT DOES GETTING BACK CHLOE'S MEMORIES HAVE TO DO WITH MAKING HER YOUR LOVER?
I'M GLAD YOU ASKED!
KOKKURI-SAN ISN'T THE *ONLY* ANSWER-TYPE URBAN LEGEND.
WHILE WONDERING WHAT I SHOULD DO TO WIN CHLOE-SAN'S HEART...
I ASKED VARIOUS QUESTIONS OF **SATORU-KUN** AND **ANGEL-SAMA.**
What a weirdo.
OOOO-KAY...
IT WORKED JUST ONCE.

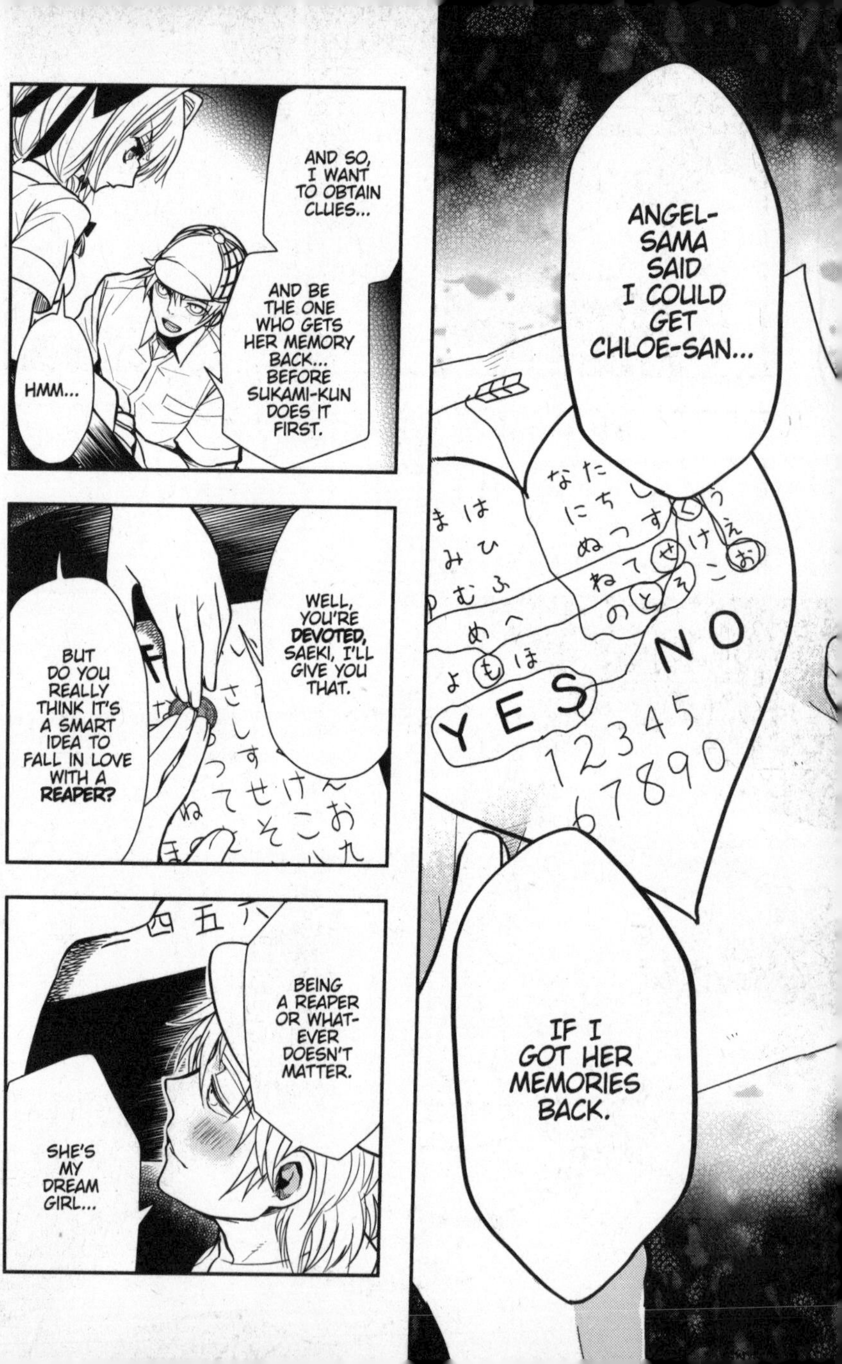
ANGEL-SAMA SAID I COULD GET CHLOE-SAN...
YES NO
12345
67890
IF I GOT HER MEMORIES BACK.
AND SO, I WANT TO OBTAIN CLUES...
AND BE THE ONE WHO GETS HER MEMORY BACK... BEFORE SUKAMI-KUN DOES IT FIRST.
HMM...
WELL, YOU'RE **DEVOTED,** SAEKI, I'LL GIVE YOU THAT.
BUT DO YOU REALLY THINK IT'S A SMART IDEA TO FALL IN LOVE WITH A **REAPER?**
BEING A REAPER OR WHATEVER DOESN'T MATTER.
SHE'S MY DREAM GIRL...

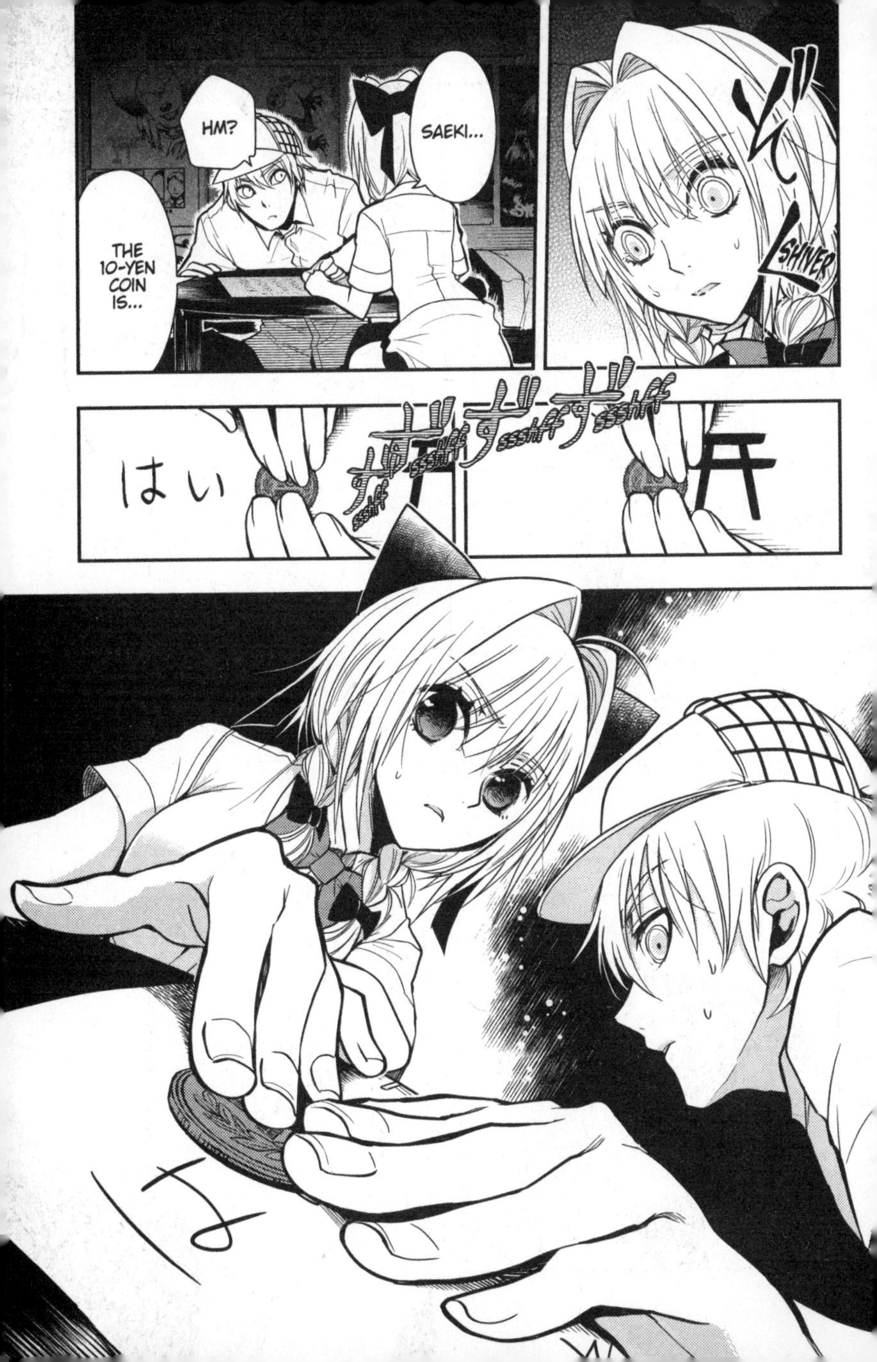
SHIVER
SAEKI...
HM?
THE 10-YEN COIN IS...
sssshiff
sssshiff
sssshiff
はい

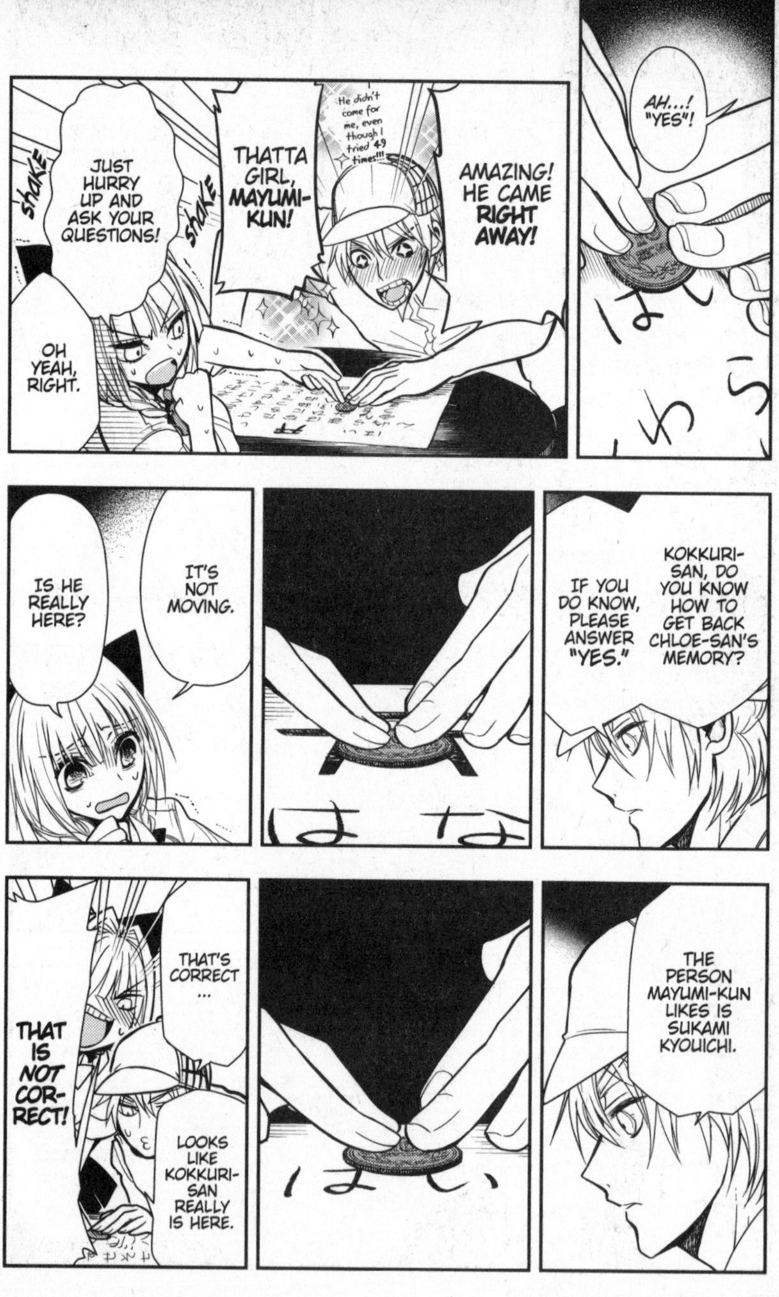
AH...! "YES"!
AMAZING! HE CAME RIGHT AWAY!
THATTA GIRL, MAYUMI-KUN!
He didn't come for me, even though I tried 49 times!!!
shake
JUST HURRY UP AND ASK YOUR QUESTIONS!
shake
OH YEAH, RIGHT.
KOKKURI-SAN, DO YOU KNOW HOW TO GET BACK CHLOE-SAN'S MEMORY?
IF YOU DO KNOW, PLEASE ANSWER "YES."
IT'S NOT MOVING.
IS HE REALLY HERE?
THE PERSON MAYUMI-KUN LIKES IS SUKAMI KYOUICHI.
THAT'S CORRECT ...
THAT IS NOT CORRECT!
LOOKS LIKE KOKKURI-SAN REALLY IS HERE.

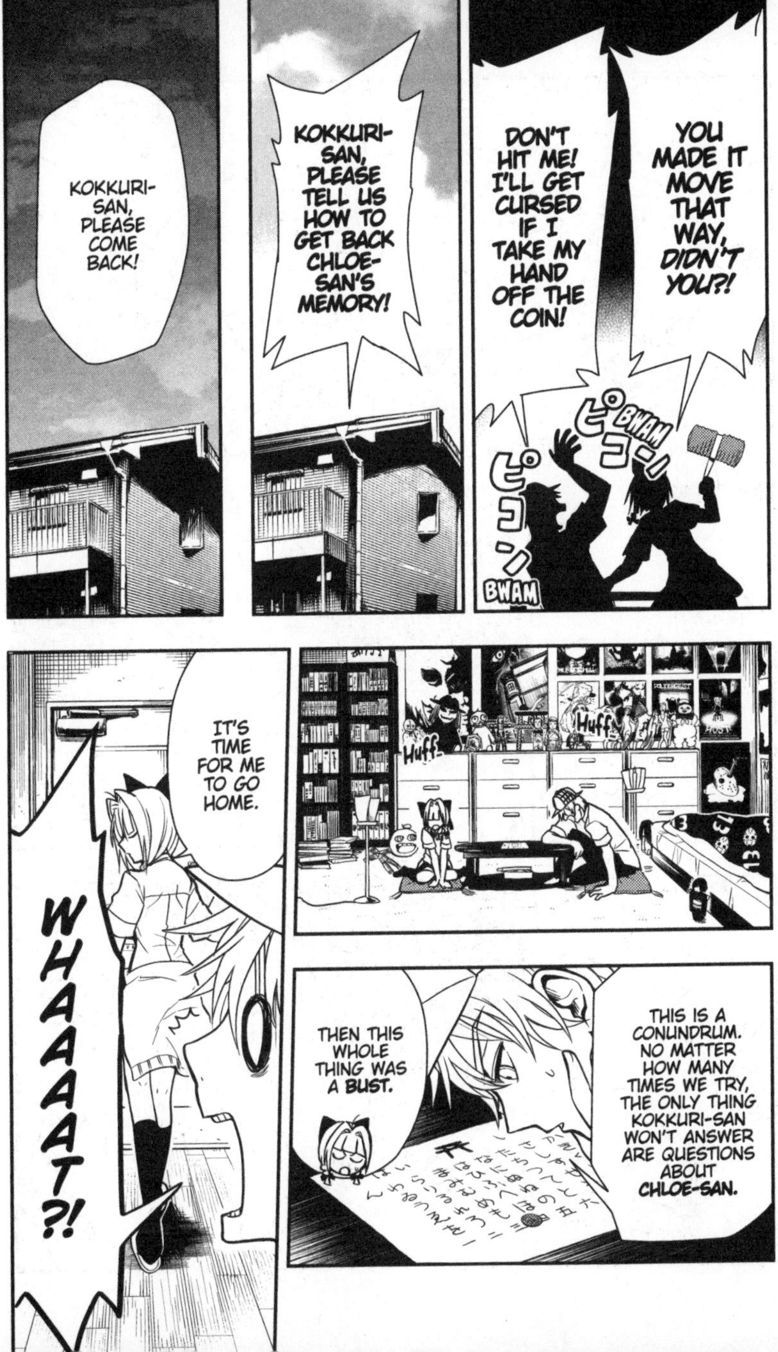
YOU MADE IT MOVE THAT WAY, DIDN'T YOU?!
DON'T HIT ME! I'LL GET CURSED IF I TAKE MY HAND OFF THE COIN!
ピコーン
BWAM
ピコーン
BWAM
KOKKURI-SAN, PLEASE TELL US HOW TO GET BACK CHLOE-SAN'S MEMORY!
KOKKURI-SAN, PLEASE COME BACK!
Huff
Huff
THIS IS A CONUNDRUM. NO MATTER HOW MANY TIMES WE TRY, THE ONLY THING KOKKURI-SAN WON'T ANSWER ARE QUESTIONS ABOUT CHLOE-SAN.
THEN THIS WHOLE THING WAS A BUST.
IT'S TIME FOR ME TO GO HOME.
WHAAAAAT?!

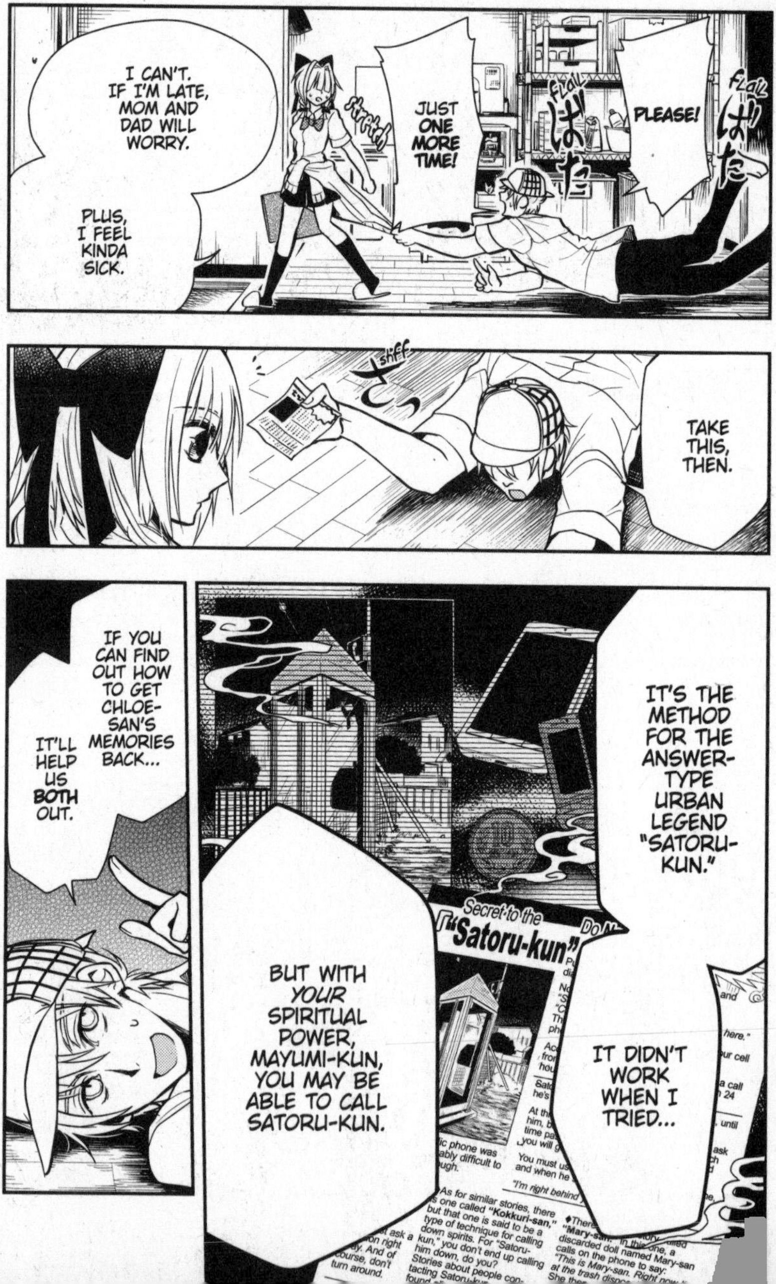
FLAIL
PLEASE!
FLAIL
JUST ONE MORE TIME!
stretch
I CAN'T. IF I'M LATE, MOM AND DAD WILL WORRY.
PLUS, I FEEL KINDA SICK.
TAKE THIS, THEN.
shiff
IT'S THE METHOD FOR THE ANSWER-TYPE URBAN LEGEND "SATORU-KUN."
Secret to the "Satoru-kun"
IT DIDN'T WORK WHEN I TRIED...
BUT WITH *YOUR* SPIRITUAL POWER, MAYUMI-KUN, YOU MAY BE ABLE TO CALL SATORU-KUN.
IF YOU CAN FIND OUT HOW TO GET CHLOE-SAN'S MEMORIES BACK...
IT'LL HELP US BOTH OUT.

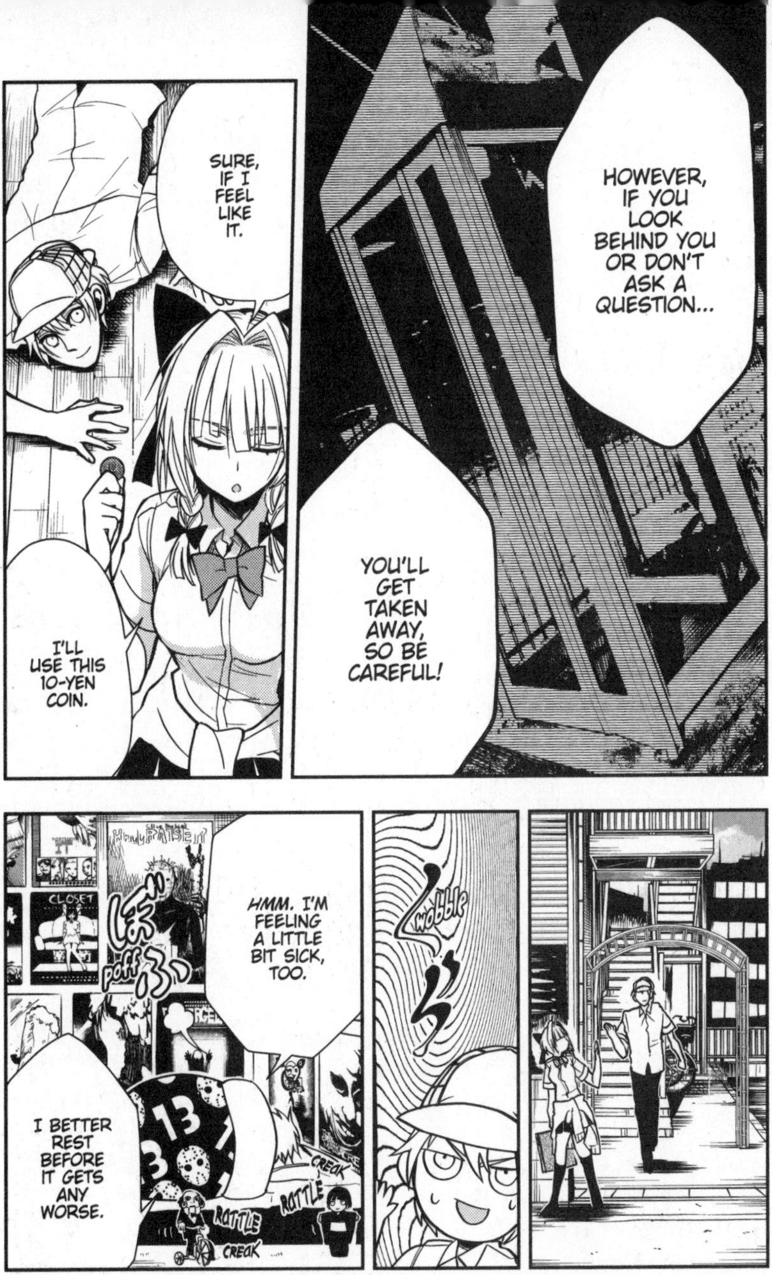
HOWEVER, IF YOU LOOK BEHIND YOU OR DON'T ASK A QUESTION...
YOU'LL GET TAKEN AWAY, SO BE CAREFUL!
SURE, IF I FEEL LIKE IT.
I'LL USE THIS 10-YEN COIN.
wobble
HMM. I'M FEELING A LITTLE BIT SICK, TOO.
I BETTER REST BEFORE IT GETS ANY WORSE.
poff
CLOSET
CREAK
RATTLE
RATTLE
CREAK

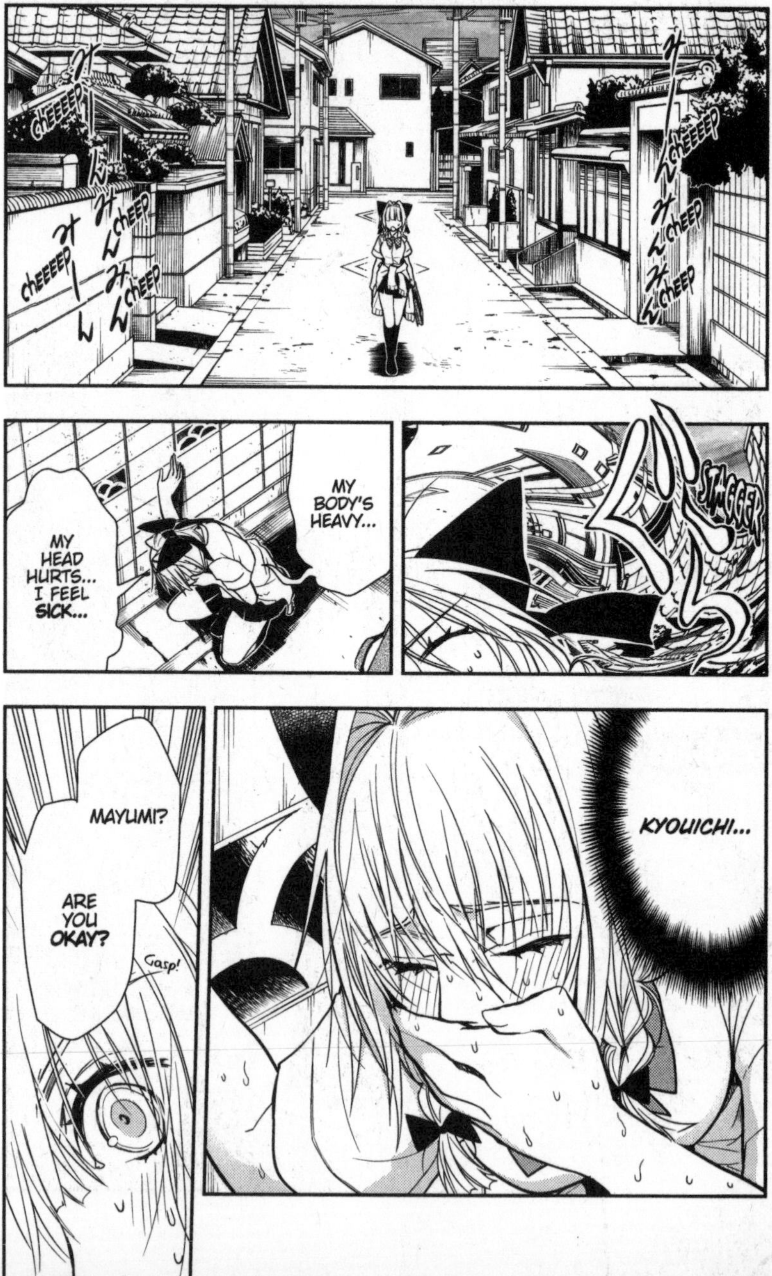
みーんみんみん
cheeeeep
cheep
cheep
みーんみんみん
cheeeep
cheep
cheeeep
cheep
STAGGER
MY BODY'S HEAVY...
MY HEAD HURTS... I FEEL SICK...
KYOUICHI...
MAYUMI?
ARE YOU OKAY?
Gasp!

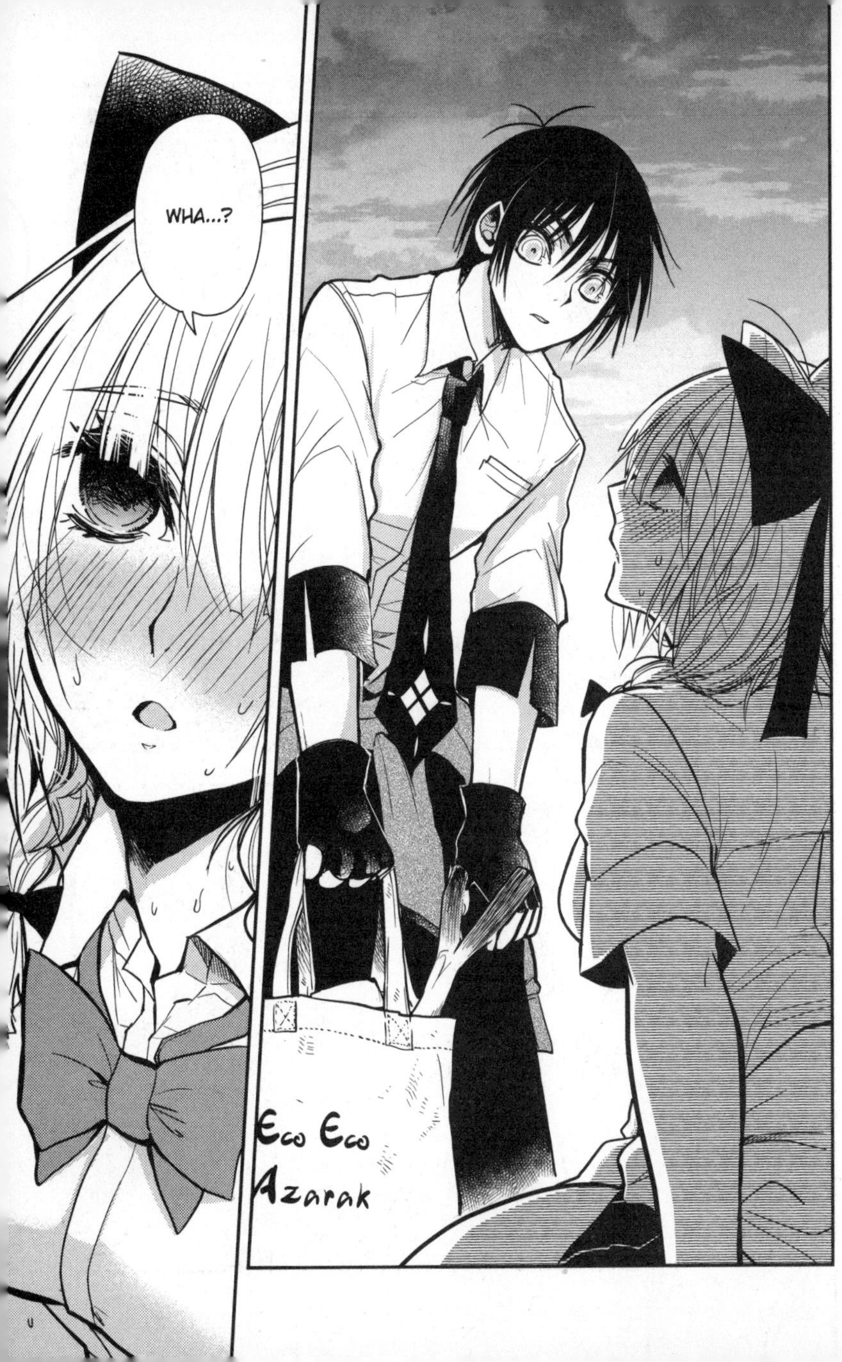
Eco Eco
Azarak
WHA...?

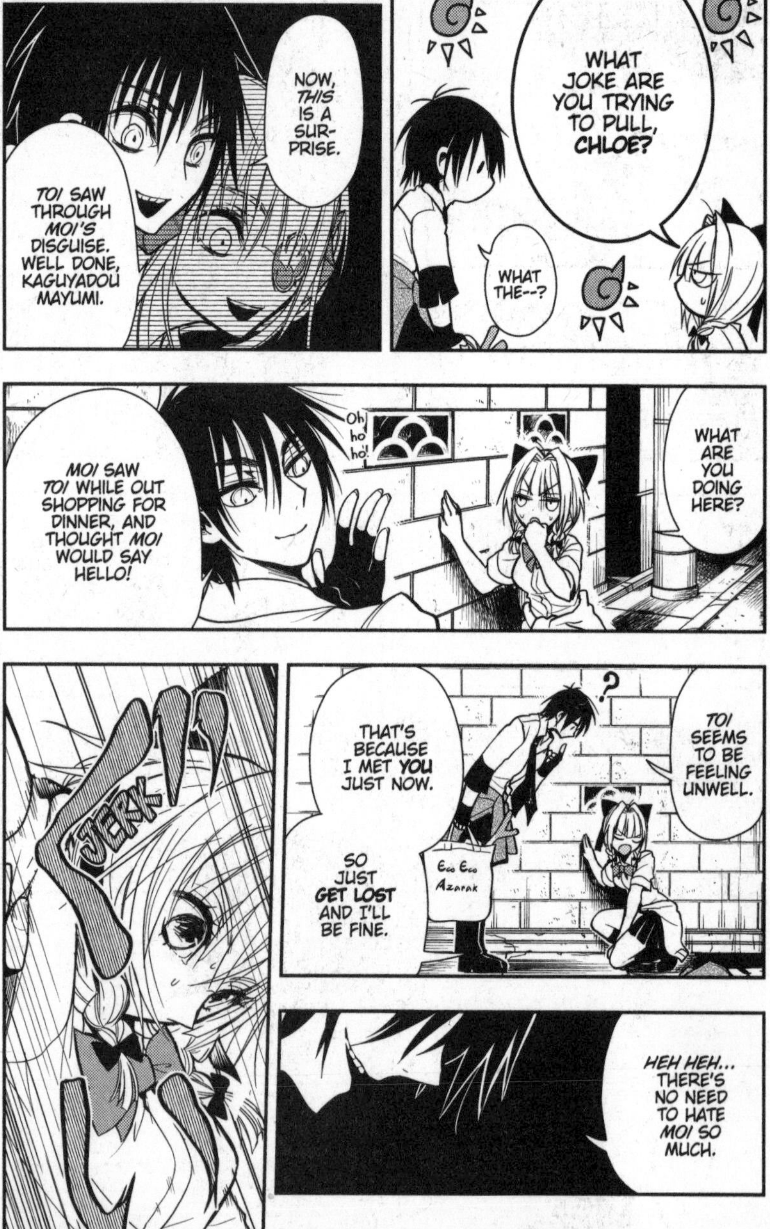
WHAT JOKE ARE YOU TRYING TO PULL, CHLOE?
WHAT THE--?
NOW, THIS IS A SURPRISE.
TOI SAW THROUGH MOI'S DISGUISE. WELL DONE, KAGUYADOU MAYUMI.
WHAT ARE YOU DOING HERE?
Oh ho ho!
MOI SAW TOI WHILE OUT SHOPPING FOR DINNER, AND THOUGHT MOI WOULD SAY HELLO!
TOI SEEMS TO BE FEELING UNWELL.
THAT'S BECAUSE I MET YOU JUST NOW.
SO JUST GET LOST AND I'LL BE FINE.
Eco Eco Azarak
HEH HEH... THERE'S NO NEED TO HATE MOI SO MUCH.
JERK

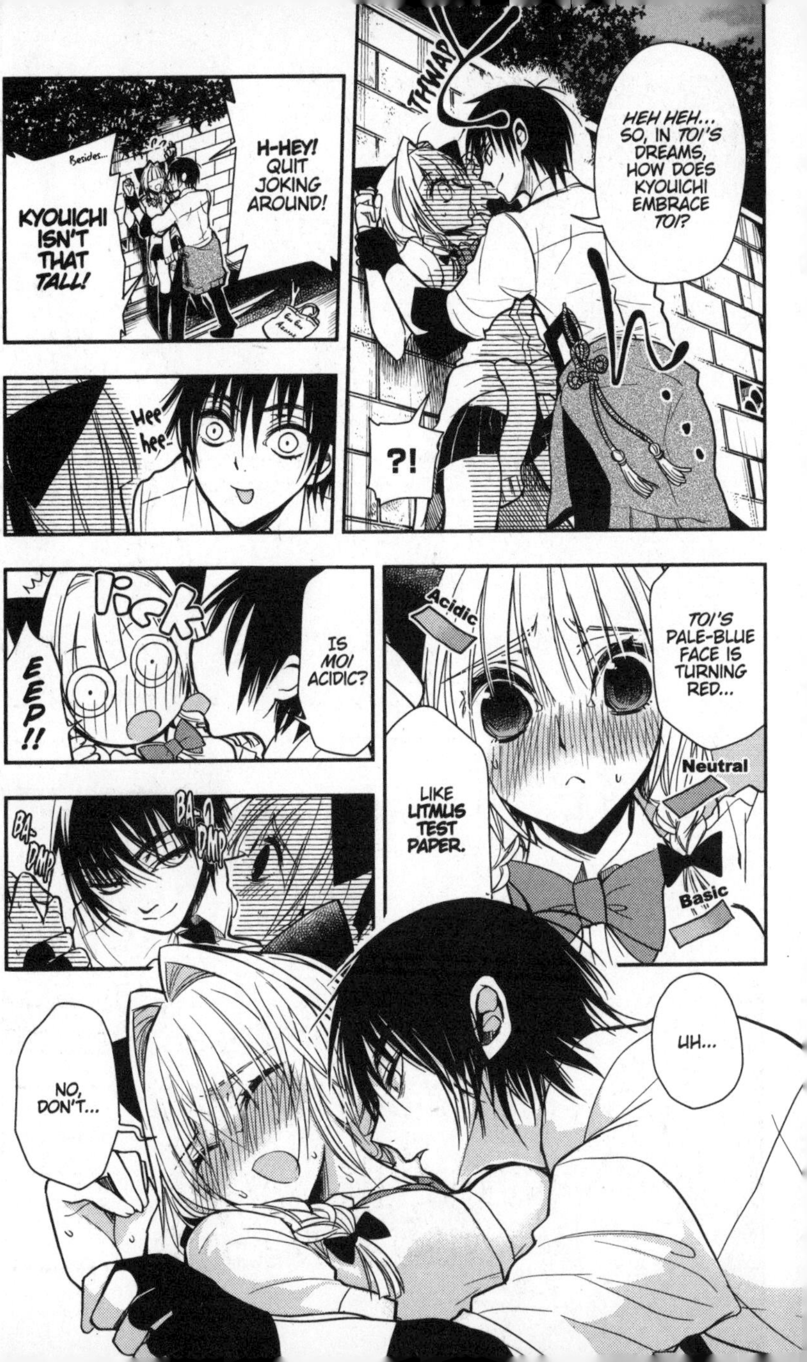
THWAP
HEH HEH... SO, IN TOI'S DREAMS, HOW DOES KYOUICHI EMBRACE TOI?
?!
H-HEY! QUIT JOKING AROUND!
Besides...
KYOUICHI ISN'T THAT TALL!
Hee hee
TOI'S PALE-BLUE FACE IS TURNING RED...
Acidic
Neutral
LIKE LITMUS TEST PAPER.
Basic
IS MOI ACIDIC?
EEP!!
BA-DMP
BA-DMP
UH...
NO, DON'T...

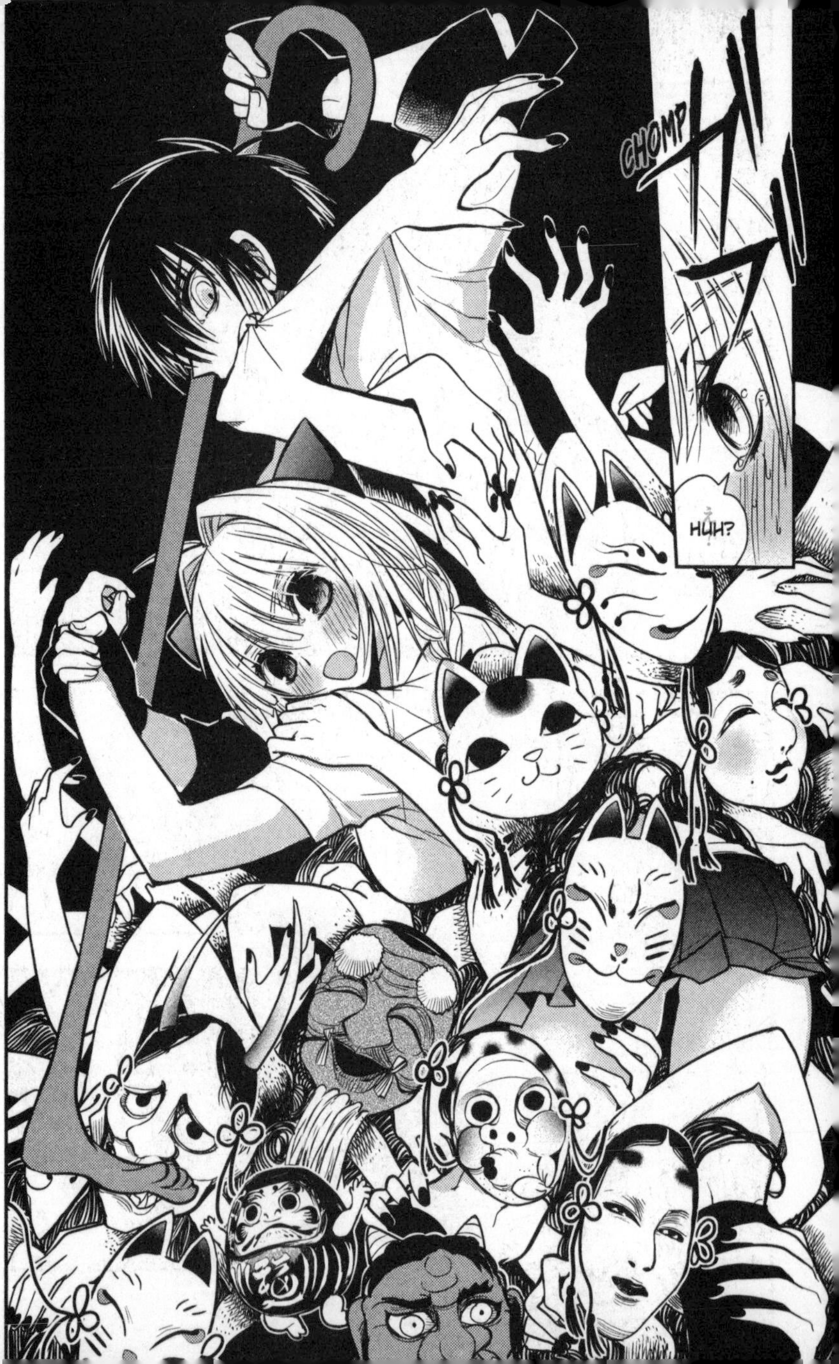
CHOMP
HUH?

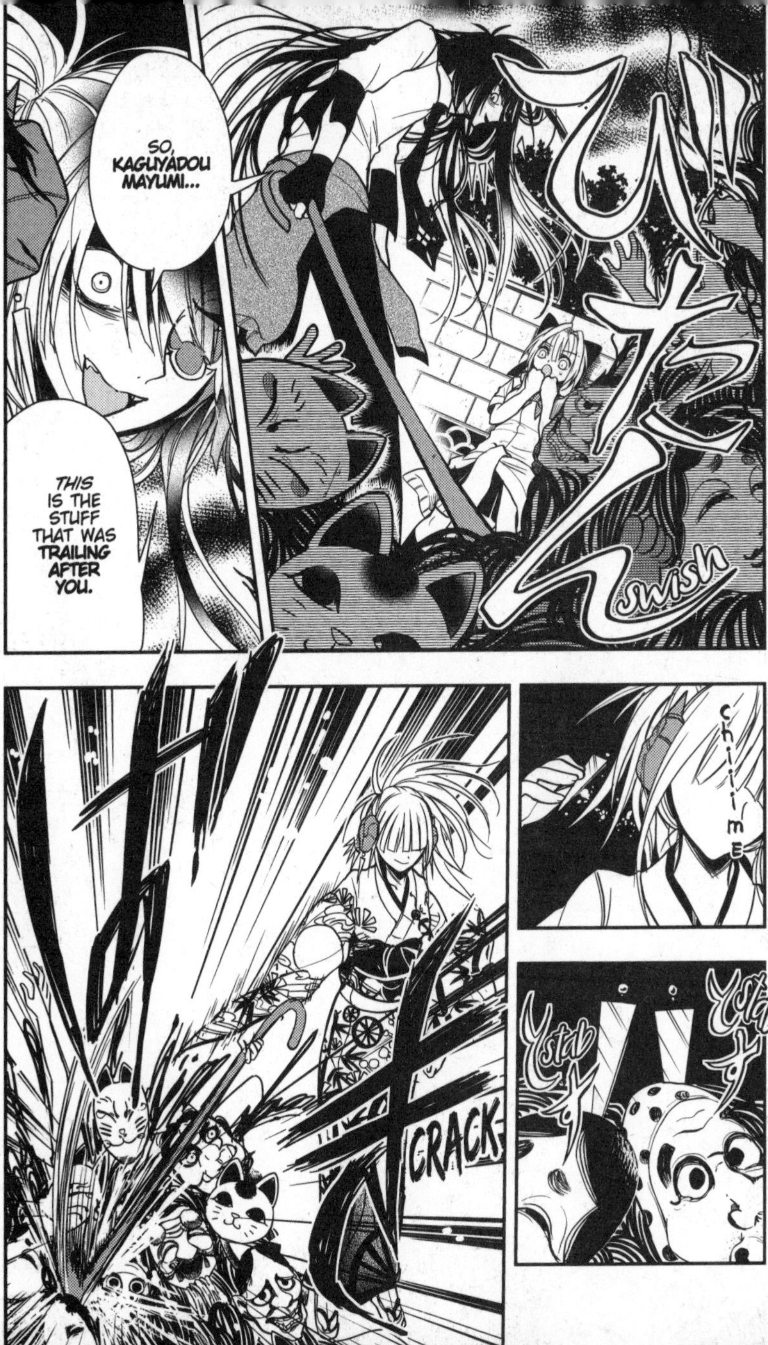
swish
SO, KAGUYADOU MAYUMI...
THIS IS THE STUFF THAT WAS TRAILING AFTER YOU.
chiiiime
stab
stab
CRACK

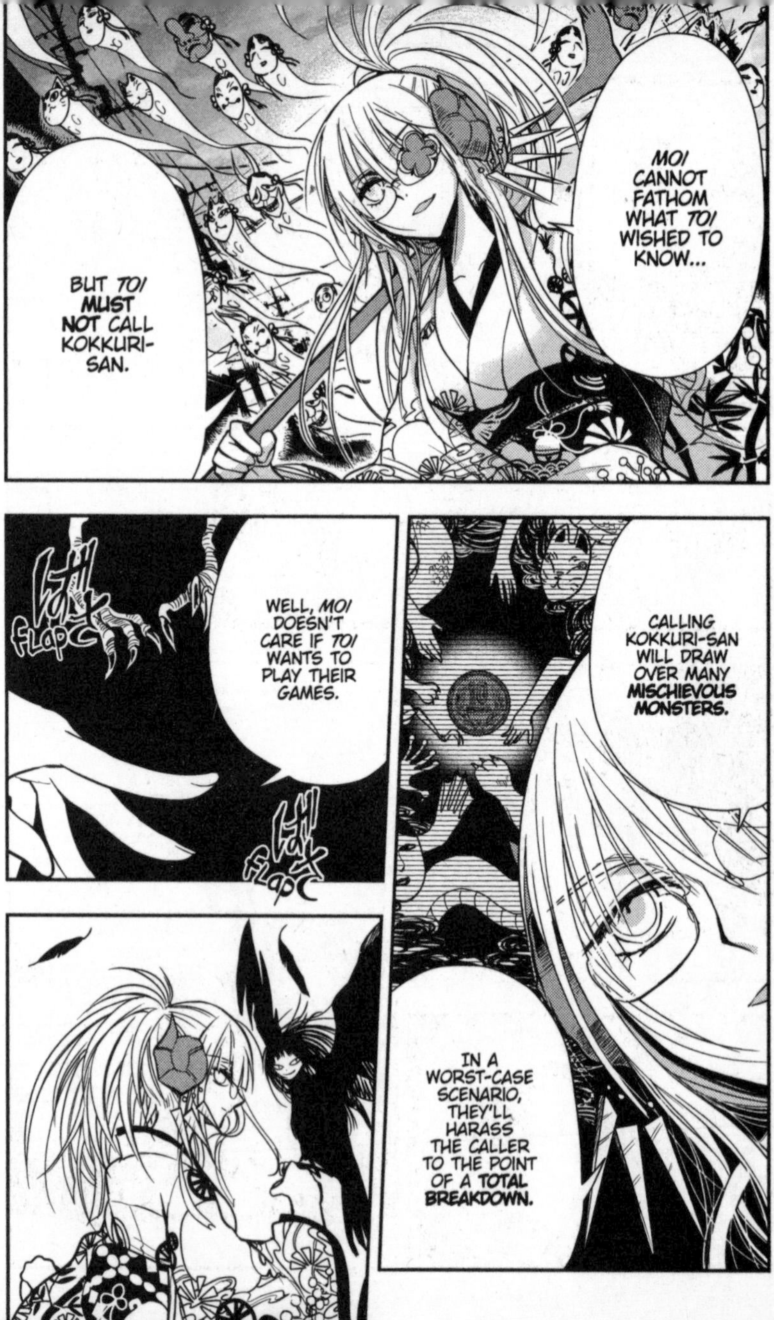
MOI CANNOT FATHOM WHAT *TOI* WISHED TO KNOW...
BUT *TOI* **MUST NOT** CALL KOKKURI-SAN.
CALLING KOKKURI-SAN WILL DRAW OVER MANY **MISCHIEVOUS MONSTERS.**
IN A WORST-CASE SCENARIO, THEY'LL HARASS THE CALLER TO THE POINT OF A **TOTAL BREAKDOWN.**
WELL, *MOI* DOESN'T CARE IF *TOI* WANTS TO PLAY THEIR GAMES.
FLAP
FLAP

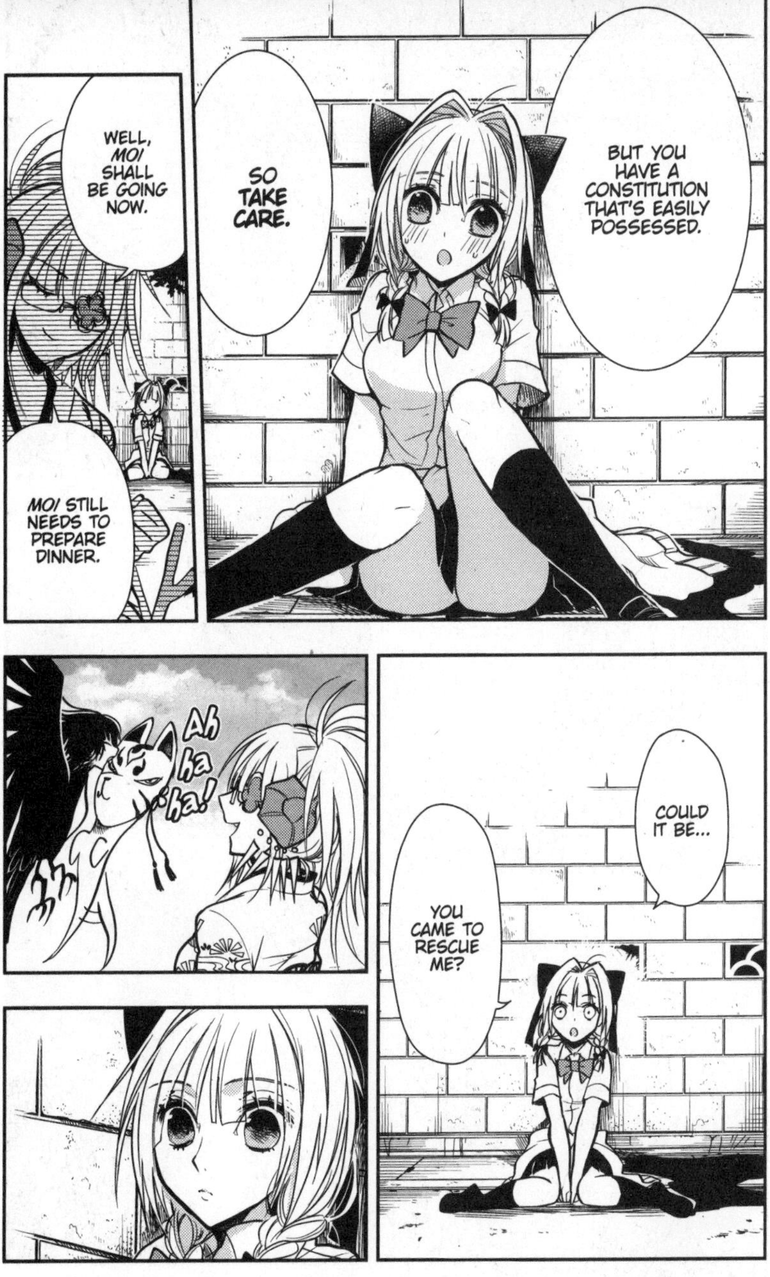
BUT YOU HAVE A CONSTITUTION THAT'S EASILY POSSESSED.
SO TAKE CARE.
WELL, *MOI* SHALL BE GOING NOW.
MOI STILL NEEDS TO PREPARE DINNER.
COULD IT BE...
YOU CAME TO RESCUE ME?
Ah ha ha!

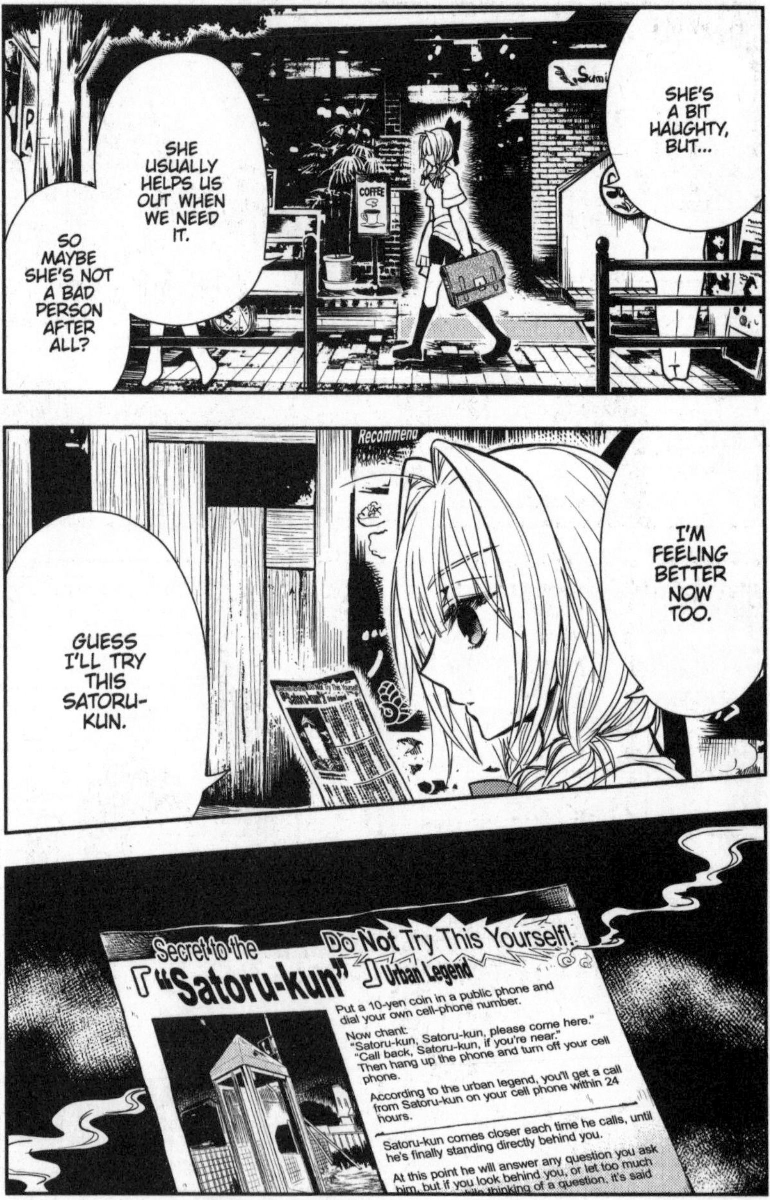
SHE'S A BIT HAUGHTY, BUT...
SHE USUALLY HELPS US OUT WHEN WE NEED IT.
COFFEE
SO MAYBE SHE'S NOT A BAD PERSON AFTER ALL?
I'M FEELING BETTER NOW TOO.
GUESS I'LL TRY THIS SATORU-KUN.
Secret to the 「"Satoru-kun"」 Urban Legend
Do Not Try This Yourself!
Put a 10-yen coin in a public phone and dial your own cell-phone number.
Now chant: "Satoru-kun, Satoru-kun, please come here." "Call back, Satoru-kun, if you're near." Then hang up the phone and turn off your cell phone.
According to the urban legend, you'll get a call from Satoru-kun on your cell phone within 24 hours.
Satoru-kun comes closer each time he calls, until he's finally standing directly behind you.
At this point he will answer any question you ask him, but if you look behind you, or let too much

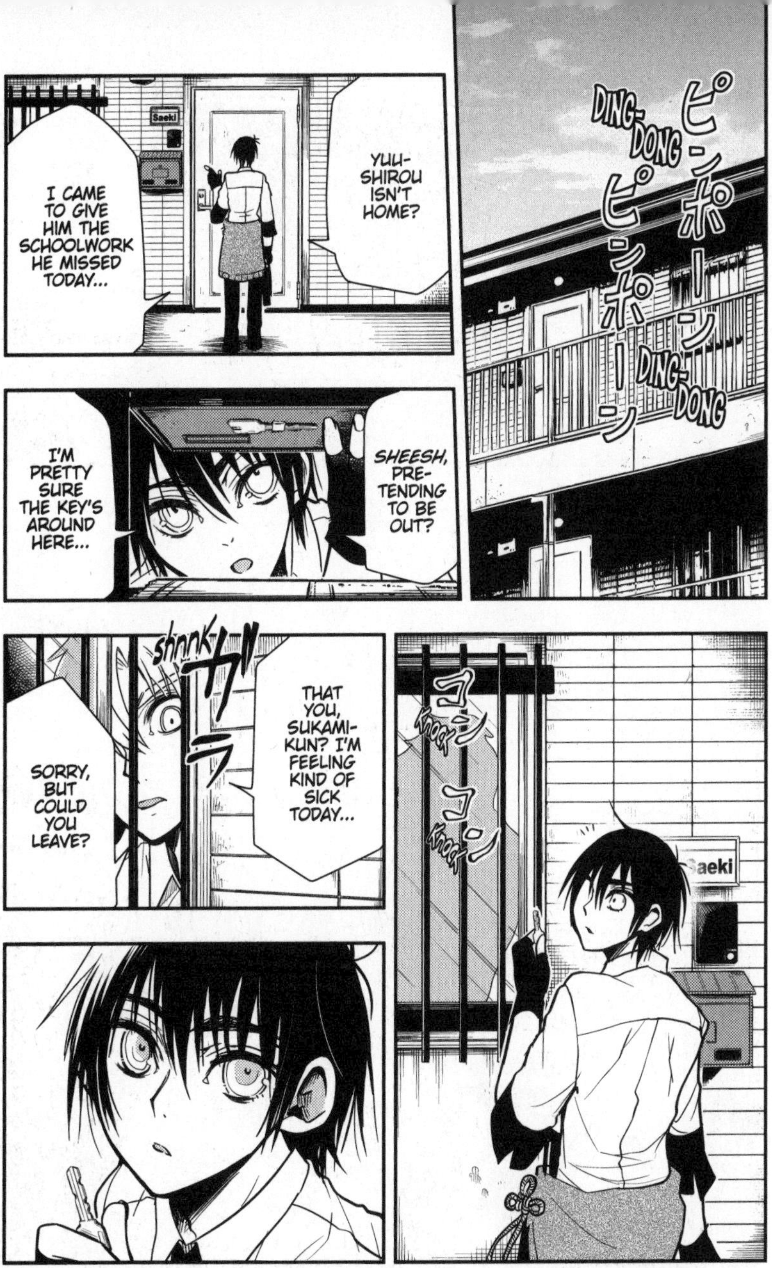
ピーンポーン
DING-DONG
ピンポーン
DING-DONG
YUU-SHIROU ISN'T HOME?
I CAME TO GIVE HIM THE SCHOOLWORK HE MISSED TODAY...
SHEESH, PRE-TENDING TO BE OUT?
I'M PRETTY SURE THE KEY'S AROUND HERE...
Saeki
コン
Knock
コン
Knock
shrnk
ガラ
THAT YOU, SUKAMI-KUN? I'M FEELING KIND OF SICK TODAY...
SORRY, BUT COULD YOU LEAVE?

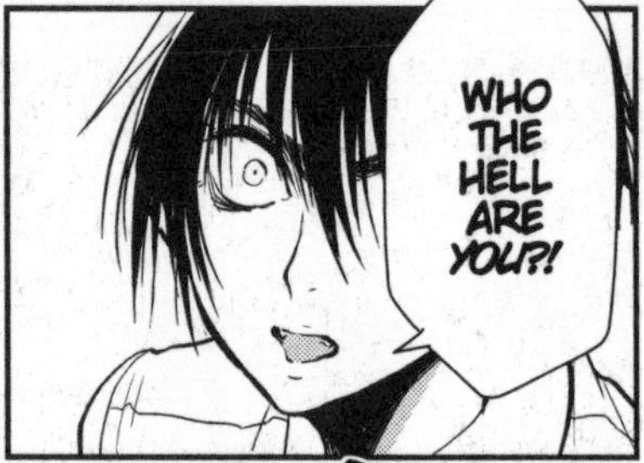
WHO THE HELL ARE YOU?!
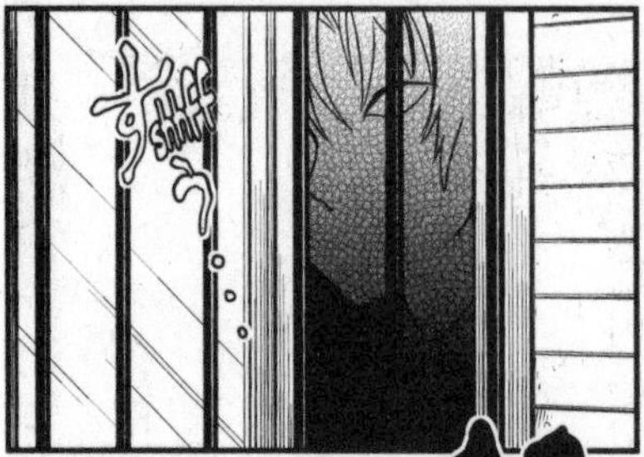
sniff
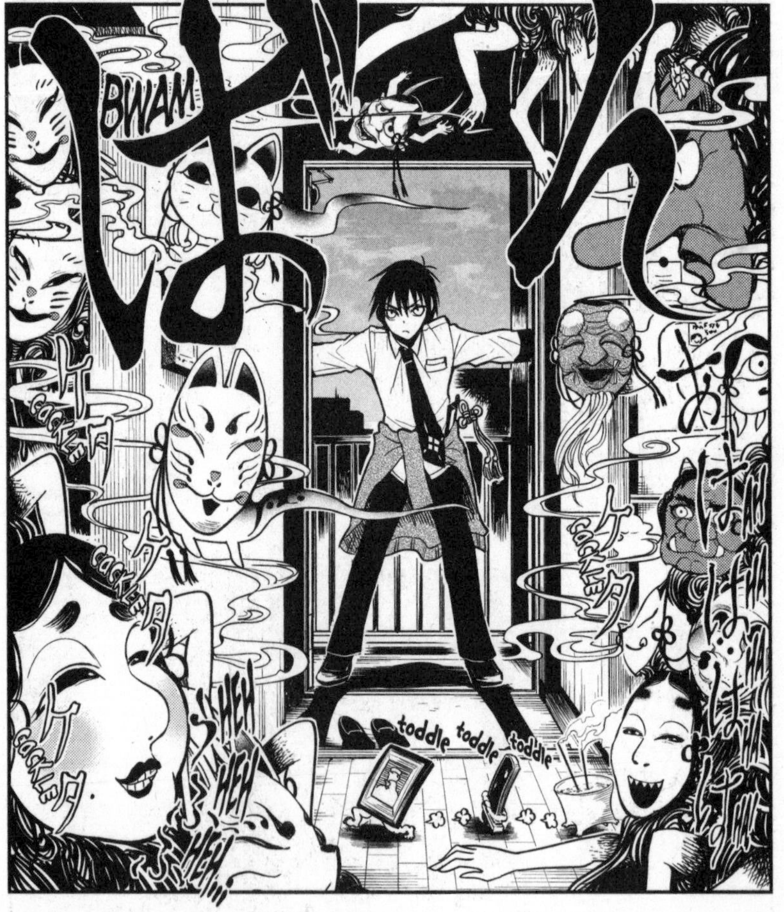
BWAM
cackle
cackle
cackle
cackle
toddle toddle toddle
HEH HEH HEH
HA HA HA HA

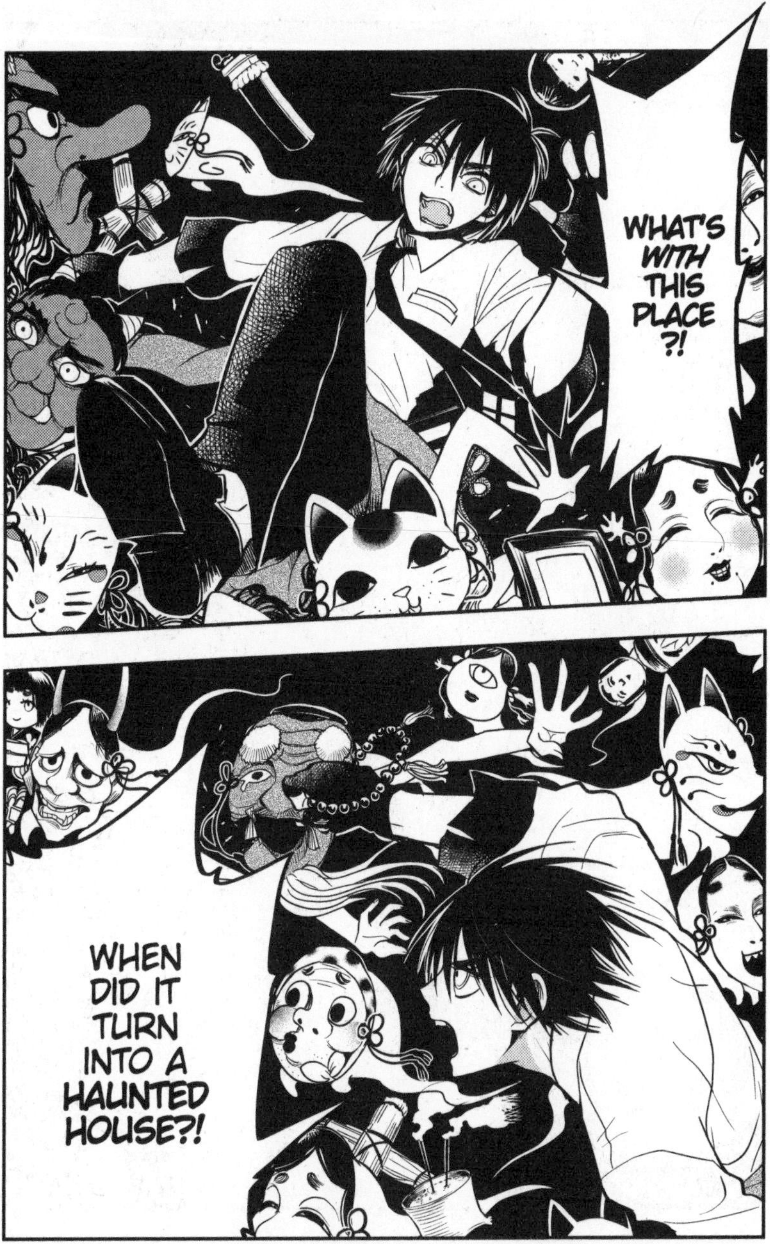
WHAT'S *WITH* THIS PLACE ?!
WHEN DID IT TURN INTO A HAUNTED HOUSE?!

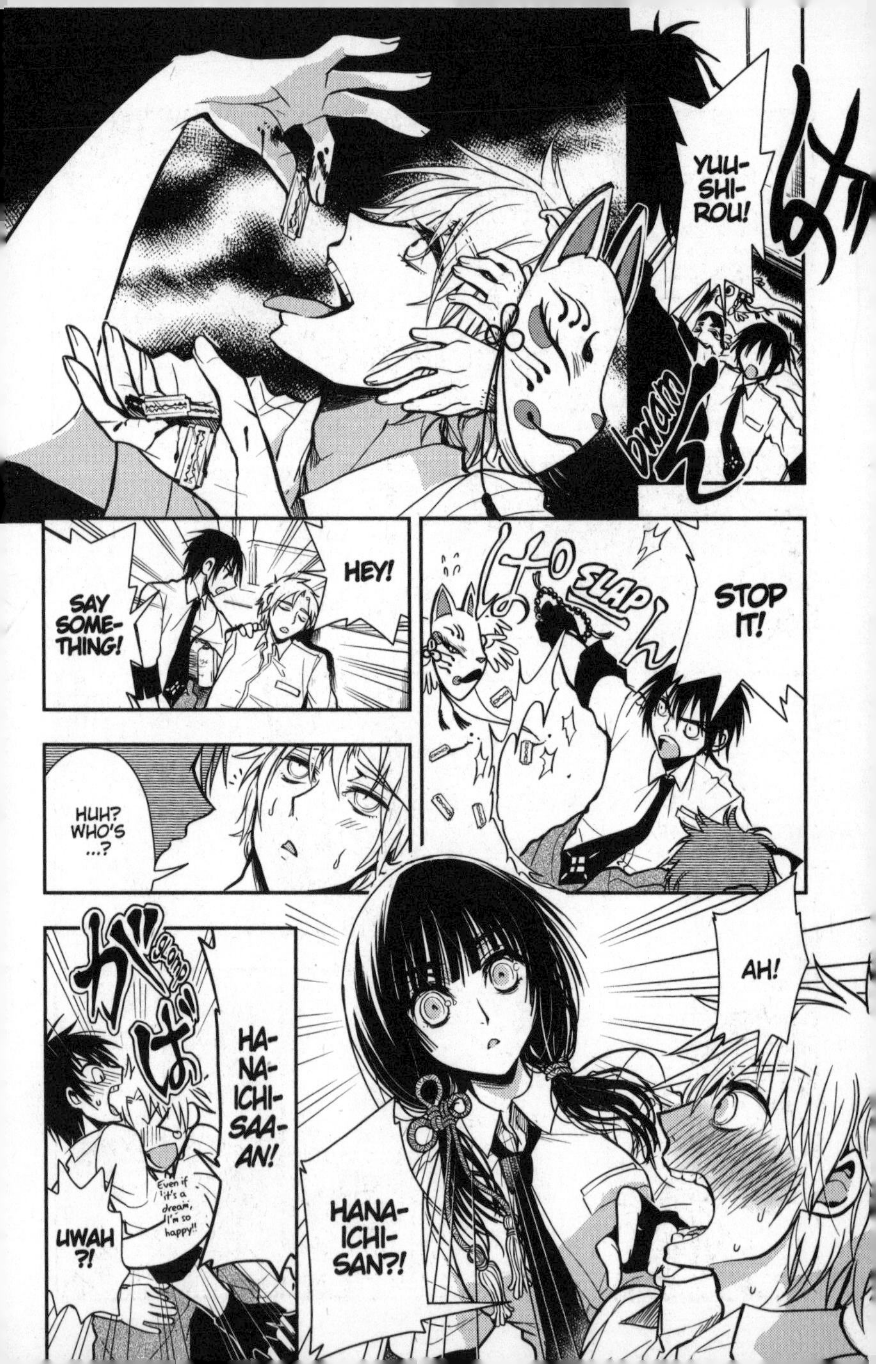
YUU-SHI-ROU!
bwam
STOP IT!
SLAP
HEY!
SAY SOME-THING!
HUH? WHO'S ...?
AH!
HANA-ICHI-SAN?!
HANA-ICHI-SAAAN!
glomp
Even if it's a dream, I'm so happy!!
UWAH?!

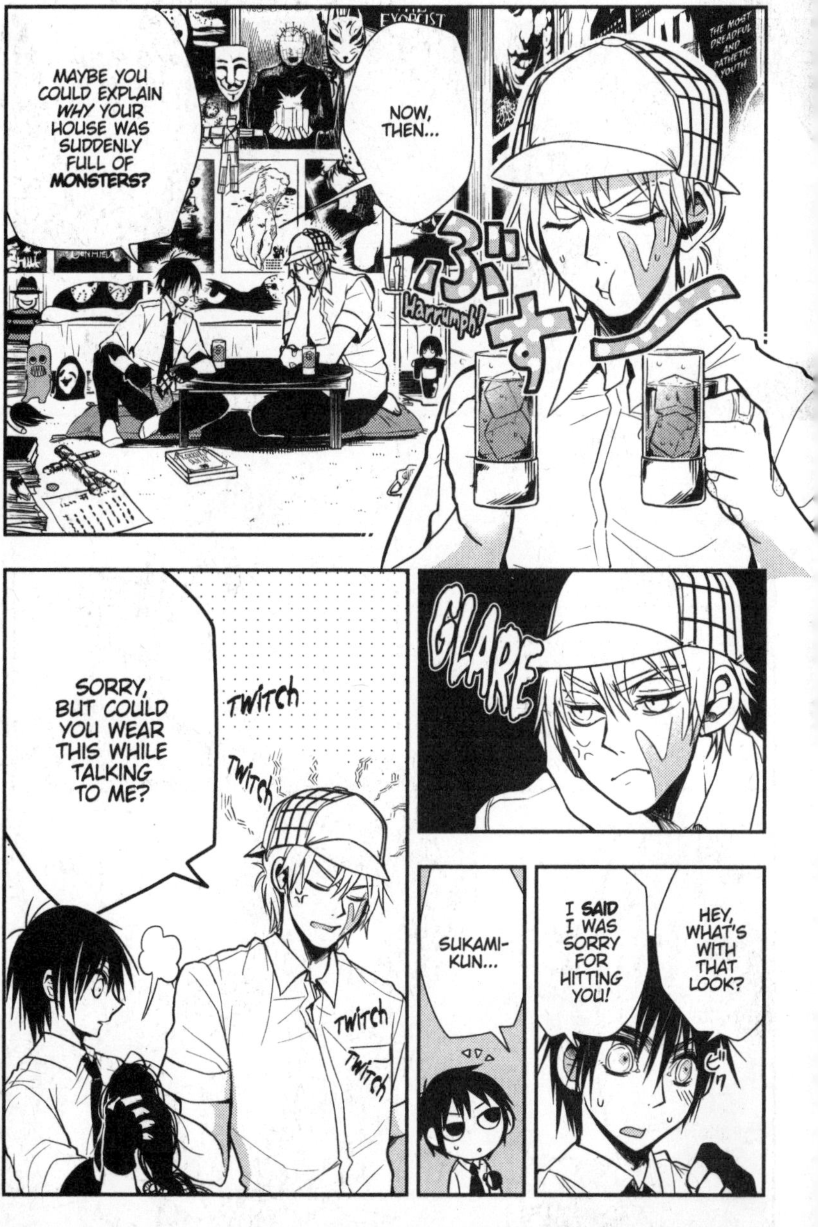
THE MOST DREADFUL AND PATHETIC YOUTH
EXORCIST
NOW, THEN...
MAYBE YOU COULD EXPLAIN *WHY* YOUR HOUSE WAS SUDDENLY FULL OF **MONSTERS?**
Harrumph!
GLARE
HEY, WHAT'S WITH THAT LOOK?
I **SAID** I WAS SORRY FOR HITTING YOU!
SUKAMI-KUN...
TWITCH
TWITCH
SORRY, BUT COULD YOU WEAR THIS WHILE TALKING TO ME?
TWITCH
TWITCH

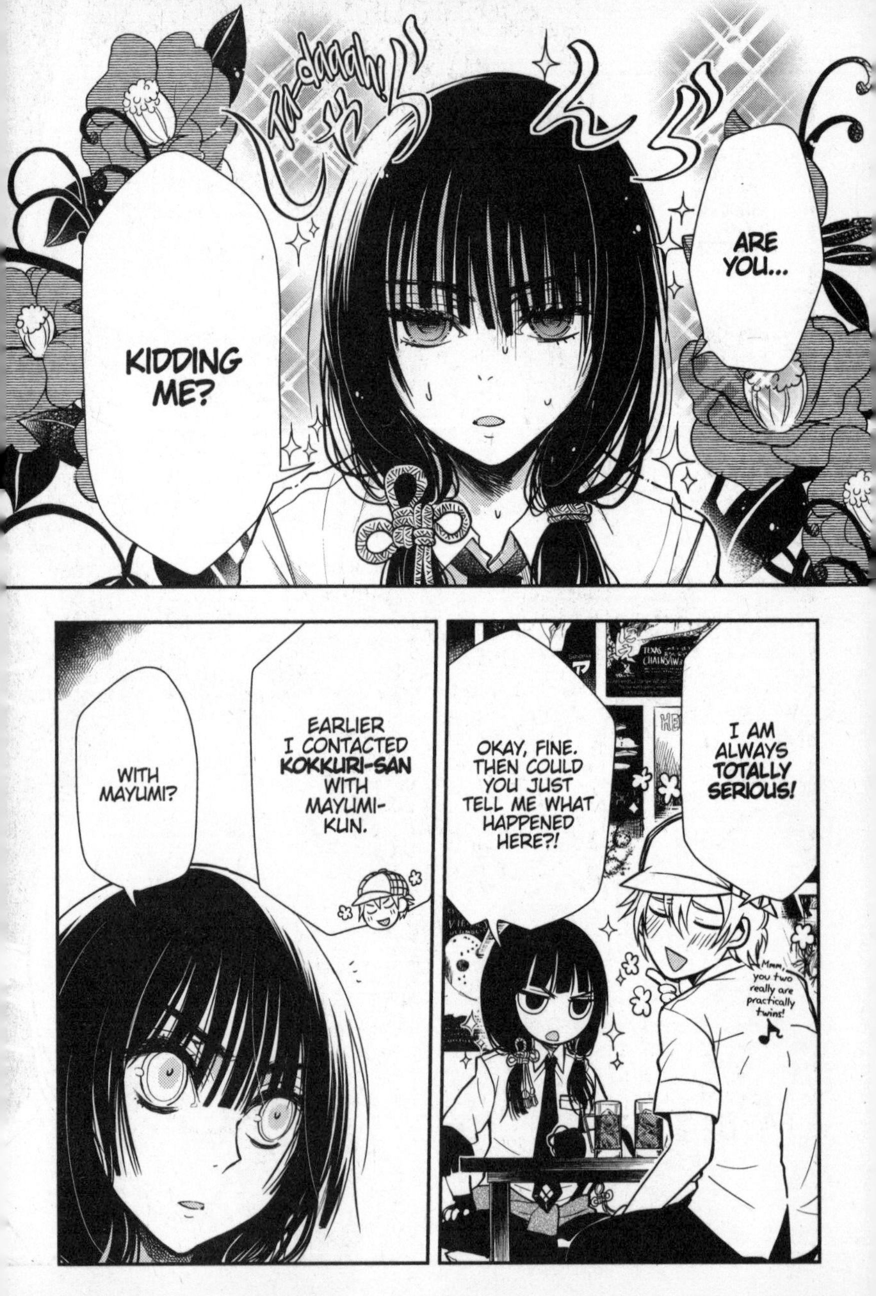
Ta-daaah!
ARE YOU...
KIDDING ME?
I AM ALWAYS TOTALLY SERIOUS!
OKAY, FINE. THEN COULD YOU JUST TELL ME WHAT HAPPENED HERE?!
Mmm, you two really are practically twins!
EARLIER I CONTACTED KOKKURI-SAN WITH MAYUMI-KUN.
WITH MAYUMI?

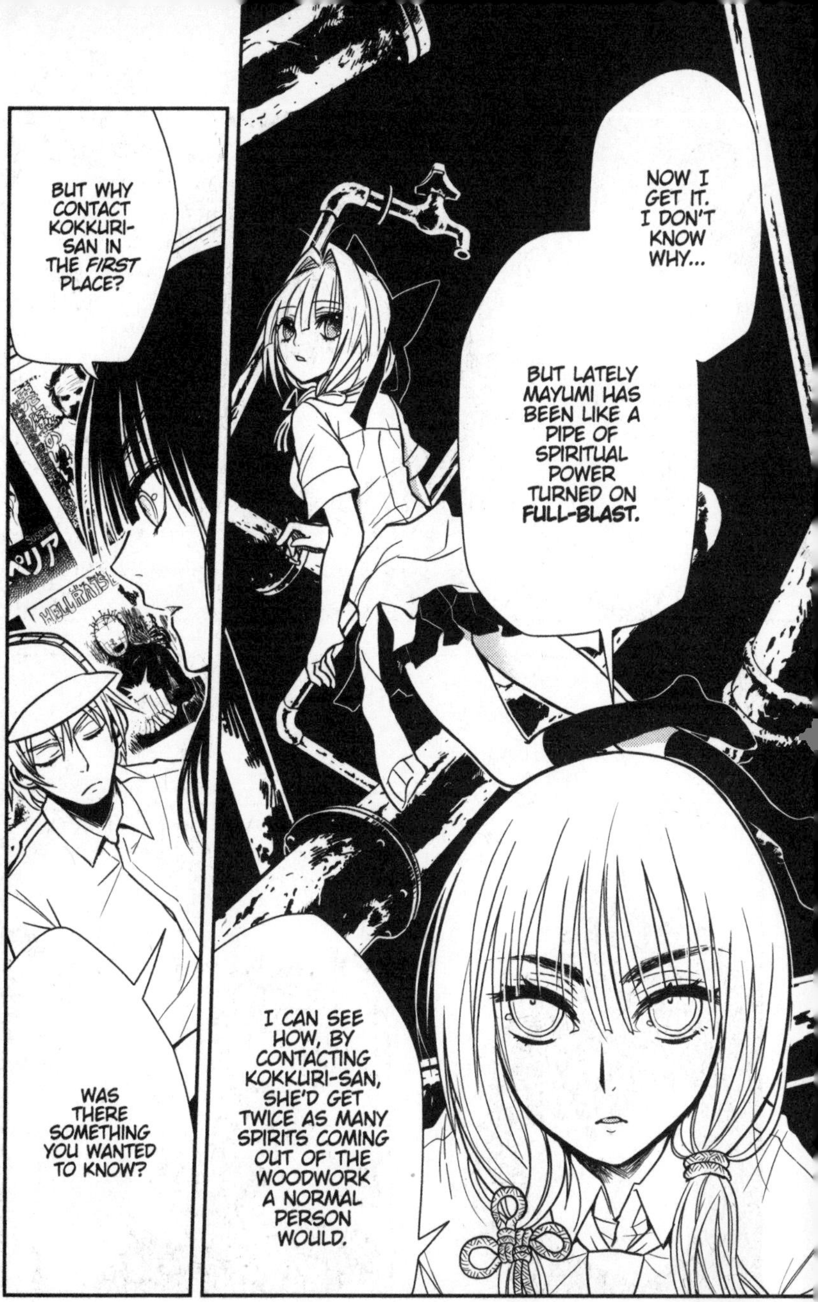
NOW I GET IT. I DON'T KNOW WHY...
BUT LATELY MAYUMI HAS BEEN LIKE A PIPE OF SPIRITUAL POWER TURNED ON **FULL-BLAST.**
I CAN SEE HOW, BY CONTACTING KOKKURI-SAN, SHE'D GET TWICE AS MANY SPIRITS COMING OUT OF THE WOODWORK A NORMAL PERSON WOULD.
BUT WHY CONTACT KOKKURI-SAN IN THE *FIRST* PLACE?
WAS THERE SOMETHING YOU WANTED TO KNOW?

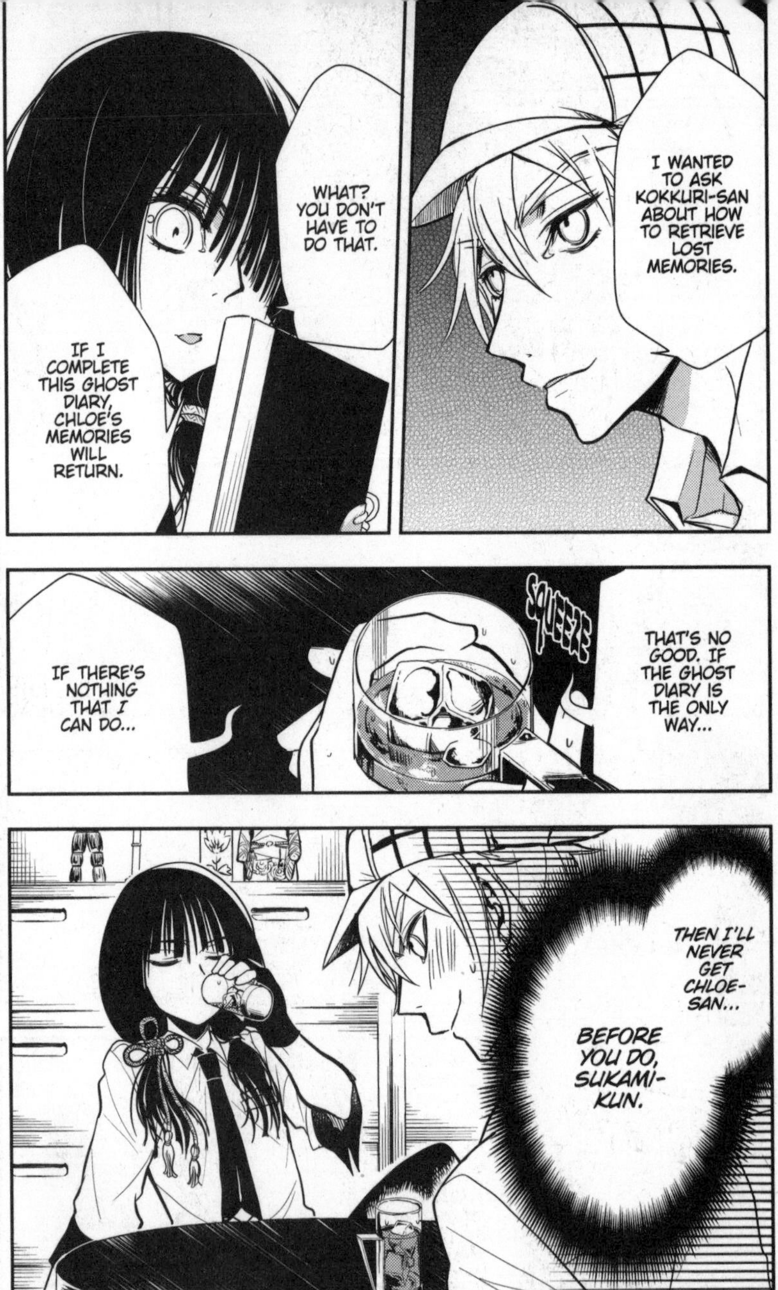
I WANTED TO ASK KOKKURI-SAN ABOUT HOW TO RETRIEVE LOST MEMORIES.
WHAT? YOU DON'T HAVE TO DO THAT.
IF I COMPLETE THIS GHOST DIARY, CHLOE'S MEMORIES WILL RETURN.
SQUEEZE
THAT'S NO GOOD. IF THE GHOST DIARY IS THE ONLY WAY...
IF THERE'S NOTHING THAT *I* CAN DO...
THEN I'LL NEVER GET CHLOE-SAN...
BEFORE YOU DO, SUKAMI-KUN.

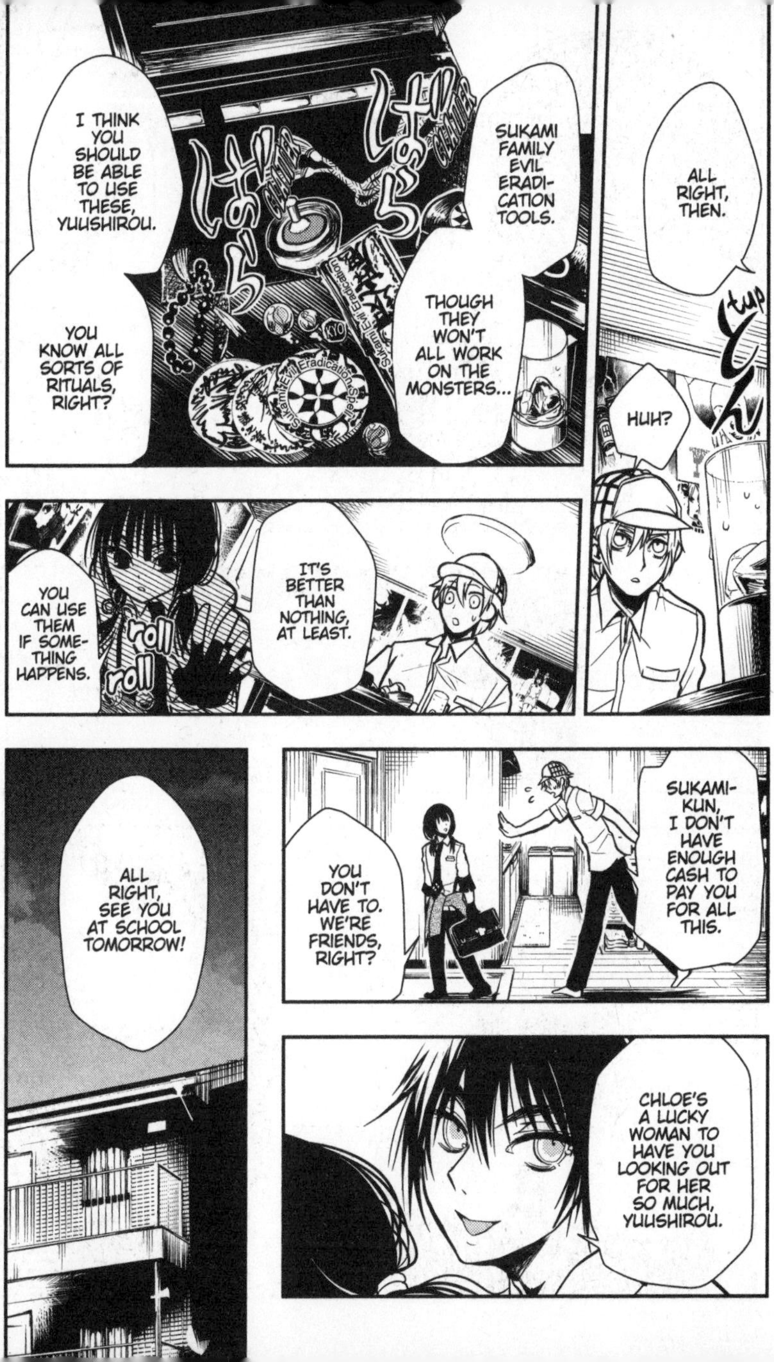
ALL RIGHT, THEN.
tup
HUH?
SUKAMI FAMILY EVIL ERADICATION TOOLS.
THOUGH THEY WON'T ALL WORK ON THE MONSTERS...
I THINK YOU SHOULD BE ABLE TO USE THESE, YUUSHIROU.
YOU KNOW ALL SORTS OF RITUALS, RIGHT?
IT'S BETTER THAN NOTHING, AT LEAST.
YOU CAN USE THEM IF SOMETHING HAPPENS.
roll roll
SUKAMI-KUN, I DON'T HAVE ENOUGH CASH TO PAY YOU FOR ALL THIS.
YOU DON'T HAVE TO. WE'RE FRIENDS, RIGHT?
CHLOE'S A LUCKY WOMAN TO HAVE YOU LOOKING OUT FOR HER SO MUCH, YUUSHIROU.
ALL RIGHT, SEE YOU AT SCHOOL TOMORROW!

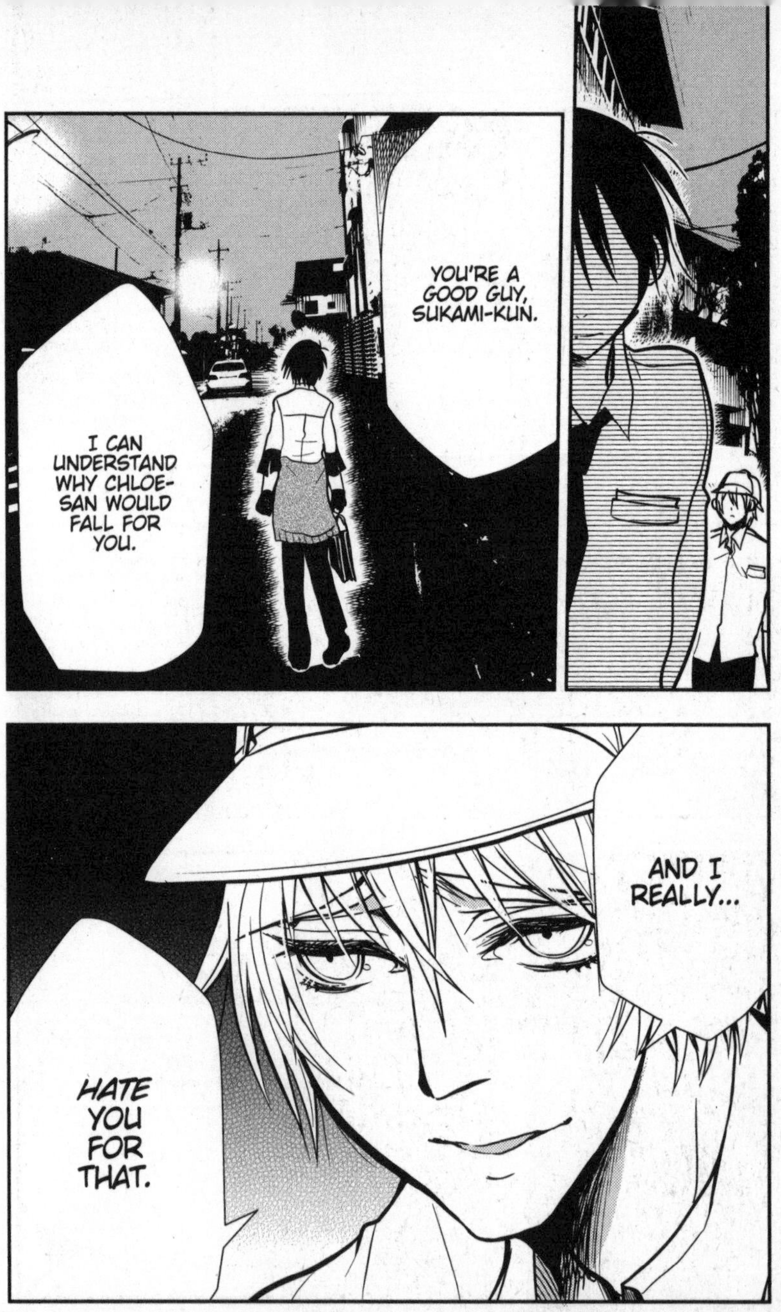
YOU'RE A GOOD GUY, SUKAMI-KUN.
I CAN UNDERSTAND WHY CHLOE-SAN WOULD FALL FOR YOU.
AND I REALLY...
HATE YOU FOR THAT.

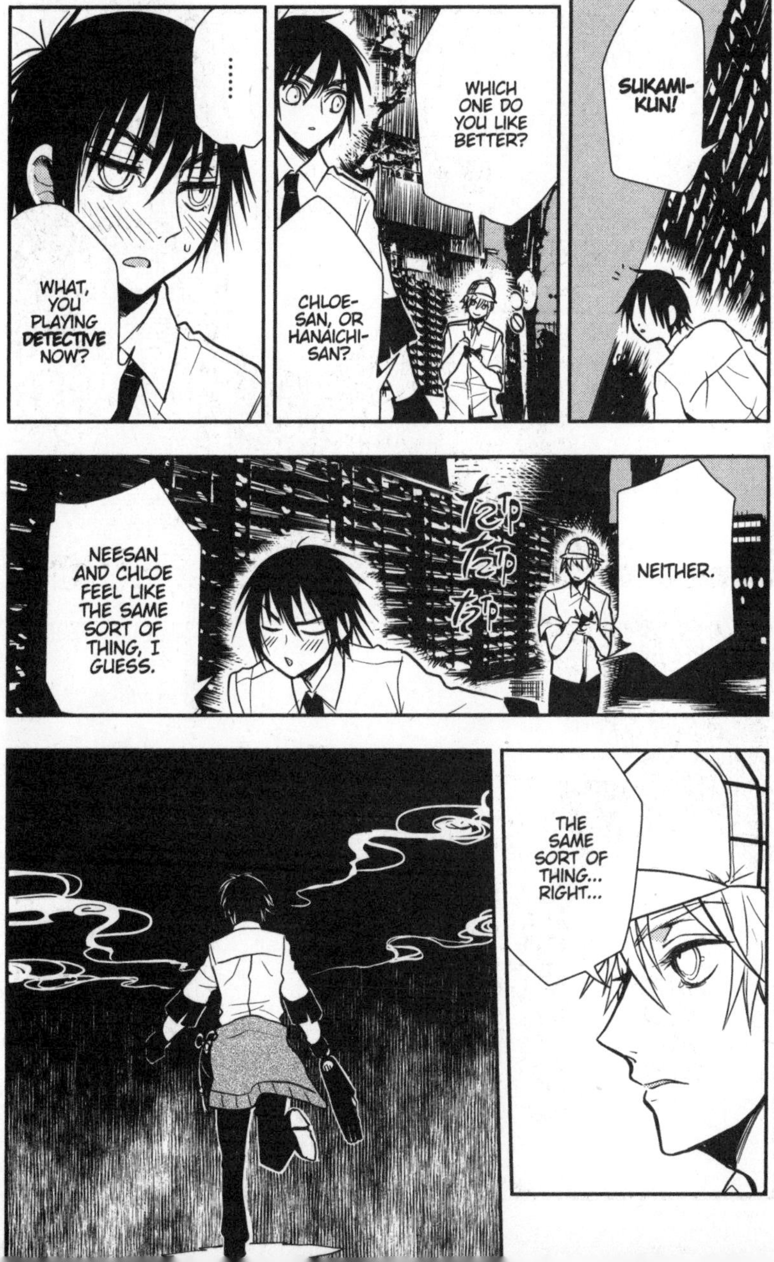
SUKAMI-KUN!
WHICH ONE DO YOU LIKE BETTER?
CHLOE-SAN, OR HANAICHI-SAN?
......
WHAT, YOU PLAYING DETECTIVE NOW?
NEITHER.
NEESAN AND CHLOE FEEL LIKE THE SAME SORT OF THING, I GUESS.
THE SAME SORT OF THING... RIGHT...

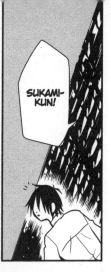

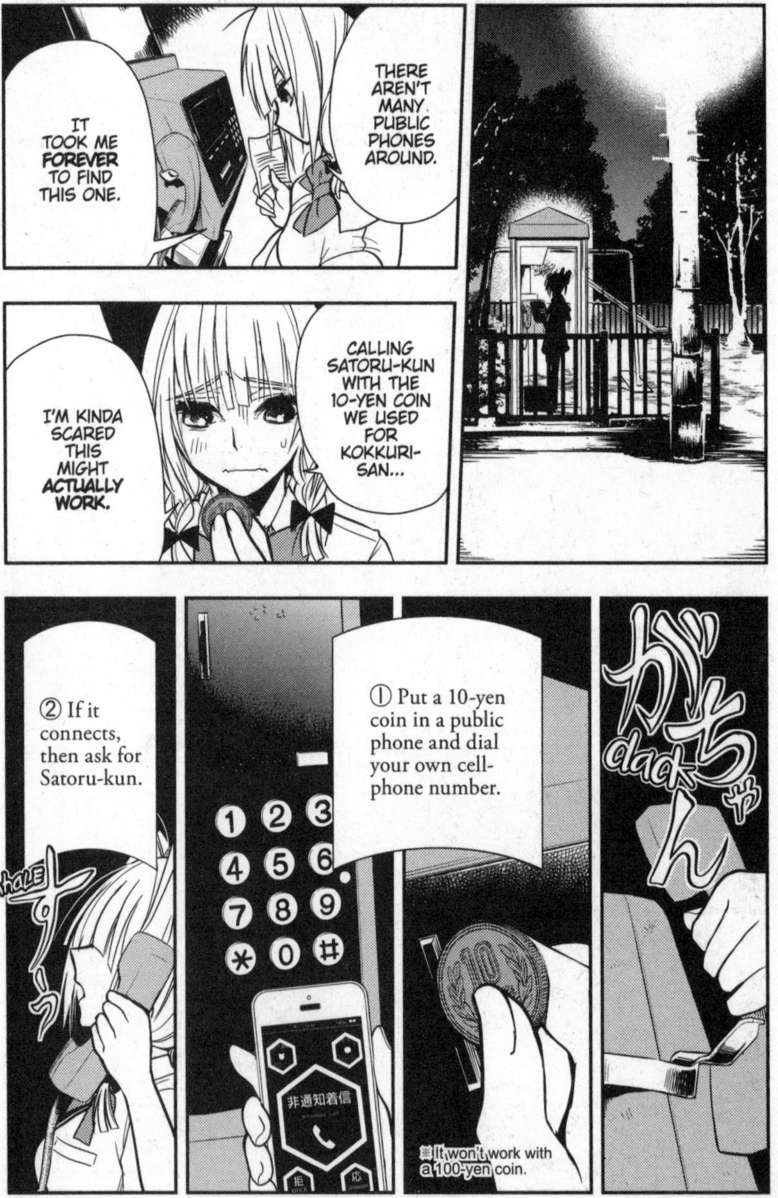
THERE AREN'T MANY PUBLIC PHONES AROUND.
IT TOOK ME **FOREVER** TO FIND THIS ONE.
CALLING SATORU-KUN WITH THE 10-YEN COIN WE USED FOR KOKKURI-SAN...
I'M KINDA SCARED THIS MIGHT **ACTUALLY WORK.**
がちゃん
clack
※It won't work with a 100-yen coin.
① Put a 10-yen coin in a public phone and dial your own cell-phone number.
非通知着信
② If it connects, then ask for Satoru-kun.
inhale
すーっ

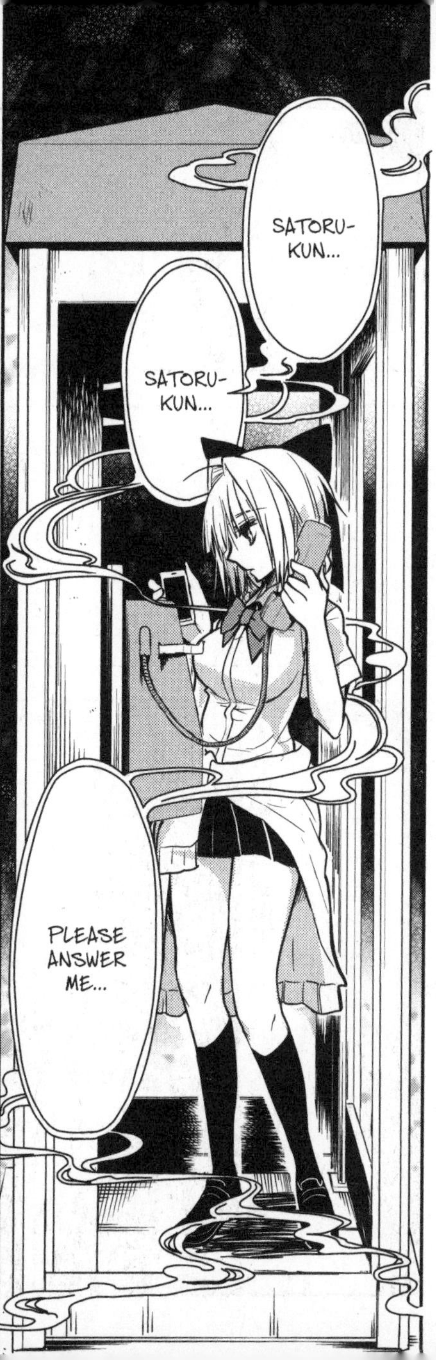
SATORU-KUN...
SATORU-KUN...
PLEASE ANSWER ME...

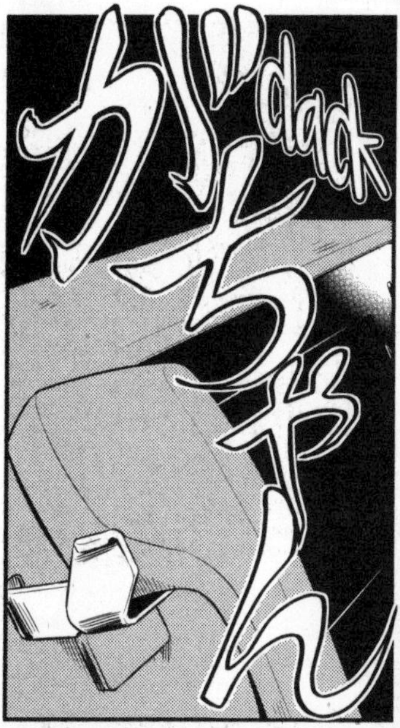
ガちゃん
clack

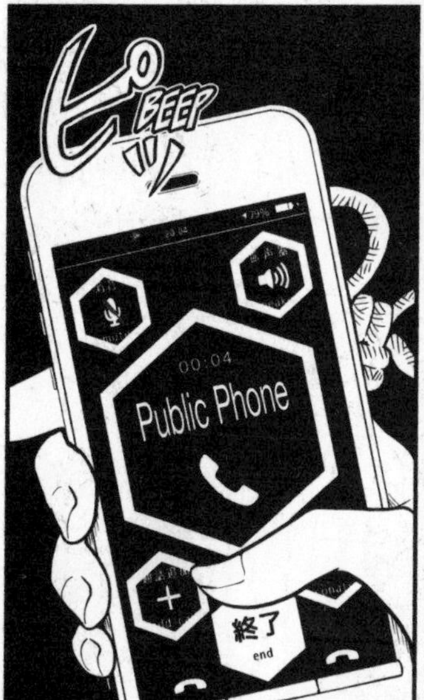
ピッ
BEEP
00:04
Public Phone
終了
end

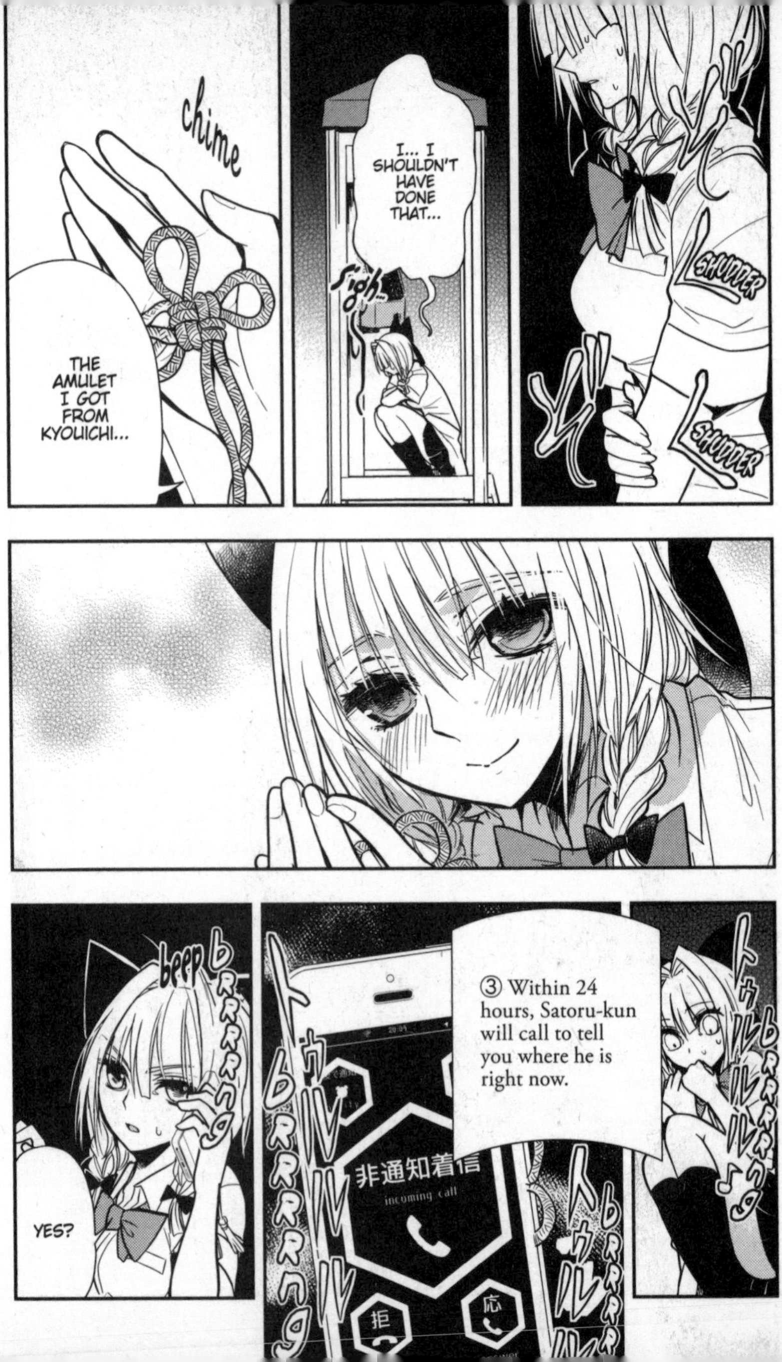
SHUDDER
SHUDDER
I... I SHOULDN'T HAVE DONE THAT...
sigh...
chime
THE AMULET I GOT FROM KYOUICHI...
brrrrng
トゥルル
③ Within 24 hours, Satoru-kun will call to tell you where he is right now.
非通知着信
incoming call
拒
応
brrrrng
beep
YES?

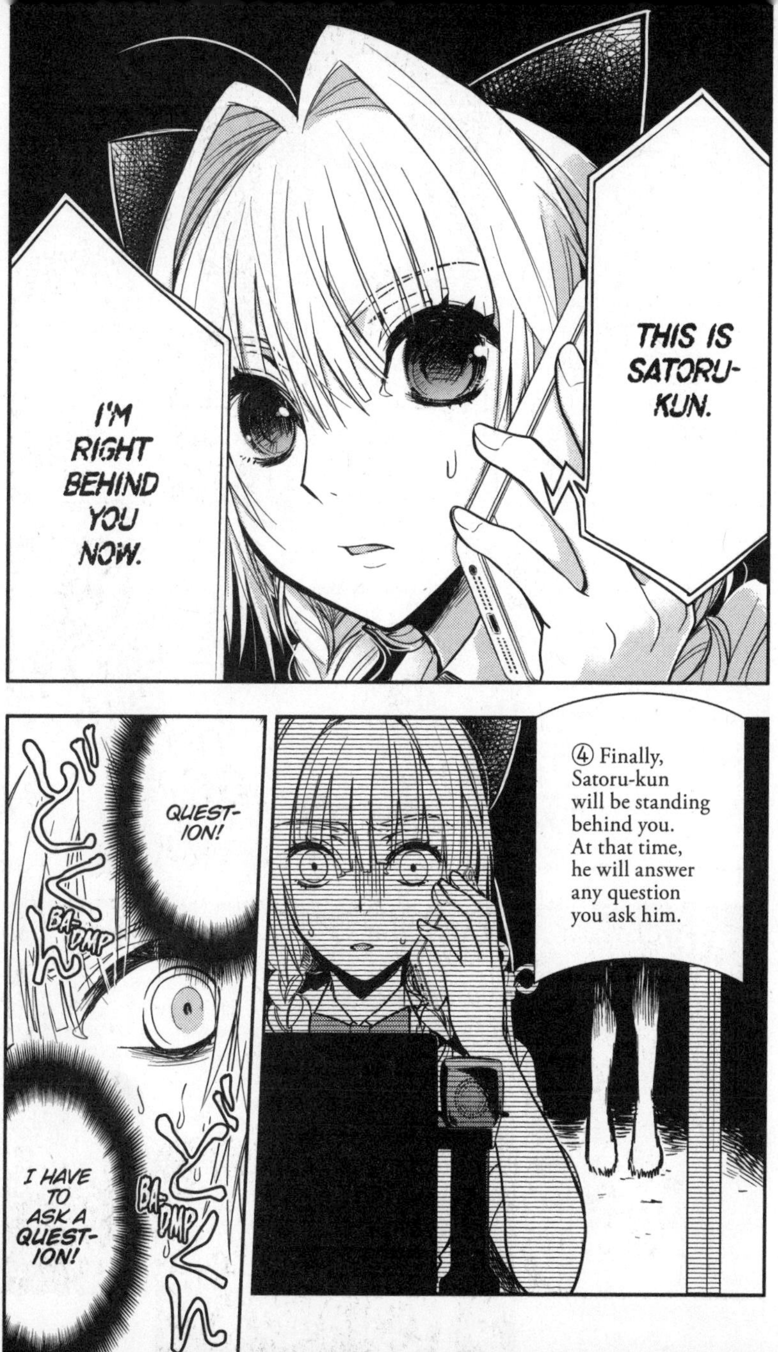
THIS IS SATORU-KUN.
I'M RIGHT BEHIND YOU NOW.
④ Finally, Satoru-kun will be standing behind you. At that time, he will answer any question you ask him.
QUESTION-ION!
BA-DMP
I HAVE TO ASK A QUESTION!
BA-DMP

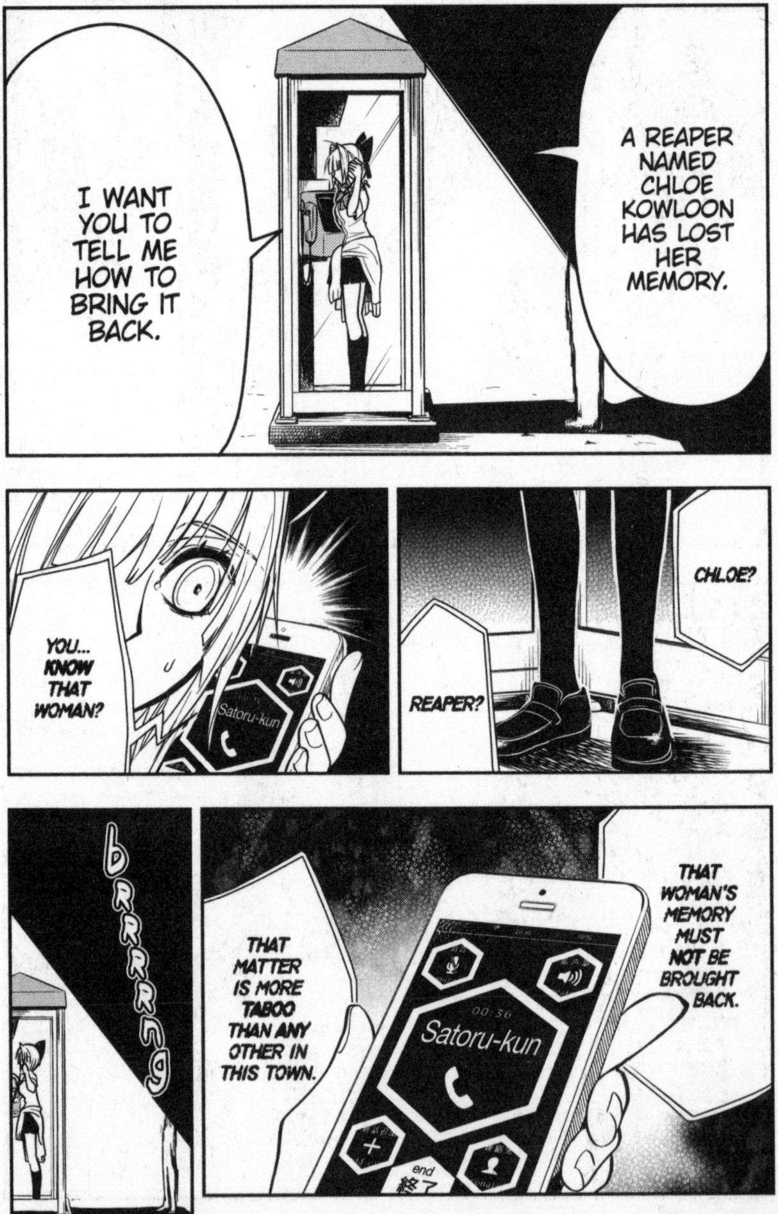
A REAPER NAMED CHLOE KOWLOON HAS LOST HER MEMORY.
I WANT YOU TO TELL ME HOW TO BRING IT BACK.
CHLOE?
REAPER?
YOU... KNOW THAT WOMAN?
Satoru-kun
THAT WOMAN'S MEMORY MUST NOT BE BROUGHT BACK.
THAT MATTER IS MORE TABOO THAN ANY OTHER IN THIS TOWN.
00:36
Satoru-kun
end
終了
brrrrng

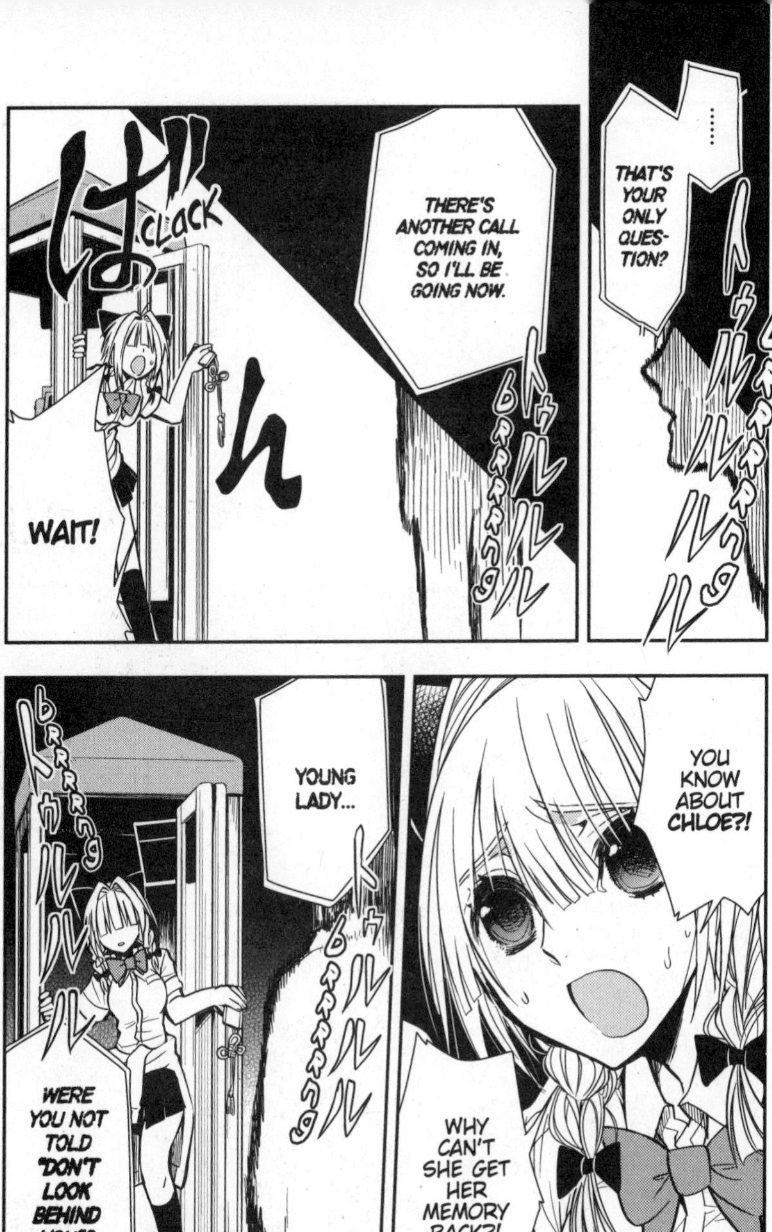
......
THAT'S YOUR ONLY QUES-TION?
BRRRRRNG
THERE'S ANOTHER CALL COMING IN, SO I'LL BE GOING NOW.
BRRRRRNG
CLACK
WAIT!
YOU KNOW ABOUT CHLOE?!
WHY CAN'T SHE GET HER MEMORY BACK?!
YOUNG LADY...
BRRRRRNG
BRRRRNG
WERE YOU NOT TOLD "DON'T LOOK BEHIND YOU"?

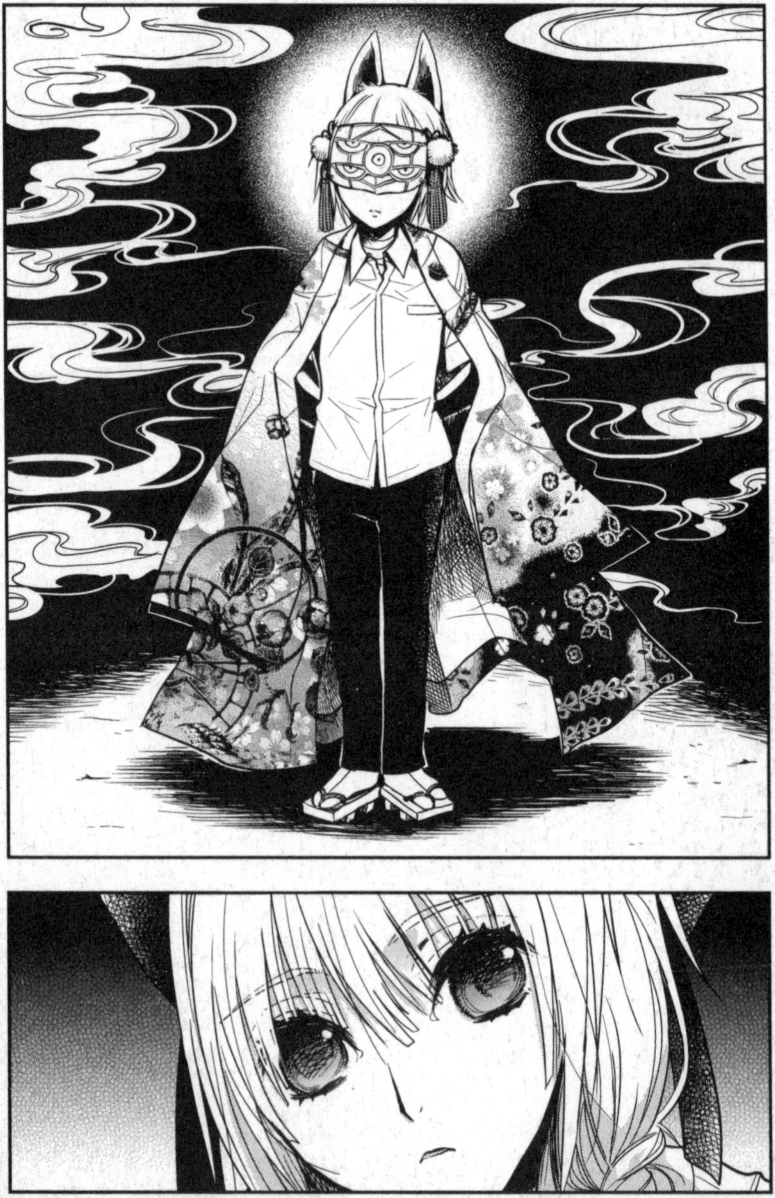

To Be Continued...

K a i d a n n i k k i

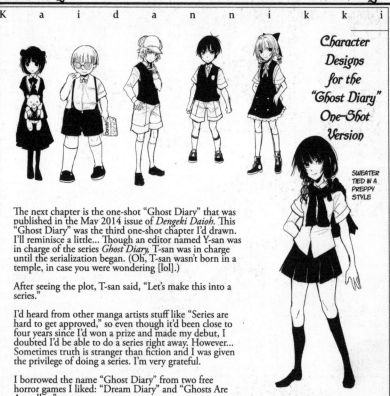

Character Designs for the "Ghost Diary" One-Shot Version

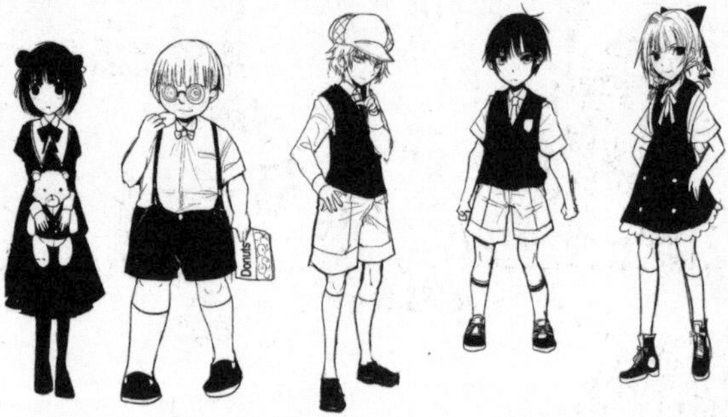
Donuts

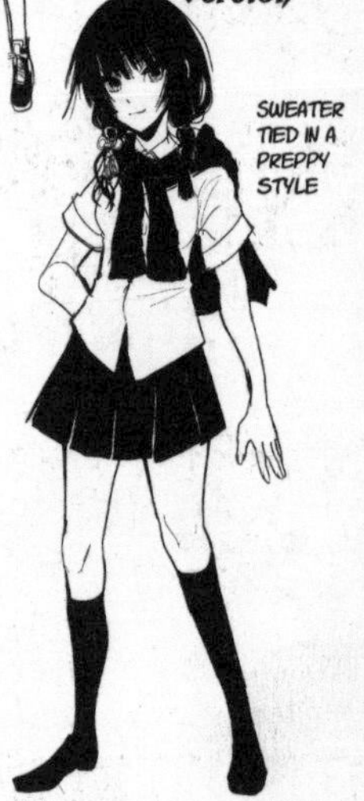
SWEATER TIED IN A PREPPY STYLE

The next chapter is the one-shot "Ghost Diary" that was published in the May 2014 issue of *Dengeki Daioh*. This "Ghost Diary" was the third one-shot chapter I'd drawn. I'll reminisce a little... Though an editor named Y-san was in charge of the series *Ghost Diary*, T-san was in charge until the serialization began. (Oh, T-san wasn't born in a temple, in case you were wondering [lol].)

After seeing the plot, T-san said, "Let's make this into a series."

I'd heard from other manga artists stuff like "Series are hard to get approved," so even though it'd been close to four years since I'd won a prize and made my debut, I doubted I'd be able to do a series right away. However... Sometimes truth is stranger than fiction and I was given the privilege of doing a series. I'm very grateful.

I borrowed the name "Ghost Diary" from two free horror games I liked: "Dream Diary" and "Ghosts Are Actually..."

"Dream Diary" is a game where a girl walks around in an eerie dream. It is a wonderful work with an eerie worldview and charming characters. The music is very lovely too. It's very eerie (lol).

"Ghosts Are Actually..." is a horror adventure game that made use of a particular quality—not showing visuals for its character. In it, you get different developments and characters appearing depending on your choices, even though it's the same story. These two can be played online even now, I think. I highly recommend these free horror games, so please try them out.

After hearing the one-shot version of "Ghost Diary" was to be included in Volume 2, I tried taking out the sample magazine from that time. Seeing it this way, I'm surprised that the characters' personalities are actually very similiar to how they are now (lol).

Since I wanted it to be read as a historical document from that time, I haven't made any revisions to it or touched it up. Now then, please enjoy my half-baked "Ghost Diary" one-shot chapter as is.

Today's Theme: Ghost Diary

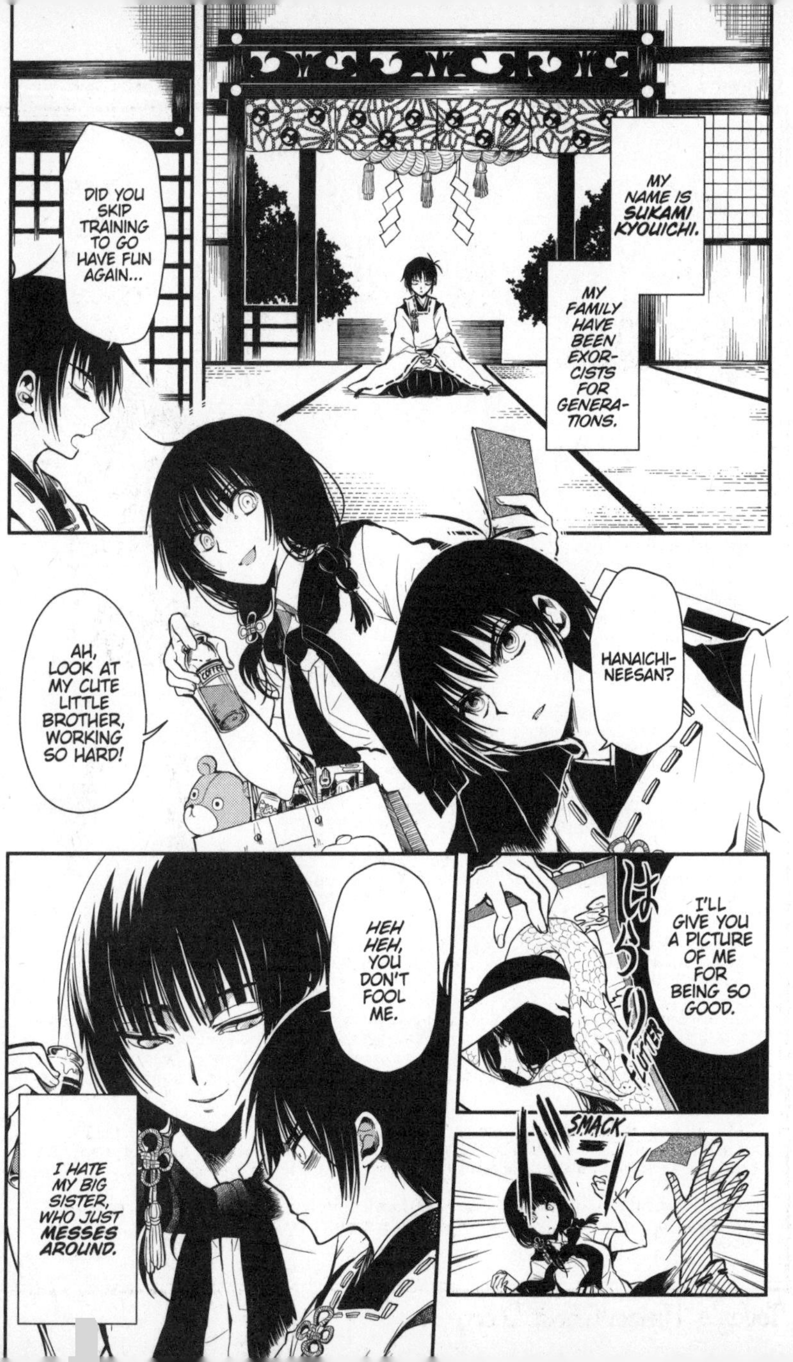
MY NAME IS SUKAMI KYOUICHI.
MY FAMILY HAVE BEEN EXORCISTS FOR GENERATIONS.
DID YOU SKIP TRAINING TO GO HAVE FUN AGAIN...
HANAICHI-NEESAN?
AH, LOOK AT MY CUTE LITTLE BROTHER, WORKING SO HARD!
I'LL GIVE YOU A PICTURE OF ME FOR BEING SO GOOD.
はらり
FLUTTER
SMACK
HEH HEH, YOU DON'T FOOL ME.
I HATE MY BIG SISTER, WHO JUST MESSES AROUND.

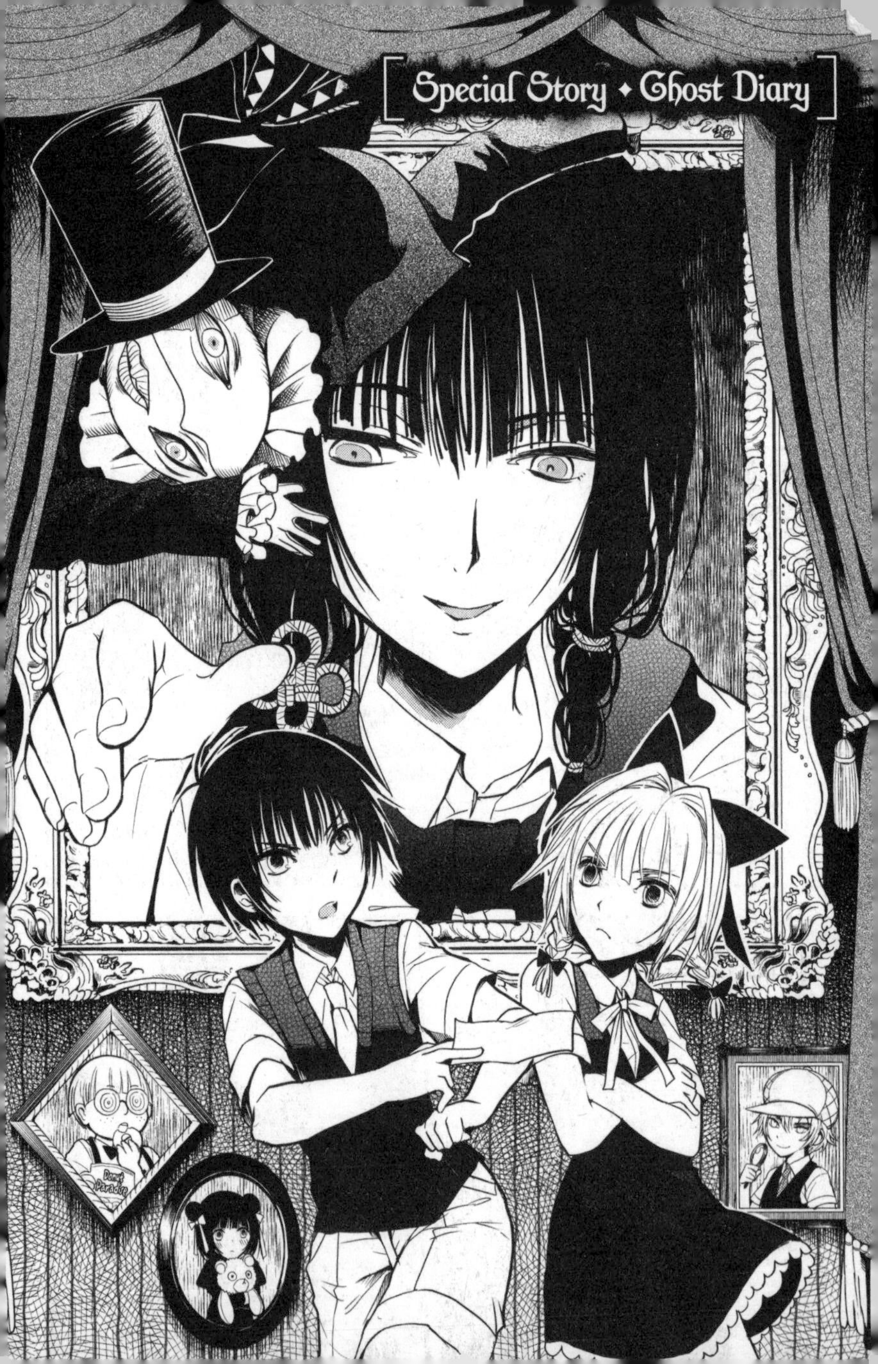
Special Story ◆ Ghost Diary

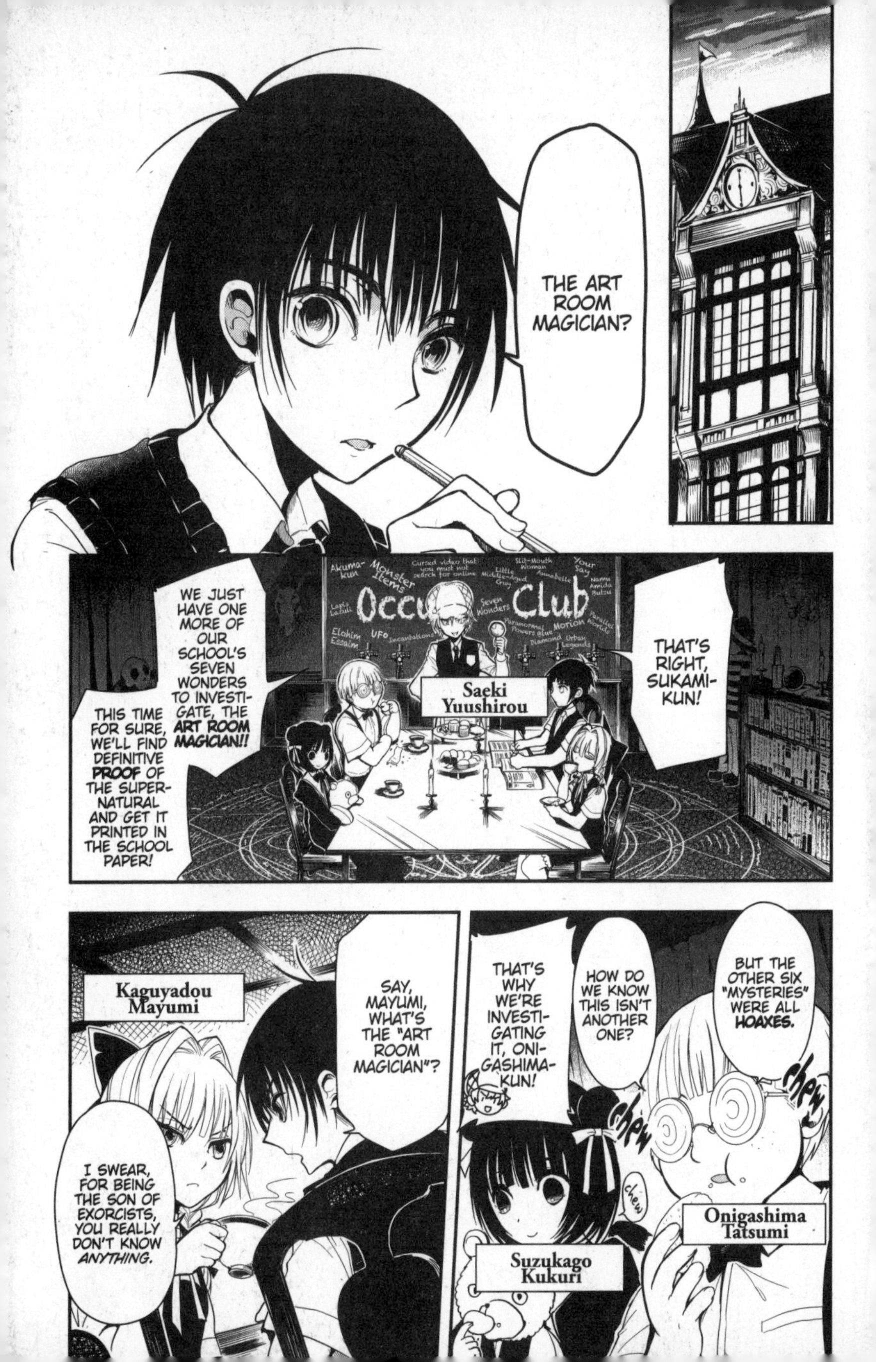
THE ART ROOM MAGICIAN?
Occu Club
Akuma-kun
Monster Items
Cursed video that you must not search for online
Slit-Mouth Woman
Little Middle-Aged Guy
Annabelle
Namu Amida Butsu
Lapis Lazuli
Seven Wonders
Elohim Essaim
UFO
Incantations
Urban Legends
Saeki Yuushirou
THAT'S RIGHT, SUKAMI-KUN!
WE JUST HAVE ONE MORE OF OUR SCHOOL'S SEVEN WONDERS TO INVESTIGATE, THE **ART ROOM MAGICIAN!!**
THIS TIME FOR SURE, WE'LL FIND DEFINITIVE **PROOF** OF THE SUPERNATURAL AND GET IT PRINTED IN THE SCHOOL PAPER!
BUT THE OTHER SIX "MYSTERIES" WERE ALL **HOAXES.**
HOW DO WE KNOW THIS ISN'T ANOTHER ONE?
THAT'S WHY WE'RE INVESTIGATING IT, ONIGASHIMA-KUN!
chew
chew
chew
Onigashima Tatsumi
Suzukago Kukuri
Kaguyadou Mayumi
SAY, MAYUMI, WHAT'S THE "ART ROOM MAGICIAN"?
I SWEAR, FOR BEING THE SON OF EXORCISTS, YOU REALLY DON'T KNOW *ANYTHING.*

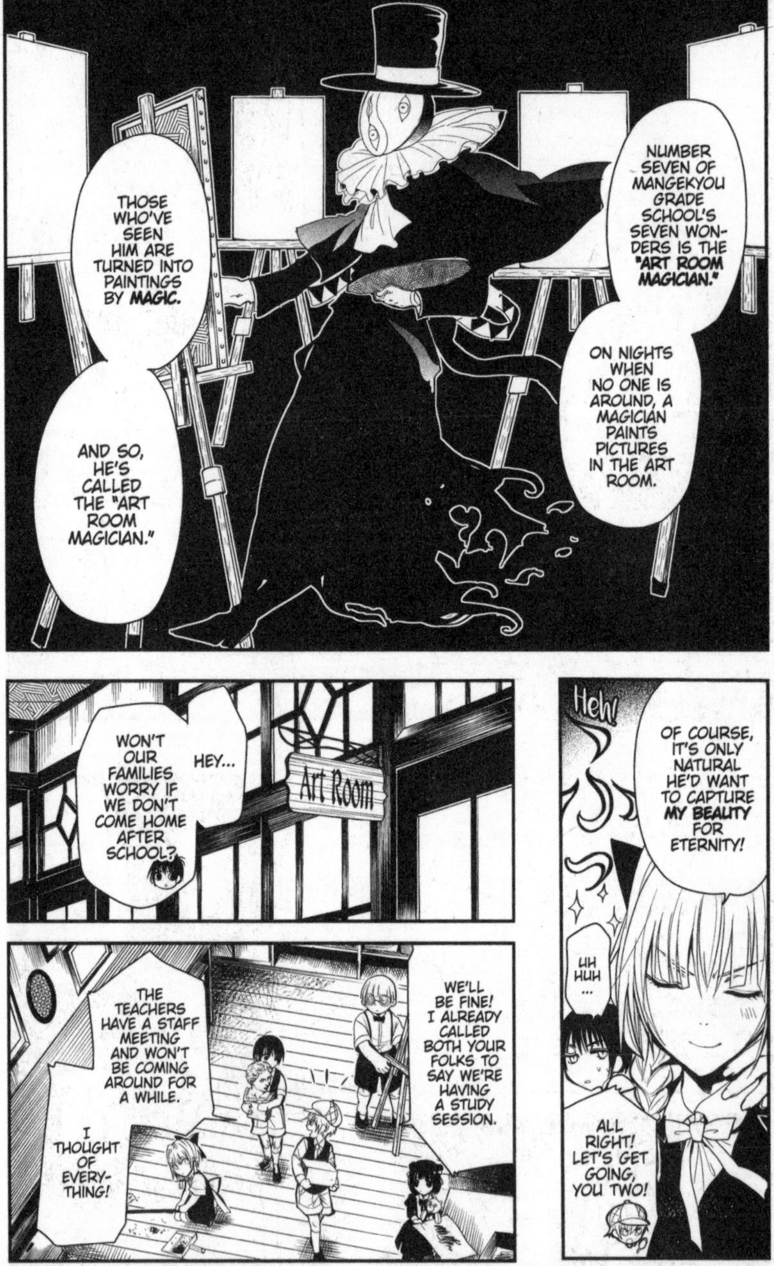
NUMBER SEVEN OF MANGEKYOU GRADE SCHOOL'S SEVEN WONDERS IS THE "ART ROOM MAGICIAN."
ON NIGHTS WHEN NO ONE IS AROUND, A MAGICIAN PAINTS PICTURES IN THE ART ROOM.
THOSE WHO'VE SEEN HIM ARE TURNED INTO PAINTINGS BY MAGIC.
AND SO, HE'S CALLED THE "ART ROOM MAGICIAN."
Heh!
OF COURSE, IT'S ONLY NATURAL HE'D WANT TO CAPTURE MY BEAUTY FOR ETERNITY!
UH HUH ...
ALL RIGHT! LET'S GET GOING, YOU TWO!
Art Room
HEY...
WON'T OUR FAMILIES WORRY IF WE DON'T COME HOME AFTER SCHOOL?
WE'LL BE FINE! I ALREADY CALLED BOTH YOUR FOLKS TO SAY WE'RE HAVING A STUDY SESSION.
THE TEACHERS HAVE A STAFF MEETING AND WON'T BE COMING AROUND FOR A WHILE.
I THOUGHT OF EVERY-THING!

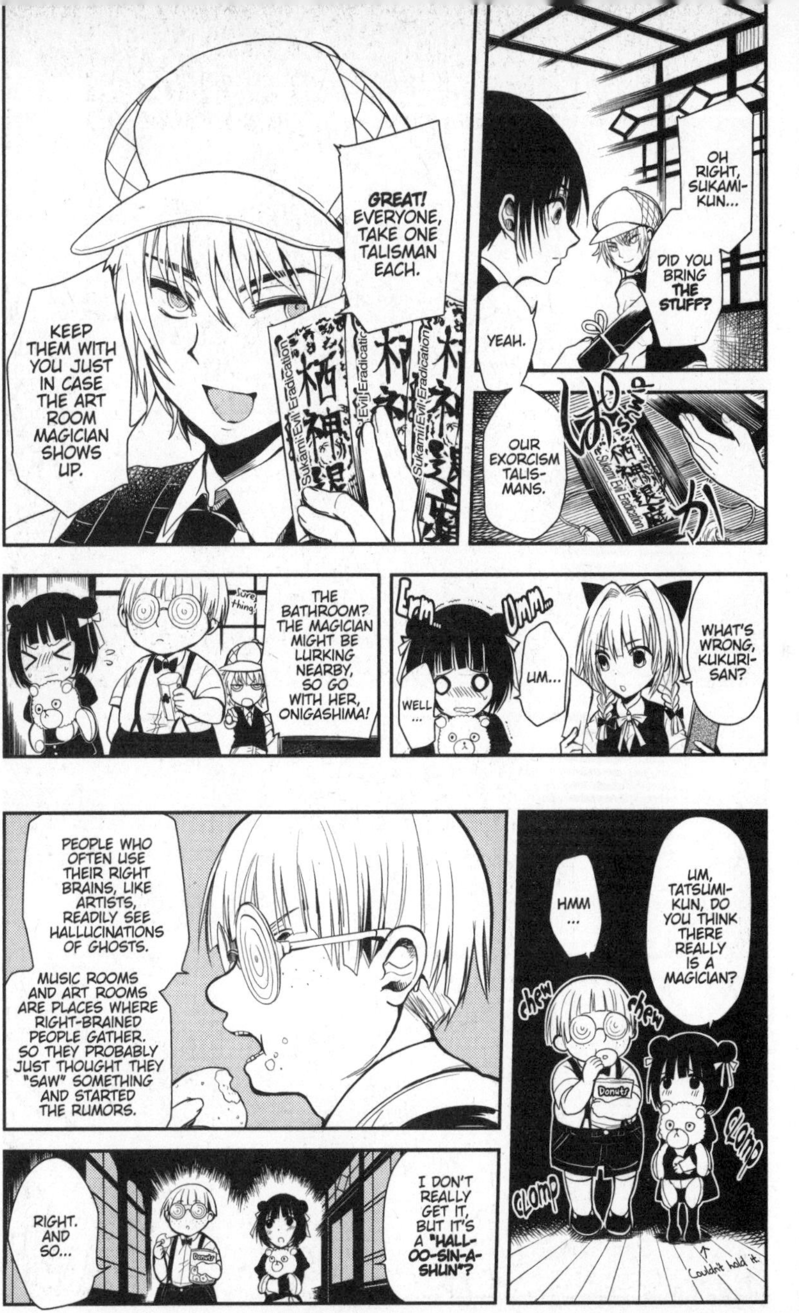
OH RIGHT, SUKAMI-KUN...
DID YOU BRING THE STUFF?
YEAH.
SHWIP
OUR EXORCISM TALIS-MANS.
Sukami Evil Eradication
GREAT! EVERYONE, TAKE ONE TALISMAN EACH.
KEEP THEM WITH YOU JUST IN CASE THE ART ROOM MAGICIAN SHOWS UP.
Sukami Evil Eradication
Evil Eradication
Sukami Evil Eradication
WHAT'S WRONG, KUKURI-SAN?
Umm...
UM...
Erm...
WELL...
THE BATHROOM? THE MAGICIAN MIGHT BE LURKING NEARBY, SO GO WITH HER, ONIGASHIMA!
Sure thing!
UM, TATSUMI-KUN, DO YOU THINK THERE REALLY IS A MAGICIAN?
HMM...
chew
chew
clomp
clomp
Donuts
Couldn't hold it.
PEOPLE WHO OFTEN USE THEIR RIGHT BRAINS, LIKE ARTISTS, READILY SEE HALLUCINATIONS OF GHOSTS.
MUSIC ROOMS AND ART ROOMS ARE PLACES WHERE RIGHT-BRAINED PEOPLE GATHER. SO THEY PROBABLY JUST THOUGHT THEY "SAW" SOMETHING AND STARTED THE RUMORS.
I DON'T REALLY GET IT, BUT IT'S A "HALL-OO-SIN-A-SHUN"?
RIGHT. AND SO...
Donuts

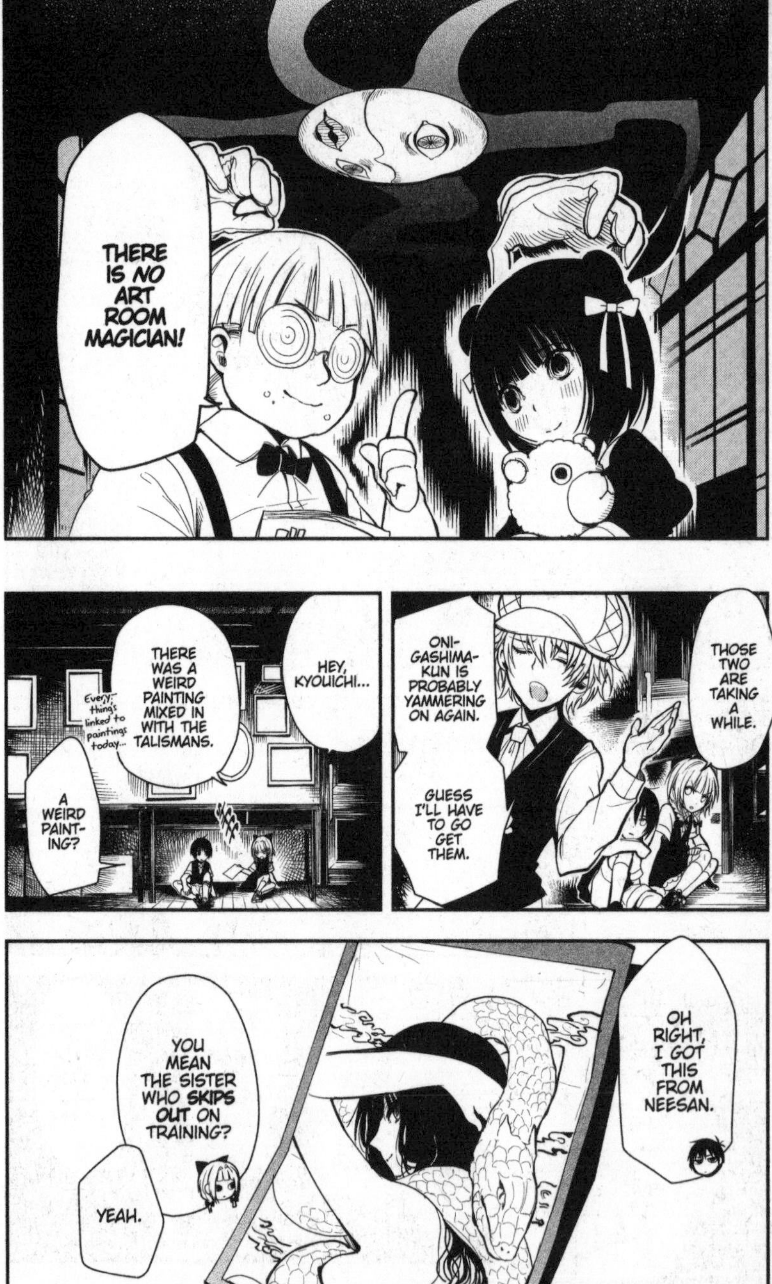
THERE IS NO ART ROOM MAGICIAN!
THOSE TWO ARE TAKING A WHILE.
ONI-GASHIMA-KUN IS PROBABLY YAMMERING ON AGAIN.
GUESS I'LL HAVE TO GO GET THEM.
HEY, KYOUICHI...
THERE WAS A WEIRD PAINTING MIXED IN WITH THE TALISMANS.
Every-thing's linked to paintings today...
A WEIRD PAINT-ING?
OH RIGHT, I GOT THIS FROM NEESAN.
YOU MEAN THE SISTER WHO **SKIPS OUT** ON TRAINING?
YEAH.

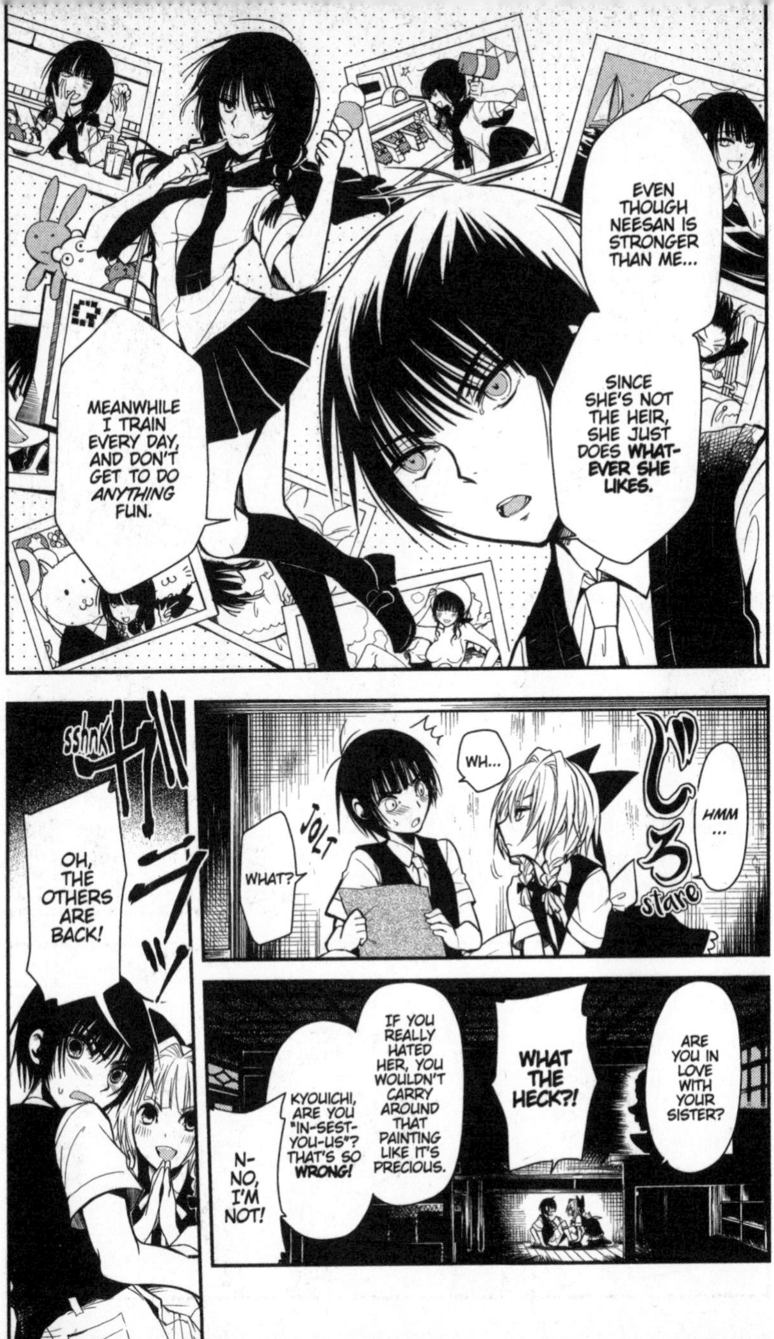
EVEN THOUGH NEESAN IS STRONGER THAN ME...
SINCE SHE'S NOT THE HEIR, SHE JUST DOES WHATEVER SHE LIKES.
MEANWHILE I TRAIN EVERY DAY, AND DON'T GET TO DO ANYTHING FUN.
じろ
stare
HMM...
WH...
JOLT
WHAT?
ARE YOU IN LOVE WITH YOUR SISTER?
WHAT THE HECK?!
IF YOU REALLY HATED HER, YOU WOULDN'T CARRY AROUND THAT PAINTING LIKE IT'S PRECIOUS.
KYOUICHI, ARE YOU "IN-SEST-YOU-US"? THAT'S SO WRONG!
N-NO, I'M NOT!
sshnk
OH, THE OTHERS ARE BACK!

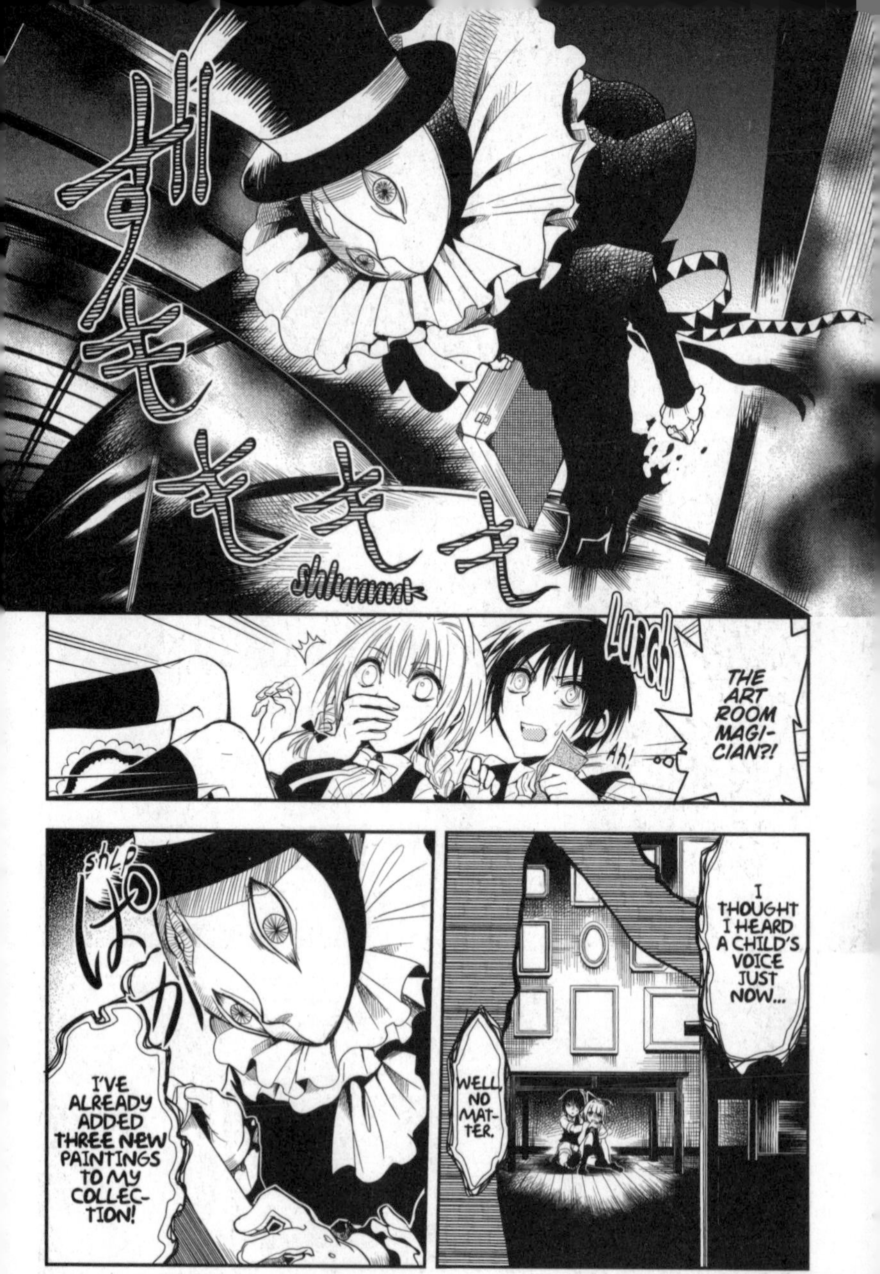
shhhhhhk
LURCH
THE ART ROOM MAGICIAN?!
AH!
I THOUGHT I HEARD A CHILD'S VOICE JUST NOW...
WELL, NO MATTER.
SHLP
I'VE ALREADY ADDED THREE NEW PAINTINGS TO MY COLLECTION!

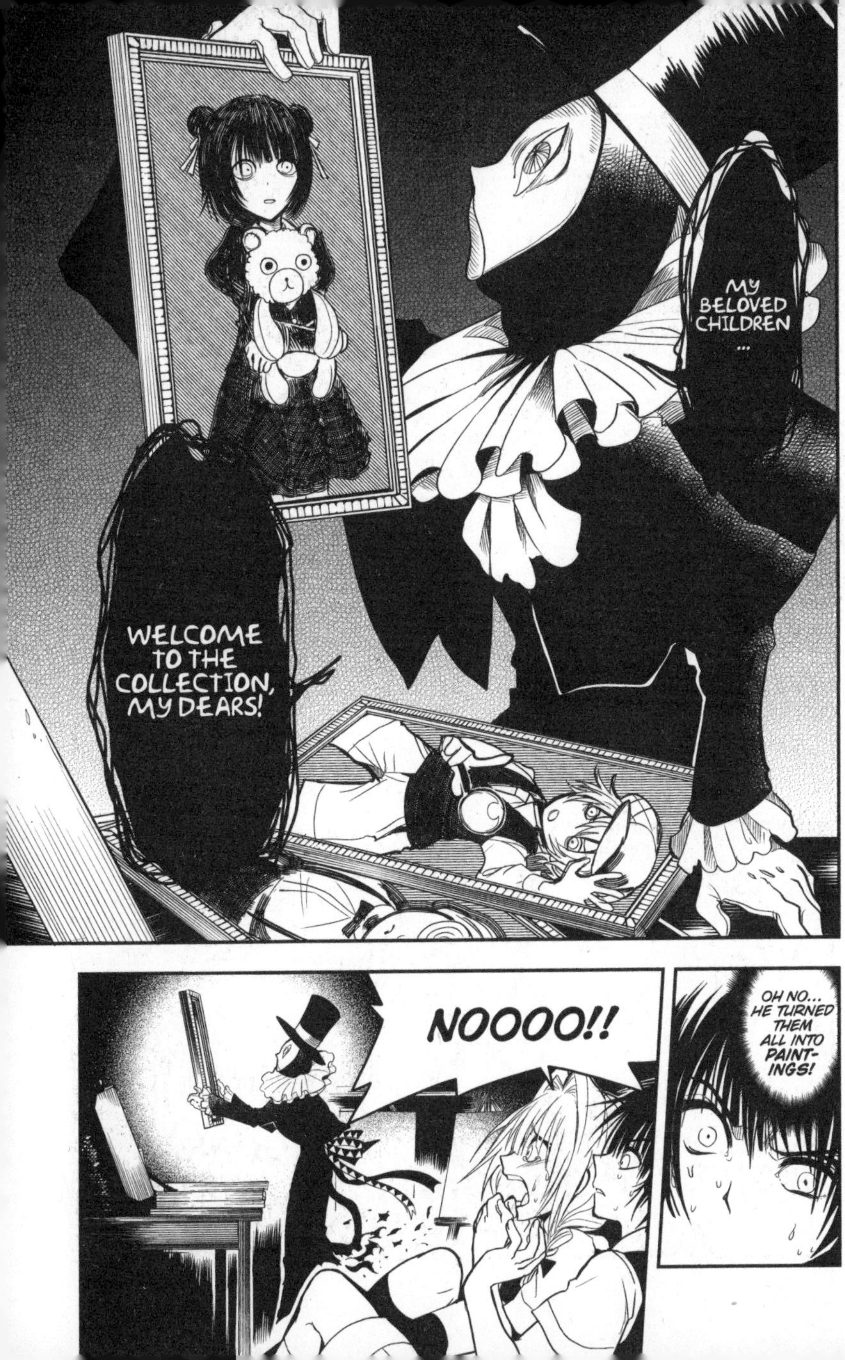
MY BELOVED CHILDREN ...
WELCOME TO THE COLLECTION, MY DEARS!
OH NO... HE TURNED THEM ALL INTO PAINT-INGS!
NOOOO!!

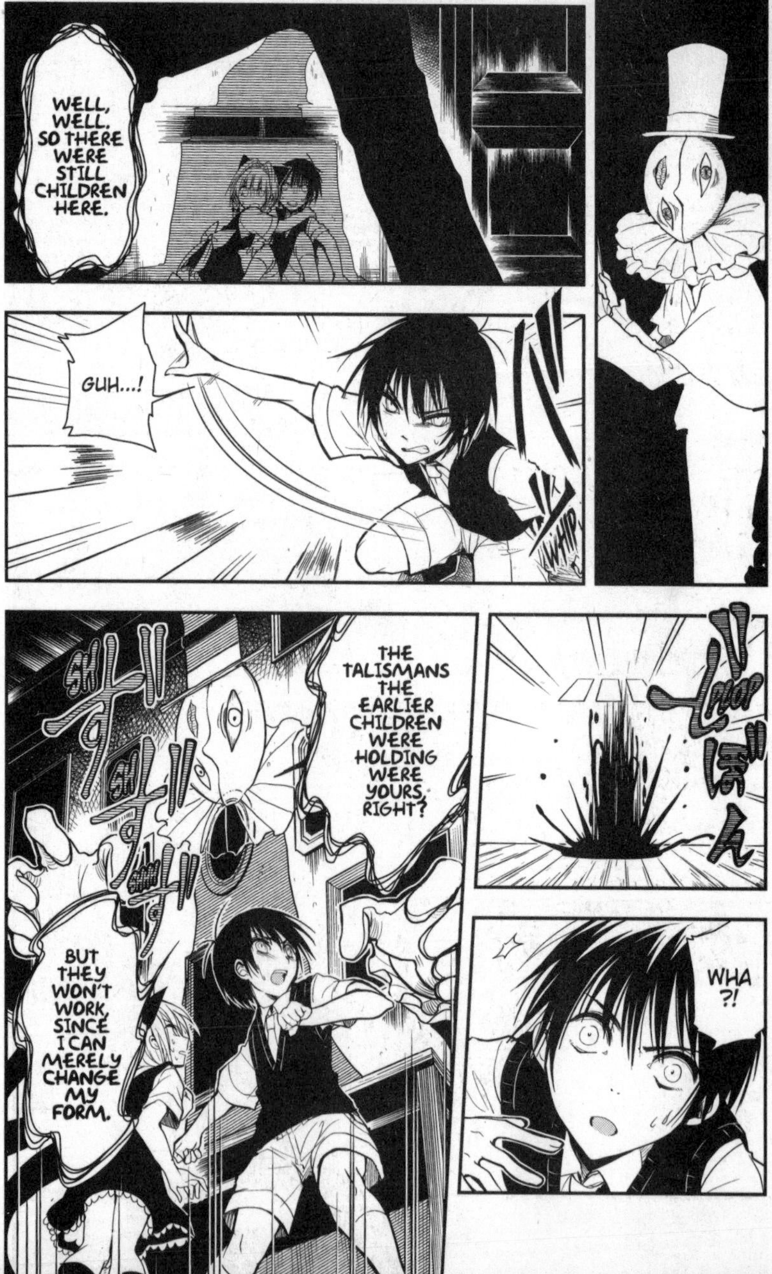
WELL, WELL. SO THERE WERE STILL CHILDREN HERE.
GUH...!
WHIP
WHA ?!
THE TALISMANS THE EARLIER CHILDREN WERE HOLDING WERE YOURS, RIGHT?
SHH
SHH
SHHH
BUT THEY WON'T WORK, SINCE I CAN MERELY CHANGE MY FORM.

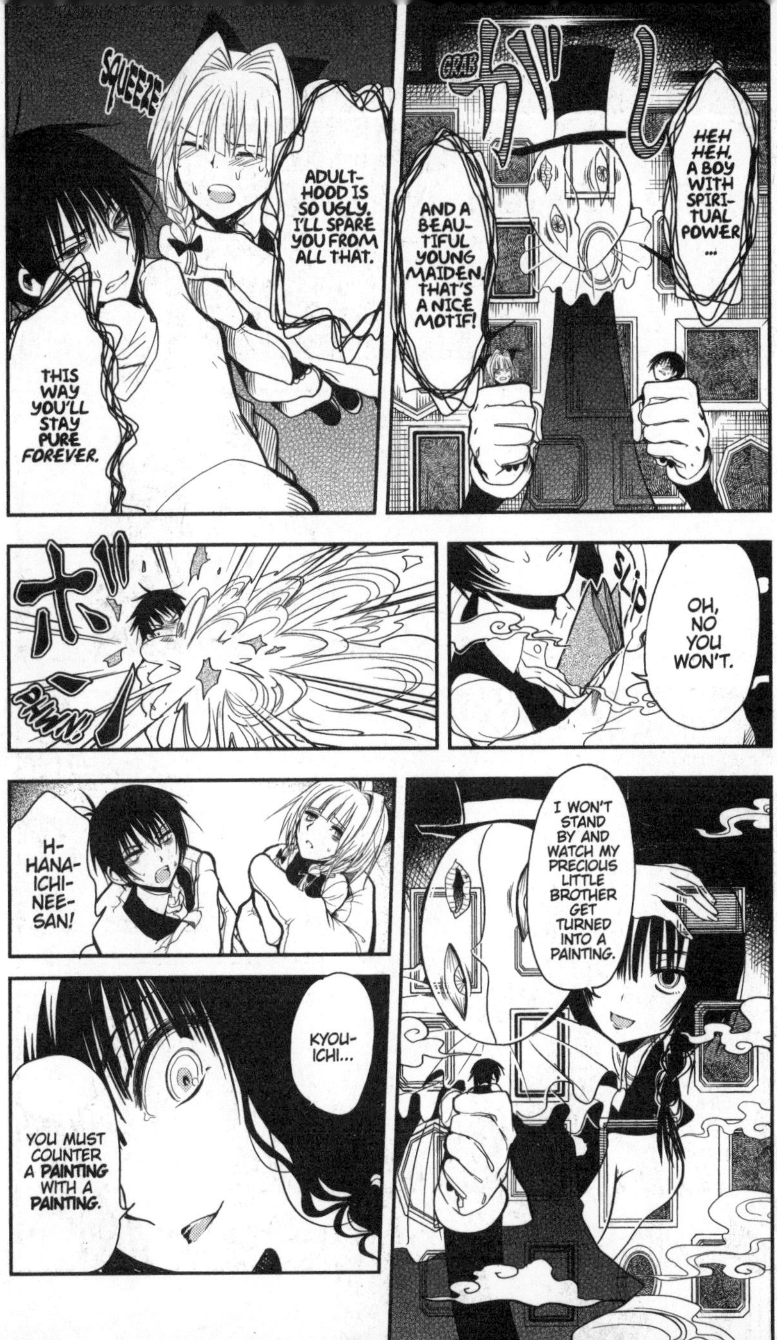
GRAB
HEH HEH. A BOY WITH SPIRITUAL POWER...
AND A BEAUTIFUL YOUNG MAIDEN. THAT'S A NICE MOTIF!
SQUEEZE
ADULTHOOD IS SO UGLY. I'LL SPARE YOU FROM ALL THAT.
THIS WAY YOU'LL STAY PURE FOREVER.
SLIP
OH, NO YOU WON'T.
PHWN!
I WON'T STAND BY AND WATCH MY PRECIOUS LITTLE BROTHER GET TURNED INTO A PAINTING.
H-HANAICHI-NEESAN!
KYOUICHI...
YOU MUST COUNTER A **PAINTING** WITH A **PAINTING**.

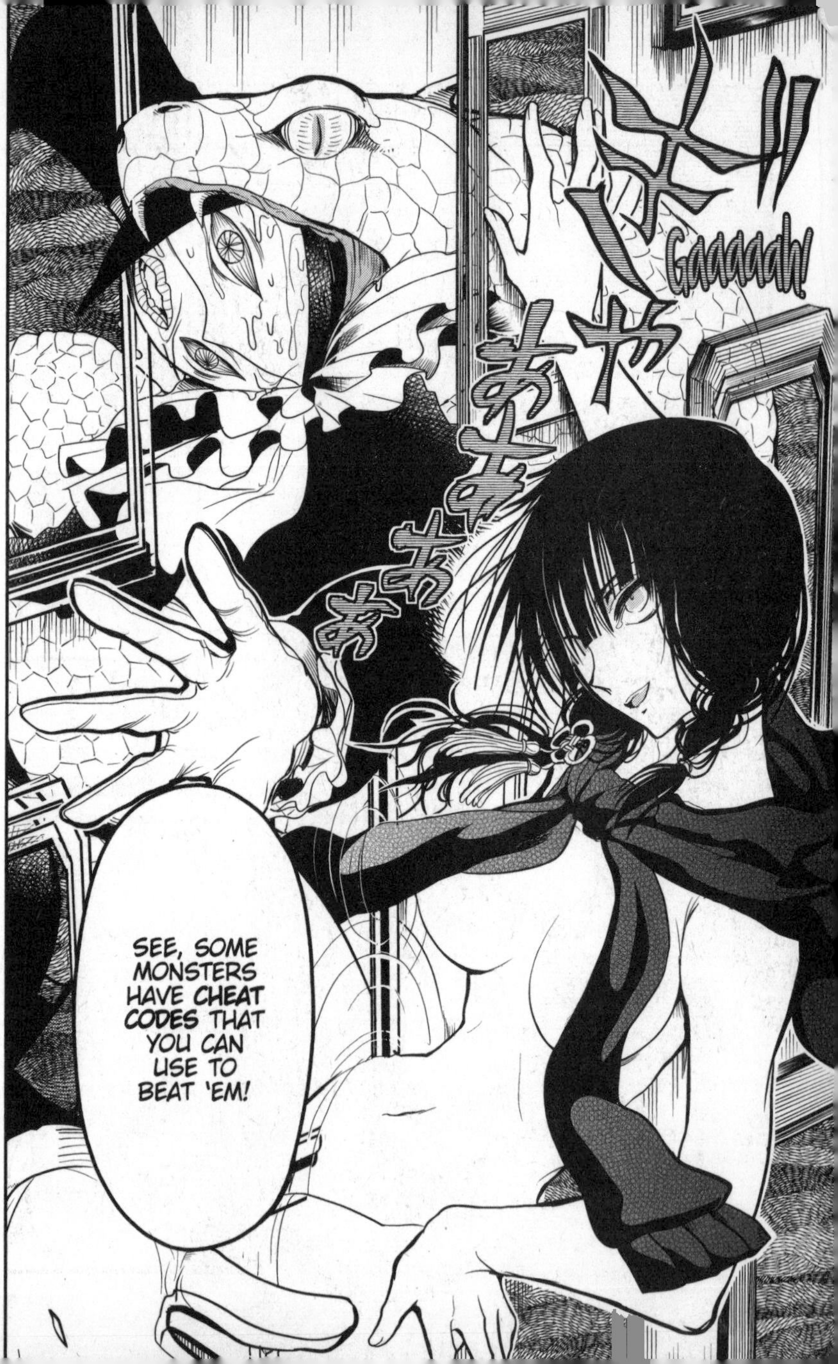
Gaaaaah!
SEE, SOME MONSTERS HAVE CHEAT CODES THAT YOU CAN USE TO BEAT 'EM!

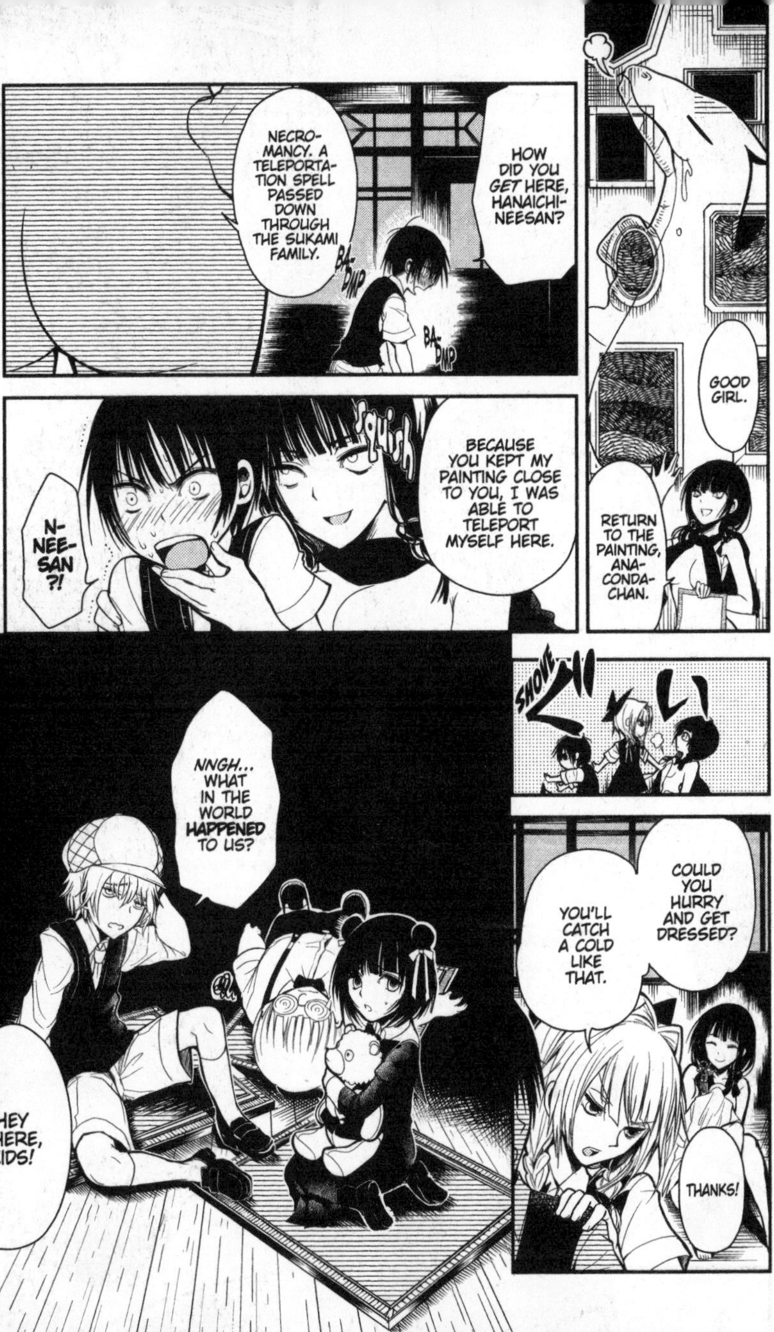
GOOD GIRL.
RETURN TO THE PAINTING, ANACONDA-CHAN.
HOW DID YOU GET HERE, HANAICHI-NEESAN?
NECRO-MANCY. A TELEPORTA-TION SPELL PASSED DOWN THROUGH THE SUKAMI FAMILY.
BA-DMP
BA-DMP
squish
BECAUSE YOU KEPT MY PAINTING CLOSE TO YOU, I WAS ABLE TO TELEPORT MYSELF HERE.
N-NEE-SAN?!
SHOVE
COULD YOU HURRY AND GET DRESSED?
YOU'LL CATCH A COLD LIKE THAT.
THANKS!
NNGH... WHAT IN THE WORLD HAPPENED TO US?
HEY THERE, KIDS!

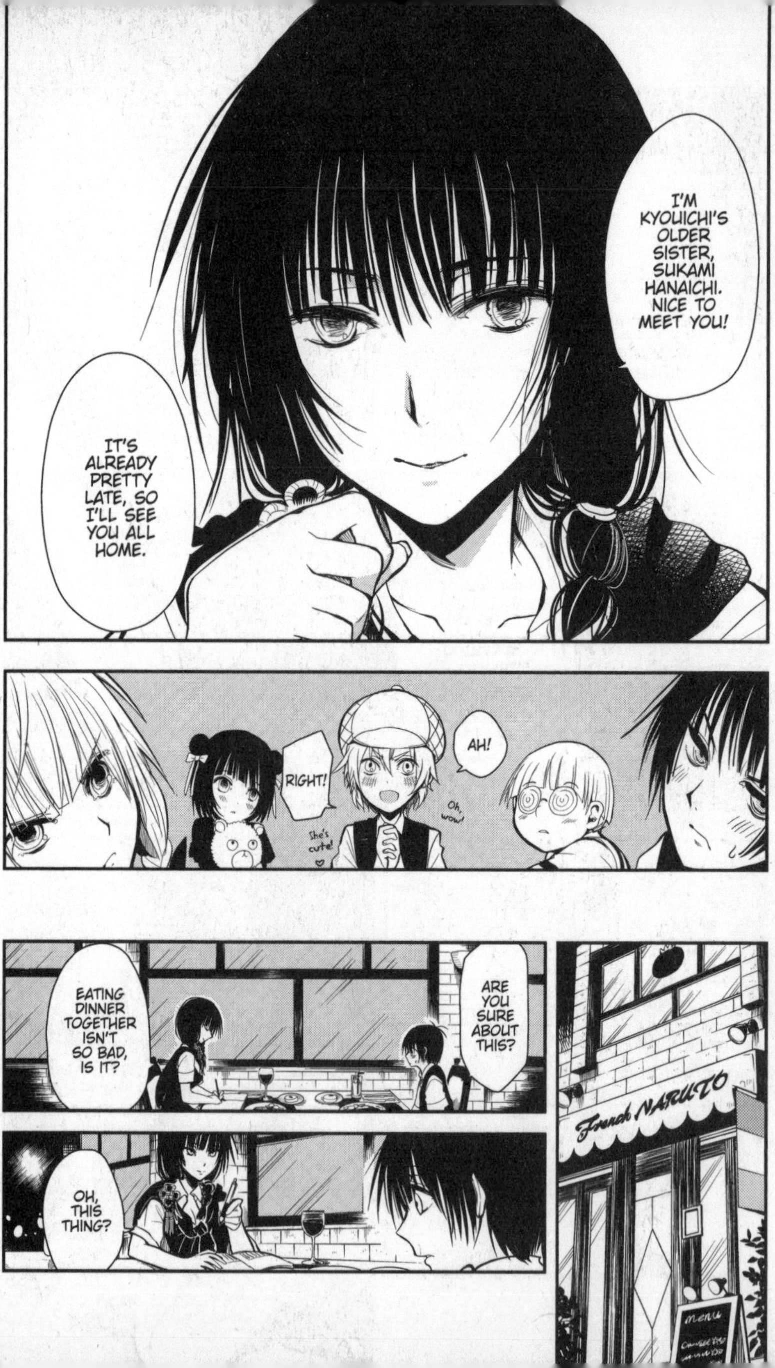
I'M KYOUICHI'S OLDER SISTER, SUKAMI HANAICHI. NICE TO MEET YOU!
IT'S ALREADY PRETTY LATE, SO I'LL SEE YOU ALL HOME.
AH!
Oh, wow!
RIGHT!
She's cute!
French NARUTO
menu
ARE YOU SURE ABOUT THIS?
EATING DINNER TOGETHER ISN'T SO BAD, IS IT?
OH, THIS THING?

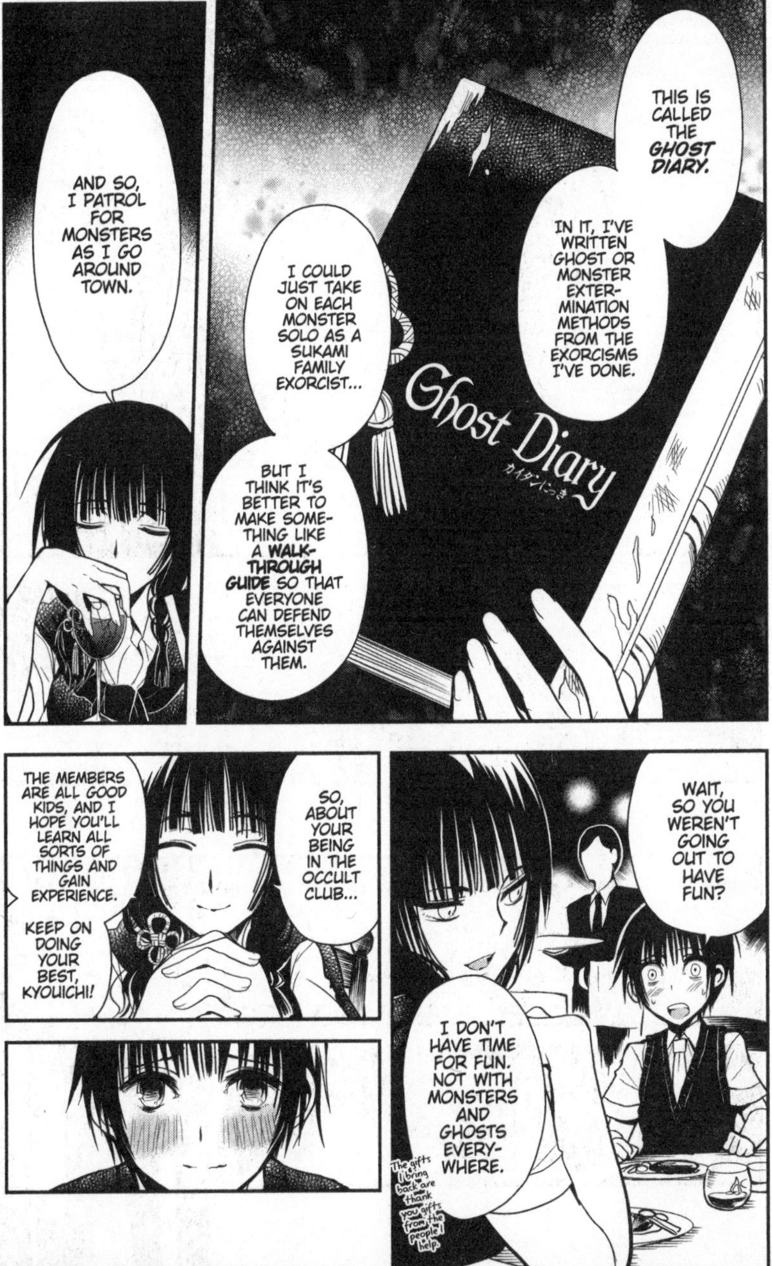
THIS IS CALLED THE GHOST DIARY.
IN IT, I'VE WRITTEN GHOST OR MONSTER EXTER-MINATION METHODS FROM THE EXORCISMS I'VE DONE.
I COULD JUST TAKE ON EACH MONSTER SOLO AS A SUKAMI FAMILY EXORCIST...
BUT I THINK IT'S BETTER TO MAKE SOME-THING LIKE A WALK-THROUGH GUIDE SO THAT EVERYONE CAN DEFEND THEMSELVES AGAINST THEM.
Ghost Diary
カイダンにっき
AND SO, I PATROL FOR MONSTERS AS I GO AROUND TOWN.
WAIT, SO YOU WEREN'T GOING OUT TO HAVE FUN?
I DON'T HAVE TIME FOR FUN. NOT WITH MONSTERS AND GHOSTS EVERY-WHERE.
The gifts I bring back are thank you gifts from the people I help.
SO, ABOUT YOUR BEING IN THE OCCULT CLUB...
THE MEMBERS ARE ALL GOOD KIDS, AND I HOPE YOU'LL LEARN ALL SORTS OF THINGS AND GAIN EXPERIENCE.
KEEP ON DOING YOUR BEST, KYOUICHI!

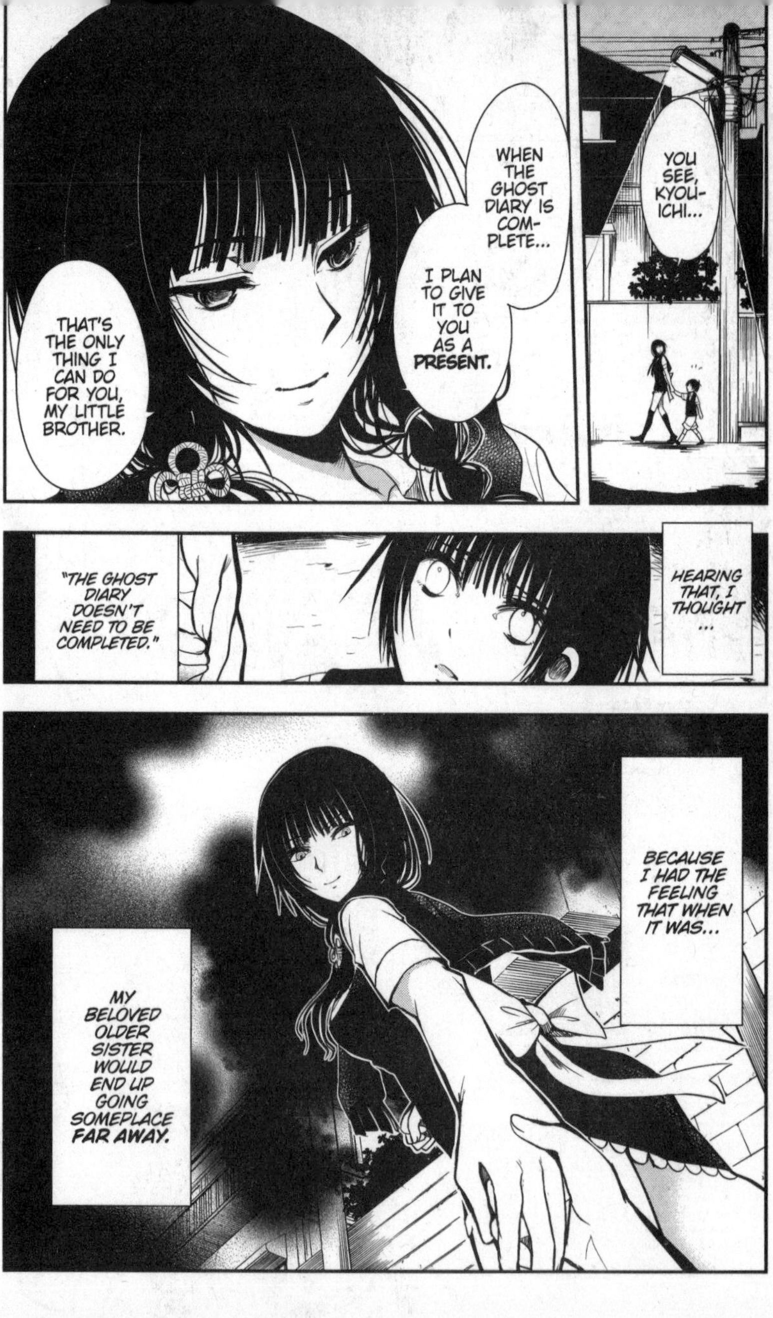
YOU SEE, KYOUICHI...
WHEN THE GHOST DIARY IS COMPLETE...
I PLAN TO GIVE IT TO YOU AS A **PRESENT.**
THAT'S THE ONLY THING I CAN DO FOR YOU, MY LITTLE BROTHER.
HEARING THAT, I THOUGHT...
"THE GHOST DIARY DOESN'T NEED TO BE COMPLETED."
BECAUSE I HAD THE FEELING THAT WHEN IT WAS...
MY BELOVED OLDER SISTER WOULD END UP GOING SOMEPLACE **FAR AWAY.**

Commentary on the Work

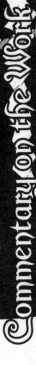

6th Page ◆ { Sea-Turtle Soup }
I drew this because I wanted to do a chapter like a detective novel. It has a western-mansion horror setting, riddles, action scenes, and sex appeal. A sublime chapter, if I do say so myself. The "Sea-Turtle Soup" author, Paul Sloane, has written a variety of other deductive quizzes. His books have been translated and published in Japan as well, so why not try solving a tricky lateral thinking puzzle yourself?

7th Page ◆ { Rubber Man }
In this chapter the characters spend a lot of time loitering around love hotels. I was asked, "Rubber Man and love hotels--are you making a pun?" but that wasn't my intention at all (lol)! At any rate, I wanted to try drawing this because I thought that love hotel exteriors are kind of funny in a crass way. Plus, there are quite a few ghost stories set in love hotels...

8th Page ◆ { Women in Black }
The material for this comes from the urban legend about the "Men in Black." Since just ordinary male aliens don't make for an interesting image, I went with girls wearing men's tailcoats. At first I planned to draw some cute girls' love this chapter, but it's kinda different from my original idea... But I rather like it, as it gives the sub-plot a pleasantly weird vibe (lol).

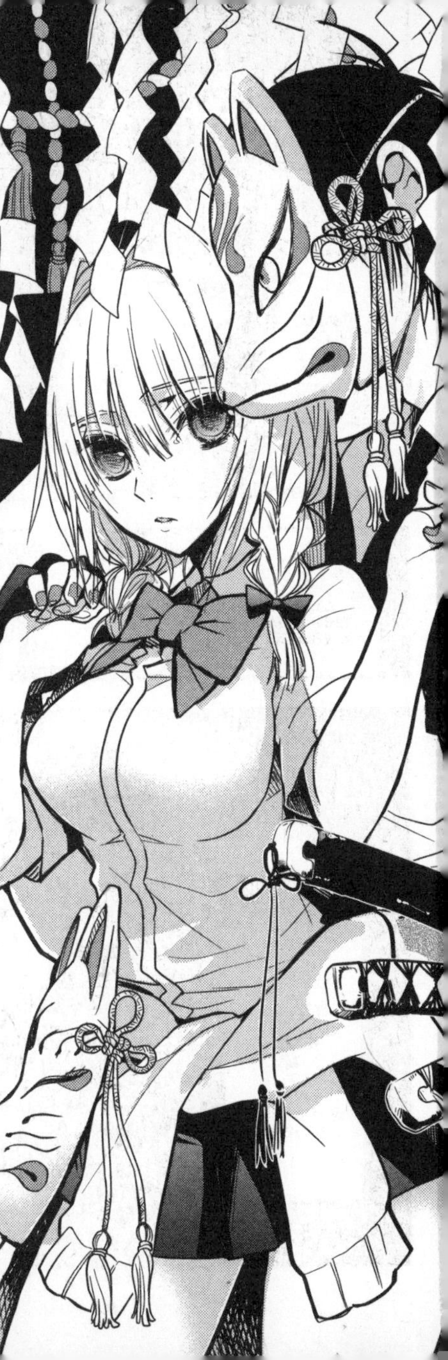

9th Page ◆ { Kokkuri-san }
Kokkuri-san, Satoru-kun--this chapter is about answer-type urban legends, where you'll get an answer if you ask a question. Incidentally, "answer-type urban legend" is my own made-up term. Wanting public phone reference material, I went out in the middle of the night to take photographs. Good time, good times (lol).
Personally, I wonder if the story and urban legends work well entwined together.
To find out what happened to Mayumi after looking behind her, be sure to read Volume 3!

Special Story ◆ { Ghost Diary }
I borrowed the Art Room Magician's ability to turn into a painting from *Legend of Zelda: A Link Between Worlds*, since I'd been playing it at the time. I wavered over whether or not to apply screentone to Hanaichi-neesan's naked body, but since the eye is drawn towards screentone anyway, I didn't use it.

{ Final Commentary }
◇ That finishes the afterword. I get the feeling Volume 2 had a bit too many sexy elements in it, but horror and sexy are inseparable, so hey, it's fine, right? At any rate, I'd be happy if you would also read Volume 3. See you next time!

SEVEN SEAS ENTERTAINMENT PRESENTS

Ghost Diary
カイダンにっき

story and art by SEIJU NATSUMEGU　　VOLUME 2

TRANSLATION
Krista Shipley

ADAPTATION
Shannon Fay

LETTERING AND RETOUCH
Karis Page
Gwen Silver

COVER DESIGN
Nicky Lim

PROOFREADER
Danielle King
Brett Hallahan

ASSISTANT EDITOR
Jenn Grunigen

PRODUCTION ASSISTANT
CK Russell

PRODUCTION MANAGER
Lissa Pattillo

EDITOR-IN-CHIEF
Adam Arnold

PUBLISHER
Jason DeAngelis

GHOST DIARY VOL. 2
© SEIJU NATSUMEGU 2015
Edited by ASCII MEDIA WORKS.
First published in Japan in 2015 by KADOKAWA CORPORATION, Tokyo.
English translation rights reserved by Seven Seas Entertainment, LLC.
under the license from KADOKAWA CORPORATION, Tokyo.

Seven Seas books may be purchased in bulk for promotional, educational, or business use. Please contact your local bookseller or the Macmillan Corporate and Premium Sales Department at 1-800-221-7945, extension 5442, or by e-mail at MacmillanSpecialMarkets@macmillan.com.

Seven Seas and the Seven Seas logo are trademarks of Seven Seas Entertainment, LLC. All rights reserved.

ISBN: 978-1-626925-00-7

Printed in Canada

First Printing: July 2017

10 9 8 7 6 5 4 3 2 1

FOLLOW US ONLINE: *www.gomanga.com*

READING DIRECTIONS

This book reads from *right to left*, Japanese style. If this is your first time reading manga, you start reading from the top right panel on each page and take it from there. If you get lost, just follow the numbered diagram here. It may seem backwards at first, but you'll get the hang of it! Have fun!!

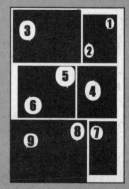

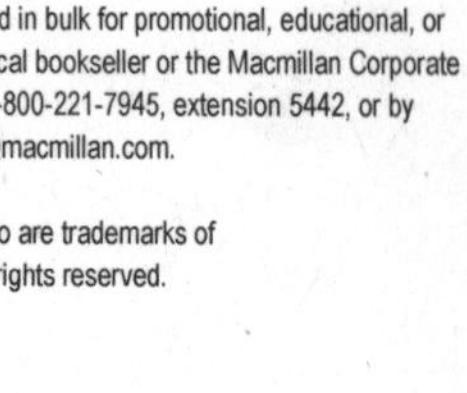